The Dragon's Promise

Jeanette McCarthy

To Terry
with my best wishes
Jeanette x

British Library Cataloguing-in-Publication Data:
A catalogue record for this book is available from
the British Library

Cover design by *Briarcal Solutions*

ISBN: 978-0-9556911-1-9

Printed and bound in Great Britain by
CPI Antony Rowe, Chippenham and Eastbourne

Also by Jeanette McCarthy:

Abandoned
A novel of survival

Brilliant. Well crafted, beautifully written and exciting. A good book for a long weekend as I found it hard to put down once I started reading. Sometimes when I did, it was hard to leave the Scottish Highlands behind and get back to my familiar surroundings.

Morelle Cowan

A tight narrative style... no words wasted, no long descriptive passages, and plenty of dialogue

David Gardiner

I put it down at 3am this morning, about halfway through, and found myself wondering where the time had gone. A wonderful cast of characters.

John Craggs

All the characters, including the minor ones, are well rounded and convincing. This for me is the mark of a very high standard of writing. I think Jeanette McCarthy is a name we are going to hear a lot more of in years to come

Gold Dust Magazine

Jeanette's writing is graceful. Her book covers are wistful. Her stories lay on feelings as well as betrayal, abuse, murder, and the kind of beastliness that you almost only ever find in fiction... I don't want to spoil the story by telling you too much about what happens next, but if, like me, you'd been turning the pages over avidly up until that point, from this point onwards they'll positively fly through your fingers. I have to congratulate Jeanette on writing a very enthralling story. I look forward to her next one.

Litarena

3

This one was always going to be for John

You glow in my heart
like the flames of uncounted candles
but when I go to warm my hands
my clumsiness overturns the light
and then I stumble
against the tables and chairs

Amy Lowell

PROLOGUE

This, then, is the legend:

Long ago, in the far north-west, there lived a dragon. He was very lonely, being the only one of his kind, and as the long years passed, he longed for company.

Eventually people came to his lands. The dragon was overcome with curiosity, and would watch them secretly, fascinated by their little lives. One day the chieftain of the people was hunting on the mountainside when he came upon the dragon, asleep. At first the chieftain was confused by what he saw, and, thinking it must be just an unusual rock formation, he looked closer. The dragon opened one huge amber eye. The chieftain let out a cry and drew his sword, but the dragon merely blinked sleepily and sighed.

'You woke me up,' he said.

'What?'

'I was asleep. You woke me up.'

'What are you doing here!' The chieftain shouted, to hide his fear.

'I *was* sleeping,' the dragon replied.

'I mean what are you doing in my lands?'

'*Your* lands? This is my country. And I have been here a long, long time.'

The dragon gave another sad sigh.

'I was here to watch the islands appear out of the sea, the mountains thrust through the earth in fire and smoke. I have seen great lands break apart, the seas rise and fall, and now all is calm, and you have come.'

The chieftain looked at the giant eye and saw the sadness there.

'And you are all alone?'

A big tear rolled out of the dragon's eye, causing a minor flood on the plateau below.

'Well,' the chieftain said thoughtfully, 'we would like to hear your stories, if you would tell them, and we will tell you ours.'

The dragon's eye grew brighter. 'Really?'

'Yes. But you must promise never to harm us, for we are small and you could squash us without thinking.'

As he spoke, the chieftain thought, *uh oh, maybe that was not the smartest thing to say.*

The dragon sat up, felling a small copse of birch trees. He held one giant claw high in the air.

'Upon my life, I give you my word,' he said.

And so the dragon came to live with the humans. They were afraid at first, but soon grew used to him, and the dragon was delighted to have so much attention. The children would climb his spiny legs, and he would put his head on the ground and let them sit on his nose, crossing his eyes to look at them, making them laugh.

And the chieftain was well pleased too, for the dragon helped them, felling trees for their boats, and clearing the land for crops. And there were raiders in the country now, searching for lands of their own. What better protection could his clan have?

The chieftain had a young son, Baran, who was clever and curious, and in a very short time he and the dragon were firm friends. Baran would sit with him for hours, telling him tales of the clan, their many journeys, their troubles and joys, and the dragon would tell him about the way the earth came to be, and the travels of the stars around the night sky. Sometimes, Baran would fall asleep, and the dragon's great claw would fold protectively around him. Baran's mother did not approve, but the chieftain saw how much the boy and dragon loved each other, and thought this was a good thing. Baran would be the chieftain, one day. The alliance would continue, and his people would flourish.

The summer was drawing on to autumn when Baran first asked the question. The dragon looked at him in surprise.

'You want to fly?'

'Yes. I want you to take me. Will you?'

The dragon blinked in alarm. 'I will not, Baran. For the winds are strong and treacherous, and you will fall.'

'I will hold on very tight.'

But the dragon refused, again and again, and Baran was disappointed.

But not disheartened. The next day he came back carrying a length of twine.

'I will not fall. I will tie myself to you.'

'The twine is thin, and will break,' the dragon said. 'It is not strong enough.'

And Baran went away again.

Time passed, and every day Baran brought something else: the gut the hunters used for their bows; the wool the women wove into garments, and every time, the dragon refused.

Baran was at his wit's end. But one day he went down to the beach and watched the fishermen, and when they had pulled their boat in to shore and left it, he hurried down and stole the rope that lay on the foredeck.

'This is strong enough,' he said, laying it before the dragon. The great amber eye turned to him.

8

'Do not make me do this, Baran,' he said. 'I swore an oath never to hurt your people, and even had I not, I would never harm you.'

'You won't,' Baran said, with the confidence of the very young. 'It'll be fine. Come on, let me try, and you can take me up the mountain. You'll see I won't fall off.'

So Baran climbed on to the dragon's back and tied himself to the front ridge of his spine. The dragon got to his feet and ran up the mountainside, clearing a wide path in the young trees. Baran held tight to the great ridge, which was smooth and black as velvet moss, speckled with silver. The dragon smelt of fern and bark, of growing things. Baran had never felt more content. They reached the mountaintop and Baran laughed.

'You see? I am still here. Now will you take me flying?'

And the dragon looked down at the sea below, and knew he had no choice. He spread his great black wings and leapt off into the sky, and Baran let out a yell of delight.

They sailed across the autumn sky, creating a huge shadow on the land, so that the people came to see what it was. Baran could hear them all yelling, and felt smug. The dragon heard the cries, and knew there'd be hell to pay.

'Higher, dragon my friend, take me higher!'

The dragon turned and found the thermals, riding them higher and higher, until they could see the whole of their small and beautiful country, far below. Baran twisted this way and that, eager to see everything. But although the rope around him was strong, the knot with which it was tied was not. As Baran leaned over to see the chain of islands far below, it gave way suddenly, and he fell.

He screamed, and the dragon let out a roar of anguish. Pulling his wings in tight he dropped after the boy, They dropped like stones from the pale blue sky, the dragon's wings making the air scream, his forelegs outstretched, his claws only inches from Baran's small body. 'No!' the dragon roared, as Baran hit the water. The dragon followed him down, down, into the chill depths.

He found the small broken body and lifted it gently in his claw. He rose out of the water and roared his despair to the stars.

The dragon laid Baran's body on the soft white sand, and rose again into the sky. When he was high enough, he looked back and saw the chieftain standing on the sand, the body of his son cradled in his arms. The dragon roared once more, and then he plunged into the sea.

Years passed.

9

The grief lay heavy on the chieftain's shoulders, and not only for the loss of his son. He knew the dragon had loved the boy, that there had been no evil in him. When the sun sank low in the sky, he would go the most westerly point of his lands, and he would call out:

'Come back, dragon. All is forgiven. Come back and claim your lands.'

But the dragon never came.

After one long, fierce winter, the spring tides were very low, and when the chieftain went into the west, he saw that a new island had appeared. It lay opposite the beach where Baran's body had lain. It was small, but mountainous, and atop the mountain were a series of sharp spines, like a dragon's back. The island looked into the west, into the sunset, and the chieftain knew he need call the dragon no more.

Many long years passed, and the story was told from father to son, from generation to generation. But a time came when finally there were no longer children to tell the story to. The young left the islands and did not return, and the old ones left behind told the tale amongst themselves, until at last the ending changed. The dragon had not returned, but he was there, on the island they now called Baranpay. Perhaps he was not dead, but sleeping. Perhaps some day he might return, and when he did, he would bring their children with him, riding on his back like little Baran.

For the years of men are hard, and hope is often all there is.

PART ONE

ONE

Griff came out of the movie theatre and stood on the sidewalk. He listened to what the other moviegoers were saying about his film, and was reminded of the Simpsons episode, when Homer and Bart are walking out past the ingoing queue, and Homer says: 'who'd have guessed Darth Vader would turn out to be Luke's father!'

He tried to gauge the atmosphere. It was – well, OK. No one was raving about what a brilliant piece of art they'd just seen. No one was saying it had been utter crap. It was just OK. He began to walk down towards Figueroa, following two twenty-something men.

'That chick was hot,' one of them said. 'What's her name again?'

It seemed not even the actors had made much of an impression.

He had come out of the same cinema as a teenager, having seen a film called *Blade Runner*, and stood on this same sidewalk, and stared into space, overwhelmed by what he had seen. The film's imagery haunted him, drove him back to watch it over and over, to seek out all the director's other work. The film changed him. He had always loved writing, but after that his stories grew darker, harder, and he longed to write something that would touch people, the way he himself had been touched. In the years to come, he would sometimes joke that Harrison Ford had changed his life.

He looked back, but there was no one standing on the sidewalk staring into space.

He walked away, and deep in his heart, a little hollow place began to form.

TWO

Friday night, and the pub was heaving. A fine mist of smoke and laughter hung low in the room. Ellie, being the smallest, snuck through a gap in the crowd.

'Hoy! Billy! Three and a half!'

The barman saw her and nodded, his lips moving as he tallied up the present round.

'Haven't you got them in yet?' Hannah complained behind her.

'Give us a chance.'

She pushed against a woman at the bar, smiling in apology. The woman turned to her, her face angry, and Ellie felt a perverse pleasure when the woman's expression suddenly changed. There were odd occasions when the scars were useful.

Why thank you!

Ellie grimaced, grabbing the drinks. She carried them in front of her like a talisman to clear her path.

'Here we go, ladies.'

'Fee, why don't you drink pints?' Lara complained, sneering at the half-pint of cider. 'It's pathetic. You're letting the side down.'

Ellie grinned. 'Fiona's the token female among us. Aren't you?'

Fiona raised a delicately plucked blonde eyebrow. 'At least there is one,' she said.

'Look, there's Pete Ross,' Lara took off through the crowd towards the local dealer.

'I'll be back in a minute.'

Fiona's face turned dark. 'She'll kill herself with that stuff-'

'Oh, leave it,' Ellie said, sighing. 'Look, there's a seat by the juke box. Let's go.'

Hannah raised her pint glass once they had squeezed round the tiny table. 'Here's to your new desert island job, Ellie.'

'Cheers! I'm looking forward to a better class of male talent than we have here.'

'Wouldn't be hard,' Hannah replied, looking round. 'Look at that bloke over there. Face like a bulldog chewing a wasp.' She bit her lip, still staring at the bulldog as Lara returned, smiling widely. Her teeth looked very white against her dark skin.

Ellie grinned back. Lara was skinny. She'd been skinny before her illness, and had gotten even thinner during it. Now that she was well again, she could afford to put on some weight, but her lifestyle wouldn't allow it. She was taller than Ellie and the others, tall enough that she could have been a model, with her jet hair and come-to-bed

14

eyes. She'd inherited those eyes from her Jamaican mother, together with her laid back attitude. Her high cheekbones and thin, angular face she'd got from her Glaswegian father, from whom she had also received all her bad habits. There were lots of them, Ellie mused. In fact, Lara had the full set.

There were no spare seats, so she knelt down.

'You'll get filthy down there!' Fiona said.

Lara shrugged. 'Hey Ellie, when are you going?'

'Tomorrow. When I wake up.' Ellie grinned again. Now that the decision was made, she was looking forward to the move. It was always like this; the sense of hope and anticipation. Absently she wondered why the past few shitty jobs hadn't dulled her expectations. She touched her face in case the scars had somehow vanished. They hadn't.

Of course we're here! Where else would we be?

'And do they have, like, phones up there?'

'Of course. It's not the bloody Congo, you know.'

Lara shrugged again. Her dark eyes were starting to look glazed. 'But I bet they don't have decent pubs in the Highlands. Not like this.'

'They will when I get there,' said Ellie.

The crowd in the *Lismore* was transient. People stopped in for a pint and then went somewhere else. Ellie had another beer and people-watched as the night wore on and the regulars began to outnumber the strangers. Hannah was now talking to the bulldog at the bar, her body language, as usual, contradictory; Han was flicking her straight blonde hair and smiling, but her body was turned into the bar, away from her companion. It looked to Ellie as if she'd learned how to flirt out of a book. Hell, maybe she had. Ellie smiled as she wondered how good her own technique was. She knew what rule number one was, anyway: *find a dark corner.*

She tried to remember what she had looked like before. Of course, she was almost the same.

Almost.

Ellie had dark brown hair that she kept long to hide her damaged cheek, and greyish -green eyes with perhaps more lines round them than were normal for a twenty-seven year old. Laughter lines, they called them. What the hell had been *that* funny? When she looked in the mirror at her right profile, she sometimes had the hopeless little idea that she wasn't bad looking. Until she turned face on, of course, when it looked as if part of her had melted.

Fiona broke into her thoughts.

'So, you're determined.'

'What?'

15

'Baranpay. You're determined to go.'

Ellie looked up. Fiona had tied her long blonde hair up in a neat clasp, and not one single hair had dared to escape. The pale blue eyes were still outrageously sober, and despite herself, Ellie had to laugh.

'Fee, why don't you lighten up. Have a drink.'

Fiona's lips drew into a thin line. No mean task. Ellie considered Fiona the most beautiful woman she had ever seen. Like a blonde Demi Moore, with an unfortunate side order of Julie Andrews. One night the two of them had gone out to a pub, and she had overheard two men whispering about them. They had called them *Beauty and the beast,* and Ellie had turned to them in a quiet fury.

'How dare you say that about my friend!'

She smiled to herself at the memory.

'What are you grinning at? Honestly, Ellie. How many drinks have you had?'

'Just the even dozen.' Ellie took another sip just to annoy her. 'Where's Fred tonight? How is the old man anyway. Haven't seen him for ages.'

'He's fine. Don't change the subject.'

Ellie shrugged, glancing round for Lara. She spotted her in a corner with her tongue down some guy's throat. Nice. Ellie stole her drink.

'And what about you, Fee. How are you? Any happy news yet?'

Ellie saw the hurt appear in her friend's eyes, and immediately regretted her words.

She was about to apologise, but Fiona leaned forward, the hurt turned to anger.

'Never mind me. Don't think I don't know why you're leaving.'

Ellie was surprised. 'What?'

'You can't keep running away from things. You have to stand and face them.'

'And is that what you're doing?'

'I told you. Never mind me.'

Ellie felt the warm happy drunkenness wave goodbye. Fiona carried on talking, but she no longer heard her. The noise of the pub blurred around her like a mangled ancient cassette tape. She was back once more in the shell of Ellie, the scarred survivor, and a question occurred to her: survival requires effort, but does effort equal survival? She wasn't sure. She was too drunk to think it through.

'-not even listening!' she heard suddenly. She looked up. Fiona's eyes were furious, but there was something else there, as always. Ellie found a smile.

'I'm going, Fee,' she said. Her voice sounded as if it came from far

16

away. 'I'm even looking forward to it.'

Fiona looked away. 'It's a tiny island a long way from anywhere. You'll be lonely.'

'Maybe,' she said. 'Actually it doesn't sound so bad.' She finished Lara's drink and stood up.

'I think it's time-' she said, and stopped. Time for what? She had no idea. The next tune started up on the juke box. It was the Pogues' version of *The Irish Rover*. As she looked around the bar, she spotted Billy the landlord collecting glasses. She hurried over and grabbed his arms as he put the empties on the bar.

'On the fourth of July eighteen hundred and six -' she sang, waltzing him round the room. Billy laughed, joining in. Before long everyone was singing the chorus, which were the only words they knew: *in the hull of the Irish Rover!*

Ellie danced until all the alcohol made her dizzy, and she hurried to the toilet in a haze of nausea. Leaning over the cracked basin, she splashed water on her face. Someone had spilled perfume in the sink, and the reek of it made her feel even more sick.

'Are you all right, Ellie?'

She looked round. Hannah was sitting in a cubicle with the door open. Her face was streaked with tears.

'Han, what's wrong?' She said.

Hannah just shook her head. She never wore make up, and amidst all the tears she looked like a child. Ellie crouched and put her arm round her. Someone came into the toilet, and Ellie kicked the cubicle door closed. She stroked her friend's hair until Hannah stopped sobbing.

'That's better,' she said. Hannah looked up, but her eyes were sad.

'If you don't want to talk about it, that's fine,' Ellie said. 'I understand.' *And how,* she thought.

'You're going away tomorrow.'

Ellie nodded. Her knees were aching now from crouching low, and she knelt down, ignoring the rough and dirty tiles.

'Can't you take me with you?'

Ellie searched her eyes, and then smiled. Eventually Hannah smiled too, and then they both laughed.

'Come on,' Ellie said.

As Hannah washed her face, a woman came into the toilet, drunk and singing to herself. She looked at Ellie and her face twisted in disgust. Ellie felt the familiar sensation as her heart dropped. The woman realised what she had done and put her hand to her mouth.

'I'm so sorry,' she said.

Ellie nodded. As they left, she saw Hannah give the woman a filthy

17

look, and that made her smile.

Back at the bar, Fiona was waiting alone. It was gone closing time, and all the lights were on. Billy was shouting unintelligibly, but his meaning was clear.

'Where's Laz?'

Fiona shrugged.

Ellie looked around the pub, but couldn't see her friend. Ah well, she thought, it was typical for Lara. She'd see her next time.

'Fred's here,' Fiona said. 'Do you guys want a lift?'

Ellie shook her head. She thought it was typical that Fiona's husband would wait in the car, not even coming in for one drink. He didn't like her, but Ellie had no idea why. Maybe he was just embarrassed by her scarred face.

'Well, Han,' Ellie said, steeling herself. 'I'll see you in a few months.'

Hannah looked as if she might cry again. *Honestly*, Ellie thought, reaching out to hug her.

'You've got my number, and I'll tell you my address when I get there.'

'You take care,' Hannah said. 'And I hope you love it there. I really do.'

Ellie grinned.

Fiona reached out and hugged her too.

'And be careful on that bike. You always go way too fast.'

'Yes mother.'

'And if you don't like it, come back.'

Ellie nodded, stepping back. Like that was going to happen.

'I hate goodbyes,' she said. 'So just bugger off, will you?'

*

Let the eye of the traveller roam over the grey waves, across the quiet minch where seals bask on the rocks, and on to the island of Baranpay. The sea there is rough, breaking over the treacherous underwater ridges, and tall cliffs rise to a fortress of rock. Now turn north and west, where the rocks give way to grass and heather, and a white house stands at the northern point. There is a shingle beach, with two elderly donkeys rubbing each others' back with their soft muzzles.

Now turn south, past the sharp jutting rocks they call the wingtip, towards the harbour and the masts of the boats, to a lone house by the water's edge. There's a row of cars, some of them very old and battered, and as you swoop lower you will see that one of them has an open bonnet, and someone is tinkering with the engine. Pass over,

18

and you will have to climb now, for the land rises to the western cliffs. Out to sea is another tiny island, just a patch of sand pushed above the waves, where grasses wave in the wind, and a rocky outcrop stands like a milestone. The cliffs are full of birds of all brands, squabbling and screaming. The noise is deafening. There is a sudden gap in the granite, and there below is another beach, sand rising to shingle, and above it, a tiny white cottage. The mountain rises past it, crowned with spikes of rock like a dragon's dorsal ridges. There is a single light in the cottage.

Now turn north again, and follow a deer track down the hillside, down to the harbour with its lights and houses. There is a pub there, and someone is pushing open the door. The pub is busy. Move lower, and the conversation can be heard...

'You're the new bird person then?' the barman said. He had a very long face, with sad grey bloodhound eyes, and a single eyebrow that went right across the bridge of his nose. Ellie nodded. She had that fluttering in her chest that she knew was nerves. Any second now she'd start giggling.

'Christ, lassie, that's a lonely job.'

She looked round. The man who had spoken was tall and broad, his dark hair just starting to turn grey, although he looked to be in his late fifties. He had large pale blue eyes above a big nose and small mouth that contrived to make him look solemn. But then he smiled, and the rough lines round his eyes and mouth crinkled like the careless folds of his clothes, transforming him into a seriously attractive man. It was a trusting face, and he looked at her without giving any sign that there was anything wrong with her, which was intriguing. She gave a little shrug, and the man stood up.

'Donnie MacLeod,' he said, reaching out his hand. 'This is my son Conor.'

Conor didn't have his father's skill. He looked at her and smiled, but his gaze lingered on her scars.

Ha ha! In the limelight again!

'What happened to your face, gal?' Donnie said.

Ellie raised an eyebrow. This directness was a surprise as well. She was aware of all the faces in the bar turned to her, and felt the tightness in her cheek as blood rushed to it. She took a deep breath.

'Och, I just lay on it funny,' she said.

Donnie smiled, and she saw what looked like approval in his eyes, as if she'd passed some sort of test. She heard a chair being scraped back, and looked over. One of the older fishermen was pulling up his smelly brown sweater, taking the T shirt underneath with it.

19

'Look at this one, lassie,' the man said, grinning. He turned his bare side to her, and she saw a huge rope of scar tissue running from the base of his rib cage to the joint of the shoulder. It looked as if someone had gathered the skin in a fist and squeezed it so tight it could never relax.

'Got caught in the boat line,' he said, a smug note in his voice.

'Ach, put it away, Roy, that's nothing. Here gal, look at this.'

Another man had now lifted the leg of his jeans to show her a great dent in the calf muscle.

Ellie felt as if she was caught in the middle of a surreal movie. The whole pub was now full of scar bravado, men comparing various limbs, detailing how deep, how many stitches, how incredibly painful it had been, how they had been back at work within the hour. For the first time Ellie felt upstaged, and as for her scars, well they itched and burned in silent anger. For the first time, she thought about telling her own story, but she dismissed that thought quickly.

'Hey lass, if you look closely, you can see I got a cockle trapped.'

'I'm sorry?' She looked at the man, who was flexing a suitably marred bicep. As he flexed the ropy muscle, it pushed up a round lump of tissue, as if a ball bearing had been inserted under the skin. Ellie raised her eyebrows, hoping she looked impressed.

'Be all right if you get hungry, then.'

The man laughed, and clapped a big hand on her shoulder. The landlord placed another pint in front of her, though she'd barely touched the last. She laughed, glancing round to see who had bought the drink, but the men were back to comparing their injuries. She caught the eye of a man in the corner, clearly not a fisherman, by his dress (and the lack of scars). He was older than the others, with cropped grey-white hair and very blue eyes, and he was looking at her intently. She smiled absently and looked back at the bar.

'You'll be here till the autumn then,' the landlord said mournfully.

She nodded. 'Is that a problem?'

'Och no. Not at all,' he said, as if she had just told him he had a month to live.

'Don't mind Murd, he was born miserable,' Conor said. 'Come and sit with us, and tell us your name.'

Ellie took the offered seat. 'I'm Ellie,' she said, feeling an unaccustomed glimmer of hope reaching into her heart.

THREE

'Whenever, wherever I find who you are
If time has forgotten me, I'll find a star
And rest my head upon it and dream a little while
I've travelled far'

Ellie listened to the words and wished she had written them. The old song was one of her favourites, the music speaking of loneliness and isolation, both of whom she joined regularly for a drink. She closed her eyes, smiling at the warmth of the May sun on her face.   There was no feeling in the world like this, and she should know, having tried plenty of them out for size. The sand beneath her fingers was as fine and white as flour, and she turned her face into it, feeling the soft warmth rub against the rough and ridged tissue of her scarred skin. Perhaps if she stayed here for a thousand years the sand would rub away all trace of those scars. She grasped a handful of the stuff and held it tightly. Geology was simpler than real life.

A lot simpler.

She opened her eyes to see a tern hovering in the blue, wings outstretched like an angel. He spotted a fish and pulled his wings tight to dive. There was barely a splash, and the silver gleamed in the dark beak like a shard of stolen sunlight.

She stood up, switching off her IPod. The tide would be turning, and it was time to go.

She walked round the tiny island towards her boat, pushed it out of the shallows and got in. As she rowed for the mainland, she looked back at the lonely speck of land, her own special place. The island was no more than half a mile across, and there was nothing but ocean between it and America. She looked back to check her position, and rowed for the landing.

As she drew nearer to the shore, the sound of the birds became louder. She couldn't see them behind her, but she knew their names from their voices; kittiwakes, gannets and fulmars, guillemots and razorbills. They covered every inch of the tall cliffs, living on top of each other in grudging accord.

Four months, she'd been here, and already the city was like another lifetime. The memory of her last night out with her friends was like the full stop at the end of the book. She'd started a new one now, and at the moment it was shaping up to be a bestseller. There was a lot of truth in what Fiona had said; that she was running away, hiding from the scars. But there were few things to rival contentment. This job was going to save her life.

She tied up and walked up the sand and shingle beach, all that remained of the former cliff face. Some twist of geological fate had dumped a weaker strata of calcite there, which the sea had steadily worn back. Seen from the sea, the cliffs looked like a mouth with a tooth missing. Ellie climbed the ancient steps cut into the rock face, counting as she climbed. There were one hundred and forty seven. A month ago she had counted to take her mind off the height, but now she paid the shore below scant heed as the tide came rolling in fast, lifting her little boat and tugging at its mooring.

The cottage was an old croft house, and had probably looked out over these cliffs for two hundred years. It had three simple rooms. The only door opened into a living room-cum-kitchen, behind which were a bedroom and small bathroom. The windows were small, to keep out the Atlantic winds, the walls a foot thick to keep in the warmth.

Inside, Ellie lit the stove and put some music on. She opened the fridge door and stared in as she did every single day. She could describe the contents of her fridge in perfect detail, but every day she performed the ritual of the door opening, in case someone might have sneaked in and filled it full of unexpected goodies. Unfortunately, there was still only milk, cheese, a mouldy tomato and a half-empty jar of mayonnaise. She closed the door again and made herself some toast, sitting down at her laptop to check her e-mails, singing along as she did:

These are my mist covered mountains
my dark loch, silence surrounding…

There was one from Fiona, and a couple from her old workmates. Ellie didn't even open them. Another was from William Ross, the warden on the isle of Rhum. He had spotted a white tailed sea eagle, and she felt the sudden thrill that the bird might come here. They were very rare. William was an enthusiastic e-mailer, and she realised he was getting more and more keen, which was a problem. He had never seen her, nor she him for that matter. It was best to keep it simple, so she kept her replies as formal as she could. Life was fine until other people got involved, then it got messy and uncomfortable.

This is my sky filled with stars

She closed the e-mail page, glancing at her saved mail. There was only one item in there; an article Jim MacGregor had sent her. Jim was a retired psychiatrist, and her best friend on the island.

'I know you might not be interested in this now,' he had said in the mail, 'but keep it. One day you might be.'

The article was all about reconstructive laser treatment for hypertrophic scars. He was right, she did not want to even think about it.

She glanced outside, where the sun was setting beyond her little island. The pale, slow moving clouds were lit up from below, and rimmed with gold like a party invitation.

in the land of my hope and my heart

Four months, to change her life. She smiled. It sounded like one of those new diet fads, or some self-help course. She had learned, and learned fast, and not only about the birds.

The music finished, and she wandered outside into the cold air, enjoying the feel of the wind on her face. Rubbing her cheek in the sand had not been a good idea, and the scars felt like they were crawling around looking for something. Escape, she hoped, sadly.

No chance.

They talked to her.

Now and then she'd reply, say things like: what's with all the itching, you got fleas? Or why can't you just give me peace, or you don't get any better looking, you know that? As if the scars were some mischievous mongrel dog that was a pain in the arse to look after, but that she loved all the same. Sometimes, she'd be laughing, and she'd feel the skin tighten round them, in a way now familiar and depressing, but still somehow reassuring.

She headed back indoors and smeared the bland smelling cream on her ravaged face. The cream numbed the skin, but she hated it, all the same. It smelt of defeat, of yet another lie. She glanced at herself in the mirror, and decided there was only one thing to do.

The evening sky was the palest of blues, and hanging there like an unwelcome blot was a big vermillion cloud. As the sun travelled south, the topmost cloud layers turned brown, smudges of darkness, like smoke against the blue. And then suddenly, Mars appeared. Of course it had always been there, but the light had died enough that it now shone out like a quiet beacon. The air smelt of summer, though it was still a way off. After another moment, the vermillion was gone, and there was nothing left but a few donkey-brown smudges against the perfect sky.

Ellie walked down the track towards the village. She rounded a bend, and there it was: the pale shapes of long-empty cottages, dimly lit windows, darker shadows of boats moored in the safe waters, their masts ticking like metronomes against the stars. Ellie smiled to herself, making for the brightest building, hearing the gentle sounds from within.

There were four people in the pub, and they all looked up as she walked in.

23

'Evening folks.'

'Ah, Ellie. It's a gentle night.'

She sat at the bar and took the drink Murd had already poured for her.

'So how are your birds?' He asked, leaning on the bar and fixing her with his doleful stare.

'There are more arriving every day,' she replied. 'Coming here from warmer places, which I will probably never understand.'

Archie Marr stood up and handed his empty glass to Murd, who took it slowly.

'I'd go somewhere warmer mesel' if I had the cash.'

'Where would you go, Archie?' Ellie said, grinning. Archie was small and stocky, with a sort of permanent stoop, as if he was carrying an invisible rucksack. He had intense eyes that were never still, and now they flitted round the room as he thought about the question.

'I've heard it said the Greek isles are just like the highlands,' piped up Donnie MacLeod. 'Only a wee bit sunnier.'

'Aye, and they speak funny there too,' Ellie agreed.

Donnie laughed. 'You softy Southerners.'

'Watch it, MacLeod,' said his wife, Lisa. She shook her head at Ellie.

'Come away and sit down.'

Ellie was happy to oblige. Lisa was a large woman with a thick Welsh accent and a fearsome head of curly black hair. Ellie had heard that she was formidably strong, with a temper to match, yet most of the time she reserved it for her brood of five sons. She had come here on holiday one year, and had danced with MacLeod at the gathering. She had never gone home.

'Well, I wouldn't mind going, some day,' Archie said wistfully.

'Aye, and leave your Flora behind,' Lisa laughed. Archie forced a smile, but his face was burning.

'So, Archie,' Donnie said, 'Did you have a look at that old banger our Iowyn's bought?'

'I did that,' Archie said, pleased at the change of subject.

'So what is wrong with it, then, can you put it right?'

'Just crap in the carburettor,' Archie said, taking a long pull of his pint.

The others took this in carefully.

'So how often does he have to do that then, Archie?' said Murd, his face twisted in a frown.

Ellie burst into laughter, feeling the skin tighten round her cheek, not caring.

The door opened before Donnie could reply, and Jim MacGregor walked in.

'Hello, Ellie,' he said, listening as the story of Iowyn's car was recounted for his benefit. Murd stood behind the bar, looking solemn.

'Knowing the state of the car,' Jim said eventually, 'I can't see it would do any harm,'

FOUR

Griff could still hear the echo of the words, could still feel the sinking sensation in his chest, the sudden rush of anger bursting out of him. He could still see the faces, turned to him in surprise, the Best Boy standing there with his mouth open. The moment was captured in his dreams now. There was no getting away from it.

He got out of bed, feeling groggy, and headed for the bathroom. He turned on the light above the sink, looking at his red-veined eyes, the grey pallor of his skin. Too many flights, too many drinks, too little sleep. And, of course, too many bad dreams.

He pulled on his jeans and got the last-but-one clean shirt out of his bag. Then he left the hotel and wandered aimlessly down dim streets lined with dark houses. The ground floor windows all had bars, which reminded him of home. He pushed his hands into the pockets of his black linen jacket, and crossed a wide street empty of all but a passing taxi cab, which slowed hopefully when it got near him. He walked on until he reached the embankment, and there he leaned on the wall and looked out at the Albert Bridge.

'What am I doing here?' he thought. Every city now appeared to him pretty much the same. The geography was different, but underneath the surface, each place had its own life that he did not feel a part of. As the light began to leach into the morning sky, he looked up and sighed. He didn't know what to do. Below him, the river flowed on, uninterested.

Well, one thing was for sure, he couldn't go back. He had left his whole life behind him, though some things had inevitably come along for the ride. Guilt was one of them, and there were others, some of them still too painful to think about. He needed to get out of the city, find somewhere he could think. Maybe then he could decide what to do, how to go on.

He looked up at the sky again. He loved to fly. Maybe that was the answer. Maybe he could just fly away.

*

Jim came walking down the hill towards the pub, and stopped short when he saw everyone sitting outside. It was a warm spring night, with the waves lapping gently against the boats. Ellie had dragged everyone outside.

'What's all this?' he said.

'It was too nice to sit inside,' Ellie said, well aware that behind her,

Donnie and Lisa were rolling their eyes. Jim nodded absently.

'I bet Murd's pleased.'

'No change there, then. Anyway, it's getting cold now, we were just coming in.'

They all regrouped back inside, where Murd gave them a baleful stare.

'And how are you this evening, girl?' Jim said, sitting down in his usual corner.

Ellie grinned. 'I'm fine, *man*. How are the chickens?'

Jim's wife Mairearadh had a soft spot for stray animals, and had recently acquired half a dozen bantams.

'Bloody things,' he said. 'They're a nuisance.' But he was smiling as he said it.

Ellie listened while Donnie and Lisa began arguing over a planned trip to Inverness, when Jim spoke quietly.

'You've overdone it a bit, today.'

She instinctively touched her cheek, looking at him anxiously, but he shook his head to reassure her.

'I know. You don't want to talk about it. It's fine.'

Ellie took a long pull of her pint, looking up at Jim as she did, just in case he changed his mind. She was fond of him, but found it hard to forget that he was a psychiatrist. Even now he was smiling as if he could read her mind.

'You've got my Gethyn interested in the wildlife now, you know,' Lisa nudged Ellie.

'I have? But I've never met your son.'

Donnie laughed. 'No need,' he said. 'Lisa's told him all about you.'

'Yes. I told him, see, about what it is you have to do, counting the birds and ringing them and so on, and he's dead into it. Wants to go with you sometime.'

'Oh,' Ellie said, smiling now. 'Sure. I'll take him.' She tried to remember which one of Donnie and Lisa's sons Gethyn was. They had alternate Scottish and Welsh names. She guessed he was number four, which would put him about seventeen.

'Gethyn's the clever one,' Jim said softly. 'But has trouble making up his mind.'

'Aye, he wanted to be a doctor a fortnight ago,' Donnie said, shaking his head. 'Can't think why.'

Jim gave him a look of mock outrage.

'How did you get into this work in the first place?' Lisa asked.

Ellie shrugged. 'I just saw the job in the paper one day. Thought it would be good. Really different, you know?'

Donnie went up for a refill. 'What did you do before?'

Ellie kept her face carefully blank.

'I was a lab tech. In a hospital. It was my job to do blood tests and so on.'

'Yuch,' Archie said. 'No wonder you wanted another job.'

'No, it was all right, actually. We used to have a laugh.' Ellie said. 'Every Monday we used to prick our fingers and do blood alcohol tests on ourselves. There was a sweep for who was the most pissed from the night before.'

Everyone laughed except Lisa.

'What, and you were supposed to be testing people's blood, in that state?'

'I know,' Ellie said. 'It was a disgrace. But the work was nearly all mechanised. All we really had to do was put the test tubes into the machine.'

'And I'm sure you never won the sweep anyway,' Jim said loyally.

Well, Ellie thought, *not at first…*

'It is a big change; a city lab tech to a bird warden on a remote island,' Jim said, not looking at her.

Ellie said nothing. The door opened then and the workers from the salmon farm came in. The air filled with the stench of fish and the sound of laughter.

'I know what you're thinking, Sigmund,' Ellie said, smiling. 'I just wanted a change, and I saw this job and thought it would be great.'

Jim nodded, his face impassive. 'Well. You must know a lot about birds, anyway.'

She smiled then, fiddling with a beer mat. 'I've always been a birder, but I still had a lot to learn in a short time.'

Jim just nodded. Ellie knew very well that he was trying to get her to talk. She had read a crime novel once in which the cops simply waited in silence until the suspect confessed. She smiled at her thoughts.

'What?' he said.

'Nothing.'

'So you've always been into bird watching?' he prompted. Ellie looked up. He had the kind of eyes that took hold and gripped tight, and she found it hard to look away. At the same time, he gave off a sense of reassurance. Years of bedside manner, she supposed.

'My father was,' she said. She waited, as if something would happen. When nothing did, she continued.

'He used to take me with him. It was incredibly boring. I'd sit there for hours drinking horrible tea out of his plastic flask, trying not to make a noise. All of a sudden there'd be a mad panic when he spotted something. He'd make me look through the binoculars, but of course I never saw what he did.'

'How old were you?'

'Dunno. About six or seven, I suppose.'

'What happened after that?'

Ellie shook her head. 'What do you mean, 'what happened'. Nothing happened.'

'I mean, did you get fed up going, or did he stop going? What?'

Ellie shrugged. 'I stopped going.'

'Why?'

She looked at him. 'Do you want another drink?'

'It's my round.' He made no attempt to get up. Ellie looked past him out of the window, to where the sky was now the colour of heather in shadow. When she looked back, Jim was still looking at her. She sighed.

'Because he left,' she said. As soon as she had said it, she felt a strange surge of relief.

'Strange, isn't it?'

She laughed, but there was no humour in it.

'He left, but out of some strange perversity I began to take an interest in the bird world. Wonder what that says about me.'

Jim smiled. 'Feels better, doesn't it? Talking about things. It helps.'

Before she could reply he got up and went to the bar. Ellie looked up and saw Donnie's son Geraint looking at her. At 23 he was the oldest of the five boys, and also the best looking. He was big and brawny, with dark George Clooney eyes. He was giving her his best 'lets-go-skinny-dipping' look, and she grinned back. Geraint didn't care about her scars. She was female; that would do nicely. Behind her, Ellie heard a sigh.

'One of these days maybe he'll settle down,' Lisa said, fixing her son with a hopeless look.

'Don't count on it,' Ellie said, laughing. 'If he runs out of Scottish women, he'll only go abroad.'

Ellie rode down to the harbour, looking for Gethyn. After Lisa had told her that her son was interested in birds, she had dug out a set of photos she thought he might like to see, the ones of the Storm Petrel chicks. But the harbour was deserted, all the boats were in for the day, and the pub was heaving. She looked in, but didn't see anyone she didn't know. Donnie and Conor were there, though.

'I'm after Gethyn,' she said.

'It's about time someone was,' Donnie said. 'He's at home, I think.'

She got back on the Yamaha and rode past the harbour towards Donnie's house. It was a big rambling place, all ramshackle sheds and sheep, and the next field was strewn with Iowyn's experiments; quad bikes, cars and tractors that he had tried unsuccessfully to fix, but refused to get rid of. Lisa was hanging out her washing, and waved as Ellie rode into the yard.

'Hi Lisa. I've brought some photos for Gethyn.'

Lisa took the peg out of her mouth. 'He's about somewhere. Oh hell, will you listen to that!'

Ellie grinned at the scream of a tormented engine.

'He's got a motor bike now, see,' she said sadly, shaking her head. 'Got it from some bloke on Mull.'

'Don't knock it,' Ellie said. 'One day he might be a millionaire inventor.'

Lisa gave her a sour look, and Ellie laughed and rode round to the back of the house. Iowyn was mad about engines, cars, motorbikes, anything fast, which was kind of ironic on an island twelve miles long. He was sitting on the cobbles, his hands inside the workings of the bike. He was skinny for a fourteen-year-old, and had inherited his mother's wild black hair. When he stood up, he looked like a used match.

'Hi Ellie,' he said.

'What are you doing? No, on second thoughts, don't tell me.'

He looked up. There was a smear of grease across his right cheek where he'd obviously wiped the back of his hand. He looked very young.

Ellie left her bike by the corner and walked over.

'Have you seen my mum about?'

'Yeah, she's hanging out the washing.'

'Well, don't tell her I'm here. I'm not supposed to bring my stuff near the house, but it's so sheltered here out of the wind.'

Ellie nodded. Although the sun was warm today, the wind was

coming straight from Greenland. Iowyn had pushed the bike up to the back of the house where the wall of a cowshed and the L shape of the kitchen extension protected him on both sides. He was facing the new patio doors Lisa had been begging Donnie to fit for years. Ellie nodded towards them.

'You better be careful with the new doors.'

'God, yes,' he said in hushed voice. 'Right, let's try that.'

As he stood up and reached for the key, a young man appeared on the other side of the doors. He was a younger, softer version of Geraint. He opened them and stepped out.

'Hi. I'm Gethyn. You must be Ellie.'

The scars preened under his gaze. Ellie tried not to sigh.

'Iowyn, you shouldn't be so close to the house-'

'I know, I know,' Iowyn ignored his brother and started the engine. 'Shut the doors or mum will hear.'

Gethyn did as he was told. He stood beside Ellie while Iowyn messed about with the bike.

'Your mum said you were into birdwatching. I brought you some photos I thought you might like.'

'Oh right. Great!'

Ellie reached into her bag for the pictures, hearing the engine sound suddenly change. She and Gethyn looked over at the bike just as it leapt forward, Iowyn still hanging desperately to the handlebars, and headed straight for the new doors. Ellie put her arms up to her face as the glass exploded, Iowyn let out a single anguished yell of 'No!' and Gethyn just stared, mouth open in horror. No one moved for a long minute, and then Ellie realised Iowyn was hurt. She hurried forward and leaned over him.

'Iowyn, are you all right? You're bleeding.'

Iowyn looked numb. He stared at the broken glass as Lisa came thundering through. She let out a furious scream and Gethyn winced.

'What the fuck! What have you done!'

Iowyn looked down, noticing his cut arm for the first time. Ellie gave Gethyn a little push. 'Go and call Jim.'

Gethyn was only too glad to get out of the way.

'How many times have I told you!' Lisa yelled. 'My doors. My new doors!'

She stood looking at the wreckage as if it might somehow repair itself. Iowyn stood up slowly.

'I don't know what happened,' he said in a confused voice. 'It must have slipped into gear. I don't know how.'

'This is the end, Iowyn,' Lisa said in a suddenly calm voice. 'No more tinkering with old junk. Not in this house.'

31

She went back inside and a few minutes later Ellie heard her telephoning Donnie.

'I'm really in the shit now,' Iowyn said.

Ellie sighed. 'We need to get that cut seen to. Don't worry, she'll calm down.'

Iowyn looked down gloomily. 'You don't know her,' he said darkly.

Jim arrived ten minutes later, by which time Lisa had calmed down enough to start clearing up the glass. The bike had collapsed on the dining room floor, and Ellie had found some kitchen towels to mop up the spilled petrol. The house stank of it, and Ellie saw Lisa sniffing, about to fly into another rage. She handed the stained towels to Gethyn.

'Here, get rid of these,' she hissed. Gethyn disappeared into the house, and she tried to lift the bike up to get it outside. Lisa saw what she was doing and came over. She hefted the bike onto its wheels easily, wheeled it outside and let it go at the grass. The bike collapsed in a heap, and Lisa stared at it for a long moment as if it were a drunk she'd just thrown out of the pub.

Ellie looked back at the sound of a car arriving, and Gethyn appeared at the door.

'Dad's here,' he said. Lisa nodded, and Ellie realised that Iowyn had been right. His life was about to become hell.

'What in God's name happened?'

Donnie looked at Gethyn, who shrugged. 'I don't know really. The bike just seemed to leap forward.'

'Iowyn's got a bad cut,' Ellie said, in an effort to defuse matters. Donnie said nothing, looking at Lisa, who was staring at him in silent fury. Donnie's eyes turned to Ellie, and she saw that Iowyn's life wasn't the only one that was going to be miserable for a while.

'He was told not to bring his junk near the house. I want all those old cars out of here, and I want those doors repaired before the weekend.'

She folded her arms, and Donnie's eyebrows met in an angry frown.

'Here's Jim,' Gethyn warned, before a shouting match ensued.

Jim walked up, looking round the faces and smiling in a grim way.

'Iowyn's going to be fine,' he said. It didn't have the desired effect. He looked at Ellie and she tried not to smile. It was pretty funny really, but if Lisa saw her smiling she'd probably give herself a heart attack.

Donnie turned to walk away.

'Where do you think you're going? Come back here!'

'I'm going for a smoke and a think, woman. Be at peace!'

Donnie managed a tight smile as he walked past Ellie. She looked past him to see Iowyn walking towards them, his arm bandaged. He smiled awkwardly, but couldn't meet his mother's eyes.

'You all right?' she asked quietly.

'He's not all right in the head,' Lisa snapped. 'You get your pals up here right away, Iowyn, and get all those old cars moved. I'm not joking.'

Iowyn looked as if he might cry, and Ellie felt a huge well of sympathy for him.

'Donnie'll see the glass gets fixed,' Jim said.

'Damn right he will! The length of time I've waited-'

Everyone ducked as a huge *whumph* shook the house, followed by a scream.

'Jesus!' Ellie said. They all looked back at the house from where the sound had come. Jim started to run inside and they all followed.

Ellie felt her heart pounding. That sound had been all too familiar. They pelted through the broken doors to see Donnie, hobbling forward, bent over, trousers round his ankles. There was a smell of petrol and something burning, something Ellie didn't want to think about. Lisa screamed, and Gethyn reached out and put his hand on Ellie's arm.

'Oh no,' he whispered.

Ellie looked at his face.

'Gethyn, where did you put the paper towels?'

He looked at her. 'Down the toilet.'

'And your dad's just been for a smoke.'

There were no prizes for guessing where he'd dumped the fag end.

Jim crouched down to where Donnie had now dropped to his knees. Jim yelled for someone to call the ambulance.

'No!' Donnie yelled. 'No ambulance. I'm not going to the mainland, not like this.'

'Donnie-'

'Just take me to my room.' Donnie closed his eyes.

Ellie looked back to the forlorn bike crumpled on the grass. A curious sheep was nosing at it. Her heart was still pounding, and she knew that the nightmare would never go away, not really. She was destined to relive the scene forever.

'If any of you breathe a word about this, your lives won't be worth living!' Donnie yelled. They managed to get him into the bedroom, and Ellie and the boys were left outside. They looked at each other sheepishly. Iowyn glanced back at the broken doors.

'This is all my fault.'

Gethyn swallowed. 'Well, I think we'd better just get out of the way.'

'Good idea,' Ellie said. She could feel the irrational beginnings of a giggle starting deep in her chest, and looking at Gethyn saw that he

33

too was struggling not to laugh.

Ellie retrieved her bike and rode it quickly along the dirt track. It was only when she reached the cliff path that the laughter overtook her, stretching her ruined cheek.

Just as well there's no one here to see, the scars whispered, wiping the smile from her face.

SIX

Next morning, the sun slanted gradually across the window until at last it fell on Ellie's face and woke her up. She dragged on her jeans and a T shirt and walked outside to the clifftop.

The sun was warm again today, though the wind was still biting, and she turned her ravaged cheek into it, enjoying the coolness. She could hear the gulls on the outside cliffs, but they seemed quieter today, as if they weren't quite awake yet. She grabbed her stuff and went down the cliff stairs, ready to check her charges and see how many had arrived. It was a sign of the summer to come, she knew, how quickly the seabirds were arriving.

And coming they were, in their hundreds. She marvelled at why they all chose these particular cliffs, when there were others all up and down the coast and on the western isles, but perhaps they were just like humans, and old habits died hard.

It was hard work, picking her way between the nests, as virtually every space was taken, and the birds screamed at her in outrage. They were not afraid of her though, and, she thought privately, not one of them ever winced at the sight of her hideous face.

They're birds, Ellie. In case you hadn't noticed, the scars taunted.

She ignored them.

It was pretty much the perfect job. She watched as a pair of gannets slapped their

bright yellow bills together in their own special kiss, before taking to the skies, their tail

feathers spread out like white stars, and the now-familiar feeling of contentment stole

into her heart.

In the afternoon, Ellie took a walk down past the pub and up the dirt track towards the church. On the southern hillside above she could see a cluster of white fishermen's cottages, windows gazing out to sea, so the women could watch for the returning crews. The cottages had been empty a long time. On the northern side, the little church was a far older building, with a small graveyard sheltered by the cliff wall. The road forked half way up, beside another small building, a neglected little house with its own garden cut out of the turf, but long since left to the elements. It was a forlorn place, and Ellie felt a deep and unidentified sense of sadness looking at the empty windows. She turned round and headed back to the harbour, where she could see Flora Marr, arms folded, watching her.

'Exploring, are we? There's not much to see,' Flora said. She looked disapproving, her natural state. Archie's wife had eyes that seemed at once bitter and angry, but Ellie sensed that it was not directed at her. When Flora looked past her, it seemed she was looking a long, long way.

Ellie heard a shout, and looked past to see the fishing boats returning. Flora pursed her lips and walked back to her little shop. The bell tinkled forlornly as the door banged.

Ellie waved at the boatmen and looked down the northerly track rising from the harbour. There was another small group of cottages, the dirt road running to Donnie's croft, and the remains of the road rising past the playing field into the hills.

There was something on her mind, but she couldn't identify it. She glanced walked back to the harbour, where a small group had gathered to watch the boats tie up. Murd was there, and two old men, one leaning on a stick, and a group of three women, who were the only people talking. She spotted Iowyn too, as it was half term, and he wasn't at school.

That was when she realised what was on her mind. The children. Where were the children?

Conor leapt from the deck, shouting her name.

'Got you some scallops, today.'

'Great, Conor. Thank you.'

She took the bag he offered, looking at him. He was grinning. Conor had a wide happy mouth. When he smiled, everyone joined in.

'Good catch today?'

He nodded. 'Brilliant today. Dad says he thinks this is going to be a good summer.'

Ellie lowered her voice. 'How is your dad?'

Conor grinned. 'He's OK. Mortified, but OK.'

He started to laugh. 'I wish I'd been there.'

'Don't,' Ellie said, 'It was awful.'

'Well anyway, we're all on notice never to breathe a word of it. Not that it'll make any difference on this island.'

Ellie smiled. 'Conor-'

'Iowyn, get your lazy arse over here and help me clean up.'

Iowyn walked over slowly, shoulders slumped. Conor looked quizzically back at her.

'Conor, where are all the children?'

'Children? What children?'

'There must be children on the island.'

Iowyn arrived, and gave her a quick smile. Conor reached up and ruffled his messy hair. Iowyn ducked away.

'This is the only one we have,' he said.

'Aww, Conor.'

'Here you go.' He handed Iowyn a broom, and the boy jumped down on to the deck. Conor looked at her.

'They've all grown up,' he said.

'There are no children *at all?*'

He shook his head. 'Nothing here for young folks. They grow up and move away.'

He nodded towards the hill road.

'That building you were looking at. That's the school house. For the young 'uns.'

Ellie followed his gaze, remembering how sad the building felt. A school with no children.

'Flora used to teach them. But –'

He shrugged, and Ellie looked back at him.

'Flora and Archie had no children?'

Conor shook his head. 'It's why she's so miserable. No kids of her own. No kids to teach.'

Ellie sighed. 'Oh, poor Flora.'

'We'll just have to hope Geraint and Angus settle down,' Conor continued with a grin. 'They'll never leave. But Gethyn'll be off to university soon, and Iowyn can't wait to leave.'

'What about you?'

'Me? Well. I've an understanding with a lass on the mainland, but she's only eighteen, three years younger than me, and she wants me to move to Lochinver, where her folks are.'

Ellie looked again at the abandoned house. She thought she understood the sadness she had sensed now. The island was slowly dying. She sighed.

'There's always the legend,' she said.

Conor's youngest brother Angus was a keen musician, and she'd heard him sing a song he'd written about the legend of the dragon.

'Aye, right,' Conor said. He grinned suddenly. 'There's always you,' he said.

'What? What do you mean, 'me''

He laughed. 'Well, you could stay and add to the population. Plenty of eligible bachelors here.' He winked and nodded over at Murd and the old men.

Ellie felt herself grinning. 'I'll give that the consideration it deserves,' she said.

Back at her cottage, she wrote up her log before going back outside. She got her motorbike out of the shed and took it for a ride round the cliffs. The wind felt good on her sore face and in her hair, and by the time she got back to her own cliffs, she was smiling. The sun was going down in a sky streaked with orange and gold, and she left the bike and walked to the cliff edge, looking down at the beach, where the tide was well out. She was about to go back in when something caught her eye off to the side. She scanned the cliffside, unable to see anything unusual, when suddenly a bird took off from half-way up, and headed out to sea. Ellie felt her heart skip. It looked like a peregrine.

'Oh wow,' she said, rushing inside to grab her binoculars and camera, then scanning the cliffside until at last she found signs of what might be a nest, lodged in a crevice. The peregrine had chosen the sheltered face, shunning the open sea wall with its other many inhabitants. She scanned the sky, waiting for the bird to return.

Ellie sat there a long time, watching the falcon. Try as she might, she could see neither eggs nor chicks. The nest had been built too well into a sloping crevice in the rock, and though the mother bird came and went regularly, she never saw as much as a feather. Ellie began to time the bird, working out how long she was gone for, an idea burning in her mind. Her face was very itchy and sore now, but she ignored it. She stood up, thinking, when she heard the sound of her phone ringing. She decided to ignore it, but it rang on and on, while the peregrine stayed put on her nest, as if wary of the new noise. Cursing under her breath, Ellie ran inside and grabbed the phone from her desk.

'Yes, hello.'

'Ellie. You know, don't you? You know what it's like.'

Ellie tried to identify who it was. The woman was sobbing, her words barely intelligible.

'What?' she said, listening to the sobs, her impatience ebbing away as she realised who it was.

'Lara, is that you? What's wrong?'

There was no reply, just more racking sobs.

'Lara? Laz?'

'You know what it's like,' Lara said, taking a deep breath, 'to think you are dying.'

Ellie held back a sigh.

'But you didn't die,' Ellie said. 'Neither of us did. Why are you so sad?'

She waited while Lara breathed hard, getting a grip of herself.

'Sometimes,' Lara said,' sometimes I wish I had died.'

Ellie waited. She had known Lara most of her life. She had never been strong, in body or mind. When the cancer had taken hold, no one expected Lara to make it. No one except Lara.

'I don't know what's wrong with me. Everyone says I ought to be happy, I should be dead, but I'm not. It's as if, I don't know; I didn't die, but *something* did. Do you understand?'

Ellie nodded, touching her own face. Nothing would ever be the same.

'Laz,' Ellie said. 'Why do you think everyone calls you that?'

There was a long silence, broken by a sniff. 'It's just easier than Lara.'

'No. You're our Lazarus, you came back to us from the grave. We won't let you go. I won't let you.'

'Something came back, but it wasn't me.'

'It was, Lara, it was you, but you'd changed. I came back, and people could see the change. It was there on my face. Yours is inside. But you're still Lara. You just need to look inside yourself, you'll find what you're looking for.'

'Have you?'

'You know the answer to that.'

'But you're still looking?'

'Yes.'

Another long silence, then –

'I wish you'd come back. I miss you. We all do. It's not the same here.'

Ellie laughed in relief at the end of the gloomy conversation.

'I don't think Fiona misses me.'

'Sure she does. She needs you to talk to. You know she won't talk to the rest of us.'

'I take it Fred's still being an arse?'

'And then some. Frankly I think she should cut her losses and find someone else, but...'

Ellie smiled, glancing out of the window. The sun had gone down, and the sky now was palest blue, patched with shocking pink clouds. Looking at the sky, she felt as if Lara and all her other friends were on another planet, one she couldn't visit. She might not be able to breathe.

'Are you all right, Ellie?'

Ellie smiled. 'Oh yes, Lara. I'm good. I really am.'

When she finally put the phone down and walked back outside, it was too dark to look for the peregrine. But it didn't matter, there was always tomorrow. Ellie sat on the damp grass and felt the contentment leach into her soul. There would always be tomorrow. She thought about what she had told Lara: that she was feeling good, and realised that she had never been happier. She was a lonely, scarred woman, living by herself on an isolated island, and utterly content.

39

*

Griff looked down at the sea beneath him. The noise of the machine intruded on the beauty surrounding him, and he wished he was in a glider, not a helicopter. He throttled back and banked the machine over the long narrow islands as the sun gleamed on the windshield and runners. He turned east then south, towards land, and away from the sun as it slipped down the sky.

This was not his own machine, he'd had to leave that behind, and the chances were he'd never fly it again. At this moment in time, he was never going back there. He was realistic enough to know that such feelings often dimmed with time, nevertheless, he was a long way from home, and that's the way he liked it.

He had left from LAX with nothing but his wallet and a hastily filled rucksack. He took the first flight he could get out of Los Angeles, before he could change his mind, or have it changed for him. The plane took him to Oklahoma City, and as he waited in the terminal for the next flight to Boston he saw a poster advertising his last film: *Passages*.

Or at least it had been his film, to start with, before the producer had pulled the plug on him and replaced him with another director, someone who would make the film more commercial to placate the creative administrators. Creative administrators! If that wasn't an oxymoron he didn't know what was.

The last flight had been to London, England. That had been a week ago, and now he was a long way from anywhere. It felt good.

The machine was responsive, and he smiled to himself as it obeyed him, dipping down to ride a few meters above the waves. From here he could see the little islands as they approached, some flat, some hilly, the farthest north dominated by a blue-purple mountain. The sea was laced with rocks, tall columns of granite giving shelter to countless seabirds. He flew around one such rock, so covered in birds it appeared to be moving, and for a moment the cries of the gulls almost overwhelmed the engine noise. He pulled the machine up, now following a lone black bird as it headed for land. He had grown up in the mid west and knew nothing about the sea, nothing, except that he liked being here. He felt at peace, and that was an unfamiliar feeling.

He flew over a tiny blip of land, no more than a stony beach among the waves, and seconds later he reached a bigger island, with rocky cliffs also full of birds. This island had a bite out of it, where a shingle beach rose to a tiny cottage far above. Beyond that, the land rose again to a knife-edged mountain. The sun dappled the land in greens and rusts, with here and there the fluorescent yellow splash of broom.

40

Close up, the mountain peak was made of shards of rock, a stonehenge built by the earth itself, both stark and beautiful. Griff banked north and the land fell away to a glen, and then a small harbour, facing the open sea to the glowing western sky once more.

He pulled the machine into a climb. It would be better to be on the mainland come dark, and he didn't know when that would be. They said the light remained long into the night this far north, but as he set course due east, something made him look back. The island looked like a whole other world there in the vastness of the sea, an innocent place, without profit margins and angry recriminations, hard words and harder truths. On an impulse he pulled the throttle back and turned again for the cliffs.

Ten minutes later he walked along the cliff edge, alone with the sound of the sea and the birds. And he felt his spirits lifting as he looked out at the waves. In the bright afternoon light they looked heavy and viscous, and the thought occurred to him that these waves might have travelled all the way from his homeland.

America: the home of the brave, whoever they were.

The grass here was thin and pale, struggling to survive in the wind, but it was full of tiny pink flowers. He crouched and touched one. He liked the idea that life carried on, no matter how difficult. The wind tugged his short brown hair, and he stood up again. To hell with good sense. He'd seen a harbour from above. There was bound to be a hotel, or at least a bar. The helicopter would be safe on the cliff for tonight. He started to walk north, along a deer track, towards the little cottage he'd seen from the sky. He wondered who lived in such a lonely place. Probably no one. Hell, maybe he could live there himself. The way he felt right now, loneliness would be an improvement.

SEVEN

Next day Ellie got her work done early, then hunted around in the shed until she found the spare boat rope. She looped it and her camera over her shoulder, and went to the cliff edge to watch the peregrine.

As the falcon took off from the nest, she timed it until it returned. She did this patiently, again and again as the day wore on, until she had worked out that the bird was gone an average of twelve minutes each time. In the late afternoon, she got to her feet as the bird prepared to take off again, and when it did, she ran as quickly as she could to the northern cliff, and fixed a loop of the rope to an outcrop. She tied the other end round herself, and before she could change her mind, lowered herself down the cliff.

After a few feet, she changed her mind. This was a truly stupid idea. She discovered very quickly that she wasn't strong enough to pull herself all the way back up, so she would have to climb hand-over-hand down to the shore, and then climb back up the cliff stairs and pull up the rope. By that time the mother bird would be back, and she would not be pleased.

Moron, the scars taunted.

'Well, I've done it now,' she said aloud. She lowered herself slowly, realising that she was too far left of the crevice where the nest was. She drew nearly level, and tried to reach over to pull herself towards the ridge. The rope above rubbed against the cliff edge as she swung in, once, twice, until she could finally grab a protruding rock and haul herself over. She looked down on the nest with its load of pale eggs. A thrill ran through her at the sight of them.

Her arm quickly grew tired with holding her at the ridge, and she let go of the rock, swinging back to the left, the rope above again rubbing against the edge. Reaching with her right hand to bring her camera round, and careful to keep the lens clear of the sharp rock face, she swung the rope again and grabbed the rock, clicking off half a dozen shots with one hand before her muscles began to scream and she had to let go again.

She hung there for a long moment, feeling elated. Her arms were sore, but it had been well worth it. When the worst of the ache abated, she carefully untied the knot fastening the rope round her waist and began to let herself down slowly. Within seconds her muscles were screaming at her. She looked down as the rope threatened to slip, burning her hands. It was still a long way down, at least twenty feet, and the sand below was littered with spiky rocks. She paused to rest, bracing her feet against the cliff wall, when at last her weight coupled with all the rubbing to and fro against the clifftop was too much for the old rope, and it snapped.

'Shit!' She held her camera out as she fell, trying to protect it. The thud when she hit the beach knocked the wind out of her, and she felt a sharp stab of pain as the rope coiled on top of her.

'Great,' she thought, looking down. For the most part she had been fortunate to land on the soft sand, but her feet had landed amongst the rocks. She tested her neck and arms before sitting up, feeling another stab of pain but this time recognising what it was. Her left foot was caught between two boulders.

Ellie let out a sigh. Typical

Well, it's your own stupid fault.

'Shut up!'

She was wearing soft leather ankle boots, and the right one was well and truly stuck. Ellie leaned forward and grabbed her ankle, testing how far it was caught, but even that small movement made her head swim with pain. She leaned back on her arms, closing her eyes.

Every time she felt pain now, it came with its very own reminder of the past. The counsellor had told her this might happen, but that didn't make it any easier. She opened her eyes again, and this time looked out to sea, where the sun was going down above her little island. The wind found its way inside her sleeves and collar, reminding her that she hadn't bothered with a coat before her little escapade. The golden light flickered on the waves as they came in…

'Oh shit!' Ellie yelled, reaching again for her trapped ankle. Her heart began to pound. She had forgotten about the tide, which was even now only a few feet away. She tried to twist her foot, wincing at the pain, but the rocks were tight against it. She loosened the laces, trying to pull her foot free, but it was no use, the boot was lodged tight. She looked back at the sea. Maybe when the tide came up, it would loosen her foot and she could get out. If not, of course, the water would be well over her head by then, and it wouldn't matter. She caught sight of movement above, and saw the dark shape of the falcon returning. She got the impression it was looking at her. Hell, it was probably grinning.

'What am I going to do?' She thought, biting her lip against the rising panic and checking her pockets, even though she knew very well her mobile phone was on the kitchen worktop. She looked up at her house in reproach, and there beheld a small miracle, for someone was walking along the clifftop.

'Hello!' she yelled, waving her arms. 'Hello. Down here! Help!'

She had to do a great deal of screaming before the figure finally saw her, and by the time it had found the cliff steps and made its slow careful way down them, she was sitting in half an inch of water. She tried to ignore her heart thudding in her chest, willing the person coming towards her to hurry. He was not someone she felt she knew.

'At least it's a bloke,' she thought. 'I hope he's strong.'

The thought occurred to her that maybe it was Gethyn, come to see her birds, but as the figure drew nearer she realised he was not a boy.

The man came up to her and sized up the situation.

'Is your foot trapped?' he said, tentatively pulling at one of the rocks.

Ellie stared up at him. 'No, actually, I'm waiting for a bus.'

The man stared back, and she looked away, biting her lip at her sarcasm. There was no need for that. He was clearly a tourist, and had come to help.

He was also extremely attractive, a fact not lost on her despite her predicament.

'Sorry,' she said.

'I'll need something to pry the rocks apart,' he said, looking round for something to use. He caught sight of her boat, now floating in the shallows, and splashed towards it. He came back with an oar, and Ellie waited, shivering, as he pushed it between the rocks like a crowbar. The rocks moved slightly, just enough for her to pull her foot painfully out.

Ellie got to her feet slowly. Now that the danger was past, she was completely embarrassed. She looked at the stranger's soaked trouser legs, then up at his face.

'Thanks very much. You're a life saver,' she said, looking away again quickly and fiddling with her camera to hide her face.

The man said nothing for a minute, then slowly he replaced her oar in the boat.

'Is your foot hurt?' he asked. She could pick up his accent now: American.

'I'll be fine,' she said, taking a few steps away from the sea. 'It's my own stupid fault anyway. Ow.'

It hurt to walk, and the man came alongside her and took her by the right arm.

Oh please don't, she thought, all the time relishing the touch. She kept her head turned away so he could not see the left side of her face, but deep down she could hear her scars laughing. *Oh yeah, like that's going to work.*

'Do you live here?' the man asked.

'Yes. That's my house up there. I work for the local Trust. I look after the birds. You know, the seabirds? My name's Ellie.'

You're babbling, girl!

'I'm Griff. Griffin Park.'

'Griff of Griffin Park? Where's that?'

'No, uh, just Griffin Park. It's my name. Griffin Park. Friends call me Griff.'

She heard a little disquiet note in his voice, but couldn't quite identify it.

'Well, thanks Griff,' she said again. 'You just stopped me drowning.'

He gave a wry chuckle. 'Glad to be able to help.'

'So are you visiting someone, or just travelling round?'

'Travelling, I guess. I saw this little island and just thought I'd take a look.'

'Where are you staying?'

They had reached the steps now, and Ellie went up first. Her foot was less painful now the pressure was removed, and in any case there was no room for two to walk side by side up the stairs.

'Uh, I'm not. I just got here, and I'll probably be off soon.'

Ellie laughed. 'Well, you've missed the ferry. We only get one a day, and Cameron likes to get back to the mainland in time for the pubs opening. I can show you to the village, if you like. There's a pub there that has rooms, and they have good food.'

Griff did not reply, and Ellie continued up the stairs to the top, where she hopelessly dragged her unruly hair over the left side of her face, putting off the inevitable.

'Well, thanks again,' she said, smiling at him. She was being a complete fool.

Yeah! And are you in for a disappointment

'Shut up. I won't let him see you.'

He'll see. I'll talk to the wind. You can't hide from us.

'Are you sure you're all right?' the man said. He was looking at her strangely, probably because she insisted on standing side-on to him.

'Me? I'm fine! No problem. Well, I'll be off then. Nice to meet you, and hope you enjoy the rest of your trip.'

Babbling again. Just leave! What, do you think he's going to find you attractive? You?

Ellie sighed, and turned to her house. As she did, the evil wind slipped up from the sea and pulled at her hair, dragging it back from her face. Ellie almost closed her eyes. Well, it had been inevitable. She looked round at the man, who was still looking at her. His eyes had a familiar light in them now, one she recognised all too well.

She knew the full gamut of reactions by now. Pity was number one, of course. Occasionally there was horror or revulsion, which at least were honest. Curiosity was one she had to grit her teeth against, and of course there were the ones who wiped their face clean and pretended nothing was wrong. But by far the worst of all was the one she saw now on the face of Griffin Park. *What sort of a name is that!* It was compassion.

'Bye,' she said, sadly.

'Wait,' he said. 'Can I take you up on your offer? I could use something to eat.'

She looked back, not hiding her face this time, searching his eyes.

He was very tall and broad, and tanned, of course, like all the American tourists she had ever seen. She guessed he was thirty something, though it was hard to tell. He had a wide mouth that twisted up at one side, as if he were trying to hide some inner amusement, and his eyes were a dark colour she couldn't quite make out. All in all, it was a very successful combination. The eyes seemed sad, though, and overall, he gave the impression of being lonely, though it flew in the face of his handsome appearance.

'Well,' she thought. 'I suppose I could cancel tonight's appointments.'

What are you, a masochist? You know he'll spend all night looking at us and ignoring you.

'You know what? I don't care.'

Griff's mouth turned up a little further.

'I'll dry out, but you might want to change.'

'No, it's fine,' she said quickly.

He might be gone by the time she had.

EIGHT

'Evening, Murd.' Ellie said, as she opened the pub door. The place was empty apart from Donnie and Conor, who had just come in from the fishing and were sitting by the window. Ellie winked at them, enjoying the surprised looks on their faces.

'This is Griff,' she added, 'who has just saved my life.'

'Why?' said Murd.

Ellie looked at him.

'Cos I was quite fond of it, you know.'

'No, I mean why did he need to? Och, you know what I mean.'

'Just pour the pints, Murd,' Ellie said, looking at Griff. 'Pint of heavy? Is that all right?'

'Sure,' he said, shrugging.

Ellie recounted the tale of her trapped foot.

'What the bloody hell did you think you were doing?' Donnie said at last. 'With a salt-eaten old boat rope. And that drop has to be sixty foot. Are you mental?'

Ellie shrugged. 'It seemed like a good idea at the time.' She looked at Griff and smiled tentatively. He was looking at her, and she could guess that he agreed with Donnie.

'Look, it was a bit daft, but I got the pictures!' She held up the camera she still had with her.

Conor shook his head.

'Just as well you were there,' he said, eyeing the stranger carefully.

'You'll be wanting some food, no doubt,' Murd said gloomily, his mono-brow creasing up like a caterpillar. 'The menu's on the blackboard.'

'Cheer up, Murd!' Conor laughed. 'Business is early this year.'

Murd looked at Griff. 'We don't usually get tourists till the summer. But you are very welcome.'

The door opened, and the crew of another fishing boat arrived. Murd retreated to the bar, and Donnie and Conor stood up.

'We're off home for our tea. Might see you later, if you're out.' Donnie winked at Ellie outrageously, making her blush.

When they had gone, she risked a glance at Griff. He was looking at her.

'People here seem very friendly.'

'Yes,' she grinned. 'We're suckers for new faces, new stories.'

He took a sip of his drink. 'Have you always lived here?'

Ellie shook her head. 'I'm from the mainland. Veni vidi velcro.'

He smiled, confused.

47

'"I came, I saw, I stuck around"' she shook her head. 'Sorry, terrible joke. But it's such a beautiful place, I don't want to leave.'

'It is beautiful.' He said softly, trying his pint. He looked at the dark liquid, then up at Ellie. 'This is a strange drink. I like it.'

She took a sip of her own pint. 'You obviously haven't been in here before. I thought you'd have checked in off the ferry.'

'I was walking. On the cliffs,' he said hesitantly. 'Um, I didn't come on the ferry.'

Ellie looked at him. That meant he had to have come in on someone's boat. She wondered whose it had been, but didn't ask.

She was aware that she was talking too much. The man was not only good looking, but he had no problem looking at her face. The two things combined to make him pretty much perfect. But she was babbling away like an old *cailleach.* Not attractive to men, sir. Anyway, he was certainly just being polite. It was stupid to get her hopes up.

He smiled suddenly, his mouth turning up at the corner. 'I came here on a helicopter.'

'What?'

'Yeah. I hired it from the mainland. I was just going to fly round and sightsee, but I saw your island and – well, here I am.'

She felt herself grinning.

Get a grip!

'Oh, be quiet,' she told the scars.

'Well. Now you're here, we better take care of you. Will you have something to eat?'

He leaned his elbows on the worn table. 'Sure. If you'll join me?'

Ellie felt the colour rush to her face, and looked down. When she blushed, her damaged cheek turned even more hideous than normal. Looking down meant her dark hair fell in front of it to hide it.

When she looked up again, Griff was studying the blackboard, and she breathed out in relief.

'I can recommend the crab,' she said. 'Do you like seafood?'

'Love it,' he replied, smiling. 'Do you like wine?'

'I think the answer to that would be a definite 'yes'.'

He laughed softly as he went to the bar.

They ate crab and prawns with salad and crusty bread, and shared a bottle of Californian Sauvignon, as the sun went down and people came and went, all of them giving Ellie the same look. The wine was making her feel warm and fuzzy, and as she talked with the American she decided that she had probably never had such a good time in her entire life. She realised how pretty sad that sounded, but she was in much too good a mood to be bothered. Save that for tomorrow, when the man was gone.

48

Which he will be. Have no doubt.

'The wine's good,' she said, looking at the pale liquid.

'Yeah. One of our better exports.'

She could sense his sudden sadness, and frowned. Murd chose that moment to clear their plates.

'Is your man here a film star, then?'

Griff laughed. 'I'm afraid not. I do work in films, though.'

'That's nice,' he said, shuffling back to the bar. Griff raised his eyebrows.

'Don't worry about Murd. You've heard of job share? Well, he's on brain share, and it's the other guy's turn tonight.'

Griff laughed again.

'Do you really work in films?'

'Yeah. I'm a writer, and director. Sometimes,' he added, looking down ruefully. 'When I'm allowed.'

'What do you mean?'

He shrugged, picking up his glass. 'The industry likes to make films that make money. Sometimes the money men come along half way through and decide my work's not commercial enough. Then they get another director in and I get fired.'

'That's terrible.'

He shrugged. 'It's business.'

She could tell there was more that he wasn't telling her.

'I'm sorry. Is that why you came here? They threw you off your film?'

He looked up. 'Well. I just - I just needed to get away.'

He looked at her, smiling. His eyes were a strange colour. No, that wasn't it; it was more like they seemed to change colour. At first she had thought they were brown, the rich brown of the peats, but then the light changed, and they would be the pale green-grey of young beech branches. She'd look again, and they were the grey of the waves under a rainy sky. Maybe she could pin him down and look hard into those eyes, see if they dared change with her gaze upon them.

Pin him down, that was a nice idea.

So this is what happens, she thought absently. This is the sledgehammer. She felt as if all her limbs had been turned to rubber. She picked up her glass to try and retain some vestige of dignity.

Too late.

'Oh, piss off.'

'What about you?' he asked. 'What brought you here?'

'Oh,' she said, shaking her head. 'I was fed up with my last job and I saw this one. I just thought I'd give it a go.'

She hesitated. 'My friends all think I'm mad.'

49

He grinned.

She laughed to herself. 'They think *I'm* mad. You should meet them.'

'What was your last job?'

'I was a lab tech,' she said, 'In a hospital.'

He shook his head. 'When I was at university, I took a job as a hospital porter. It was terrible.'

'What did you do at University?'

'English lit. I always wanted to be a writer.'

She smiled. 'I was never much good at English. I was into wildlife, and did biology. After university, my first job was at the Royal Infirmary, in Glasgow. They were good times.'

She looked up again. The sky was darkest blue outside now apart from one last line of palest turquoise on the horizon. The pub was empty apart from old Alasdair MacKinnon and his collie Reuben. The dog looked up at her and his tail swept the floor. She closed her eyes suddenly. She wanted to remember everything she could about tonight.

Griff poured the last of the wine and she picked up her glass.

'A toast! Griff to the rescue.'

He grinned. She wondered what it would be like to kiss that upturned mouth.

'How about: to adventurous Ellie. The Lara Croft of the Islands.'

She giggled. 'I don't think so.'

Then she looked down again, conscious of her ruined face.

Griff reached out and his fingers gently touched her left cheek. Ellie felt her heart take a leap into space. She looked up, astonished. Griff's smile was sad.

'What happened to you, Ellie?'

A torrent of emotions descended on her. She felt tears rush into her eyes and blinked hard.

'Car crash,' she murmured. The memory came hurtling back, and for a long moment all she could see was the rushing flower of flame. She blinked again, hard, and looked up. Griff was still looking at her, the sad smile curving his wide lips.

'They – I – ' she swallowed, and looked away.

'It was thought the scars would heal better than they have.'

He nodded.

'You should have seen me ten years ago,' Griff said softly. 'I had teeth sticking out at all angles, and a nose like a boxer.'

Ellie found herself staring at his nose. 'You can't tell.'

He chuckled. 'Where I live, appearance means a lot. These days I'm more interested in what's in here.'

50

He pulled his hand into a fist and held it to his chest.

Ellie thought for a moment that her heart was going to explode. She had never felt such affection. In the silence that followed, the only sound was Reuben's tail thumping on the floor.

The long walk back up the cliff seemed to take no time at all. Ellie had a warm hand holding hers, and the warmth seemed to pervade her whole body. She still had the weird sensation that she had walked into another dimension, and was experiencing someone else's dreams. She was sure there'd be a price to pay. But as long as it wasn't tonight, that was all right.

'The stars are amazing,' Griff said, gazing up. 'There's no smog here. No streetlights.'

Ellie followed his gaze. The milky way was a handful of pale dust thrown across the sky, bright enough to cast its own shadow. Mars shone out like a beacon. The scars had nothing to say.

'You've gone all quiet. Something wrong?'

Wait till daylight. Wait till he realises what he's done.

'Maybe. But I'll still have tonight, so shut your fat mouth.'

They reached the clifftop and stopped outside the cottage.

'My uncle had a telescope,' Griff said. 'He'd let me look at the stars when I was a boy. He taught me all their names.'

Ellie looked at him. She could tell there was another sadness hovering under the surface, but she didn't speak.

'There's Taurus, and Pegasus. And Andromeda,' he said, pointing. Ellie looked, but didn't see the pattern. Griff looked at her. 'She was chained to a rock to be eaten by a sea monster, but Perseus rescued her.'

Ellie smiled. 'So if you hadn't rescued me, would I have become a pattern in the sky?'

He squeezed her hand. 'Who knows. But I'm very glad I did rescue you.'

'So am I.'

She turned to him, and closed her eyes as his hands touched her face. A moment later his mouth touched hers, gently. She was surprised, until she realised he was making the decision hers. She made it easily. As they kissed, she wondered how many shooting stars flew overhead. Millions, she hoped, and made the same wish on every one.

The fire had gone out in the stove, but it didn't matter as they went straight to the bedroom. Ellie had only one disquiet moment, when her outraged scars screamed at her: *what do you think you're doing? You don't know anything about this man! Why is he doing this? With you, of all people!*

'I don't care,' she told them. 'I really don't.'

There were no curtains on her bedroom window: only the birds could look in, and she could see the stars as she lay back in her bed and felt the strength of his arms around her.

'Ellie?'

She smiled at his intuition. 'Nothing's wrong,' she whispered. 'It's just been a long time.'

He kissed her, and she felt his lips curve above hers.

'It has for me, too.'

Ellie was used to sexual partners who took rather than gave. She knew it was because the partners she always chose were flawed, like herself. But not Griff. Whatever skeletons were in his closet, they couldn't be all that bad. When Griff loved her, he gave everything. The lovemaking was intense, and at the moment of release, he said her name. Ellie closed her eyes to photograph the memory. If things went as usual, she would have to bring that picture out a lot in future.

When she woke, it was not quite light outside, but she was used to waking up just before the dawn. This was no different, except it was quite clear she was not alone. She looked across the bed. Griff was asleep on his side, facing her. His hand was on her hip.

Well. It had been great. She smiled to herself. It had been a night to remember.

But this was now. Time to leave the poor guy a get-out. She slid out of bed and walked outside, pulling on a T-shirt. In the pre-dawn gloom, the stars were still out, and the air was mild and smelt of seaweed and spring grass. Even the ever-present wind had died to a whisper. Summer was coming.

She looked out across the sea to her little island, just a smudge of deeper darkness. There was no sound at all apart from the waves rolling in, doing their time. On a whim she sat down on the damp grass, thinking about the night. It had been a new experience, one not to forget. She had been with men before, of course, before the accident, but not a man like Griff. She was not naïve enough to believe he was unique, she knew she had just never had any decent luck. Not until now, when it was too late. As the light leached into the sky, she felt reality poke into her thoughts. He was wonderful; kind and clever and attractive and sexy. But she was always going to be Ellie, with a face like a squashed pizza, and soon he would be gone.

She tucked her knees into her chest and pulled her arms around them. As the sun rose behind her, she saw a single black-headed gull, soaring above alone and silent in the not-quite light.

What are you thinking, she wondered. Can you see me? Do you wonder what I am?

She sighed, looking down.

Suddenly she heard a sound behind her, and before she could look round, she felt Griff's arms around her. He had dropped to the ground, and spread his legs out either side of her.

'Hi', he said. 'Good morning.'

She laughed uneasily.

'The light is strange, isn't it? It's like fake light. It's as if we're in the middle; caught between two dimensions.'

She said nothing, listening to her heart thudding as his arms held her tight.

'You thought I'd be gone by now,' he said.

She nodded. His arms tightened around her.

'What sort of life have you had, that you think I would do that to you?'

She shook her head.

'You're a good man, Griff, I think.'

'Yes, I am.'

She smiled.

'You're a writer. Have you ever heard of Robert Frost?'

'The poet.'

'Yes. He wrote that nothing gold can stay. I think that's right.'

There was a small silence.

'He also wrote: *I took the path less travelled by, and it has made all the difference.*'

Ellie felt her eyes fill with tears. She turned to him, and before they could overwhelm her she buried her head in his shoulder.

'Griff,' she whispered, as if it were a prayer.

'I'm here,' He murmured into her hair. 'I'm here.'

NINE

They spent the next day on the cliffs, walking among the birds. They were used to Ellie by now, but they protested bitterly at Griff's appearance. She showed him the eggs, the early chicks, the adult birds fishing out to sea. And all the time she watched him, waiting for the tell-tale signs that he was ready to go. But they didn't come. He seemed genuinely delighted by the city of birds. They didn't speak: conversation was impossible above the raucous cries.

Back at the cottage, Ellie noticed there were a pile of messages on her phone, but she ignored them.

'Are you hungry?'

'Yeah, sure,'

Griff came and stood behind her, looking over her shoulder as Ellie gazed hopelessly into the empty fridge. She looked round, and he grinned.

'I think I need to go to the shop.'

'There's a shop?'

'Of course.'

'Tell you what, I'll cook dinner. What do you say?'

'You can cook?'

Griff hitched his shoulders. 'I'm all right.'

Ellie wondered privately what he'd think of her aberrant diet, made up of mostly beans, toast and pot noodles. 'You're on.' She grinned.

'But not just yet...' Griff said, putting his arms round her, his fingers lightly touching the sides of her breasts. Ellie laughed.

Later, while Griff showered, Ellie checked her messages. There were three from Fiona, one from Hannah, one from Jim. Fiona was annoyed that Ellie hadn't answered any of her e-mails, while Hannah had clearly been drunk when she sent hers. Jim's was short and to the point, as always:

You guys want to have dinner tonight?

Ellie smiled. She knew it would have taken microseconds for the news to travel round the island. She heard Griff coming up behind her, and waited for the delicious moment when he would put his arms around her.

'Hey, hope you're not calling another man.'

'What do you mean: 'another man'. Other *men*, more like.'

She closed her eyes as his lips touched the nape of her neck, at the edge of her scars.

'Jim's asked us to dinner. He's a retired doctor, and a good friend.'

'Asked *us* to dinner?'

She turned to him, grinning. 'It's a small island. You'll see. Now, are we eating?'

'Sure.'

Ellie let him go, and hunted round for her rucksack, purse and keys.

'Hey, I thought you said you never locked up here.'

'I don't,' she smiled. 'Come and see'

Outside, she hauled the bike out of the shed, and Griff burst out laughing.

'You are full of surprises!'

'Come on. I'm starving.'

Griff climbed on behind Ellie and put his arms round her.

'It's not as impressive as a helicopter, but I'm not sure I believe you about that yet,' she said, laughing.

'I'll just have to show you.'

Ellie rode carefully down the cliff path, unused to having a passenger. They got to the harbour in time to see Donnie's boat coming in, and Ellie parked and waved at him, noting that Donnie was pointing them out to his crew. 'Well, sod em!' She thought. 'Let them gossip.'

You are in for a massive fall.

'Just be quiet,' she told the scars. 'No one's interested.'

'You said you like fish? The boats are all coming in. We could get something off one of them?'

Griff smiled. 'Yeah, great. What will they have?'

Conor leapt on to the dockside, tipped a wink to Ellie, and tied up the boat to a cleat.

'What have you brought in, Con?'

'We've got herring and mackerel mostly, but Murd asked us for some Bass. You after some?'

Ellie looked at Griff. 'That'd be great,' he said.

Donnie had climbed on to the harbour halfway through the conversation. He looked at Griff seriously for a long moment.

'You know, I'm honour bound to tell you, that our Ellie here is more than likely to poison you.'

'Oh, cheers, Don,' Ellie said gloomily.

Griff smiled. 'Well, I did promise to cook, so-'

Donnie and Conor exchanged a look.

'Well. I'm sure I can find you a nice fish,' Conor said, turning back to the boat.

Donnie looked from Ellie to Griff, until Ellie's face was burning. Donnie grinned.

'Well. I hope you young people have a nice meal,' he said, winking. Conor arrived with the fish, and Griff took it from him.

55

'On the house,' Donnie said, still grinning.

'Thanks. I owe you one,' Ellie said. 'Let's go.'

She turned away from the dock, while Griff looked down at the fish in his arms.

'Honestly,' Ellie murmured. 'How embarrassing was that!'

Griff laughed. 'Never mind.'

Ellie took the fish from him and put it into a plastic bag she kept in the rucksack pocket, then they turned to the shop.

The shop's sole window was obscured by the rows of packed shelves laid out inside. On the door were signs for the Easter service at the church, which had long since come and gone, a ceilidh at the pub, and a request for entries for the local show and gathering. Ellie pushed the door and the bell above it clanked. Flora Marr appeared as fast as a spider feeling a vibration on her web.

'That damn bell. I'm forever telling Archie to fix it!'

Ellie smiled at her.

'Hello Flora. How are you today?'

'Not so good, Ellie, not so good.'

It was her stock answer. Ellie had learned not to ask further. Flora's fierce eyes moved past her to the stranger behind.

'This is my friend Griff,' Ellie said, grinning to herself. 'Griff, this is Flora.'

'Nice to meet you, Flora,' Griff said.

'Ah. Are you here on holiday, then?' she said, her voice edged with curiosity.

Ellie looked at Griff, grinning. He understood and grinned back.

'Well, I've not quite decided yet,' he said, smiling at Flora. 'It's a very beautiful island.'

'Aye. Well.'

Ellie could see the colour rushing to Flora's drawn cheeks, and felt a surge of a strange emotion: pride.

'Anyway. I've promised to cook, so –'

'Och yes. Away you go.'

Flora turned away, but Ellie noticed that instead of going into the back of the shop as usual, she hovered round the till.

'Come on,' she said, picking up a wire basket and giggling to herself.

The shop was small, no bigger than Ellie's living room, but it was crammed with stuff from the floor to the ceiling. There was a refrigerated section, and a freezer that tended to be full of salmon and venison, culled from the hills by Archie and his cronies. The room was divided by racks of shelving, each of which was filled with items in strict order known only to Flora. When she first arrived, Ellie had been

56

astonished at the range of things on offer. She put milk and bread into her basket.

'Hey,' Griff whispered. 'Look at this!'

He showed her the herbs he had found. She smiled, holding out the basket as he put what he needed in it.

'How about this?' he added, holding up a bottle of wine.

'Now you're talking!'

Flora was still hovering as they approached the till. She rang through the items, scarcely looking at them, so intent was she staring at Griff. Ellie got her purse out to pay, but Griff insisted. He handed over a bank card, and as Flora went to the machine to swipe it through, he looked down at her.

'I hope there's something left in the account,' he whispered.

'Griff, I'll pay, you don't-'

'No chance,' he said, and Ellie heard the ice in his voice. 'They'll be taking everything else soon.'

She wondered what that meant, but Flora returned before she could ask. The card had worked OK, and they left the shop with Flora seeing them to the door. As they loaded the rucksack and took off, she was still standing there.

Ellie waved and shouted 'bye' as they left. The harbour was crowded with the late boats, the crews hurrying to clean up so they could get home, or to the pub. The bike climbed the hill, and at the turn for the clifftop, Ellie looked back. Despite all the activity on the harbour, most of the faces were upturned, looking at them. She laughed out loud until Griff looked back and saw what was funny.

'I told you we're seriously starved of entertainment here,' she said, throttling back and tearing across the clifftop, into the west.

Back at the cottage, Ellie gave Griff the tour of her kitchen, which took all of a minute.

'Donnie's right, I'm afraid,' she said. 'I'm not much of a cook.'

Griff put the milk in the fridge.

'Well. Maybe you should reserve judgement on me until after we've had this fish.'

'I know it's going to be great,' she said, putting her arms round him.

Griff smiled down at her, then reached down to kiss her. He was so much taller, he had to reach down a long way. Ellie felt the now-familiar warmth in her chest as he held her.

'Now. You go open the wine, and I'll cook.'

The fish was wonderful. Griff had cooked it simply in butter and herbs, and Ellie had seconds. They ate at her little kitchen table, with the sunset lighting up the sky.

'I can't believe that little shop,' Griff said. 'All the stuff they had.'

Ellie smiled. 'It's Flora's doing. She's bored stiff here, so she's always looking for other things to sell in the shop.' She hesitated, not wanting to mention the sad fact that Flora was a teacher without any pupils. 'She grows most of the vegetables and the herbs herself.'

She topped up his wine glass, looking outside to where the sky looked as if it were burning. Griff followed her gaze.

'We get skies like that in LA sometimes,' he said, 'they say it's because of the smog.'

As he gazed out, Ellie looked at his face. There was a lot to be read there, she knew, a lot of pain and sadness, and in a way, it calmed her. She was bursting with questions: why are you here? Why me? Why do you hate your home? Is this because of your films they won't let you make? What is it they are all going to take away? But just knowing that his life was full of problems made it more reasonable that he might want to be with her. After all, she was a walking psychiatrist's textbook. He probably felt right at home with her, another misfit. It stopped her asking the questions. He looked round, realising she was watching him, and smiled. It was a real smile, nothing held back, and she got up and went to him, sat on his lap and put her fingers on his face. His eyebrows were bleached almost white by the sun, making his eyes look very dark. She was filled with the need to help, but had no idea how.

'I'm sorry,' she said. Griff reached up and touched her hand. He took it and kissed her palm. He shook his head.

'You have nothing to be sorry about. I'm the one should be sorry. There's stuff I should tell you, Ellie. Stuff about me-'

She kissed him before he could say anything else.

When at last she let him breathe, the emotion in his eyes made her feel as if she'd done something wonderful. She smiled, and it turned into a laugh.

'What's so funny, have I got spinach on my teeth?'

She shook her head.

'I don't believe you,' she said. 'You're a phantom, an apparition. I'm a lonely woman living on a clifftop, and I've conjured you out of thin air. You're not real.'

'Oh no?' he said, standing up, gathering her up in his arms and carrying her to the bedroom. 'Well, let's see if I can convince you.'

Griff made love to her as if she were a rare and marvellous thing, like an archaeologist touching an ancient and beautiful artefact. He moved slowly inside her, in a rhythm much like the waves lapping the shore, then retreating. When he kissed her, he kept his eyes open, as if he could not bear to be without the sight of her. Deep inside, Ellie knew that every time they made love was only driving another nail into the coffin she was making for herself: the dark and empty box she'd be left with when he left. Yet she was powerless to do anything about it. She loved him already. She accepted it calmly, just as she accepted that the time would come for him to leave. It was as much a truth as his gentle hands on her skin. She fell into a deep, dreamless sleep, and woke with Griff shaking her.

'Ellie, wake up.'

She opened her eyes. In the dark, she could see his eyes shining. Then she noticed the shadows moving in the tiny room.

'Come and see this. It's amazing!'

Ellie got up, already knowing what he had seen. She walked outside, and Griff was standing on the clifftop, naked, staring up at the sky.

All around, the Aurora Borealis moved across the sky on legs of green and pale gold, drifting and returning, like a flock of alien birds. She looked at Griff and knew this memory would be with her till she died, the naked man raising his arms to the colours of the sun.

'What is it?' Griff cried.

'The northern lights,' she said, taking his hand.

'It's unbelievable!'

He laughed. 'This must be a sign that I've come to the right place.'

Ellie raised an eyebrow. 'You have?'

He turned to her, and pulled her into his arms. 'In case I didn't already know it.'

*

Days passed. The cliffs became so packed that Ellie could barely make her way along them. The work was easy. After all, she had an extra pair of hands to help her. She kept her log and made her reports, but her e-mails and texts went unanswered, as every waking moment she spent with Griff, leaving the past to look after itself. Once more, deep down, she knew the day would come when she would regret this.

TEN

On a bright morning at the end of July, Griff grabbed her hand and took her along the clifftop to his helicopter.

Ellie was not surprised. She still knew little about him, they had not talked about themselves, but she knew he was no liar.

'Come with me?'

'Try and stop me!'

Ellie climbed aboard the machine and Griff showed her how to strap herself in. The helicopter seemed to her to be mostly glass, and Ellie felt very exposed. She tried not to be afraid, waiting while Griff retrieved his mobile phone from a sling and called in his identity.

'I better call the hire company too, I guess,' he said, smiling ruefully. 'I've been kind of busy lately.'

Ellie smiled back. The second call used up the remainder of the phone's battery and he plugged it into a charger. Then he switched the engine on. The rotors began to turn, and Ellie looked up, apprehensive. Griff reached over and squeezed her hand.

'It's scary at first, but wait till we're up there.'

She nodded. There was no way she was backing down. The helicopter left the earth, and Ellie made a reflexive grab for the edge of her seat. She turned her gasp into a laugh, and then they were up and banking hard west over the cliff edge and out to sea. Griff looked at her, and she tried a smile, although her heart was thudding so hard she guessed he could probably hear it.

'We'll go out a bit, and then come in from the west, just as I did. See how beautiful your island really is.'

Ellie looked down at the grey waves passing beneath. The helicopter banked left again, and she felt her stomach lurch. She glanced up, and Griff was grinning, clearly delighted to be back in the air again. She had a moment's pang of sadness, that whatever was wrong in his life was taking all his money, and helicopters were not exactly cheap. Then her thoughts were wiped clean by fear, when Griff took the machine down low to the waves. For a moment she thought they were going to crash, but another glance at Griff told her he was doing this on purpose, for the hell of it.

'One day, I hope to meet a dolphin, eye to eye,' he said.

'I could take you out in my boat to do that,' she replied, more testily than she had intended.

'Sorry, Ellie.'

Her stomach gave another lurch as the machine rose up again, and then they were over her island, the pale machair waving in the wind, the sand as white as the wave caps. She looked ahead, and Baranpay came up fast; the cliffs, the white dot of her cottage, and then they were rising up, round the side of the mountain, Griff now careful with his controls. They flew along the edge of the jagged black rocks on the summit, startling a herd of deer grazing in a small corrie.

'Oh, look!' Ellie cried, spotting them, her fear of the machine fading.

Griff took the helicopter higher, until the island became visible in its entirety again. Over to the north west, the harbour was like a child's toy, and the spread out cottages and crofts were tiny white squares. Below the mountain, Ellie saw the helicopter reflected in the inland loch. The sun gleamed on the mountain ridges, casting the southern edges in deepest shadow. Ellie was entranced. She sensed Griff looking at her and looked back, a laugh escaping from her. He was grinning.

'Oh I have slipped the surly bonds of earth,' he said, 'and danced the skies on laughter-silvered wings.'

'Is that a poem?'

He nodded. The machine landed gently and Ellie undid her harness.

'That was amazing. Scary, but amazing.'

Griff had already unstrapped and got out. She climbed out and walked into his arms.

'No wonder you love it.'

He said nothing, just held her, and she wondered if he was thinking as she had earlier, that this might be lost to him soon.

'Griff?'

He pulled back, looking at her. 'So when do I get the boat trip to see the dolphins then?'

She searched his eyes, but the familiar shadow of sadness was nowhere to be seen.

'Any time you like,' she grinned. Her fingers traced slowly up his back.

'Only not just yet, hmm?'

It was his turn to grin.

Later, they walked down to the pub again. Donnie's son Angus was there, with a couple of the fishermen. They all had instruments and were playing quietly in one corner. Griff was intrigued.

'Hey, live music,' he said.

'Aye, but wait till you hear it,' Murd said, miserably.

'I think Angus is really good,' Ellie answered loyally. Angus gave her a grateful look.

'He would be if he stuck to the traditional stuff,' Archie said. 'Listen to that!'

The music they were playing was strangely familiar to Ellie, but while the older men played simple chords, Angus played an improvisation on top.

'What is it called?'

'*Sound the Pibroch,*' Donnie said, from behind her.

'Is it buggery,' Murd muttered.

'It's good,' Griff said. Ellie looked at him and saw his face was alight, as if some idea was taking root in his mind.

'What?'

He smiled at her. 'Nothing. Let's get a drink.'

As they sat down, Archie leaned forward curiosity all over him like a rash.

'So what is it ye do in America, then?'

Griff hesitated. 'I'm a writer.'

'Oh? A writer, is it?' Archie said, nodding.

'And a director,' Ellie said, smiling at him.

'Like a film director?' Donnie said.

'Really? What films have you made?' Conor sat forward.

'Well, only three,' Griff said.

'What sort of films? Action films?'

'Not really.'

Conor's face fell.

'Sorry, You might not have heard of them,' Griff said.

Ellie laughed. 'He was expecting you to get him Arnold Schwarzenegger's autograph.'

'Not at all!' Conor protested.

'But I expect you do know all the film stars?' Archie said.

Griff shook his head. 'I'm a pretty lowly director, I'm afraid.' He smiled.

They all looked at him as if he was a big disappointment. It should have felt like a kick in the teeth to Griff, but Ellie sensed it didn't. It was as if he, Griff, was right there with them, looking at this stranger and wondering what he was all about.

'So what's it like then, Los Angeles?' Lisa asked. 'Is there lots of crime?'

'Compared to here?'

Donnie laughed. 'Have we had a crime round these parts?'

'Well, Roy MacKinnon stole all those woolly hats out of the shop,' Archie said.

'Ach, that was just to wind Flora up,' Murd said. 'They were bloody daft hats, anyway.'

Archie said nothing. Flora had knitted the hats herself.

'I've heard tell Wullie Ross has more than a passing attraction to one of his sheep.'

'That's not a crime, is it?' said Archie.

'Depends,' Donnie said, through the laughter. 'Ewes get very jealous, you know.'

Griff put his hand on Ellie's arm, and she could almost feel his laughter through her skin. Archie leaned forward.

'Aye, and how about Gethyn MacLeod setting fire to his dad's arse.'

The laughter died suddenly, and all eyes turned to Donnie. For a long few seconds, he said nothing, his face impassive as stone, then slowly he grinned, and everyone started to laugh again.

ELEVEN

The mountain up here looked as though many years ago it had been covered by a brown velvet cloak. The new cloak, and the softness it lent to the gneiss and ancient sandstone could still be imagined, but millennia of wind, water and ice had worn it threadbare, and in the tattered fabric strange fungi and moss had prospered. In the lowlands, the cloak remained, still with a vestige of the opulence it once had, but among the high peaks, the fabric had been torn away, and the bare rock stood stark against the sky, like a naked spine hunched over against the cold.

Ellie was fond of finding such shapes in the landscape. She stood now on the dragon's backbone and looked ahead at the jagged rock spines

Where had the weeks gone? Ellie had no idea. And had Spring ever really been here? It seemed to her now that they had gone from winter straight into summer. Or perhaps that was Griff's doing. The yellow broom was fluorescent on the hillsides, the sky clear blue, pale and dark, day and night. This year's lambs were many and strong, and the fishermen came in from the warm seas with record catches. It was a good year for everyone.

'But for me more than anyone,' Ellie thought, as she climbed the scree-covered path up the mountain. The sun was hot and irritating on her cheek, but the wind up here was cool and welcoming as she turned into it. She scrambled to the top and stood catching her breath until Griff arrived.

She reached out a hand to help him up, not that he needed it, but he grabbed it anyway, using the excuse to pull her close. Ellie felt the familiar thrill his arms around her evoked. She looked up at him, grinning. There was nothing else she could do.

'I'm, not as fit as I thought I was,' he said eventually.

'I wouldn't say that,' she replied. He chuckled, looking past her, and releasing her.

'Wow. The rocks look like they're made of silver.'

She nodded. 'It's called mica. It's a mineral deposit.' Ellie the scientist, oh yes.

As Griff touched the rock, he looked out past them to the sea far below. Ellie watched him.

'It's so beautiful.'

'As beautiful as your home?'

He put his arms round her shoulders. 'More beautiful.' He smiled. 'More wild and empty. It's a place that doesn't need humans at all.'

Ellie looked out at the dark blue smudge of sea, reaching up and taking his hand. There had been many such moments as this in the past weeks, long silent contented pauses, where they simply stood and stared. Ellie felt as if her heart might burst with love for this man, and wondered what would happen then. She smiled at her foolish thoughts.

She realised he was looking at her.

'What are you thinking?'

She leaned her head against his chest. 'Just how good this is.'

He said nothing, his fingers gently stroking her hair. Ellie closed her eyes, and as she did so, the dark and hopeless feeling rose up inside her. She opened her eyes quickly, but it was too late. The bright morning no longer sparkled with life and light.

Face the truth, said the scars. She nodded to herself.

'You will be going soon, I suppose,' she said.

Griff turned so he could look at her.

'Why do you say that? Do you want me to go?'

'No, of course not,' Ellie could not meet his eyes, not wanting to see what she expected to see. She looked down, letting her hair fall over her cheek. Griff suddenly crouched before her. Surprised, she looked at him.

'That's better,' he said. 'When you won't look at me, I think I must have done something wrong.'

'Oh no-'

He took both her hands.

'Good. Because I don't want to go either.'

Ellie felt a flicker of hope. 'Really?'

'Really. Now-' He stood up again, not relinquishing her hands. He looked around until he saw something he was looking for. Then he leaned over and lifted her into his arms. Ellie yelled in surprise, and it turned into a laugh.

'What are you doing, idiot!'

He didn't reply, but carried her through the rocks to where a waterfall tumbled down the sheer face. Below it, the water gathered in a small pool, where grass and heather and small trees grew strong in the lee of the mountain. He laid her on the grass, and followed her down, his hands touching her damaged face as his lips reached for hers. Ellie felt the return of the warmth to her bones. He might still leave, but he wanted to stay, and that was good enough for now. His lips found her neck, his tongue tracing the ridge of her collar bone. Their fingers fumbled with each others clothes, and Ellie kissed his chest, the soft hairs there tickling her nose. She breathed in the warm musky scent of him, breathed it in deep as if she could somehow keep

65

it there. His lips closed round a nipple, his tongue gently tasting it. She reached for him, stroking down his lean body until her hands closed around him, sighing. She felt his fingers on the inside of her thighs, and then his lips were on hers again, and she felt the smile in the kiss.

'I love you,' she whispered. 'I do.'

'I know, Ellie,' he said.

She laughed softly.

They made love watched only by eagles, and afterwards they lay gazing up at the empty blue, the wind playing in Ellie's hair and cooling her sore cheek.

'It's a totally different colour, you know,' Griff murmured.

'What is?'

'The sky. In California. It's darker blue, more intense. Up here, it's as if we are closer to the edge of the world.' He laughed softly. 'It's as if we're almost in space.'

Ellie stared up at the pale sky.

'I love to fly,' he said, and she sensed the sadness in his voice. 'Up there, you're free, there's nothing but the sky and you. Nothing else matters. Everything makes perfect sense.'

Ellie leaned on her elbow to look at him. She sensed he wanted to talk. She laid her hand flat on his chest, above his heart.

'What brought you here, Griff?' She asked softly. 'What were you flying away from?'

As he looked at her, she saw the hesitation in his dark eyes, and felt her own heart begin to pound. Why had she asked, when she dreaded the answer. Griff covered her hand with his own.

'I woke up one morning, Ellie, and felt as if – I don't know. As if the world had moved on and left me behind.'

His fingers tightened round hers.

'I had it all. And somehow, it all turned to shit.'

Ellie lay down, resting her head on his shoulder.

'Tell me,' she said.

He hesitated. 'Not much to say, really. I woke up one day and my career was a real nightmare, my writing was rubbish, my wife was divorcing me. I was estranged from my parents, and for the life of me I couldn't think of a single person I could call a real friend. And my brother-'

He stopped, and she heard him sigh. 'Well. Everything was just a mess.'

It was Ellie's turn to sigh. The word *divorce* had put a jolt of electricity through her.

'So you left.'

She felt him nodding.

'I flew away, as far as I could, left it all behind. As far as I know, they're all back there now, squabbling. I got to England and rented a helicopter. Between the divorce and the breach of contract, by the time the lawyers get done I guess I won't have much money left. I doubt I'll ever see my own helicopter again.'

Still grasping her hand, he leaned on his side. Ellie looked into his eyes and saw they were smiling.

'And you know what? I don't care. It won't bother me if I never see it again, if I never see California again. I can start again, Ellie. You make me feel as if I've had a second chance.'

Ellie stared at him. The thought of being someone's second chance was frightening. But his eyes were filled with hope and resolution. She tried a smile.

'What about-' she hesitated. 'Your wife. What about her?'

Griff's eyebrows rose. 'You're worried about whether I still love her?'

Ellie looked away.

'Ellie. It's a hard thing to admit, but I never loved her.'

He looked at her, and she felt a tug in her heart at the pain in his eyes.

'All my life I've chosen the path of least resistance. Mel wanted to get married, and I went along with it. I did try to be what she wanted, at first, but then I was always working. I never had any time. I drove her away.'

He sat up, drawing his knees up to his chest.

'I'm badly flawed, Ellie. I should have told you this before. I didn't love her, but I didn't try to love her. I-'

'Hush,' Ellie put her finger to his lips. 'Hush. It doesn't matter.'

She drew him back down to the mossy grass and kissed him. As he held her, she could feel his heart beating next to hers. They were beating in time. Ellie took that as a sign, and closed her eyes. They made love again, only this time the intensity of it left them both holding each other as if they were in danger of falling off the world. Ellie knew she was lost. She could feel the dread deep inside, that when this man went away, he'd take a good chunk of her with him.

He won't leave, she told herself, as she leaned her head once more into his shoulder. But she already knew that he must leave. Even if what he said was genuine, that he wanted to stay, his old life was too much of a mess to simply abandon it. One day, he would have to go, to sort it all out, and that would be that.

Now you're talking sense.

'Be quiet,' she told the scars. 'No one's paying you any attention.

Paying attention? They're always paying us attention. They can't

67

help themselves!

'Shut up,' she gritted her teeth, but all at once a strange truth came to her in a sudden moment of clarity, and she felt a smile come to her face unbidden.

'He doesn't see you,' she said. 'He doesn't see you, therefore you don't exist.'

You're fooling yourself!

Ellie turned and looked at Griff. He had his right arm round her shoulders, his left folded above his head, which rested on his left palm. His eyes were closed. He sensed her looking and smiled, opening his eyes.

Griff looked at her, and Ellie knew that she was right.

'He sees me, not you.'

He sees us, all right –

She could sense the twinge of doubt, and pounced upon it.

'No. He doesn't. Be quiet now, and go away. Don't speak to me again.'

You need-

'I said shut up!'

She sat upright, and for a moment waited for the rejoinder. None came. She lifted her hand to her face, touched the ridges and valleys of her face.

But the scars had nothing to say.

She looked round. Griff was watching her, a confused look on his face.

'Are you all right?'

'Oh yes!' she said, turning to him. 'Oh yes, I'm fine.'

She held him close, under the pale sky. The sky so near to the stars.

'Sometimes you can see them,' she said.

What?' he whispered. 'What can you see?'

'The stars. In daylight. Sometimes, they're just there. You don't expect them, but you look up, and there they are. Stars in the blue.'

It was the best moment of her entire life.

TWELVE

It was a long walk back down the mountain and across the lowland fields to the clifftop. They got back to the cottage just as the sky was turning gold. Jim was waiting for them in his Land Rover. Ellie hurried over.

'At last. Where have you two been?'

'We climbed the Sgurr. Are you all right, Jim?'

He nodded, looking past her to Griff, who was standing behind Ellie, his hands on her shoulders.

'Well. I've been told to fetch you both for dinner, and I'm not allowed to take no for an answer.'

Ellie grinned, and looked back at Griff.

'Mairearadh figured the only way you'd accept the invitation was if I came and got you, so here I am.'

'Well, we'd better go then,' Ellie said. 'Can we at least get cleaned up first?'

'All right,' he climbed out of the Land Rover. 'I don't suppose there's anything wet in the house, is there?'

Griff laughed. 'I'm sure we can find something. Come on in.'

Ellie hurried in the shower, trying to listen to what Jim and Griff were talking about, with little success. She pulled on her best jeans and took her favourite black T shirt from the radiator, wincing as she put it on, as it wasn't quite dry. Then she rushed through to the kitchen, where the two men were drinking whisky. Griff was laughing.

'What are you two conspiring about?'

'Men's talk, woman,' Jim said in his best Presbyterian voice. Griff put a hand on Ellie's shoulder as he walked past her.

'I'll not be long.'

Ellie smiled. Griff was beginning to talk like an Islander. He was losing his American drawl. When she heard the sound of the shower, she poured herself a whisky and sat down. Jim was looking at her intently.

'So what's all this about, then?'

Jim shrugged. 'Mairearadh wants to hear all the gossip.'

Ellie grinned. 'You mean you do.'

He shrugged. 'I'll admit to a certain idle curiosity.'

'At least you're honest. Well there isn't much gossip, I'm afraid.'

Jim shook his head. 'Lass, on an island like this, *everything's* gossip. And you two? Well, it's like *Gone with the wind.*'

Ellie laughed out loud. 'What, without the dresses.'

Jim grinned, looking down at the table top, which was cluttered with

Ellie's log books, binoculars, dead coffee mugs and junk mail. He picked up her phone, abandoned on the window ledge.

'You've got a pile of messages waiting.'

She nodded. 'I was going to go through them all tonight, but-' she held her arms out, in a gesture of 'what can you do.' Jim simply nodded.

'My kids are always e-mailing me, or texting, that's the latest fad, isn't it? No one speaks any more, it's too old-fashioned.'

'Where are your children?' Ellie asked.

He smiled. 'My son's a doctor in Edinburgh. Married, three kids of his own. My daughter Hayley lives in Canada with her husband. They have a baby daughter. Hayley's a nurse. I suppose it must run in the family.'

Ellie nodded. 'You must miss them.'

Jim looked out of the window.

'Yes, but we talk and e-mail all the time. My son brings his gang over once a year to visit, and we go over to see them a couple of times too. We went out to see Hayley last year.'

He sighed, looking at her. 'It's easy to let too much time pass without seeing each other. Everyone's busy, but it's important to keep in touch.'

She wanted to ask why, but remembered he was a psychiatrist. She knew it would sound strange and provoke awkward questions.

'It's like that song, you know the one: 'cat's in the cradle'?'

She shook her head.

'I suppose it's before your time. It's a song about being too busy to notice the important things until it's too late.'

It was Ellie's turn to look out of the window. She wondered what he was telling her, if anything.

'Any brothers or sisters?' he asked.

'No. Just me.'

He nodded, and she studied his face. His pale blue eyes were looking out at the clifftop again, and she couldn't read him. Thankfully, Griff arrived then, dressed in his black jeans and the new smokey blue shirt she had bought him on a day trip to Inverness, 'to match his eyes.' She felt her face going red at the thought of that, and hoped to God he didn't tell Jim.

'You ready?'

'As we'll ever be,' Ellie said, as they piled into the Land Rover.

The sun was on the water now, like a child's ball floating out over the horizon. Jim drove them down to the harbour and up the other side, across lowland fields filled with sheep, and past the loch, where the dusk was filled with the mournful sound of curlews. It was the softer side of the island, despite being the north side. Jim's house nestled in a hollow, with the loch at its back, facing out to the west. Beyond the house, the grass sloped down until it became rock, and then shingle, stirred up by the waves. The house was surrounded by sheds and smaller structures, which Ellie knew housed all Mairearadh's animals; she had a few sheep, two jersey cows, goats and chickens, and two elderly donkeys. Only the chickens could be seen, pecking round the yard as they drew up. Mairearadh came out of the house, drying her hands on a cloth.

'Well done, Jim,' she said. 'So this is Griff. We meet at last!'

Mairearadh had clearly been a very beautiful woman in her youth. The grey mixed in her blonde hair made it look like the soft island sand.

Griff smiled. 'Hello, Mairearadh.'

Ellie noticed that his accent came back when he was with other people, and wondered why. They went inside, where the dinner table had been laid, and a bottle of red wine was already open on the fireplace. Jim poured all four of them whisky, and held his glass in a toast:

'To better days.'

Ellie had always thought it a sad toast, a toast for bad days, but Jim always said, if today was good, what was the harm in hoping for even better? She could see from Griff's face that she'd have to explain that to him later.

Mairearadh had cooked a venison pie, which was delicious. Ellie, as usual, had seconds, much to Mairearadh's delight.

'Got to build you up, girl, you're skin and bone.'

Ellie said nothing. Mairearadh thought Bernard Manning was a healthy weight. She sipped her wine and looked at Griff. She was trying to ration out her glances, aware that Jim was watching her every move. Griff's eyes met hers as if drawn by a wire, and they both smiled and looked away. *Gone with the wind*, Ellie thought, smiling to herself. Mairearadh stood up to clear the table, and Griff gallantly offered to help.

'I know what's coming next,' Jim leaned forward and whispered. He laid his head on one side, as if listening.

'Jim, will you bring the chickens in?' Mairearadh called.

Jim nodded sadly. 'You could set your watch by her.'

Ellie grinned. 'I'll help, if you like.'

The chickens were quite happy to go to bed, especially when Jim rattled their grain bag. Ellie counted them in and then latched the door to their little house.

'They're so sweet,' she said. 'One day, I'm going to have some of my own.'

'They're a total pain in the arse,' Jim said mildly. 'Come on, Foghorn, you too,' he said, shooing the cockerel in. Ellie saw he was grinning.

'I didn't know you had a rooster too.'

Jim looked sheepish. 'Well, we've got so many animals now, I thought I might as well join in. Mairearadh's none too pleased, though. He's a right noisy bugger. Crows all night long. Anyway, come on and let's have a seat on my throne, and you can tell me all the news.'

Jim's throne was an outcrop of rock above the shingle below, where he was fond of sitting and watching the sunset. The sun had long gone now, but the sky was still sharp blue and gold, streaked with indigo clouds.

'Do you know why it never gets dark in summer?' Jim asked, sitting on the rock.

'Yup. It's the angle of the Earth,' Ellie replied. 'This time of year our part of the world is tilted towards the sun. As the world turns, we barely reach the earth's shadow. But you know this, Jim.'

Jim nodded. 'No I didn't. I'm impressed.'

'Well, thank you, doctor.'

They both laughed softly. Ellie looked up to where the stars looked hard and brittle and a long way away. Mars, in contrast, looked as though she could reach up and touch it.

'So. You two are doing well, I'd say,' Jim said.

'Yes,' Ellie said, nodding, 'We are.'

'Do you know anything about him yet?'

Ellie looked at him. Always straight to the point. 'Some,' she admitted. 'I think he's in denial.'

'A river in Egypt?'

'Very funny. He's left a lot of problems behind.'

Jim nodded. 'Just as you have.'

Ellie looked out at the waves, rolling in gently and carrying the warm breeze to touch her face. Things had changed. A couple of months ago, she would have left Jim alone as soon as he started to ask about her personal life. Now, it didn't seem such a problem.

'Yes. I have.'

'But you know that they haven't left you.'

She sighed, looking at him. 'Enough of the psychobabble, hmm Sigmund?' She smiled. 'I'm happy, and that's good enough for me.'

'For now,' he said quietly. 'Ellie, I only want to help.'

'I know you do. But I'm fine.'

'OK, if you're fine, will you answer me a question?'

'Depends what it is,' she said, warily.

'A personal question, obviously. I'm curious, that's all, after our last conversation.'

Ellie thought back. Her job, the birds, her father. She could guess what it was going to be.

'You're going to ask me about my father.'

Jim nodded. 'Why did he leave?'

'I don't know.'

'Well, surely he told you, explained-'

'What. You think he took a nine year old child aside and said, 'look here dear, I know you won't understand, but I'm off'

Jim just looked at her.

'You mean you've not seen him since.'

Ellie shook her head, sudden anger welling up inside. 'He's long gone.'

She folded her arms, turning away, trying to calm down. So much for it not mattering.

'What about your mother, did she never tell you why?'

Ellie pulled her knees up to her chest. 'I don't think she ever knew why. Besides-'

She looked at him, trying a smile that didn't quite work.

Jim leaned against her so their shoulders touched.

'You haven't seen her in a long time either, have you?'

Ellie stared out over the water. The breeze ebbed and flowed like the whisper of the stones. As if they were telling the wind her story, to carry it away.

'She turned up at the hospital, two years ago.' Ellie tried to keep her voice calm.

Jim nodded to himself.

'I expect you were close, you and your mother, after your father left.'

Ellie looked at him. 'Yes. We were.'

'And then she found someone else.'

'How do you know that?'

Jim looked at her, and she saw the compassion in his eyes.

'It was just a guess, Ellie. People are lonely. It's what being human is all about. Of course your mother wanted to find love. We all do.'

Ellie took a deep breath. She knew it was irrational to blame her mother, who had done nothing wrong except fall for someone she shouldn't. But there was something inside Ellie that did blame her. Something deep and old and nameless, that she didn't even want to acknowledge. And then there was the guilt. Sometimes it felt like a bitter sort of revenge, one that left her feeling sour and old.

'What happened then?' Jim said in his quiet voice. He was looking out across the sea now, as if her reply didn't matter. Ellie looked down at her hands.

'He was a piece of work. He used to get drunk all the time and hit her. I went away to the furthest university I could find.'

Ellie looked at Jim carefully, waiting to see his reaction. She expected to see disappointment there, to reinforce the self-loathing that was filling her. Jim met her gaze steadily. His pale eyes were smiling. He reached out and put his arm round her.

'I understand,' Jim said. 'You loved her so much, and then suddenly there was someone else. A usurper. And not only that, but he was an evil man.'

'Yes,' she whispered. She was suddenly shaking, and a tear escaped and fell on to her knee.

'I hated him. I hated them both. And now I hate myself.'

'You did the only thing you could. What would have happened if you'd stayed?'

She shook her head.

'I was selfish. I didn't care about what happened to her. I just had to get away.'

'Well done,' he said.

'Why?' she said angrily, 'Because I left?'

'No. Because you've finally told it.'

He held her eyes until Ellie finally felt her heart slowing down. His hand tightened round her shoulder.

'Your mother was a grown woman who could take care of herself. She wasn't and isn't your responsibility. In fact, she was the one who should have taken care of you. She should have been the one to leave, and she should have taken you with her.'

It wasn't what Ellie wanted to hear. This was an old wound, but one that had never healed, and Ellie couldn't help but pick at the scab.

'Sometimes I think – what happened to me. The accident. I deserved it.'

And she felt a sudden sense of déjà vu, and examining it, remembered that Lara had said much the same thing to her, months before.

'Deep down, you know the truth,' Jim said, letting her go. She looked at him. 'Don't you?'

Ellie didn't know what was true and what was not. She only knew that some nights she lay awake and saw her whole life as one big spread-out accident, her father, her mother, the accident, the aftermath. Sometimes she felt that the next instalment was just round the corner, and she'd better brace for the impact. Griff had taken all of that pain away, but she knew, all the same, that it had not gone for good.

'So this is where you are!'

They both jumped at Mairearadh's voice.

'Are you coming in now?'

'Yes, in a minute.' Jim looked at Ellie again. 'All right?'

She nodded. As all right as she'd ever be, she supposed. She watched the door close as Mairearadh left.

'Your man will be looking for you.'

She smiled.

'Ellie, I know he has problems of his own. But I believe he's a good man. You should hang on to this one.'

She stood up, wiping the grass from her jeans.

'That's if he wants to hang on to me.'

Jim looped her arm in his, grinning. 'Have you seen the way he looks at you?'

Ellie shook her head.

'He can't take his eyes off you. He's smitten, Ellie, believe me.'

She laughed, embarrassed, as Jim opened the door. Griff and Mairearadh were in the kitchen, leaning on opposite worktops.

'Here they are.'

Griff came towards Ellie and took her hands. She looked up and saw the smile in his eyes. Jim's right, she thought. He really does love me. *But why?*

'Are you OK?' he whispered, and she nodded. At that moment her past seemed far away and insignificant. She had loved, but no one had ever loved her back, not until now. It felt almost surreal. She realised Jim and Mairearadh were looking at her. Jim raised an eyebrow and nodded almost imperceptibly. She knew what he was thinking: *seize the day.* He was right, of course. She closed her hands round Griff's and smiled up at him.

THIRTEEN

The morning of the annual Baranpay July Gathering dawned clear and warm, just like all the days of this summer had been. Ellie was awake first, and she woke Griff up in her usual fashion, by slipping down the bed and making use of her mouth. Griff stopped her, as always, before it was too late. He held her so tightly when they made love, that he might have been clinging to a life raft. It made Ellie feel fragile and powerful all at the same time.

Afterwards she lay with his arms around her, stroking the fine hairs there. Even his arms were attractive, and she told him so.

He laughed. 'I have nice looking arms? Is that it?'

'You have nice looking everything,' she said, her fingers now stroking his chest.

'Well, I am flattered, my love,' he said, kissing her cheek. His lips brushed the ridged and pitted flesh, and she closed her eyes. The scars had had nothing to say for a long time now.

They left the cottage and walked down the hillside, the sound of music on the air as it had been all night. Mainlanders had started to arrive the previous afternoon, crowding the tiny island and filling it with unaccustomed human sounds. The pub was packed, although it was not yet ten o'clock. Cameron had just brought the morning ferry over from the mainland, full to bursting, and was downing a swift half before he took it back across. Conor and Geraint were leaning on the bar in full highland dress, Geraint grinning at his own handsome reflection in the bar mirror. Ellie saw him and laughed out loud. He looked over and gave her a little bow.

'He's so vain,' she murmured to Griff.

'Well, he's a good looking man,' Griff replied equably. Ellie raised an eyebrow.

'Is there something you're not telling me?'

A group in one corner started up an eightsome reel, and every foot in the place began to stamp. The atmosphere was full of anticipation.

'Does everyone start drinking so early?' Griff whispered.

Ellie nodded. 'It's part of life here. Especially today.'

The band broke off, the accordionist complaining that the fiddler was going too fast, and an argument started. A piper in the opposite corner poked his bag awake and began a sombre version of *The Mist Covered Mountains*.

'Ach, for God's sake play something cheerful, Wullie,' Murd shouted above the mournful sound. 'You'd think it was a funeral, not a Gathering.'

76

'Come on,' Ellie said, grabbing Griff's hand and leading him out.

The harbour boats had been decorated with balloons and bunting, and Flora was carefully pinning up a row of flags outside her shop. She was standing on a chair and struggling to loop the end over a nail, when Griff took the end from her and did the job.

'Och, thank you, Mr Park,' she said. Griff smiled, but Ellie raised an eyebrow. She didn't remember telling anyone Griff's surname. How did Flora know? She assumed Griff must have told someone, Mairearadh perhaps, and of course it had spread like a virus across the island. Flora was now blushing furiously as Griff had taken her chair to even up the row of flags.

'Flags of all nations, Flora. Very cosmopolitan.'

Flora looked at Ellie, searching for sarcasm, Ellie kept her features carefully bland.

'Aye well. People come from all over to the Gathering.'

Ellie smiled. 'They do this year.' Flora actually smiled back, and Ellie was strangely pleased.

'Where's Archie today?'

'Och, he's up with his damn sheep, the useless article.'

She turned away halfway through the sentence, and Ellie felt the happy moment disappear like air out of a balloon.

Griff handed the chair back to Flora, who thanked him, but her smile was gone.

'Did I do something wrong?' Griff murmured as Flora disappeared inside.

Ellie shook her head. 'Not you, me,' she said. 'Come on, let's go see the tent.'

A marquee had been raised on the flat area beyond the harbour, before the hills rose again to the north. The land had been used by the school for football, rugby, hockey, hurling, or anything that needed a flat space. These days it was only used for the gathering, and today it was home to the beer tent, a stage for dancing, various stalls, and pens where animals would be shown off, bought and sold. Ellie felt the excitement in the air, for this one day when everyone could cut loose and have fun. It was a hard life, fishing and crofting, and the islanders played as hard as they worked.

A group of fishermen including Donnie MacLeod and his younger sons were struggling with one of the tent supports, which had clearly seen far better days. Griff went off to help again, and Ellie watched them happily. Griff looked different from the local men; his skin was tanned by sun, theirs by wind. He was taller and broader, whereas they were lithe and lean, their arms and legs driven by ropy muscles, forged by hard graft.

The tent went up eventually, and all the men shook hands, their teeth very white in their broad grins. A half-bottle of whisky was passed round, and Griff dutifully took a swig, looking round for her. Ellie put on her best disapproving fishwife stance. As he began to walk over, she laughed.

'Stay. Have a drink with the men!'

Griff's grin returned when he realised she was kidding. Donnie pushed the bottle into his hands again. Ellie turned to look for Jim and Mairearadh, and she heard a rough voice say: aye well, he's no' bad for a foreigner. That made her laugh again.

The Baranpay Gathering brought people from all over the Highlands. They brought whatever they had to sell, and they brought their instruments to play in the biggest jam session ever. Tourists came, for it was the heart of the season, bringing much needed revenue. They camped in Davie Murchison's fields (for a very large fee), ate in the pub, browsed Flora's straining shelves, had tea and scones baked up by Mairearadh and the other crofting wives. And they went away happy, and hopefully told their friends, so that next year the whole thing would start all over again.

Ellie walked along the edge of the field until she saw Archie with a group of spring lambs, struggling to get them into a pen. His sheepdog seemed to be enjoying the fact that things weren't going to plan.

'You useless mutt!' Archie yelled. The dog wagged his tail happily. Ellie laughed.

Archie looked up at the sound and smiled ruefully.

'He's only six months old, and his brain is slow in growing.'

Ellie put her hand on the handsome dog's head, and he pulled back his ears and gave her a big doggy smile, his tail lashing so hard his whole back end moved.

'What's his name?'

'Fred.'

'Hello Fred,' she said, as the dog gave her hand an enthusiastic lick. The name reminded her of her friends back in the south. Fiona's husband Fred, another man in denial. She felt a shiver run through her, though there was no wind to explain it. She looked up, determined to avoid unquiet thoughts today.

'You selling the lambs, Archie?'

'Aye, if I can get a good price.'

'They look good and strong.'

Archie grinned, the lines on his face deepening. 'It's been a very good year.'

'I know,' she smiled. They looked at each other for a long moment, until Ellie remembered her conversation with Flora earlier.

'You dancing tonight?'

'Och, I cannae dance.'

'That's not what I've heard,' Ellie said quickly.

'What-?' Archie looked genuinely surprised.

'I heard you could dance for Scotland, Archie. Why don't you get Flora up there tonight, and do a bit of showing off. After all, everyone else will.'

'Who told you-' Archie started, but Ellie shook her head, grinning, as she moved away. When she looked back, he was gazing at the grass, his hand cupping his jaw.

Ellie had no idea where the idea had come from, it just seemed right. She grinned. The big lambs had moved down the field, and one was trying to eat the tablecloth from the next stall. Fred the dog watched, contented.

That little piece of subterfuge cleared away Ellie's unpleasant thoughts of her past life, and she walked up to the next stall, where a woman she didn't know was busy setting up her displays of silver jewellery. Ellie looked down at the pretty earrings and brooches. She had never been very fond of jewellery, and now, well, what was the point? But she spotted a pendant, a small square of amber, on which a silver wave had been crafted. It looked like the tide rolling in before the sunset, and she loved it at first sight. She looked up, smiling.

'That's beautiful! How much-'

She broke off when she saw the look of fascinated horror on the woman's face. For a moment she wondered what had happened, then realisation dawned. How could she have forgotten! She quickly pulled her hair across her cheek, and turned to go. The woman called after her: 'Oh, God, I'm so sorry. Please don't go!'

Ellie gritted her teeth, and kept on walking. She walked past the other stalls, the groups of musicians laughing and drinking in between songs, the bleating lambs and tourists with their cameras, and on across the road to where the field dropped to the shingle beach. She stopped at the water's edge and looked out. The tide was well out, the rock pools full of the life left behind. She tried to blink back the tears, but it was no good.

Just as everything had seemed to be going so well, there was always a tripwire waiting. She remembered those dreams that used to haunt her; that the next accident was just round the corner. They had been banished by Griff's unqualified love, but now they were back.

She picked up a handful of stones and began to throw them one by one into the water.

As if aware of the return of her preoccupation, her cheek began to itch. Ellie clenched her fists round the remaining stones, anger overcoming her tears.

I don't deserve this! She told herself.

Oh yes you do.

'Hey Ellie!'

She blinked hard, turning. Angus MacLeod was standing on the grass above. He had his guitar on his back, and was holding a penny whistle.

'Will you not come and hear my new song?'

She smiled as brightly as she could. 'Course I will, Angus.'

*

Griff leaned against the bar, his hand clutching his whisky glass. It seemed every time he let it go someone filled it up again. Conor MacLeod was holding forth:

'-so Agnes Larssen told me that Callum MacPhee won first prize last week at Tobermory show with the same tatties he's brought here today-'

'Aye, well, so what?' Donnie said. 'Lisa told me they looked fine tatties.'

'Aye, dad, but Agnes says they won first prize at Mallaig show a fortnight ago, and Callum pinched them off the stand.'

'He did not!'

'Aye!'

Griff laughed, and they all turned serious faces to him.

'It is not a laughing matter, Griff, potato theft.'

But that just made him laugh all the more. The band in the corner finished 'the Garry Strathspey' and started on 'the Black Isle', and Griff looked round, thinking he recognised the song.

'So what do you play, Griff?' asked Roy MacKinnon, one of Donnie's fishing crew.

'Play? Oh you mean an instrument. I don't, I'm afraid.'

Donnie gave him a scathing look. 'Well. If you can't play, you'll have to sing, or tell a tale.'

'Sing! I don't think so!'

'Aye. Everyone plays or sings. Do you not have music in America, then?'

Griff hesitated. The music coming from the corner was haunting and gentle, like the mist rolling in from the sea. No, he thought. We don't have anything like this.

'Ach, don't torment the man,' Roy said.

'Well,' Conor said, winking. 'You've plenty of time to learn.'

Griff felt a blush rising up his cheeks.

80

'That's if our Ellie'll let ye out of the house,' Donnie said, grinning. The others began to laugh at his blushes, and he grinned, feeling strangely comforted by the teasing.

'They say you're never too old to stop learning,' Roy said.

There was a brief and confused silence. Then the band struck up 'Scotland the Brave', and the tent was filled with the sound of male voices pledging fierce allegiance to their country, whether it needed it or not.

It took a while before Ellie could hear Angus's music, as Gethyn arrived, and began to ask Ellie questions about her work with the birds. Then Jim arrived with his pipes and he and Angus began tuning up and messing about. Ellie didn't mind in the least, as it took her mind off the dark gloom that seemed to have had dropped on her from a great height. She was quite sure that Jim could see it, and questions would be asked, but at the moment she was powerless to fight it. Eventually, Angus butted in.

'You can still talk, Ellie, but will you let me play?'

Ellie looked at Gethyn. 'Hey, I'll take you with me one day next week, show you what I do, how would that be?'

'Oh wow! Yes please.'

She smiled. 'OK, now let's hear Angus's song.'

Angus grinned, nodded at Jim, and began to play. It was a ballad, and he sang in Gaelic, so Ellie couldn't tell the words, but she knew this was a sad and melancholy song. Angus was singing about loss, and grief. She listened, entranced by his skill, his soft young tenor voice, and the power of the song to reach deep inside and tug at the very gut. When he had finished, a small crowd of people who had gathered round applauded. Ellie had not even noticed them arrive.

Angus looked at her with his big dark hopeful eyes. He looked very young for his sixteen years, with his soft pale skin and fair hair sticking up on one side where he'd slept on it.

'Did you not like it?' he asked tentatively.

Ellie nodded. 'You have a rare talent, Angus. That song is stunning.'

Angus seemed to glow from within. Jim put his hand on the boy's shoulder.

'You're not to listen to the older men, Angus. You keep writing your own stuff. It's good. The best I've heard in a very long time.'

Angus began to look embarrassed. Jim stood up.

'I have to go, I promised I'd play along with Mairearadh's cousins from Mull.'

He made a face as he left, waving to Ellie. She turned back to Angus.

'Listen. Why don't you put some of your songs on tape, see if you

81

can't send them round to a studio? Look at all these musicians here, I bet some of them record stuff. We could ask?'

'Och no.' Angus was looking down now, stroking the pale blond wood of his guitar as if it were a pet. 'I don't like to put myself forward.'

'Angus, if you don't, no one else will. In fact, scrub that. If you don't, I will.'

He looked up.

'You really think my stuff's any good?'

'I know it is. Listen, you have to do this, otherwise you'll regret it. Believe me.'

He smiled, but she could tell he wasn't convinced. Angus looked past her.

'Here's your man.'

Ellie glanced round to see Griff coming towards her. She looked back.

'Angus, believe in yourself,' she said.

'Och, I'll try.'

She ruffled his hair as she stood up.

'Hi Angus,' Griff said, as he put his arm around her waist. Ellie felt a smile come to her lips uncalled-for. She looked up and into Griff's eyes, and it felt like homecoming. She looked back at Angus and winked.

'All morning in the beer tent,' she said. 'He must be turning into a Scotsman, hmm?'

82

FOURTEEN

The sun burned down on the capped heads of the pipers as they sweated through their songs, and the young girls looked grim in their heavy kilts as they worked through their dances. Everyone had worked hard for this day, and the fact that it turned out to be 90 degrees wasn't going to spoil it. The crowds lazed on the grass and drank beer, or sauntered round the stalls while their children chased each other round the sheep pens. It was the first time in a long time that the island had rung to the sound of a child's laughter, and it was all the more poignant for that.

Ellie and Griff walked hand-in-hand down to the shingle beach, where a group of older children were swimming in the little bay. The sun glazed the water, making it hard to look at. The kids were screaming and laughing, not quite drowning out the music coming from the grassy bank, where their parents kept one eye on them and the other on their music. Ellie had known the tradition of music on the islands was strong, but hadn't quite realised how strong until now. She felt sorry that there was nothing she could play to join in, but then, neither could Griff. She looked up at him, and he pulled her hand up to his lips and kissed it.

He was looking at her intently, his eyes screwed up against the bright sunlight. His eyes were the grey of the incoming waves today. She smiled.

'What?'

He shook his head. 'Have you ever been married, Ellie?'

She raised an eyebrow. 'No.'

He hesitated, and she felt her heart suddenly skip. As always when she felt insecure, her mouth went off on its own.

'You got married. Was it a big Hollywood wedding?'

He laughed. 'What does that mean?'

'You know, wedding organisers, rose petals, everyone coordinated.'

He looked at her as if she'd asked him to explain the big bang theory.

'I'm sorry, you don't want to talk about-'

'No, it's not that. I can't remember. I really can't.'

'What? You must remember your wedding.'

'The wedding – well yes. I remember the vows and so on, but I don't remember the rest - the surroundings.' He looked at her. 'That's terrible, isn't it?'

Ellie shrugged. 'Maybe you were just too much in love. All you could see was your new wife.'

83

He shook his head. She looked again into his eyes. They had changed colour once more. They were darker now, and she was sorry she'd brought the subject up.

The band on the grass began to play: 'She moved through the fair'

'I know this one,' Griff said, putting his arms round her. They played it three-time like a waltz, and Griff danced her round the grassy bank, to the childrens' amusement. After a few minutes, some of the kids joined in, making Ellie laugh as Griff spun her round. She didn't know the dance steps, but it didn't seem to matter. The sun beat down on them, and they breathed in the smell of the sea, the hot still air, and the faint hint of whisky. The world gleamed bright and clear, and Ellie smiled, the memory of the jewellery stall fading fast. She felt that today was perhaps the final day, that things were so good at this minute that they could never get better if she lived another hundred years. Angus arrived and began to play, and the music grew faster and stronger.

Griff pulled Ellie into his arms and out of the circle of dancing children, and he kissed her as if he could not stop himself.

And she closed her eyes and let the emotion carry her, feeling her heart as light as the air beneath a tern's wing, holding her easily in the sky, like a dream.

*

The light dimmed from the sky, and the stars appeared, but there was no pause in the music, and it grew faster and wilder now, as the dancers took to the floor. Some of the revellers had succumbed to the consequences of drinking for twelve hours straight, and there were a few quiet corners with the inhabitants peacefully asleep. Otherwise, the younger people had claimed the floor, and the fiddlers and accordion players blew sweat from the end of their noses as they played, stopping whenever they could to drink from the pint pots at their feet. Ellie pulled Griff to the floor for some of the easier dances, but he still got hopelessly lost and ended up alone in a corner, while the other dancers had moved on. Ellie laughed, for she had not been able to do the dances before coming here, and knew how hard it was to pick them up. Eventually he admitted defeat, and they retreated to the bar.

Murd had ordered twenty extra barrels of beer from his brewery for the day, and it looked like it might not be enough. The volunteers manning the bar were working non-stop with the steady determination to see the day over with and have a hell of a drink themselves. Ellie struggled through the crowd, losing sight of Griff. She managed to catch the eye of one of the volunteers, and two pints arrived before Griff did.

She looked round, but couldn't see him.

'Hello Ellie, you're looking lovely tonight.'

She looked round into Geraint's dark eyes. She was wearing the same T shirt and shorts she'd put on that morning, and a whole day of sweating in the sun could not have been kind. She grinned.

'Oh yes. I'm sure I am. And you're looking very debonair. Or is that still a word?'

He raised an eyebrow. 'Got to make an effort.'

She sipped her pint. 'What's the catch of the day, then?'

He twirled an imaginary moustache.

'There's a young lady from Ardnamurchan I've been chatting to.'

'Oh yes, and I expect she's in the toilet, or you wouldn't be talking to me.'

'Now Ellie, as if. Ah, here she is.'

He grinned as he turned away, and Ellie chuckled. She caught sight of Archie heading tentatively for the dance floor, and searched among the bobbing faces for Flora. She was in the middle of the floor, her mouth a thin line as she danced the *strip the willow*, giving no impression of enjoyment whatsoever. The tune finished with a flourish, and while the fiddler exercised his elbow in a different way, Angus got up with his whistle and began to play *Ae fond kiss*. The crowd booed good-naturedly at the soppy song as they too headed for their pints, and Ellie saw Flora shaking her head as she left. Archie stopped her, and Ellie saw the amazement on her face as Archie took her hand and looped her arm round his. They moved out on to the dance floor, and there was a brief lull in the conversation at this most unusual of sights. The music was bitter sweet, and as the fiddler joined back in it took on a different feel, as if the two instruments were the lovers in the poem.

Ae fond kiss, and then we sever, Ellie thought. Rabbie Burns had written with heartfelt passion about his love affairs, and there had been many of them. But no one could doubt the truth and sadness of the words:

Had we never loved so kindly; had we never loved so blindly!

Archie was smiling, and Ellie noticed that his features seemed totally different, as if at last he had let himself go. Flora was looking at him as if he might turn into a monster any minute. The two figures waltzed on as the music wound down to its wistful conclusion. As the last notes died away, Archie whispered something to Flora, and as the accordionist swung into 'Bonnie Dundee' and the dancers all returned, Ellie saw the couple walk through the crowd and out of the tent. A flood of warm feelings swept through her. Then she caught sight of Griff struggling through the crowd, and waved. She looked at his face and saw something was wrong.

'What is it?'

He shook his head. 'A lady, in the crowd there. She asked me to give you this.'

Ellie looked down. The amber pendant sat in his big palm like a pearl in an oyster. Ellie felt herself sag.

'She said to tell you she was very sorry.'

Ellie couldn't look away from the necklace. She could never wear it. It would forever remind her of her devastated face.

'What is she sorry for, Ellie?'

She looked up. 'Never mind,' she said grimly. 'You keep it for me, Griff, and let's have a drink.'

*

A visitor to the island the next morning might have thought it had been deserted, as if the dragon had returned to chase all the people away. The Gathering ground was littered with plastic beer glasses and forgotten sandwich wrappers. The tent itself flapped gently in the morning breeze, the only sound apart from the sea. Ellie woke early, hungover, and got up for water. Out to sea, her little island was swathed in a pale, ethereal mist, which the sun would burn away in an hour or so. For now, the world looked as if it were between time and space. It was her favourite time.

'Hey.'

She looked round. Griff's hair was sticking up at the front, and his eyes were red-veined and puffy. He was wearing nothing but his boxers, and they were inside out. She found herself grinning.

'I don't know how you manage it,' she said. 'You still look sexy, even hungover.'

He groaned. 'I don't feel it.' He put his arms round her, resting his chin on her head as they both looked out to sea.

'How do you feel? You look fine.'

She shook her head, enjoying the feel of his spiky stubble on her scalp.

'I feel and look terrible, Griff. Admit it.'

'Aye wull not,' he said, in his best Scottish accent, making her laugh.

She turned to face him. In the pale light, he looked older and wiser, the lines in his face more pronounced. He smiled, and the corner of his lip turned up in the way she loved.

'I feel as if I've known you forever,' she whispered. She leaned her face into his chest, breathing him in.

'Do you ever think about destiny?'

86

'Destiny?' he said, smiling. 'I think we make our own.'

She nodded. 'So did I. But I'm not so sure now. I mean what are the chances of you being there that day when I got trapped in the rocks?'

She remembered that she had intended to look at the nest the night before, but Lara's phone call had stopped her. If she had, Griff would not have been there, and she would have drowned. It was a sobering thought.

'You came all the way from America to save me.'

He laughed then. 'It was worth it.' He touched her chin and lifted her face. As always, he had to bend a long way down to kiss her.

'Why are you –' she began. She felt tears lurking behind her eyes. She didn't know what she wanted to say, or rather, she did know, but she couldn't find the words.

'Hush,' he said, and bending down, he put his arms round her and lifted her up. She put the flat of her hand on his chest, feeling for his heart.

'My Ellie,' he whispered. 'I love you. You know that, don't you?'

She smiled. 'I think so.'

'You think so?'

'Ok. I know so.' She looked into his dark eyes. He looked tired and weary, and she was overwhelmed with love for him.

'I don't love you,' she said softly.

'You don't?' He smiled, anticipating a tease.

'No. It's more than that,' she said. 'It's as if you're part of me. You don't love parts of yourself. They just are.'

His eyebrows rose as he looked at her, and she saw in his face a desperate emotion.

'I have upset you,' she said.

He shook his head. 'No. You just reminded me of something. Something from the past.'

She nodded. She knew all about that.

'I'm sorry.'

'No. Hush.' He held her tightly, so she could not see his face. This, also, she understood.

'Hey,' he said. 'Let's go out in the boat. Clear away the cobwebs.'

She let him go reluctantly. 'Ok, why not.'

As her hands slipped from his, she looked down and noticed the little amber pendant on the table. She swallowed, looking at it.

'It's very pretty,' Griff said. She looked up.

'Yes, it is. But I don't want it.'

'OK,' he said, smiling. She loved that about him, that he knew when to leave a subject alone. She watched as he wandered off to the shower, and after a few seconds she joined him, so desperate to be

87

with him she couldn't let him out of her sight.

The sea was choppy as the wind bore down from the west, fighting against them as they rode out into the waves. They beached the little boat and walked up the white sand to the dunes, where they collapsed, still tired and hungover. They had dressed in sweat pants and T shirts, like joggers, only a long way from home.

'The Gathering was great,' Griff said.

'Yes, it was,' Ellie agreed. *Most of it*, she added privately.

'Conor MacLeod is funny.'

Ellie grinned. 'He tells the most outrageous jokes. All the MacLeods are talented. Angus has his music, Iowyn is mechanical, Gethyn is academic, and Geraint. Well, you know Geraint.'

He chuckled. 'The Valentino of the Islands. It must be nice to have a big family like that.'

Ellie looked at him. 'You don't have brothers and sisters?'

He hesitated. 'What about you?'

'Only child,' she said quickly.

They lay in silence for a while. Then Griff took a deep breath.

'My home life wasn't all that great,' he said.

Ellie reached over and took his hand.

'My parents, well, they fought a lot-' he chuckled. 'Well, more than a lot.'

She looked at him. His eyes looked pretty bleak, but he seemed determined to continue.

'I left,' he said. 'I didn't go back.'

She blinked. He had done the same as she had, walked out on his parents. She remembered what she had told him that morning, about his being part of her. It had just seemed right to say it at the time, but now, it was spooky.

'What?' he said.

She shook her head.

'Some things we do,' she said, 'haunt us forever.'

They lay in silence for a long time, and Ellie closed her eyes. The wind was rustling about in the machair, urging the tide in.

'Tell me a poem,' she said. They were lying on the east face of the dunes, looking back to the cliffs and the mountain.

'I wandered lonely as a cloud –'

She elbowed him, grinning. 'A better one than that.'

'What's wrong with Wordsworth?'

'Nothing,' Ellie leaned her bad cheek into the curve of his neck and shoulder.

'Something – I don't know. More appropriate.'

'More appropriate,' he said.

'Yeah. He wrote about the Lake District. We need a poem about here.'

'I see. Something about geology, perhaps, or maybe weather systems? The gulf stream and its effect on local wildlife?'

'Yeah all right. I'm the scientist, remember? You're the writer.'

'And fare thee weel my only love, and fare thee weel a while,
and I will come again, my love, tho' it were ten thousand mile.'

Ellie laughed. 'Where did you pick that one up?'

Griff looked offended. 'I read Burns at University, I'll have you know.'

She grinned. 'Well, all right, but not that one either. It's too sad.'

He laughed softly. 'I'm not a poet. I was a writer, once.'

His voice was wistful. She looked at him, and he smiled.

'That's like saying you could ride a bike once. Once you can, you always can.'

He sighed. 'I don't know. I haven't written anything in a long time.'

'Maybe you should.'

'Maybe,' he nodded. 'I'll need to do something to make a living. Not much use round here, am I? I can't fish, can't sail, don't know anything about sheep, and I can't even play an instrument.'

'Neither can I.'

'Ah, but you take care of the birds.'

'Well, you can take care of me.'

She felt his fingers in her hair. 'I'll take care of you, Ellie.'

But she sensed his unease, and sat up.

'What's wrong? You're worried about what's happening back in America?'

He shook his head. 'I should be, but I'm not. I've got my head in the sand here, Ellie, I've run away from all my responsibilities, and I don't care. I just want to stay here with you.'

Ellie looked up at the clouds rolling gently in, great tumbling cumulus piles. Suddenly she grinned.

'Look at that cloud. It looks like Murd from the pub. It's got his big nose.'

Griff chuckled. 'That one looks like a woman combing her hair.'

Ellie tried, but couldn't see what he meant. A sudden wind high up began to tear the cloud apart, and she was reminded of her own face.

'It looks like me, now,' she said softly.

Griff looked at her, his dark eyes full of sadness.

'When I came here at first, and went in the pub, I didn't get the reaction I expected.' She laughed to herself. Griff's arms tightened round her.

'One of the fishermen took his shirt off to show me his back and shoulder where he'd been trapped in a trawler line. It was awful, as bad as my face, but he seemed proud of it.' She shook her head at the strange memory.

'It sparked a whole session of 'my scar's better than yours'. It's the first time I ever felt comfortable with my own scars. Up here, everyone had scars. They didn't matter. They *really* didn't matter.'

Griff rested his head on top of hers.

'I don't know how you can bear to look at me. I can barely look at myself.'

He shook his head. 'I told you. It doesn't matter. Not to me.'

'It does matter. You know it does.'

'Is that why you're here? Are we both doing the same thing: hiding?'

Ellie drew her lips into a thin line.

'You don't know what it's like,' she murmured. 'All the pitying looks, sometimes people are horrified, sometimes they are fascinated and can't look away.'

She felt his arms tighten harder round her.

'It doesn't matter to me,' he said again.

'Maybe not here,' she whispered. 'But it does everywhere else.'

'What are you saying?'

She turned and sat across his legs, facing him. She reached her hands inside his shirt and touched his warm skin.

'If we were anywhere else, you would see the looks I get, and you might think now that you wouldn't care, or that it wouldn't affect you, but it would.'

She looked up, and saw the hurt in his eyes, but there was nothing else for it.

'It would make you angry, and there's nothing you can do about it. It would get to you, and soon you'd have to leave.'

He put his palms on either side of her head. 'Look at me,' he said, 'I hear you, but no matter what, I won't leave. I'm in for the duration. I promise.'

She smiled and kissed him softly, but she knew he saw her disbelief.

'I don't know what's happened to you in the past, Ellie,' he murmured. 'If you don't want to tell me, that's OK, but I don't make promises lightly.'

And there have been some that I've broken, she thought sadly.

She thought about that first night, walking home from the pub hand in hand, as he showed her the constellations and she made hopeless wishes. Back then all she had wanted was that one night. Now, of course, it wasn't good enough. She felt like a spoilt child, wanting more and more, forever unsatisfied. Griff touched her chin again, making her look up.

'I love you, Ellie,' he said.

She smiled. She did believe him. She just knew the world wasn't perfect.

'I love you too Griff. I really do.'

'Well, will you do something for me?'

'Of course. Anything. What is it?'

'Get off my legs before all circulation is lost.'

She laughed, collapsing off him on to the sand. His hands reached up inside her T shirt, and she tugged at his sweatpants. He seemed none the worse for yesterday's bingeing, and she climbed aboard happily.

She felt relieved that he had talked about his other life. The knowledge of it was always there, waiting for a chance to sneak into her heart and remind her that one day he'd be gone. She knew he meant what he said, but she also knew that things could easily get out of control. One day, the matter would be taken out of his hands. But she forgot all about it as he suddenly rose up to kiss her, pushing her back on to the soft sand as the urgency hit them both at once. The waves roared in her ears as she closed her eyes, letting the unchained moment wash over her like the waves, taking her away to another place.

FIFTEEN

Summer passed.

The young birds learned to fly, to fish, to follow the flock, and one by one they started to leave. The cliff cities turned suburban, and the sea was full of seals, swimming in perfect graceful arcs around their mates. Before long there would be young seals crying on the rocks while their parents fished for them. In the high corries, the young deer tried out their antlers amongst the purpled heather, and the eagles watched the days grow shorter, and darkness return to the nights.

Ellie knew it would only be a matter of weeks before the cliffs were empty once more, as they had been when she had arrived. That seemed like years ago now, not months. Her job would be finished, and it would be time to do something else.

She could not think of anything else she would ever want to do again.

Griff still showed no signs of leaving, and she was reluctant to tell him that she would have to find other work. Secretly she hoped the RSPB would renew her position, and she could hopefully work in the pub all winter, and start again in the spring. But any talk of change was to be resisted. She had no desire to remind him that time moves on, for then, so might he.

Even now, she still could not accept he would stay. She held him at night in her little bed, and wondered if this would be the last night. And every morning, there he was, loving her awake, looking at her as if her face held no resemblance to a Hammer horror film. It was all just too unbelievable.

And this morning she had completed her log of birds leaving, and returned home to find he had packed a picnic. It was still warm, the September sun low in the sky, but the wind was catching.

'I thought we could make the most of the sunshine,' he said.

And they took the boat out to the island, Ellie bringing her camera, for the seas were filled with whales now. Like the seals, it was time for them to breed, and she hoped to get a picture of one. They beached the boat and picnicked on the dunes, looking back at the cliffs.

The waves rolled in gently, the colour of stormy clouds. The cries of the seabirds ebbed and flowed as the wind gusted, sometimes carrying the songs far out to sea, sometimes bringing them direct to the ears of the humans.

Ellie felt Griff's fingers tangling in her hair.

'I wonder what they're saying,' he murmured.

Ellie closed her eyes.

'That puffin's scream is a protest,' she said. 'Some other bird has stolen her food or her space.'

She leaned her head on his shoulder, smiling to herself.

'That one, that machine-gun cry, that's a shag.'

'A shag?'

He chuckled. 'What about that one?'

The gull's cry was loneliness turned to sound. The wind brought it to them and then carried it away, and they both looked way out to sea, where the bird was already out of sight. A lone seal watched them from a rock.

'That's the sadness left when all the children have gone.'

As soon as she had said it, she wondered what had put that thought in her head. Griff's arm tightened round her.

'But there'll always be next year,' she said in an attempt to cheer things. Change the subject, she thought. 'Tell me about your films,' she said.

'What? What do you want to know?'

'Well, what were they about?'

'I only wrote two of them, and one of them got changed a lot.'

She sighed. She sensed he did not want to talk about this.

'All right, then. You're a writer. Tell me a story.'

He laughed softly. 'Just like that? It's like being back at school.'

'Well, there might be a reward at the end, if it's a good one.'

'Well, it's a tempting offer… all right.'

She adjusted her position so she could stay in his arms but still look at him. His eyes were blue today, like the autumn sky. He thought for a moment, looking out at where the seal was still bobbing in the water, curious.

'Once there was a lonely fisherman, who lived alone on an island.'

Ellie smiled, watching him conjure up the tale.

'One day he left the island for a while, and when he came back, he brought a wife with him. She was quiet and kind, with big gentle dark brown eyes, but all the islanders knew there was something strange about her.'

'Strange?'

'Yeah. Not quite right. But she loved him, loved him more than the world.'

'More than the world?'

'More than the world.' He smiled at her.

'Well, it was a bad year for the fishermen. There were not many fish to be had, and the people went hungry. One day in the late autumn, the fisherman got his nets together, and his wife came to him and told him not to go. There was a storm coming. It was dangerous. Well, he

93

should have listened to her, but he didn't.'

Ellie pulled his arm tighter around her.

'He went to his boat, and his wife stood on the shore and watched him sail away. Then the storm rose, and it tore first the sails, and then the masts from his boat, and then the wind died and left him drifting far out to sea, ice cold and helpless, dying.'

He was still looking out at the grey waves, but there was nothing to see now.

'And die he would have. But in the morning, the other fishermen went to search for him, and when they found him, there in his boat was a seal, with gentle big dark brown eyes, lying on him and keeping him warm and alive. And when the men arrived, she dove back into the sea, and was not seen again.'

Ellie sighed.

'And the moral of that story is?'

He grinned. 'I don't know. Listen to your wife?'

'Or don't marry a silky. It's an old legend, you know. Like the dragon.'

She had told him the legend of the island. 'We are lying on the dragon's nose.'

She felt him nodding. 'I saw it, as I flew in from the sea. It does look like a dragon.'

'They say the dragon will return one day to reclaim his lands.'

Ellie touched her hand to the sand, as if feeling for a pulse.

'Or maybe,' Griff said, 'Maybe not to reclaim his land, but to make amends. Don't they say the dragon will bring back the children? Have you noticed there are no children here at all?'

She nodded. 'No children, and no hope of any.'

He said nothing, and she wondered what he was thinking. Ellie looked at him and saw he looked sad. He realised she was watching him and grinned.

'Come on, let's go back, and I'll buy you a pint.'

SIXTEEN

They rode the bike down to the harbour, where Flora was outside her shop talking to Mairearadh. As Ellie kicked the stand down, she saw Jim in his Land Rover.

'Oh, Mr Park!' Flora said, as Griff climbed off.

'Hello Flora,' he said, giving her his best smile. Ellie was still annoyed about her knowing his last name.

'Hey Griff,' Jim called out of the car window. Griff smiled at Ellie. 'Won't be a minute.' He went to see what Jim wanted, and Ellie walked over to the women.

'Hello Mairearadh,' she said. 'Are you all right? You look tired.'

Mairearadh made a face. 'Ach, that cock of Jim's was up all night.'

Ellie felt her mouth quivering and bit back the laughter. She looked at Flora, who appeared oblivious to the comment. She was looking at Griff, and smiling.

'He's such a nice man. And I don't care what he's done.'

Ellie blinked.

'Flora? What do you mean, 'what he's done'?'

Flora looked at her in surprise. 'Well, you know. Why he's here.'

Ellie felt her mouth go dry. Her mind began to work overtime.

'Flora, who told you his last name?'

'What? No one told me. It was on the telly.'

On the telly!?

Flora gave her a confused look. 'You must have seen it.'

'Why don't you just tell me,' Ellie said.

Flora shrugged. 'Well, he's a famous film writer, and no one except us knows where he is.'

Her heart started to pound. Events were moving out of her control.

'Well, if he doesn't want anyone to know, it's his business.'

Flora was well versed in the subject. 'There was all this stuff about him, his divorce, and some argument with a film company. There was talk that he might have killed himself and someone else came up with the idea that he might have committed a crime.'

Ellie swallowed hard.

'But now they know he's in Britain. It's because of his helicopter, they say.'

Ellie wondered if this was how fugitives felt when the knock on the door finally came. She looked across, but Griff and Jim were both laughing.

'Does everyone know this?'

'Och, I think so,' Flora said contentedly. Of course they do, Ellie

95

thought savagely, because you've told them all, you gossiping old hag.

But wait a minute. Everyone might know, but no one had said anything. She felt a small surge of hope. Maybe they wouldn't say anything, and they could just go on as before.

'But it's urgent they find him now, you see, because-'

She felt Griff's hands on her shoulders. Flora stuttered to a halt, simpering up at him. Ellie looked at Mairearadh, who shrugged.

'Mr Park, do you think you could maybe help me with the ladders in my shop? If it's not too much trouble.'

Griff gave a little laugh. 'No trouble, Flora, and call me Griff. You don't mind, do you, Ellie?'

Ellie shook her head, watching him follow the older woman into the shop. When the door closed, she ran over to Jim's car.

'Did you know about Griff being on the TV?'

Jim looked surprised. 'Well, yes. You didn't, I take it.'

'I can't remember the last time I watched TV.' She looked at Jim, who was grinning.

'Oh lay off. That Flora, I could strangle her!'

'Calm down,' Mairearadh said, arriving behind her. 'People were worried about him, that's all.'

'No they weren't,' Ellie said, remembering everything he had told her. *They'll clean me out.* 'They just want his money.' She ran her fingers through her hair, but it was tangled from the bike ride, and her fingers caught painfully.

'Ellie,' Jim said. He reached out and grasped her arm. 'There's no need to panic.'

'I'm not panicking!'

She turned and ran back to the shop. Griff was just leaving, and he hurried towards her.

'What's wrong!'

'Nothing. Let's go. Let's go home, Griff, please.'

'Sure, whatever you want. Calm down. I'll drive.'

She was shaking so much, she let him, holding him tight as the bike climbed the path to the cliffs. He drove fast, and the chill wind bit at her cheek until it felt completely numb.

They reached the cottage and Ellie leapt off and ran inside. Griff hurried after her.

'Ellie, what is it?'

She couldn't stand still, but paced in the little kitchen. She had no idea what to say.

Griff slowly walked towards her and took her in his arms.

'Whatever it is, it can't be that bad. Tell me.'

She leaned into his chest, feeling her heart thudding against it. This is it, she thought. This is the last time.

'Flora said that people have been on the TV trying to find you. You're a missing person.'

She felt him stiffen, and then he took her by the shoulders and looked at her.

'Is that what's upset you?'

She looked at him as if he was mad. What else?

'Well,' he said, and then he smiled. 'I suppose that was inevitable. After all, I did leave suddenly, and in the middle of a row. And a divorce.' His smile grew wider. 'But I'm not a missing person. The helicopter company know where I am. They're still taking my money.'

Ellie looked away. 'Yes. She said they knew you were in the UK.'

'Well, there you are.'

'What do you mean: 'there you are''

Griff looked utterly confused. 'I don't understand, Ellie. Why is this such a big deal?'

She pulled away from him.

'She said they had to contact you urgently.'

He laughed. 'I bet they did. I bet they're just desperate to get me into Court.'

He hesitated, and then reached out to touch her shoulders.

'Ellie? Did you think I would leave, is that it?'

She turned, and saw in his face the same compassion she had seen the day they first met. The tears rushed to her eyes and he held her close. She tried to stop the sobbing, but it had hold of her. *Out of control again!* She thought angrily.

'I'm not leaving, Ellie,' he said softly.

Ellie's phone rang, and they both looked over at the table at it. Neither of them made any effort to answer it.

They stood there for a long time, until at last Ellie got a grip of herself and pulled away, wiping her eyes. Her face was burning, and she suppressed the urge to scratch it. One day, she thought, one day I'll scratch it so hard I'll tear the rotten mangled skin away, leave myself with nothing. That'll be nice, won't it.

'I'm sorry for being so pathetic,' she said.

'Hey,' he said. She looked up. 'We're both pretty good at that.'

She managed to smile.

'I never did buy you that pint.'

'I'll live. And I bet that was Jim on the phone, worried about you.'

Ellie nodded. She was certain of it.

'Yeah. I'll ring him,' she picked up the phone and saw Jim's name. There was also another list of messages that she had once more ignored for weeks. If she carried on like this, she'd have no friends left.

No friends but Griff.

And that was just fine.

After Flora's bombshell, Ellie decided to have done with it and put the TV on. There was nothing about Griff whatsoever, and she realised that, as he himself had said, it was minor news. They lay on the couch in each others arms, drinking red wine and flicking channels, until Ellie had to laugh. She snuggled into him, until the snuggling became more urgent. Afterwards they lay together naked in the saggy couch and watched soap operas on TV.

'What are we like! We're like an old married couple.'

'What's wrong with that?'

She sighed, as the news came on. They watched in silence.

'Look, there's nothing about it. Satisfied?'

'All right.'

'Tell you what, tomorrow I'll get my phone from the helicopter and call the rental people. Tell them under no circumstances are they to divulge where I am.'

Ellie giggled. 'It's like Bonnie and Clyde.'

'Yeah. You make a good Clyde.'

'Cheek!'

'Ow. Anyway, maybe I'll take the helicopter back to Inverness, pay for them to pick it up from there. We can come back on your bike.'

'You'll never get my bike in the helicopter. It's too big!'

'Well, we'll get a taxi then, or, I know! We'll buy a car, an old banger, and Iowyn can have it when we get back.'

She looked at him. 'But you love flying.'

He nodded, smiling. 'I love you more.'

Ellie closed her eyes. 'I wish I had lots of money, I'd buy you a helicopter.'

'Hey. My career's not over yet, you know. One day I'll get back into film-making, I'll make enough money for both of us.'

Ellie sighed. *One day…*

'Until then, well, we're happy here, aren't we?'

'Oh, yes.'

And it was true, and Ellie knew he loved her, knew he wouldn't leave her, knew they would sort things out. But she was also aware that in the pitch dark of the night, when Griff was breathing evenly beside her, and sleep was far away, she knew the opposite. Nothing gold can stay.

She stood up suddenly, holding out her hand.

'I want to show you something.'

Griff wiggled his eyebrows. 'Oh yes?'

Ellie smiled, shaking her head. 'Something special.'

'More special than just now?'

She grinned, pulling her clothes back on. 'Different. Come on.'

She took him by the hand and led him across the cliff path. The sun was just beginning its descent into the west, and was warm on their backs. The wind, however, carried with it the first chill notes that summer was drawing to an end. Ellie felt it on her scars, reminding her again that nothing lasts. She shivered at the thought, and Griff put his arm round her, thinking her cold.

Ellie led him to the place where cliffs became rocky and rough, and the rocks rose above the cliff path, holding up the mountain. There was the last piece of flat land, where Griff had left his helicopter, and beyond it, the cliff path ended and the rocks rose above their heads. She took him to the wall of rock, and then she stopped.

'This is a secret,' she said.

He gave her a quizzical look. 'I can keep secrets,' he said.

'I know. Come on.'

She took his hand again, and led him to where the rocks parted slightly. The fissure was cut at a slant, and was not noticeable unless you were right upon it. She led him through it between the granite walls with the sea a distant murmur, and down a barely noticeable path, treacherous with loose scree. Ellie remembered the first time she had found the path, the excitement she felt, wondering what she would find at the other end: a beach, maybe, or a jetty. Maybe an old smugglers cave. Certainly not what she did find.

The path wound inwards, and became narrower so they had to go single file. The sea grew even quieter. At last there was another split in the rock, similar to the one at the clifftop, and Ellie looked round at Griff. He had a bemused smile on his face. She had a moment of doubt, that he might be unimpressed, but she shrugged it off, taking his hand again and walking between the columns of stone.

She stopped and looked around, smiling.

The valley sat in a circle of protecting stone, ancient rocks of Torridon sandstone and gneiss. Rocks that were around when Scotland and Canada were one country, and England was across the sea. The cliffs were shot through with diagonal bands of colour, from some upheaval in a time when walking upright was a far distant dream. Fresh water rolled off the mountain above, and had worn through the softer rock before it hit the harder, and there it fell in a sheet of white to a pool below, and then to a river running through another gap in the rocks, to the sea. The valley was tiny, but lush, protected from wind and sea, a gathering place of soil and silt, and here trees had taken root. There were poplar trees with their silver-and-gold leaves, rowans and beeches and ash, oaks and birches, none of them very tall, but all of them thriving, like a forest kindergarten.

Ellie felt Griff's hand squeezing hers.

'It's the only place the trees can grow,' she said. 'Out of the wind and weather.'

'It's beautiful.'

They walked across the grass and between the young trees to the waterfall.

'Jim told me that everyone who finds this place plants something here, as if answering a request made by the trees themselves.'

She looked up. Griff was nodding, as if that made perfect sense. He looked at her.

'What did you plant?'

She took him to the water's edge, where a tiny tree hung its long branches over the water.

'White willow,' she said. '*Salix Alba*. In ages past the bark of this tree was used to heal pain.'

She smiled at him. 'It still works.'

He put his arms around her, and she closed her eyes, leaning into his chest and breathing in the warm scent of him. The sun fell lower, until the valley was cast in shadow, and the falling water looked ghostly.

'What shall I plant?' he whispered.

Ellie looked at him. 'Yourself,' she said.

100

SEVENTEEN

Next morning Ellie took Gethyn MacLeod down the cliffs to see the remaining inhabitants. The night before, all the Puffins had left as one, as if answering some call. Ellie explained all about the job while he examined the deserted nests and looked out to sea, as if he thought he might see the birds returning.

'They'll all be back next year,' she told him.

'So why does someone have to do all this checking up?' he asked.

'Well, so we can tell how healthy the returning birds are, and how many there are. We can keep track of whether the sea's getting warmer, and what sea life is in there. Then we can check that data against the year before's, and tell whether things are improving for the birds, or not.'

'I see. And what about this year?'

'This year,' Ellie said, grinning. 'Was a bumper year for everyone.'

Gethyn nodded. 'My father said he's caught more fish in this year than in any since he started fishing.'

Ellie nodded. It had been a hell of a year all round.

'But why?'

'Who knows? Maybe it was the good weather: warm tides, gentle winds. Lots of food in the sea, no harsh conditions to kill off the vulnerable young.'

Gethyn looked at her.

'You know an awful lot about it. I wish I did.'

She laughed. 'I have to put my report in at the end of this month. I'll let you read it, if you like.'

'Oh yes please.'

'You want to do this sort of work, Geth?'

He nodded. 'Do you think I could?'

'I think you could do whatever you wanted. Your mother tells me you're very smart.'

He smiled, embarrassed. 'I don't think she's very impressed by me wanting to be a warden.'

They started back up the cliffside, Ellie pulling her fleece tight against the chill wind.

'If there's one thing I have learned -' she said, grinning, 'it's that there's nothing worse than doing a miserable job. Being content is worth an awful lot. I'm sure you don't want to hear any advice from an old fart like me, but that has to be rule number one.'

Gethyn looked at her solemnly, making her laugh.

'Hey, lecture over. Come back to the house. I've got something for

101

you.'

The sun was dazzling as they reached the clifftop, casting long shadows behind them.

'Where's Griff this morning?'

'Oh he's messing about in his helicopter.'

Gethyn sighed. 'Flying. That must be wonderful.'

Ellie pushed the door open. 'Scary, is what it is. Come on in.'

The house was messy, as always. Ellie rooted in a box under the kitchen table, pulling out notes and lists of statistics for her final report. In the bottom she found a pouch of photographs, which she pulled out.

'Here we are.' She began to look through the photos until she found what she was looking for.

'Here. Have a look at those.'

She handed Gethyn the pictures she had almost drowned taking. She smiled to herself as she remembered.

'Those are Peregrine falcon eggs. The falcon nested on my cliffs out there this year.'

'Really!'

'Yes, and here-' she handed him another photo, one of the young falcons, too big for the nest now, almost ready to make a start on their own lives.

'And you've been able to watch them, all year?'

'Yeah, pretty much. Here, you can keep that.'

Gethyn held the photograph in both hands, as if it were fragile.

'Thanks a lot.'

Ellie smiled. 'De nada. Or so Griff tells me.'

Gethyn left clutching the photograph, not wanting to crush it in his pocket. Ellie watched him wander down the cliff path, wondering how he got to be so earnest in such a light- hearted family. Perhaps it had to do with being clever. He thought about things too much.
Whereas she tried not to think about things at all.

She watched a Great Skua hovering above the cliffs, and thought about Griff in his helicopter. It was only a couple of hours since she had seen him. She missed him, and decided that was pathetic. Nevertheless, she set off along the cliff to where he always landed it, to wait for him. She still couldn't get enough of him, and that was pathetic too, she thought with a smile.

The clifftop became rocky, and she scrambled over the boulders to where the land flattened off again. To her surprise, the helicopter was there. She had not heard him come in to land, which was strange. She could see Griff in the cockpit. He was leaning over the controls, looking down at something. She hurried over, sensing something wrong. He saw her coming and raised his head. The sun was slanting on the glass, and she couldn't see his face. She reached the helicopter and looked in. Griff smiled, but it didn't reach his eyes. She put her hands flat on the glass, and he reached for the catch and opened the door.

'What is it? What's happened?'

'Nothing. It's all right.'

Griff climbed out of the seat and reached for her. He held her for a long moment while she panicked quietly. When she looked at him again, he had a wry smile on his face.

'Tell me,' she said. 'You've spoken to your American friends, haven't you?'

He shook his head. 'Not exactly.'

'What, then?'

He sighed. His eyes looked tired, but there was more; they looked beaten. He looked down for a long moment, and then back at her. His dark hair gleamed in the low sun, like the mica in the rocks. His eyes fixed on hers, and suddenly she felt as if the world had stopped revolving, just for an instant, while the silent *twist* in time took place. Everything would change now, she knew.

'I called the rental place to check in. They said, as before, that people back home were trying to contact me. I told them I wasn't interested, but then they said my father was very anxious to speak to me.'

Ellie waited. Griff took a deep breath and shrugged.

'Like I told you, I haven't seen my father for nearly fifteen years. All of a sudden he wants to talk to me. So I looked at the phone, and there were a lot of voicemails. *A lot.*

I wish I hadn't listened to them, but I did.'

Ellie sighed, her heart sinking fast. 'What did they say.'

Griff looked away across the sea. 'That he's dying. Cancer. The last message was Monday. He sounded, I don't know. Desperate, maybe.'

He looked back at her, reaching for her hands. His were freezing.

'You have to go and see him,' Ellie said. *What are you saying!*

He shook his head.

'Why? What's the point? If he had anything to say to me, he should have said it long ago.'

'No. You need to go.'

Griff gave a cold laugh. 'So he can make his peace with me? So he can die content?'

'No,' Ellie said, laying her hands on his chest.

'Not for him, for you. Don't you see? You have to go. If you don't go, one night a long time from now you'll wake up and think, I should have said goodbye. No matter what had happened in the past, I should have said goodbye.'

Griff stared at her.

'You want me to go?'

'I want you to stay with me. But you have to go.'

'No. I- I know what you're saying, but I – there's nothing left between us.'

It was her turn to look out over the sea. She recalled her mother turning up at the hospital, after the accident. She had heard a nurse say that her mother was there, and had felt a lump of solid dread settle into her heart. She had come into the ward, and Ellie had waited for the anger and recriminations. She hadn't even looked up for a long time, and no one said a word, until at last Ellie did look up.

She saw the pity, the compassion. She was already sick of it, but there was something else there, something sadder and darker. Something that reached out and touched them both.

My poor Ellie, she had said. *I should have looked after you better.*

Ellie closed her eyes tightly, then reopened them to the autumn glare.

'Griff. You have to trust me on this. There's always something left. You might think there's not, but there is.'

Griff covered her hands with his. He looked into her eyes for a long time.

'I don't want to go,' he whispered.

Ellie leaned her head on his chest, closing her eyes as his arms closed round her.

'Come with me.'

She shook her head.

'Why not?'

'I can't go. You know I can't.'

'Ellie, I won't go without you.'

She looked up, smiling now.

'Yes, you will. You have to. Go, and come back to me when you can.'

He shook his head again.

'Go on, Griff, there might not be much time.'

'What, just like that? You want me to go now?'

'If you don't go now I won't be able to let you go at all.'

'That suits me.'

She reached up to kiss him. He leaned down the long way, then changed his mind and lifted her off her feet. The kiss lasted a long time, and Ellie knew it would have to last her a lot longer. In the end she looked up at him as the decision was made. She tried to capture the memory to keep forever: the sharpness of the air; the faint smell of aviation fuel; the cold wind on her face; the sun, a long way away, reaching out its shadows beyond them; the cry of a fulmar overhead; the shuffle of the waves on the shingle; Griff, his eyes dark and uncertain; the strength of his arms; the warmth of his chest under her hands.

'I'll be back as soon as I can. I'll call you.'

She nodded. He let her go, and stood there a long moment, not moving. Ellie smiled.

'Go,' she said.

Griff smiled. She watched the corner of his mouth turn up, recognising the familiar warm sensation it evoked in her. It wasn't a happy smile, but then, neither was hers. He turned away and climbed into the cockpit. She heard the engine turn over and saw him pull on his headset. He looked at her the whole time. She stepped back before the rotors began to turn, back towards the rocks until she was leaning against them. The rotors turned, ripping the air, and still he looked at her, until at last the machine tilted forward and left the clifftop. The sun glared on the glass, and she could no longer see his face. The helicopter soared out over the sea and banked towards the east, the mainland, and the rest of his life.

Ellie stood there for a long time after he had gone. The fulmar cried long and hard above her, as if in sympathy. She felt drained of feeling. Numb. She felt as if she had blown a whole lifetime's worth of emotion in one day, and there was nothing left for tomorrow. And perhaps that wasn't a bad thing, after all.

The fulmar wheeled out over the waves. It was time he was gone too.

EIGHTEEN

Ellie knew she had to go to the pub, do something. Otherwise she thought she might go mad.

It was full of the usual suspects. Jim and Mairearadh were in the corner, talking to Lisa MacLeod. They all looked up and smiled as she came in.

'Hello Ellie. What have you done with him?'

'Tired the poor man out, I'll bet,' Donnie said, grinning. Ellie grinned back, but she felt numb, as if she was watching a film of herself, she was not actually there at all. She got a drink and sat down.

'You all right?' Jim asked.

'Fine,' she said brightly, still grinning.

'Lisa tells us Gethyn's decided on his University. St Andrews.'

'That'll be great,' Ellie said.

'Of course, he could have gone to three or four, they all wanted him-' Lisa said.

Ellie looked down. Lisa was proud of him, and so she should be. She let the conversation wash over her. It was something to think about. Something else.

She sensed Jim looking at her.

'What did you do when you graduated?' he asked. She looked up, but his face was impassive.

'My first job was in Glasgow Royal Infirmary. Biochem,' she said. She hesitated, but Jim was still looking at her. *I don't want to talk about myself,* she thought. *But I don't want to think about what I've lost.*

'I did the first year, and then I met up with one of the girls I'd been at uni with. She was working for one of the big pharmaceutical companies, selling reagents to the hospital labs. She sold it to me. I looked around and got a job with a company selling drugs to doctors. It was a hoot. I was- different, I suppose, then.'

'Before the accident, you mean?'

Ellie shrugged, non committal. She took a long drink of her pint.

'One of my drugs was an alternative to Viagra. It had the added bonus that once the patient took the drug, he had the effect for 24 hours.'

'Wow.'

'Yeah.' She smiled at the memory. 'With the other drugs, you had to take it and pelt upstairs. Mine was more sophisticated. That's how I sold it, anyhow. It was great fun, and I got to go all over the country, nice car, good money, the works.'

'So what happened then?'

'You know what happened. I was in a car crash and my face melted.'

Jim put his head on one side.

'Were you driving?'

She shook her head. 'A boyfriend was.'

'How did it happen?'

Ellie shrugged. Why was she talking about this stuff? It felt as if the loss of Griff had opened her up, like a broken oyster on the beach, for the gulls to pick over.

'He was going too fast, showing off. It had been raining earlier after weeks of hot weather, the roads were greasy.'

She stopped, remembering the moment. It was baked, as it were, in her memory.

'Billy, It's not big and it's not clever. Slow down.'

'I will, Ellie wellie, I will.'

'Now, Billy! And don't call me that!'

Laughter. 'Ellie wellie the testicle tickler! Shit!'

'Billy! You're all over the road. You're going to kill us both.'

'All right, I'll slow down, I promise.'

'No, don't promise, just do-'

The most prominent part of the memory was the poor joke. Billy was always making fun of her name and job. It had been annoying. His being pissed all the time was annoying too. Yet she still went out with him, still put up with it. Stupid, stupid girl. Nothing had changed.

She looked up. Jim was watching her. 'What?'

'Nothing. What happened then?'

'He was just promising to slow down when we ran off the road. The car hit a barrier and scraped down the left side. I think that's when the fuel cap got pulled off. The car went down a bank and burst into flames.'

'What happened to the boyfriend?'

'Well he didn't get fried, if that's what you're thinking.'

'I'm not thinking anything.'

Ellie looked up warily.

'Ellie, forget that I was a psychiatrist for a minute, will you?'

She grinned. 'Kind of hard to do, Siggy.'

He shook his head, but he was grinning.

'Tell me. He got out, I take it?'

She nodded. 'He climbed the bank and got away.'

Jim waited.

'You're doing that cop thing again. Saying nothing knowing I'll fill up the silence. I've seen 'The Bill', you know.'

'Don't be so defensive.'

107

'Defensive. Good one. What do you want me to say? It's pretty obvious what happened. I got stuck in the car.'

'How? Were you trapped?'

'Seat belt. couldn't find the button.'

'But you got out eventually.'

'Hah. Yes. Eventually.'

Jim nodded again, as if he were taking mental notes.

'What treatment did you get? Did you not have a mask to wear?'

'Oh yeah. I had the mask. They promised it would make my face heal properly. Imagine what I'd have been like without that.'

She heard the bitterness in her own voice. Heard the scars laughing. She knew they'd be making a comeback round about now.

Just you have yourselves a good ole time!

'I know it must have been incredibly painful,' Jim said gently.

Ellie said nothing. There was no response to that. It was somewhere in the middle of the pain that the scars had taken on their own identity, as if the pain gave birth to them and nourished them at the same time as it was ripping her apart.

Time to move on.

'Anyway. I got treated at the Royal, where my blood samples went to my old lab. The guys there came to see me, and my old boss offered me a job any time I wanted it. It was kind of him, and with hindsight, he knew what I didn't then. That my career as a sales rep was over.'

'Why?'

Ellie felt herself getting angry.

'Why do you think? Who's going to buy drugs from Two-Face? It's not exactly good for business, is it?'

Jim nodded sadly. 'They fired you?'

'Not exactly. My boss came to see me. Promised me he'd keep my job open. Told me to take as long as I needed to recover.'

She looked up hopelessly.

'It took me a while to realise what was happening. The treatment took months, as you probably know. By the time I made a move to go back to work, there was always some excuse. I was naïve, I guess. Anyway, to cut a long story short, I eventually put my notice in. Took up my old boss's offer. Went back to the lab. Got fed up with the Royal, and started to do temping. And one fine day I spotted a job as a bird warden, and here I am.'

Jim steepled his fingers. Never a good sign.

'What are you thinking, Jim. Am I crazy?'

'There's one thing running through your story that stands out.'

'Oh? What's that?'

'All the broken promises.'

Ellie looked down. She felt as if he had reached inside her chest and closed his fist round her heart.

'That's always been the case, hasn't it?'

She folded her arms across her stomach, feeling sick.

'Hasn't it, Ellie? Your father, your mother, your boyfriend, your boss, your doctors. Everyone broke their promises.'

She stood up, a bloom of panic opening inside her.

'I have to go.'

'Ellie, don't run away!'

'Sorry.'

She hurried out of the pub and made for the cliff road. She heard the door banging behind her.

'Ellie. Wait.'

She stopped. Here in the cold air, reality had returned with a vengeance. She felt sick.

'Ellie,' Jim came up behind her. She felt him put his hands on her shoulders.

'Where's Griff?'

She closed her eyes. 'I'm sure you can guess,' she said.

Jim said nothing. Her shoulders under his hands were the only warm part of her body.

'He's gone, of course.'

'Of course?'

She looked round. 'I have to go too.'

She pulled away, and carried on up the path. She knew Jim watched her go, but he said nothing, and didn't follow her. The stars peered down at her as she walked. All those familiar constellations, with their own sad stories to tell.

NINETEEN

'So what do I tell him?' Jim said.

'What? Tell who?'

'Griff. When he comes back. What do I say?'

Ellie laughed without humour. 'I don't think that'll be a problem.'

Jim sat on the edge of the ancient sofa.

'He will be back.'

'So you keep saying.'

She finished folding the last of the clothes and carried them outside. Jim followed her.   Ellie opened the door of the Land Rover and laid the clothes on the passenger seat.

'There,' she said. 'Since you're so sure, you can give those back to him. Otherwise, Mairearadh can give them to the charity shop next time she's in Inverness.'

She walked back inside the cottage. The wind was fierce, and her cheek felt tight from the salt spray in the air.

'Ellie, can we just talk for a minute?'

She opened the kitchen cupboards and began pulling out half-empty jars and boxes, stacking them in a cardboard box.

'Lay off, Jim. There's nothing to talk about.'

He laughed then. 'That's the most ridiculous thing I've ever heard, coming from you.'

She looked up, surprised.

'Yes. Time for a few home truths, I think. If you would just talk about things a bit more, everything wouldn't end up being such a problem.'

She felt a surge of anger, and bit it back.

'That's bullshit, Jim. Problems are problems, whether you talk about them or not.'

'Agreed. But they don't have to signal the end of the world.'

'Look. I'm going. The job's finished, I've sent in my report, it'll be winter soon, there's nothing to do, and I need to eat.'

'Ach away with you. You know you could work in the pub.'

'Why would I want to work in the damn pub.'

'Because it means you could stay here!'

He leaned forward to stare at her. She shook her head in annoyance. The box-stacking grew more frantic.

'I won't say I don't love it here. I do. Maybe I'll get the warden's post next year, if I'm lucky. But I'm not staying here alone all winter-'

She hesitated. *Yes,* she thought, *say it. Say it all: alone all winter, waiting hopelessly for something that isn't going to happen.*

'I'll go back to Glasgow and sign on with an agency. Do lab work.'

'Oh, like you did before? You enjoyed that, I recall.'

She shot him a savage look. Just because he was right didn't mean there was any choice.

She struggled to force a bottle of HP sauce into the box.

'What's Griff going to think when he gets back and you're gone?'

'How many times, Jim. He's not coming back!'

The cap came off the bottle and the sauce residue gathered round the lip went all over her hands. 'Shit!' she cried. There were tears standing about a millimetre from her eyes, and there was no way she was letting them out.

Jim stood up and walked towards her. He took the box off the table and put it on the floor. Ellie threw the bottle into the black bin liner that was half-full on the floor, trying to ignore him while she washed the sauce from her hands. In the dim light, it looked like blood swirling down the drain. If only she'd been a bit more decisive, she could have already left on the morning ferry, and avoided all this awkwardness. In truth, she did not want to leave without saying goodbye to Jim, to everyone, but she just couldn't bear the thought of it; all the sympathy. She knew she was running away. She had always been running away.

'Ellie.'

Jim looked sad.

'When did you last speak to him?'

She realised there was no escape, and collapsed on the lumpy sofa.

'The day he left.'

'And have you tried to call him?'

'No.'

'So after a week you've given up on him?'

She looked up, biting back anger. 'I'm not going to chase him.'

'Anything could have happened.'

'Nothing he wants me to know about.'

Jim sighed. 'You know, you're your own worst enemy. Anyone would think you didn't want him to come back, so you could carry on being miserable.'

'Well if that's what you think, maybe you'd better go.'

She folded her arms, her heart pounding with anger.

'That's just what you want, isn't it? Everyone to leave you alone to mope.'

'I guess you insulting me is supposed to make me come to my senses, is it?'

Jim laughed. 'I don't know anything that's likely to do that. I thought Griff might have, but you're not willing to let him.'

She sighed, the anger suddenly gone.

111

'Look, Jim. It was wonderful while it lasted, but be realistic. He came here to get away from his problems, and I was a little diversion for a while. But he's back in the land of milk and honey now, with all his wealth and influence, and all the beautiful people. He's left me behind. And I'm not staying here all winter like some jilted bride, having everyone giving me pitying looks. I'm off. Anyway-'

She stopped.

'Anyway what?'

'Oh, nothing.'

Anyway, it's all spoiled, she thought. *Every cliff walk, every boat ride, every morning with the mist rising like the breath of the sea, every sunset over the whispering dunes. Everything reminds me of him. How can I stay?*

Jim sat down next to her. 'I think you're misjudging him. Griff is a good man.'

Ellie shrugged. She was tired of thinking about it, tired of talking about it. It was time to just go. She felt Jim sigh, and looked at him.

'Will you come back?'

She smiled. 'Of course I will.' But she wondered if that was true. As she spoke it she meant it, but life was never that simple. She could see from Jim's eyes that he didn't believe her.

She looked round at her packed bags. 'Any chance of a lift to the harbour?'

Jim nodded slowly. 'If I must. Don't forget your phone,' he said, and she looked behind at the windowsill where she had left it plugged into the charger. Forget the phone, she thought. There was no way she could cope with a call from Griff to tell her he was sorry.

It was raining heavily when they left, and the pub was open, so there was no one on the dock but Jim to see Ellie quietly board the ferry and wave goodbye.

PART TWO

TWENTY

Griff felt like a tramp walking through LAX. He hadn't slept since leaving Baranpay, and his clothes were creased and sweaty. He fingered the stubble on his chin, heading for the airport shops where he bought a shaving kit and a T shirt with a kitsch print of the downtown skyline. After he washed, shaved and changed in the restroom, he wandered back out into the concourse and thought about calling his father.

After all, that was the reason he was here, wasn't it? The reason he'd left Ellie and the island behind. He felt the surge of guilt rise in him: he should not have left her. He knew it instinctively, even if he couldn't explain it to himself. Yet she had been right to make him come back, and he had known it even as she had said it. He had to come, or he'd live to regret it.

Griff pulled the mobile phone out of his pocket and scrolled through the messages until he found the last one. He walked over to a waiting area filled with sad potted plants and found an empty seat. Then he pressed redial and waited.

'Hello?'

The voice was the same as he remembered it. It only needed one word to take him back to that cold house; the constant yelling, the sense of gloom. He should have stayed on Baranpay.

'Mother. It's Griff.'

'Griffin! At last. Where the hell have you been, you idiot? Have you any idea how hard we've been trying to get hold of you? Jesus!'

He had to smile. Fifteen years of silence, and that was the first thing she had to say to him.

'How's dad?'

'Not good. You'd better hurry.'

She put the phone down. Griff looked at it. He chuckled to himself, then hit redial again.

'Hello?'

'It's me again. You forgot to tell me where he is.'

There was a silence.

'Cedars. He's at Cedars. I thought you'd know.'

This time Griff closed the phone first. There was nothing else to say.

He walked over to the bank of cash machines and used his card to draw out two hundred dollars, which was more than he figured he'd need. Then he took a taxi to the hospital.

On the ride up to Beverley Hills Griff looked out at his home town and examined his heart. He felt nothing, no sense of pleasure or comfort at being back home. It had taken four separate flights to get him here, and on each he had dozed off and dreamed of the island and Ellie. When he had walked off the film set four months ago, the last thing he needed was a love affair. Yet he knew that all the pain he had been feeling back then had been smoothed away in Ellie's gentle arms. Baranpay was his home now. He could barely wait to get back.

Hospitals all seemed the same to Griff. They didn't bother him. After all, years ago he'd come in voluntarily to have his nose straightened, a procedure that had been a lot more painful than he had expected. The price of vanity, he supposed. Even back then he had known, deep down, how ridiculous it was, surgically altering yourself to try and look better. He had had his teeth straightened too. It made him think of Ellie again. He didn't know if there was anything they could do to fix her scars, but who cared? After a week or so, he had stopped noticing them at all. Ellie had something he needed, and it was more than a pretty face. He wished he'd never had the surgery. It made him feel facile and shallow. He breathed in the hospital smell, heading for the reception desk. The nurse there looked at his T shirt and smiled.

'Can I help you?'

'I'm looking for a patient, Carl Park?'

She checked her computer.

'Mr Park's on the third floor.'

As he rode up in the elevator, he wondered how he was going to feel seeing the old man again. Right now he felt nothing at all, either for the memory of his father, or the sadness of the disease killing him. Griff wondered if things would change when he saw him.

Carl Park had been a university lecturer: history and politics. It must have been a great job in the sixties. But he wondered if it hadn't been the cause of the anger and recrimination that peppered his childhood. His and his brother's. All he remembered was the bitterness on his father's face, and the hurt and betrayal on his mother's. And Peter, he remembered Peter's words before he left:

'Get out, Griff, while you can. There's nothing in this house but hate.'

Griff had never talked to his father about this, and now he probably never would.

Carl Park was sitting in a wheelchair, watching a Jerry Springer rerun on TV. He was hunched over a half-filled glass of water on a tray on his lap. Carl had never been a big man, but he looked now as if he was disappearing inside himself, the incredible shrinking man. Griff was shocked by his assessment of the man, and tried to find something positive about the person who had fathered him. Carl was

117

wearing a lemon checked shirt. It was open at the collar, but even if he had fastened it, the shirt could still have been pulled off over his head. His skin was so pale that the veins in his arms stood out sharply like blue worms. His eyes were fixed on the screen, but otherwise he might have been asleep.

'Dad?'

Carl blinked, then he looked down at the glass in his lap. After a moment he seemed to decide that he had heard something after all, and looked up.

Griff saw little of himself in the old man's face. His eyes were cloudy blue, heavily lidded. His mouth was wide, and he had an overshot jaw which made his lower lip protrude. It had always made him appear belligerent, and that had been no lie. Griff searched inside himself for a hint of affection, or failing that, at least sympathy.

'So you've come.' Carl's voice cracked on the last word, and he reached out to the tray for his glass of water. As he drank, Griff saw the effort of swallowing was clearly painful. He put the glass back down and looked up again.

'Where have you been?'

'What, for the last fifteen years?'

The old man tried a smile. 'Yeah, I guess I deserved that.'

Griff shook his head. 'I've been travelling.'

'Ah.'

Carl looked back at the TV. Two women were now pulling each other's hair, while a security guard attempted to separate them. The audience clapped and yelled.

Griff bit back annoyance. 'Dad, if you're going to watch TV, I'll leave you to it.'

'No. Don't go. I'm sorry.'

Carl put his thin hands on the wheels and tried to turn the chair away from the screen. Griff walked behind him to help.

'Wheel me on to the balcony. It's private there.'

Griff pushed the chair outside. His father looked even worse under the sunlight, shrunken and white, like a creature that never saw daylight. He squinted up, raising one hand to shield his eyes.

'Nice T shirt.'

Griff nodded at the sarcasm, looking out at the hazy smog.

'I know what you're thinking,' Carl said. 'I look like shit.'

Griff looked down at him, but said nothing.

'Cancer of the oesophagus. They gave me twelve weeks. That was four months ago, so you could say I'm on seriously borrowed time.'

Carl looked up into his face, and Griff saw that there were things he wanted to say, perhaps needed to say, but in that instant he also knew that he would not say them. The old man's bottom lip jutted out stubbornly, and he smiled.

'Well, I'm glad you came,' he said.

Griff wondered why. There was nothing between them, no spark of affection, no fond memories.

'You've done well, with your life,' Carl said. 'I should be proud of you.'

Should be? Griff thought. *What the hell does that mean?* And in any case, he wasn't exactly proud of himself. What had he done that was so great? Direct films he didn't like. Abandon his writing. Marry a woman he didn't love. And leave the best thing he had ever found to come and say goodbye to a man who cared nothing for him.

'Dad, why did you want me to come here?'

Carl reached for his glass of water again. It was stifling hot in the sun, but the old man's hand was shaking.

'Just to say goodbye,' he said.

Griff took hold of the wheelchair handles and pushed his father back inside. He positioned the chair back in front of the TV. The old man didn't look at him again.

'Goodbye, dad,' Griff said. He hesitated for a moment, but Carl stayed staring at his bony hands. Griff turned and left.

As he reached the landing, the elevator opened, and his mother walked out. She stopped when she saw him, her mouth open in surprise.

'What, you done already?' she said.

Griff shook his head. 'Hello mother.'

She narrowed her eyes. 'Come back in with me. We all ought to talk.'

'I don't think so.'

She walked closer and looked up into his face.

'So what? After all these years you finally turn up, and now you're leaving again.'

'What do you want to talk to me about, mother?'

Her fierce little eyes screwed up in anger. She was wearing a lot of make up, and he could see where she had run the lipstick round the outside of her lips, to make them appear bigger.

'I want to tell you not to be such an asshole. Go back in there and speak to your father.'

'And say what? He wanted me to come, and yet he has nothing to say to me.'

'He's dying, for Christ's sake.'

'The disease doesn't affect his mind.'

She glanced past him to where a few patients in chairs were

listening intently. She leaned close and spoke in a savage whisper.

'God dammit, you'll do as I say!'

He looked down and saw she had clenched her fists.

'What are you going to do, mother, hit me? Again?'

She recoiled as if he had struck her. She looked down and he saw her shoulders slump.

'I'll see you around,' he said, pushing past her. The elevator was on its way down, so he made for the stairs. He ran down them three at a time, and by the time he was back out in daylight, he was breathing hard.

Griff stood outside the hospital for a long minute. He noticed a man in a dark suit and sunglasses looking at him, and figured he must look terrible. He had no idea what to do. He needed to think. He wondered if that little episode had been better than not coming at all. He desperately wanted to speak to Ellie, but decided not to call her, not yet. He'd calm down a bit first.

He started walking, looking round his home town with a heavy heart. In the heat and
gas-tainted air, it felt as if he'd never been away. He felt both exhausted and depressed. By the time he got down to Sunset he decided he'd better check into a hotel and take stock.

When Mel had thrown him out, Griff had gone to stay with his friend Dave, who also happened to be his lawyer. Dave was alone, having just gone through a messy divorce of his own, and neither of them spent much time indoors except to sleep. It had worked fine, but Griff didn't want to impose on his only good friend any more, even for a short time.

Now that he was here, he would sort out all the mess of the divorce, clean out his bank accounts, (what was left in them) and say goodbye for good. He caught a cab to the Holiday Inn on South Figueroa, mindful that his funds were limited, and checked in at reception. The teller took his bank card to make the reservation, and came back a few minutes later with a sneer on her face.

'I'm sorry sir, your card's been declined.'

'What?' It couldn't be. He'd used it at the airport not two hours before.

'Are you sure? Could you try it again?'

The receptionist gave him a tired, seen-it-all-before look, then looked past him. He followed her gaze and saw the man in the suit from the hospital. He still had his sunglasses on. He smiled in a businesslike way and handed Griff a card.

Griff looked at it without seeing. Now what? Why was this man following him? Was there something else that could go wrong today?

'I'm employed by Lincoln Przwalski and Partners.' The suit said. Griff read the card. The man was a private investigator. He looked up, confused.

'Who the hell are Lincoln Prez-'

'Przwalski. And Partners.' The suit bared his teeth again. 'I understand they act for your wife.'

Griff looked at the card again. His wife? And then it hit him. Of course. When he left, the divorce had been rumbling along in ways known only to lawyers. His disappearance must have sowed panic in dear Mel's breast. Griff, disappeared off the face of the planet, unavailable to settle the little matter of the divorce settlement. That explained the cancelled bank card. The lawyers had frozen his account. The suit coughed meaningfully, and Griff looked up.

'If you want my advice, I think you ought to call your lawyer,' he said.

TWENTY ONE

'Not even a phone call!' Dave Ross said, holding his head in his hands.

'Look, I'm sorry. I said I was sorry!'

'I mean, did you never stop to think people might be worried? I might be worried?'

Griff sighed. 'No. I didn't figure anyone would care much.'

'Oh. Nice. I'm your friend, I put you up when your wife kicks you out, I tear my hair out trying to stop the bitch freezing your accounts, and you 'didn't figure I'd care much."

Dave threw himself down on the black leather sofa. It made a farting noise, and Griff felt a smile come unbidden to his mouth.

'And now it's funny? Jesus!'

Griff looked at his friend until Dave started to smile too. Dave looked away to show he was still not happy.

'I don't know what to do with you, I really don't.'

'Dave. I'm sorry.'

They were in the living room of Dave's Monterey Park apartment. The place was done out with crisp white walls and solid black furniture, and Griff knew Dave had employed an interior designer to set the place out, having neither time nor inclination to do it himself.

'Well, at least you're here now.'

'Not for long,' Griff said. Might as well get it all over with. Dave sat up straighter, looking at him.

'Okay, let's have the story.'

Griff told him. Dave was the only real friend he had, so he missed nothing out. Dave listened without interrupting. He had dark brown eyes with heavy lids that made him look slightly sleepy, but the truth was that he was as sharp as they came. Dave sipped his drink and rubbed the crease in his Savile Row suit pants, while Griff got to the bit about his father and the investigator, and the embarrassment at the Holiday Inn.

'So, again, you didn't think to call me. You checked into a hotel.'

Griff smiled. Dave stood up and poured two glasses of whisky from a bottle on the sideboard, handing one to Griff.

'So what have I missed?' Griff asked.

'Okay, here's where we're at,' Dave said.

'You storm out of the set in a bloody rage, and everyone in Hollywood hears it. You were heard to say, and I quote: 'Fuck it. That's enough, I'm out of here permanently.'

He paused, and Griff shrugged. He couldn't remember if he'd said that or not. He remembered the day now as if it had happened to someone else: Mel screaming down the phone at him because of some papers he'd signed in the wrong place, the usual waste-of-time hassle with the leading man, and then the suits arriving en masse, George Collins putting his arm round him to give him the bad news. Why he had chosen that day to flip out? After all, it was just one bad day in a run of the same.

No, he thought sadly. It had been the worst day of his life.

Dave coughed, and Griff looked up, embarrassed at having drifted off.

'So, a week passes, then two. Word gets round, and your ex gets nervous. Starts calling me asking where you are. So I tell her you've gone on vacation, tell her not to panic. The hearing comes and goes, and I'm winging it by now, because even I don't know where my client is.'

Griff sighed, and tried to look contrite. 'I thought it was all sorted, it just had to go to Court and they'd decide what happened.'

'There's a little matter of ne-go-ti-ation.' Dave said slowly, as if he were an idiot. 'You don't just say, sure Mel, you take whatever you want.'

Griff shrugged again. 'I don't care.'

'Well I do. I negotiated you a damn good deal, if I say so myself, but that's where it backfired.'

'Why?'

'Because I still thought you'd be back any day. If I'd known you'd gone off to Timbuc-fucking-too I'd have asked for something outrageous, dragged the whole thing out. But no, I was trying to save you money, trying to do the right thing.'

'I still don't understand.'

Dave gave a theatrical sigh.

'I came up with an offer and Mel accepted. We got an Order of the Court, and it went through without a ripple. Costs awarded, settlement reached. Only you weren't there to pay up.'

'Oh.'

'Oh? Is that all you can say? Have you any idea how *embarrassing* that was?'

Griff finished his drink. It tasted bitter. He thought about how he'd feel if the positions were reversed, and decided he probably wouldn't even be speaking to Dave now.

'So then it all came out. You had disappeared, and then Mel's lawyers decided that you had no intention of coming back. They decided to go back to Court for an order to grab your assets.'

Griff rubbed his hand through his hair.

123

'But you stopped them.'

Dave leaned forward. 'Yeah, I stopped them. Until now, that is. Now they know you're back, they're forcing the issue.'

'How did you stop them before?'

'Oh, I made them a payment on account.'

'You paid them with your own money?'

Dave raised an eyebrow. 'Certainly not,' he said. 'You gave me power of attorney, remember?'

Griff laughed. 'So why didn't you just pay them everything.'

'Because you hadn't agreed to it, remember? You were still off on the island of lurvve.'

'But you knew I'd agree. I told you to let her have whatever she wants.'

'And I'm your attorney, not to mention your friend. Professionally, I couldn't just do that. And anyway, if you didn't agree, you would come back and sue me.'

Griff shook his head. 'You can't think that?'

Dave gave him a long careful look. 'Right now, Griff, I don't know what I think. You're not acting like the man I remember from UCLA. You want my advice?'

'Sure.'

'I think you ought to get some counselling.'

Griff felt his heart sink. 'Oh Dave, I don't need a shrink. I-'

Dave held his hands out in front of his chest. 'Look, it's just a suggestion. Anyway, let's go eat, I'm starved.'

Griff did a quick mental inventory of his pockets. 'Uh-'

'Yeah, I know, it's my treat.'

Griff smiled. The lawyers had not only frozen his bank accounts, but also his phone account and credit cards. Back at the Holiday Inn, he'd had to use a public phone to call Dave, another serious embarrassment that he felt in the circumstances was quite deserved.

He followed his friend out of the apartment and down to the basement. His Lexus was still there where he'd left it, four months ago, but they took Dave's Boxster and drove for less than three minutes to a downtown restaurant. It took almost ten minutes to find a parking spot. Only in LA.

It was a restaurant the two of them had often visited in the strange days when they were sharing the apartment. Dave, a man who spent all his working life talking, never seemed to be able to shut up. Griff, on the other hand, knew he was pretty much the opposite, and he was sure that was why Dave insisted he move in.

The maitre d' recognised them and showed them to their table, while Dave explained about the ongoing argument he'd been having with the landlord about maintenance of the apartment's swimming pool.

'- said he'd better just call another damn pool company, or I'd bring a case against him.'

Griff picked up on what he was saying.

'A case? For what?'

'Breach of contract. A clean and fully maintained pool is included in the rental agreement. If he fails to provide that, he's in breach, and I can not only sue him, I won't be paying any more rent.'

Griff laughed. 'You can't do that.' He looked at Dave's face. 'Can you?'

'You bet. He huffed and puffed a bit, but in the end he got a new pool man like I asked. The pool's fine now, you'll see.'

Since Griff had never used the pool, it wasn't something that he was likely to notice, but Dave swam every morning, and besides, he just couldn't resist the fun of the confrontation.

'So tomorrow, I'll arrange a meeting with the other side, and get things straightened out.'

Griff smiled. 'Thanks Dave. How about the phone, will they release that too?'

The phone worried him, as it had Ellie's number programmed into the memory, and he didn't know it off by heart. The phone had stopped working altogether, and being a technophobe, he assumed that was down to the lawyers.

'Oh sure. So are you serious, about going back to this place?'

Griff nodded. The last couple of days had been a nightmare, and thinking about it here and now, he was more certain even than before. He smiled to himself, and looked up to see Dave shaking his head.

'She must be some woman, is all I can say.'

Griff felt his smile grow wider. 'She is. She's perfect.'

'What does she do?'

'She's the warden of the nature reserve. She looks after the birds.'

Dave nodded, not interested. 'And is she pretty, you got any photos?'

'No, no photos. I never got the chance. But yes, she's pretty.'

It didn't occur to him to mention her scarred face.

'So, Griff, what are you going to do there? I saved you some cash on the settlement, but it won't last you forever.'

'I don't know.' Griff said. He wished Dave hadn't asked, because it did worry him. 'I'll think of something.'

'Why don't you go back to writing, forget all this directing crap? Writing's what you were best at.'

'Don't mince words, Dave, say what you feel.'

125

Dave made his hands-off gesture again.

'Writers do what they like. Directors have to toe the money line.'

'You don't need to tell me.'

The food arrived. Dave had ordered a rare steak. Griff had sea bass, just to remind him of Ellie. He wanted to speak to her so badly that it was like an ache inside him. He wondered where she was, what she was doing, whether she was thinking of him. He had an image of her, lying on the white sand, her thick dark brown hair spread out around her like seaweed, her green eyes grinning at him suggestively. His very own mermaid, she was, come from the sea to save him.

He realised that he had drifted off into a daydream, and looked up. Dave glanced down at Griff's untouched plate, and then back up, shaking his head.

'You've really got it bad, haven't you?'

*

Griff was up before the dawn, and he walked out on to the roof terrace to look over the city. He could already hear the hiss of the freeway, the sound that never seemed to die away. It looked like being another hot day, and his thoughts were drawn back to the island; the mist that rode in on the waves each morning, the wind that stroked your skin with chill fingers, the ozone smell of the sea. He was impatient to get his phone working again. It was now four days since he had left Ellie, and she would be wondering why he hadn't called. She might even think he had abandoned her. That brought a lump to his throat. Guilt. He knew all about that.

He glanced over at the pale green pool. He thought he heard Dave moving round, and he went back inside to brew some coffee. For four months he hadn't had a single cup of coffee, the islanders all drank tea when they weren't drinking alcohol. He smiled to himself. The coffee tasted bitter.

Dave appeared half an hour later after his swim, dressed in a bathrobe. He sat down as Griff poured him coffee, saying nothing. Dave always needed the first coffee to make himself sociable.

'What's the plan today?'

Dave winced at the taste of the coffee.

'Jesus. You wouldn't make anyone a good wife. What did you make this with, grit?'

Griff smiled. 'Sorry, darling.'

Dave drank more of the coffee, glaring at him.

'The plan today is to get the other side to agree to meet.'

'Can't we just pay them the money?'

Dave shook his head.

'They'll be dicks about it, guaranteed. The idea is we meet up, you're all apologetic. We agree to pay, they agree to drop the big freeze, everyone's happy.'

Griff nodded. 'So when will you call them?'

'When I get in to work, Griff. Give me a break, will you?'

'Sorry. It's just, I can't call Ellie.'

He explained about the number being stored in the phone. Dave just stared at him.

'That's got nothing to do with the law suit. The phone should still work, you just can't make calls.'

Griff felt his heart lurch. He got up and hurried to his room where he pulled out the phone. It was still totally dead. He carried it back to the kitchen.

'How can I get this fixed?'

Dave shrugged. 'No idea. Isn't there anyone else you can call?'

Griff thought about it. He could probably get a listing for the pub. It was worth a try.

Dave stood up. 'Well, I'll get dressed and we'll go.'

'Thanks Dave.'

Dave put his hands out in his usual gesture. 'De nada.'

Dave's downtown office was a building made mostly out of glass. Ross Kothlis Partners had the tenth floor suite, and Dave's corner room would have had spectacular views if they had been ten floors higher. It was a nice office, well furnished and giving off the sweet smell of success. Griff knew Dave was a good lawyer, but the room itself would have told anyone else.

'You're thinking I'd get a better view higher up, aren't you?'

Griff felt his face reddening. Dave grinned.

'Yeah, but ten floors up is easy to escape from, know what I mean?'

Griff shook his head. After 9/11, nothing would ever be the same. He sat down in a leather armchair that smelled brand new, while Dave started to make calls. After a few minutes he got restless and went out into the hallway, one wall of which was glass and looked out on to 7th Street. It was lunchtime, and a deli across the street was doing a good trade. Griff didn't even feel hungry, although he hadn't eaten since the night before.

He grew impatient and walked back into Dave's office, where his friend was having a shouting match on the phone.

'You seriously need to get help!' he yelled, slamming the receiver down. He looked up, running his hand through his hair and fixing Griff with a baleful stare.

'Problems?'

Dave shook his head. 'One of my clients. Ten buck Tony.'

'Ten buck-?'

'Yeah. He sells all that crap you see in the back of the newspapers, you know: a comb that also cuts your hair, or a coat hanger that fits your car seat? Everything's ten bucks.'

Griff sat back in the leather chair. 'So what's a small timer like that doing employing Ross Kothlis?'

Dave grimaced. 'He's my sister's husband. The trouble is, he's nuts. Look at this.'

Griff threw a glossy black and white photograph across the desk. Griff picked it up. It was a photo of Catherine Zeta Jones, her name scrawled in black marker diagonally across the bottom right.

'Don't tell me,' Griff said, 'He's selling these without approval?'

'Without approval?' Dave roared. 'I wish it was that easy! Signed photo of the actress, ten dollars. Only guess who signed the photo.'

Griff looked again at the signature. On closer inspection it didn't look like a woman's signature. In fact, it looked as if-

'You mean he just signed her name on the photos?'

'You bet,' Dave said. 'You know what he said to me? He said: "well, I never said they were signed by *her*".'

Griff tried not to grin.

'He has got a point.'

'This is worse than the last time.' Dave stood and began to pace round the room.

'What happened last time?'

'A hundred cigarette lighters, ten bucks.'

Griff thought about it. 'Well, that doesn't sound too unreason-'

'It was a box of fucking matches, Griff! A hundred fucking matches! Jesus!'

He threw himself down in his chair again.

Griff couldn't help it, the laughter burst out of him like a release.

'Yeah, laugh it up, pal. See the shit I've had to put up with when you were getting laid on passion island.'

That washed all the laughter out of Griff like a bucket of cold water. He stood up as Dave's phone rang and he snatched up the receiver, getting up and walking to the window so he had his back to Griff. He didn't say much, but when he turned back to Griff his face said *bad news*.

'What is it?' Griff asked, feeling his chest tighten.

'Uh, your ex's lawyers don't want to meet us. They've decided the deal's off.'

'What? Why?'

Dave sat down heavily, looking down at the blotter on his desk.

'It seems Mel is totally pissed. She's told her attorney not to play ball.'

Griff leaned his hands on Dave's desk, looking behind his friend to the offices beyond. He knew this was all his fault. He had disappeared and made things difficult for Mel, so now she was having some payback. He looked down to see Dave looking at him, concern on his face.

'There's only one thing for it, I guess.' Griff said. 'I'll have to go see her.'

Dave looked down again. Griff remembered that Dave's own divorce had been tortuous. At the end, the thought of having to even talk to his ex-wife made him go quiet, not a natural state of affairs for the garrulous lawyer. Griff tried a smile.

'I'll keep trying. I know a few moves,' Dave said in a subdued voice.

'Hey, it's not that bad,' Griff said. 'She loved me once, you know.'

Dave shook his head. 'They stop loving you, they start hating you.'

TWENTY TWO

It was late afternoon by the time Griff pulled up outside the house in Brentwood. He had gone first to the music shop where Mel had worked, but the manager told him she had quit some time ago. The manager remembered Griff, and went out of his way to be unhelpful.

'Do you know where she works now?'

The man shrugged. 'Don't know if she works at all. She didn't say.'

He was in his late fifties with close cropped salt and pepper hair, and an incongruous row of seven gold rings in one earlobe. Griff felt his eyes drawn to them.

'I don't know what went wrong with you two,' the man said. 'But it sure fucked her up.'

Griff just nodded and left. That was all he needed, another guilt trip.

So he took the chance and drove up to Brentwood, to the house they had bought together four years ago. It was a pretty white building with window shutters that had been dark green, but had now been painted aquamarine. Griff thought it looked cheap, but what the hell did he know. Not enough to save his marriage, that was for sure. He parked on the street and walked down the sloping gray driveway, thoughts roiling in his head. What if she wasn't there, where else could he try? What if she was with someone else now? The potential for hurt and embarrassment was huge, but he had no choice. He reached the porch, but before he could press the bell, the door opened.

Mel hadn't changed, she was still beautiful. Her shaggy dark blonde hair was cut round her face, softening the high cheekbones, emphasising her perfect lips. She wore little makeup, and was dressed in sweatpants and a pink T shirt, her feet bare. Only her eyes betrayed her. They were a soft hazel brown, but the anger and bitterness there made them look as hard as pebbles. Griff wanted to look away from those eyes, but knew he deserved the look.

'I wondered when you'd be round,' she said shortly. She stepped back to let him in.

Griff noticed that she had decorated since he had moved out, and by the looks of it, she'd used the same designer as Dave. Everything was stark white and chrome. It felt like an empty factory. She closed the door and walked past him through the living room to the kitchen beyond. Griff felt strange being in the house again. It was like visiting the house where he'd grown up.

I'm sorry about your father,' she said over her shoulder as she filled the coffee machine.

'But then I suppose I should be glad he's ill, or you wouldn't be back.'

The bitterness was coming off her in waves. Griff just wanted to leave, but knew he had this one chance. He couldn't blow it.

'Mel, I'm sorry. I don't expect you to believe me, but I thought Dave was sorting it all, and he didn't need me for anything.'

She gave a snort. 'Not sure if that's naïve or plain stupid.'

'Probably both. Look Mel, I didn't come here to fight.'

She slammed two coffee mugs on the worktop.

'I know why you came here. You want your own way, just as you always have.'

She looked down at the worktop, and her hair fell across her cheek, reminding him of the way Ellie had of covering her scarred face. He felt a surge of warmth in his heart, and immediately the guilt started again. Mel had deserved better from him.

'I'm sorry,' he said again.

'Is that it? That all you can say?'

'What do you want me to say? That it's all my fault? It is. I admit it.'

She laughed without humour. 'It's a little late.'

She handed him a mug, and he noticed her hand was shaking. He tried to meet her eyes, but she wouldn't look at him. She swept past him into the dining room and sat at the table, looking out at the garden. The sun was going down, and the swimming pool reflected the pink and red of the sky. Griff thought irrelevantly that he had never used that pool when he lived here, either. Mel's shoulders were hunched over, and she held her mug with two hands. He could see how toned her arms were, and guessed that a lot of her anger at him had been taken out on the gym equipment. He sat down slowly opposite her, wondering what to say. She turned to him suddenly and he saw tears in her eyes.

'Where the hell did you go?'

e was taken aback. 'I-'

'Did it not occur to you that people might be worried?'

It was the second time that accusation had been raised against him. Again he felt the guilt bearing down on him.

'I mean, never mind the damn divorce, it was like you'd fallen off the world.'

He looked at her carefully. The last time they had spoken, he had come home to find her going through his clothes with a pair of scissors, cutting the arms and legs off his shirts and pants. The row had been furious, and the neighbours had been delighted by the sight of him backing hastily out of the drive, while she threw the remains of his clothes after him. When they stop loving you, they start hating you, Dave had said. So what was happening now?

131

'After our last meeting, I didn't think you'd be bothered.'

She gritted her teeth. 'I just knew you'd try and blame me.'

'I'm not blaming you!'

'You never loved me!'

She spat the phrase out, and it hung there in the air.

'I know,' Griff whispered.

e looked up, and she was staring at him, tears on her cheeks, clearly surprised by the admission.

'I was too obsessed with myself, with the work. I didn't know it then, but I do now. I never meant to hurt you, but I did nothing to stop you hurting, either.'

He hesitated. She was still staring at him. The sunset was turning her hair to copper.

'When I – after I left the last film set, I went to pieces. I ran away. And I thought about things, and met people who made me see things in a different way. I owe you big time, Mel, and there's nothing I can do to make it up to you.'

He looked down at the grain of the walnut table. He had sat here at nights before, going through scripts and changing things. He couldn't remember ever eating a meal here.

Mel reached over suddenly and grasped his hand. He looked up. The anger was gone from her face.

'Do you realise that's the most you've said to me in four years?'

He gave a mirthless chuckle. She squeezed his hand.

'What happened, Griff?' she said softly. 'What drove you away?'

And as he looked at her, he knew he had to tell her. If anyone deserved to hear it, she did. He owed her that much. He had told no one else, not even Ellie. And he thought about the things Ellie couldn't tell him, or anyone for that matter, and the fact that sometimes people needed to hear the truth, however unpleasant it was.

'Peter died.'

Mel frowned for a moment, remembering. 'Peter, your brother?'

He nodded. 'He left home when he was seventeen. You know things weren't so good at home. Mom and dad screaming and fighting all the time. Well Peter got in the way, sometimes.'

'You mean they hit him?'

Griff nodded. The memory was like an insect fluttering in his chest.

'You too?'

'Not often. I was too big. But I never did anything to help Pete. He left, and then so did I. And I got into the work, and things were going well, until I started to direct. We got married, and then I lost one project after another. I started to think I really didn't have it, you know? I worked harder and harder, and I know it must have been bad for you.

The day you cut up my clothes-'

She sat up straighter, and he shook his head in a gesture of: no, forget it.

That day, I found Pete. He'd gotten into trouble. Drugs, mainly. He was in a mess. I tried to help. I put him up in an apartment, got him into rehab. He seemed to be doing better, and then one night I went along there to see him and he was dead. The needle was still in his arm.'

He could still recall the odor of death in the room, his brother's white face pressed into the cheap orange nylon carpet. Griff closed his eyes, and Mel squeezed his hand again.

'Next morning they threw me off the project, and that was it. I left.'

'It wasn't your fault,' Mel said.

'Yes it was. I never tried to help him when he was a beaten up kid. Maybe if I had, he never would have gone down that road.'

You don't know that.'

He shrugged. He had had enough of talking now, he felt drained. The sun had set, and the room was filled with shadows.

'I am sorry, Mel,' he said again.

She shook her head. 'Maybe if you could have talked to me more-'

He smiled wryly. 'I never could, could I?'

She smiled back.

He waited a beat before asking.

'You got someone else now?'

She hesitated, then nodded.

'I'm glad. I hope he takes good care of you.'

They looked at each other for a long moment. It was the end of things, and Griff felt strangely content. However he might have fucked things up, at least in the end he had managed to do something right. Mel laughed softly.

What?'

'You remember that time we went camping, up in the hills?'

e grinned. 'You tore the tent, and I blew up the stove.'

'And it rained, could you believe it. And the tent wasn't waterproof.'

'We packed the lot up and went to a hotel.'

They both laughed softly at the memory. When they lapsed into silence, their eyes met again.

'What made you think of that?' Griff said.

She shrugged. 'I don't know. It's just- well, we had some good times, didn't we?'

He smiled at her. 'Yes, I think so.'

It was time to leave. He stood up and she walked with him to the door. He opened it, and they looked at each other again.

133

'Look, I'm sorry about the lawyers. I'll call them first thing.'

He reached forward and hugged her, kissed her cheek. She smelt faintly of the vanilla perfume she always wore.

'All the best, Mel,' he said. He walked up the driveway, and on to the sidewalk, but he didn't hear the door close, even when he got back into the Lexus.

*

Ellie rode south, leaving the mountains and lochs behind. She made good time, although there was nothing to rush back for. She eased the bike round the sweeping bends and curves of the mountains, enjoying the speed, the easy maneuverability of the machine, the feeling of being part of the landscape instead of simply passing through it. Darkness fell, and she stayed the night at the Kings House on Rannoch Moor, sharing the whole place with four hill walkers, whom she couldn't have met even if she wanted to as they went to bed at six o'clock. She propped up the bar for an hour chatting to the Ukrainian bartender before giving up and going to bed.

She got up early, and rattled south down the A82 as fast as she could. She rolled over the Erskine bridge as the mid-morning sun lit up the murky Clyde, and on to the bland motorway and the city. First things first, she had to find somewhere to stay.

It was a choice between Fiona (too judgemental), Lara, (too stoned), or Hannah, (too depressed). She opted for option number four: rent somewhere. She rode along Great Western Road, heading for the student part of town. It was October, the start of the new term, and flats would be thin on the ground, but she had enough money to go for something more expensive than most students could manage. Sure enough, there was a small furnished flat to rent along Dumbarton Road. It was on the top floor of the tenement building, and had views towards the Art Gallery and Kelvingrove Park. Ellie said she'd have it right away. She had to leave a bond and pay a month in advance, and the agent looked surprised as she readily agreed. Ellie wondered how she looked to the agent: she was a bit old for an impoverished student. Perhaps she was wondering if Ellie was paying for the flat with compensation from whatever accident messed up her face.

The next step was work. The agency she'd used before was on the other side of town, and it was getting on for late afternoon, but she wanted to get it sorted, and anyway, she had nothing else to do.

Janice, the agency clerk, did not seem to remember her, which Ellie found strange. Most people had no difficulty remembering the woman with the melted face, she thought savagely, as Janice pulled Ellie's records and read through them quickly.

'Have you got much on?' Ellie asked.

Janice looked up, but her eyes flitted behind Ellie to the window and the street outside.

'Bits and bobs,' she said in a cheerful voice. 'I'm sure we can find you something suitable.'

Ellie wished she'd cut to the chase. Actually looking at her might be an improvement as well. The familiar depression had already started, the knowledge that everyone in the whole world that she would ever meet, would stare.

You bloody things, she told her scars. *I'm sick of you.*

The scars said nothing, but she felt them preening.

'I have a vacancy here at Yorkhill that might do,' Janice said. She had now put Ellie's papers aside and was looking through her lists for the right page. 'Have you worked Biochemistry before?'

'Yes,' she replied. 'Should be a reference from the Royal here.'

'Oh yes, I did read that. Here we are.'

Janice read out the job description. It was cover for a lab tech on sick leave with two broken legs. Perfect. She knew very well that she'd be ready to move on before the tech was ready to come back.

'I'll take it,' she said.

'It's the standard rate of pay-'

'I know. That's fine. When do they want someone to start?'

Janice looked up, surprised, but again her eyes didn't quite find Ellie's face.

'I've just put a bond down on a flat, and I need to start earning,' she said, wondering why she was bothering to explain.

'Oh right. Well, I'll call them.'

Eventually it was arranged that Ellie go along for an interview the next morning. In her experience, it was a slam dunk. It was a simple fact that no one wanted someone with a disfigurement working with them, it make them feel awkward. But no one had ever had the balls to say it, and Ellie's references and experience always told. She always got the job.

On the way back to her new flat she celebrated with a take away curry from the Ashoka. The food was good, but did nothing to fill the hollow part inside herself. The loss of Griff was something she couldn't think about yet. Just the idea of him brought tears to her eyes, and so she tried not to think. She gazed round the pristine flat. She had left her few belongings in Fiona's garage, before she left. She'd have to ring her tomorrow and retrieve them.

Tomorrow, she thought. That's the way, one day at a time. All these sad thoughts will soon be in the past, and I won't remember them any more.

TWENTY THREE

Griff watched the light leach into the sky. The night had felt endless, with sleep a long way off, but rather than get up he simply lay there and thought about everything that had happened to him lately. The meeting with Mel had left him with strange emotions. He now accepted how foolish it had been; running off to a far corner of the world, as if he could leave all his problems behind. And he had not realised that he had friends. He had told Ellie that he had none, and that was simply not true.

And so it was time for re-evaluation. This was his city. He had spent the last thirteen years here, and up till now had made a good living . The point was he hadn't enjoyed it. Dave was right, he had only really been happy as a writer. Directing films was frustrating. He knew what he wanted to say, and how it needed to be said, but it rarely seemed to jibe with what it seemed the public wanted. He was wealthy, but not wealthy enough to call the shots. Of the two films he had directed all the way through, the first had become a cult film almost overnight. The second had been less successful, but both had done well at the box office. The trouble was that he didn't see why he had to compromise for the sake of money, and, he thought gloomily, that meant he'd never do really well in this city.

And Pete. Well, that was a suitcase of guilt that he'd carry all his life, whether he ended up living in LA, or on a little island twelve miles long.

It was here, in the dark still of the night, that reality had a habit of turning up like a drunken party crasher, who drinks all the best booze and leaves behind a trashed room and a half-empty bottle of Thunderbird with a cigarette end in it.

So Griff searched his thoughts for the truth. Did he really want to leave all this behind?
All the money and acclaim? His beautiful clothes and snazzy car? And for what: a place where no one cared what car you had or where you lived, how much money you made, or how beautiful you were. He thought about his Lexus in the basement garage, and imagined driving it along what passed for roads on Baranpay. That brought a smile to his lips.

He thought about Mel, looking at him with her sad eyes, her beautiful face, telling him that they had had good times after all. And then he thought about Ellie, with whom the times had always been good. Four years with Mel, four months with Ellie. Was he still being a fool? Would he move to the island only to grow restless and bitter so far from civilisation? Wasn't it better to simply put it all down to experience and move on?

And leave Ellie alone. That was what it came down to. He didn't want to leave her alone, and not only because she deserved better, but because he loved her. He had never been in love before. He didn't have any doubt about his feelings for her.

And as he watched the sky turn blue, he considered what the gatecrasher had left behind, and decided it was time to take control. He got out of bed and walked through the silent house to the kitchen, his bare feet slapping on the Italian tiled floor. He took a pen and pad from beside Dave's phone and dialled information. He had to spell out the name of the place, and then he had to ask for the international code. Eventually he sat on one of Dave's designer stools, watching the sun gilding the buildings and holding the paper in his hand like a captured butterfly. He checked the clock and saw that it was almost eight. Late night in Baranpay. He dialled the number and waited while the line clicked and hissed, searching for the connection. Eventually there was a ringing tone, and at last someone picked up.

'Hullo.'

'Hi. Murd? Is that you?'

Silence.

'Hello, Murd? It's Griff.'

Another few seconds passed.

'Griff, f'm America?'

He smiled. 'Yeah. It's me. Are you all right? Is Ellie there?'

'It's m' birthday,' Murd said. Griff realised he was extremely drunk.

'Well, happy birthday Murd. I can tell you're celebrating.'

In the background he could hear music. He wasn't sure, but he thought it might be *the Mist Covered Mountains.* It brought a sharp pang to his chest.

'Aye, I've had a dram or two.'

The music picked up suddenly, and there was a lot of laughter and noise.

'It was nice of y't'remember me birthday,' Murd said. 'Thank you for calling.'

'Wait! Murd! Don't hang up. Can I speak to Ellie?'

'Ellie? Och, she's away.'

He glanced at the clock again. It was past midnight in Baranpay. He was too late, she'd gone home to bed.

'Well, look, tell her I called. I'll phone tomorrow.'

'Aye, aye-' Griff could tell he was no longer listening. The laughter got louder suddenly, and he could hear Murd breaking into song 'Oh I knew a lass, and a bonny one-'

138

The line went dead, and Griff found himself staring at the phone. A shaft of sunlight reflected off an office block and hit him in the face. The office itself was a dark shadowy block silhouetted against the peach and orange of the autumn sky, its windows still in darkness.

'You're up early. What happened yesterday?'

Griff turned to see Dave waking towards him in his swimming shorts. He realised he was still holding the phone. Dave noticed and looked at him.

'You all right?'

Griff nodded. 'I guess so.'

He was still back in the pub, with the singers and the laughter, and the knowledge that he had spent too long in bed this morning, thinking.

TWENTY FOUR

Ellie had a serious word with her scars before she headed out for the pub. They looked back at her, silent and morose while she lectured them.

'And no embarrassing me in public,' She wagged a finger at the mirror. 'Just keep to yourselves and don't get drunk.'

There was no response, nary an itch.

You are going seriously mental, she told herself, as she turned to leave.

The venue this Friday night was the Horseshoe Bar, and Ellie was the first there. She ordered a pint and leaned on the bar, waiting for her friends. Contrary to its name, the bar was in fact a continuous staggered circle, bar staff on the inside, customers on the outside. It was the sort of huge Victorian place where you could arrange to meet people and never actually find them. Ellie recognised a few familiar faces, as this had always been one of their regular spots.

She was determined to have a good time tonight.

Everything was running nice and level at the moment. The new job was fine, her co-workers pretty reasonable, all considered. She had a decent place to stay, and still a little money in the bank. She was aware that, in anyone else's book, life should be good.

But of course, she didn't have anyone else's book. Just her own sad pulpy paperback, a tired Mills and Boon romance. Ellie had spent a lifetime of compartmentalising her problems, forcing them into a tight box where they squirmed restlessly. She was also aware that the box was full to bursting. One more setback might smash it wide open, and who knows what would happen then.

The memory of Griff was still at the top of the box. It called to her every night, every quiet moment when her mind had nothing to focus on. It was an ache that never quite went away, like an amputee's lost limb.

She took a long pull of the Tennents, wishing the gang would hurry up. Her face began to itch suddenly, and she resisted the urge to dig her nails in and claw the skin away. She felt her heart lurch. Thoughts like that were becoming more frequent. One day, she might actually do it.

Fiona was first to arrive, and she had a big smile on her face.

'Hi,' Ellie said, giving her a quick hug. 'Looking good, Fee!'

Fiona's smile faded a bit. 'You look like you've lost weight.'

'What, since last week?'

Fiona shrugged as Ellie ordered her a drink.

'You never eat properly.'

Ellie grinned. 'Well, neither do you. Mother,' she added, for good measure.

'Ellie! You old slapper!'

Ellie looked up to see Hannah and Lara arriving. Hannah had had her hair cut short, and it made her look very young. Lara was still stick-thin, her eyes dark-circled, but the usual big grin on her face.

'Friday night in God's own city.' Lara said, before yelling at the barman for a drink. They sat down and Ellie asked what had been happening since their previous Friday night beer call.

'Well, I had a little bit of bad luck,' Lara said, her face clouding for a minute. Ellie noticed Fiona's eyes go dull. Lara laughed then.

'But in a way, it was good luck!'

'Laz, what are you talking about?' Fiona said testily. 'How can you call that good luck?'

'What happened?' Ellie asked.

'Well, I went over to Paisley last Sunday to meet up with a pal, and we had a few drinks, as you do, in that new pub in Causeyside Street.'

'She drove back,' Fiona put in.

Lara raised her eyebrows.

'You didn't get stopped?' Ellie said.

Lara nodded. 'Yeah. Coppers stopped me. I got to spend the night in the cells. But the best bit was, all I had to do was blow in the bag.'

Ellie nodded. She understood what Lara was saying. Fiona had just worked it out too, it seemed.

'You mean you were drugged up as well? Lara, for Christ's sake.'

She folded her arms, and Lara gave her a look.

'I got Court yesterday.'

'Why didn't you tell me? I'd have come with you.'

Lara shrugged as if Ellie had offered to come with her to the library.

'I got a 12 month ban, which is no big deal. Also, I got this good looking copper's phone number.'

Ellie laughed. 'You can't go out with a copper. He'll have to do you.'

'I bloody hope so.'

They all laughed except Fiona, who was shaking her head. She stood up and went to order another round.

'I wish she'd get off my case,' Lara muttered. 'She's been a total pain in the arse the whole time you've been away.'

'She worries about you,' Ellie said gently.

'Funny way of showing it.'

'And she's got her own problems.'

Lara looked at Fiona, unconvinced. Ellie turned to Hannah, who still hadn't spoken.

141

'Well, Han, why don't you shut up?'

Hannah grinned.

'What's been happening with you?'

She shrugged. 'Not a lot. Still going to work, going to the pub-'

'Going out with arseholes,' Lara added.

Hannah's face went red. She looked at Ellie and Ellie read it well: *please don't talk about this!*

'Well, I think we've all done our fair share of that, Laz,' Ellie said.

Lara laughed. 'Yeah, I suppose. So how's your love life, Ellie? Meet any decent looking highlanders up there?'

Ellie smiled, ignoring the sudden ache in her chest. 'You'd like it, Laz. There're a lot more men than women.'

They drank up and moved on to a night club in Renfield Street that had been there since the eighties, simply changing owner, décor and name every so often. To the four friends, it was like home from home. At the moment it was called Fat Larry's, and there was a live band playing some kind of nouveau jazz. The sax player was good, and Ellie dragged Hannah up to dance, partly because the music was catchy, and partly because she didn't want to get too drunk. Fiona had a way of dragging home truths out of her, and she was still hurting too much to talk about the island and Griff. It was also partly because Ellie had caught the vibe as soon as they had walked in; the crowd tonight was largely gay. Fiona had noticed it too. Ellie had seen her stiffen up as she got to the bar and took a look around. Lara had done her usual disappearing trick to the toilet to partake in whatever the latest hip drug was. Ellie moved round as more people joined the dance floor, and noticed a red haired girl squeezing closer to Hannah. As her friend didn't seem to mind, Ellie quietly moved away, until she was on the edge of the dance floor, and could return to the bar.

It was an interesting crowd. There were even numbers of men and women, but while the majority of the women were dancing, a lot of the men were standing at the bar. The dance floor was busy enough that you had to look closely to see that members of the same sex were dancing together. Ellie leaned towards Fiona, and murmured: 'Since when did this become Heaven?'

Fiona shook her head. 'I've not been in for months.'

They stood watching the dancers for a few minutes, until Lara returned from the toilet, her eyes very bright, the big grin on her face.

'Get this, you guys,' she said in a loud voice. 'This place is full of poofs!'

The bar crowd gave Lara the cold stare.

Shut up Lara!' Fiona hissed.

'What? What did I say? It is, look!'

Ellie stifled a grin, grabbing Lara by the arm and dragging her on to the dance floor.

'We know,' Ellie hissed into her ear. 'I think they do too.'

Lara looked round as they danced, fascinated. Ellie spotted Han still dancing with the red haired girl, at the same time Lara did.

'We better tell Hannah,' she said.

'She'll have guessed by now. Chill out, Lara.'

'She might need rescuing.'

That she does, Ellie thought. *But not like you think.* She noticed the redhead leaning close to talk to Hannah, who was nodding her reply. When she looked up, Ellie saw she was smiling, and that made her smile too.

'Come on, let's go back to the bar. They'll have calmed down by now.'

'I didn't mean anything, you know.'

'Yeah,' Ellie said. 'A few less E's, Laz, and you'd have a few more brain cells.'

Lara shrugged happily. 'I don't care.'

'Well, you should. You're not dying any more. You should start living.'

Lara stopped dead, and Ellie looked back, filled with sudden guilt at having said that. Lara looked more surprised that hurt.

'Sorry,' Ellie said.

'No, you're right, I suppose.' Lara looked past her into the distance, but Ellie knew it wasn't a spaced out stare, not this time. She walked back to the bar. Fiona was still boot-faced.

'Let's get out of here,' she said.

'Not yet,' Ellie replied, looking for Hannah in the crowd.

'Come on, Ellie, before Lara drops us in it again.'

Ellie studied her friend's face. There was more anger and disappointment there than could be explained away by Lara's outburst and the fact that the night had turned out to be a damp squib. More problems, she thought.

'No news from you yet?' she asked.

Fiona looked even angrier for a second, then the anger seemed to vanish. She shook her head.

'Have you spoken to Fred?'

She looked up, hopelessly.

'You know what he'll say.'

Ellie nodded. Over Fiona's shoulder she could see Lara talking to Hannah. The red haired girl was standing behind her, and as she watched, Ellie saw Lara raise her arm to the girl and wave her off like an insect. She sighed. Her own life was complicated enough without the antics of her nutty friends. She hurried over and grabbed Lara by the arm.

'We're going, Laz.'

'Yeah, about time. Come on Hannah.'

Hannah had the look of someone who had seen all six lotto numbers come up, only to realise she was checking last week's ticket.

'I told you she needed rescuing,' Lara added, putting a proprietorial arm round her friend's shoulders. Hannah shrugged her off angrily, and shoved past Ellie towards the exit.

Lara stared at her in amazement.

'Is there something I don't know?' she said as they reached the corridor.

Fiona shook her head. 'Lara, what is it you *do* know?'

'I know that you're a complete pain in the arse.'

'Oh. Nice.'

'Lay off, both of you,' Ellie said. Her head had suddenly begun to throb, and the ache was making her angry. They reached the street and the freezing October air hit them. The roads were busy with late night drinkers and clubbers, and she looked around for Hannah.

'Where we going now?' Lara said, folding her thin arms against the cold. She had no jacket.

'Home, I think.' Fiona said.

'What? But it's not two o'clock yet!'

Ellie spotted Hannah at the taxi rank outside Central Station. She hurried over, leaving the other two behind. Hannah saw her coming and looked away.

'Han.'

She looked up, her face a mixture of embarrassment and hurt.

'Did you get her number?'

'What?'

'The red haired girl. Did you get her number?'

Hannah's eyes dropped. 'Why would I want to do that.'

Ellie waited her out. Eventually she looked up again warily, and Ellie smiled.

Hannah looked over Ellie's shoulder to where Fee and Lara were arguing, then back at Ellie.

'You knew, didn't you?'

Ellie nodded. 'It's no big deal.'

Again Hannah looked back at her friends. Ellie saw the fear in her eyes.

'I'll deal with them, Han,' she said.

Two taxis arrived at once, and Hannah quickly got into the second one.

'I'll call you,' she shouted as the driver took off.

'Hey, she didn't even wait for us. What's her problem?'

Ellie turned to Lara. She had no energy left for explanations. She was tired and her head was pounding and she just wanted to go home.

'I'll tell you later,' she said.

Lara looked from Fiona to Ellie, aware that there was something she wasn't being told. Ellie shook her head.

'I think it's time I went home.'

'Well, bollocks!' Lara cried. 'I'm not going home. I'll go back in and see if I can't find a nice gay bloke to show the error of his ways.'

She stormed off, and Ellie began to laugh. Fiona shook her head.

'Well, Fee, we could nip up Hope Street for another drink?'

Fiona shook her head. 'Nah, I'm not in the mood.'

Ellie sighed, and moved back from the taxi rank where she was blocking the queue.

'What are you doing? Let's get a tax-'

'Not yet, Fee,' Ellie said. 'Look, tell me to mind my own if you like, but I know how desperate you are to get pregnant. Why don't you tell Fred how much it means to you?'

'He knows. At least, he must know! And it means a lot to him too.'

She clenched and unclenched her fists, and Ellie felt her heart lurch as her friend blinked back the tears.

'I'm getting older. Soon it will be too late.'

'Fee, you're only twenty seven.'

Fiona shook her head bitterly. 'Yeah, and already my sister has three kids. Three! And she's two years younger than me.'

Ellie put her hand on Fiona's arm, waiting until she looked up.

'Would it help if someone else spoke to Fred?'

'What? God, no. He'd get all defensive and cold.'

Ellie nodded, 'But nevertheless, it might help?'

Fiona sat down heavily on the edge of the kerb. 'I just wish he'd accept there's a problem. At least then we can move on.'

'That is the problem, isn't it? He's scared.'

Fiona looked at her. 'Scared of what?'

Ellie sat down too, and hesitated before she spoke.

'Scared that it's his fault.'

Fiona looked down, and Ellie saw her chest heave as the sobs began. She pulled her into a hug and held her until the tears waned. It made Ellie feel uneasy, her sensible, logical friend being in a state, a reminder that nothing in the world could be relied upon, ever. In case she ever needed a reminder, that was, she thought gloomily.

Fiona wiped her eyes savagely, waiting until the hitch in her chest stopped.

145

'Come on, Fee, I'll buy you a pint.'

'I think I need one.'

They began to walk slowly up the hill, and Ellie tried to think of something she could do to help, but could think of nothing. Loyalty to her friend made her want it to be Fred who had the problem, but there was no way of telling. Then she had an idea.

'Fee, I've thought of something.'

Fee pushed her hair behind her ears. 'What?'

'Fred won't go and have the tests, but there's nothing to stop you going. At least then you'll know.'

Fiona's eyes darted round the street, as if they were looking for an escape.

'I don't know,' she said. She looked up, and now her eyes were desperately sad.

'What if it's me?'

Ellie stood up and went towards her.

'Then you can do something about it,' she said. 'It might be something simple, that can be fixed easily.'

'Then again it might not.'

Ellie sighed. 'What is it you always tell me: think positive?'

Fiona flashed a small smile, which vanished quickly.

'You're right, you know,' she said.

'As usual,' Ellie said with a grin. 'After all, I'm not just a pretty face.'

Fiona looked up, raising an eyebrow, and they both laughed.

146

TWENTY FIVE

It was the seventh day since Griff had returned to LA. A whole week. He waited in the 7th Street deli for Dave to arrive, nursing a cup of English tea. Funny, he thought, they call it English tea, when it appeared they drank nothing else in Scotland. In any case, it was horrible. The tea bag had been left in the cup for too long, and too much milk had been added. Nevertheless, it was a small reminder, and therefore welcome.

He had been there almost an hour. Dave was across the road now with Mel's lawyers, and it was only a matter of time. He was sure Mel would tell the lawyers to back off. Whether the lawyers would play ball was another thing.

Last night he had booted up his laptop and sent an e-mail to Ellie, something he cursed himself for not thinking of before. He e-mailed a brief message, waiting to see if she were on line and would respond, but nothing appeared. He'd logged on again this morning, but again there was no reply. But then, when they had been together, she had checked her e-mails only when she remembered, so he shouldn't read too much into it.

Then he had visited a mobile phone retailer, who told him the phone was dead, but the data card inside should still work. Kitted out with a brand new phone, the first thing he did was write Ellie's number down. Then he had called her, but there was no reply, so he left a message, hoping she'd ring soon.

A waitress appeared, and hovered, unsure whether to ask if he wanted a refill. He put her out of her misery.

'I'll have coffee, please.'

'No wonder you can't drink that, honey, it looks like cat sick.'

She took the cup away, and Griff gazed out of the window to see Dave jaywalking. He put his hands up to the car that pulled to an angry halt, his familiar 'just a second'
gesture. He hurried in and Griff waved.

'Well?'

'All settled,' Dave said, smiling. 'We should be having a drink, not coffee.'

Griff smiled too. 'Maybe later. What about the accounts and stuff?'

'They'll arrange to remove the block today. You should be able to repay me by tonight.'

He grinned to show he was kidding. Griff shook his head

'I owe you, Dave. I really do.'

'De nada.' He gave the waitress a big smile as she appeared with

147

the coffee.

'So what are your plans?'

Griff hesitated. What were his plans? He was going back to Scotland, that was for sure, but there was stuff he had to sort out before he left: bank accounts, contracts with the producers who had dumped him, all the stuff he had stored at Dave's, the helicopter, the car, the scripts and stories his agent was dealing with, the agent himself. He hadn't told Leo anything about moving away, simply because he couldn't face the tantrum.

'I've got a lot to do,' he said.

'You're still determined to go?'

Griff nodded.

'You need a hand?'

'No, you've done enough already, Dave.'

Dave shrugged, glancing at his watch. 'I'd better get back, I've a lunch meeting. We meet up later?'

'Sure.' Griff smiled. 'I'll be buying, won't I?'

When Dave had left, Griff paid the tab and walked out into the street. He'd parked the Lexus two blocks away, and he walked through the lunchtime crowd, deciding where he should go first. In the end he went back to the car and dialled the airport where he kept the helicopter. He spoke to Michael, the controller, and told him to put out the word that he was offloading the machine. Michael told him that he knew of a potential purchaser right away, and that he'd arrange for him to look it over.

Next he dialled Leo, and waited while his secretary went through her spiel.

'Good afternoon, Leo Samuel's office, how may I help you?'

'Miriam, it's Griff. Is Leo around?'

'Hiya Griff! How's it going?'

He didn't reply.

'Leo's in, but he's snowed under with work, he's just taken on a new client, and-'

'It's really important, Miriam, can you patch me through?'

'Just hang on a sec, Griff, and I'll speak to him.'

Griff glanced around as she put him on hold. A homeless man was sitting on the sidewalk curb, a plastic carrier between his knees, staring straight up. Griff was reminded of that old adage: we're all in the gutter, but some of us are looking at the stars. He wondered what the man saw.

'Griff?'

'Yeah.'

'Sorry, Griff, he says he's really pushed. He'll ring you back.'

'Miriam, you might want to tell him that if he doesn't speak to me now, he might never get another chance.'

'Wh-what does that mean?'

'Just tell him.'

Another long hold, and then an exasperated Leo came on the phone.

'Griff, what is it man, I'm up to my neck in –'

'Listen, Leo, I need to come in and see you, go through a few things before I leave.'

'Before – what are you talking about, leave?'

'I'm leaving, Leo. Leaving Los Angeles, for good.'

'Yeah, good one, Griff. Look, I really have to-'

'I'm not joking.'

There was a silence, and Griff wondered if he was buying it. Frankly, he didn't care either way.

'Up to you, Leo, but after this week, I'm out of here.'

Leo gave a theatrical sign. 'I guess you'd better come in then. I can squeeze you in at two thirty.'

'You're all heart,' Griff said. He hung up before Leo could say anything else. As he started the car he wondered why he had been sarcastic with the man. He surely didn't deserve it. Things were still not right. They might never be right while he stayed here.

TWENTY SIX

It started to rain on Thursday night, and didn't stop. Ellie looked out of her flat at the tenements opposite, the newsagent on the street below, watching people hurrying in and out, hunched over, or fighting with umbrellas. It was proper Scottish rain, big thick pounding drops. Ellie usually quite liked the rain, but not today. It was Sunday afternoon, and she was bored, and boredom always led to other things.

She knew she ought to get up and go out, at least do something, but lethargy was upon her like a heavy weight. Why had she never been bored in Baranpay? Even before Griff –*just a wince of pain now – no more* – arrived, there was always stuff to do. Here she was in a huge, bustling, virtually 24 hour city, and she had nothing to do. She could go on a bike ride, but it wasn't much fun in the rain. Shopping was a misery at the best of times, and all her friends would be either visiting their parents or already in the pub.

Of course, she could always go out and have a walk in the rain, in true broken-hearted fashion, but why torment herself even more. She had her scars to do that.

Glad to oblige.

She sighed. 'I wondered when you'd be back.'

Never went away.

She lay back on the floor and looked straight up at the opaque sky. Maybe she should go out and take some photographs. Yeah, like, in the rain. Well, why not. They'd look arty; almost black and white. Or she could get the laptop out and have an internet browse, maybe buy some crap off Ebay.

No, maybe not. She hadn't checked her e-mails since leaving. She knew they'd all be from her friends there, asking how she was, commiserating. She shook her head. She was miserable enough.

Well, we did warn you, you never listen.

'Oh just shut the fuck up.'

In the end she took a walk across a soggy Kelvingrove Park to the art gallery, and spent what turned out to be an enjoyable afternoon looking at the paintings. In the gallery shop, she saw a postcard of Van Gogh's 'Starry Night', and stood looking at it for a long time. In the painting, the sky was alive, the stars as huge and brilliant as oncoming headlights in the rain, swirling and pulsing. It reminded her of the zillion stars up north, the pale ribbon of the Milky Way, shooting stars blazing to earth, the aurora flitting across the sky like a decision waiting to be made. It made her feel alive and warm for the first time in weeks. She bought the postcard and took it home.

Later she had a quiet pint in Tennents Bar in Byres Road, and took a pizza home; seafood special with extra anchovies. Just another small reminder.

Next morning the rain finally let up and the sun came out, and Ellie got up early and decided to walk to work. It was less than a mile, and she was feeling guilty about the fact that she'd done no exercise at all since coming back. And she felt it, as her heart pounded hard on the climb up to Yorkhill.

In a way it was good working in a hospital. Everyone there had something wrong with them, so the stares got shared round a bit. She took the lift up to the lab, figuring the walk was enough exercise for one day. She was first there apart from Dougie Laird, who had been on-call the night before and had had a call out at seven.

'Hey Dougie, what do you know?'

'Not a lot,' he said, turning the knob on his centrifuge. He glanced up.

'Had a good weekend?'

'Boring,' she said, stifling a yawn. 'You?'

He shrugged. 'The wife's mother came over for the weekend.'

She nodded, even though she knew nothing about his family. Dougie's face broke into a wry grin. 'Ach well, that's our turn over with for the year.'

'Oh, I see,' she said, returning his grin, but feeling nothing. She found it hard to empathise with other people's annoying families, not having any herself.

The centrifuge had slowed right down, and Dougie lifted the lid and stopped it with his hand.

'I think I ought to warn you,' he said quietly, 'there's a message on the answering
machine.'

'Oh?'

Dougie looked at her. 'From Belinda Carlyle. She's talking about coming back to work next week.'

Ellie bit her cheek and thought about it. It was fine, really, she'd just find another job. She looked at Dougie who was studiously examining his blood samples. The answerphone was in the chief's room, and was out of bounds, but Dougie never could resist the little flashing light.

'Looks like: "we want the same thing", eh?' Ellie quipped.

Dougie looked at her strangely, and she realised he had never heard of the girl's pop star namesake. 'Never mind.'

She went through to her work bench and sat down, looking out of the high level window which afforded a fine view of the hospital ducting

151

system. Lab workers changed tasks and therefore work benches every month, and Ellie figured it was just as well, if that was all the daylight you ever saw. Her face was incredibly itchy today, although she'd done nothing to antagonise it.

Shut up, she told the scars. Just shut up and let me get to work

My, we are touchy today...

As she loaded her sample cups into the machine tray, she noticed two of them were a different colour from the others. Her machine checked the amount of glucose in a person's blood. She already knew those two samples would be too high. She made a note of their numbers to do the test manually on them, just for backup. Too much sugar in the blood, she thought. That's my problem as well. Too many syrupy romantic notions, impossible dreams. There was still a great hollow place in her heart, and the longer time went on, the more empty it seemed. Time was supposed to patch over the cracks, not pull them further apart. Of course she still had not even acknowledged to herself what she had done, got up and left, pretending never to have known the man. She hadn't even told her friends about him, afraid that the telling would bring the pain down on her so hard that she wouldn't be able to lift it off again.

Not even Fiona, her best friend. She felt a stab of guilt at that. Fiona told her all her problems, all her hopes and dreams. Ellie would tell her. Just, not yet.

*

Much as expected, the job ran out early. Mary Law the chief came and told her the next day. She said she was sorry, and that she would have asked her to stay on if there had been a vacancy. It was kind of her, and Ellie felt a pang of regret. It had been one of her better jobs, even if it had only lasted a few weeks. All the same, Yorkhill was a children's hospital, and the little blood samples they had brought her to test had brought a giant lump to her throat.

The staff had even arranged to go out for a drink in the Lismore on Friday night, a leaving do for her, which she appreciated all the more because they hardly ever went out together. None of them had ever shown her pity or curiosity, at least not to her face. If Belinda hadn't come back, she thought she might have stayed. Ellie told her usual Friday night cronies she'd meet them later in the Islay Bar, knowing the lab staff would go home early.

It had not been a great day. Her analyser had thrown a wobbler halfway through the morning run, forcing her to do the entire test manually. A repairman had come out, diagnosed the problem, and said he couldn't fix it, so she had to do the afternoon run manually too. Then her agency had called in reply to her request for work to say they had nothing for her. She left the lab very gratefully at five, pulling her helmet on and riding down into the October rain.

She was just pulling away at the lights when the engine died. She coasted into a bus stop and checked the petrol tank. It was still half full. She turned the engine over again, but nothing was happening.

'Shit!' she said, her voice muffled inside the helmet, anger blooming in her chest. It wasn't far to her flat, but it was pissing it down. She resigned herself to the fact that she'd just have to push it. An old lady waiting for a bus came over.

'Are ye all right, son?'

She looked up blankly, before pulling off her helmet.

'Och, it's a lassie!' the old lady began to cackle. Ellie shook her head.

'Whit's the matter wi' yir motor bike?'

If I knew that, I'd be fixing it, you daft old bat, she thought. She gritted her teeth.

'I don't know.'

She pulled the helmet back on, might as well try and stay dry, and started to push the bike along Dumbarton Road. Her heart began to race angrily at the derisory toots from passing drivers, and as she passed her tenement building she had the urge to dump the damn bike and go home. But she couldn't. She needed it. She pushed it on along Sauchiehall Street towards the garage, praying they shut at six, not five. A bus came past and splashed through a puddle, and despite the leathers, she felt the water seeping down the back of her neck.

Bastard! She felt like David Banner changing the wheel on his car, hitting his hand and his eyes changing colour...

That's it, she thought. First Two-Face, now I'm the Hulk.

The garage was probably the only one in Glasgow that closed at five. She stood staring at the closed shutter, clenching her fists in fury. She had no idea where the next garage would be, and no intention of pushing the damn bike any further. She wheeled it into the MOT waiting zone and locked it. She would come back in the morning and talk to the mechanics. Then she went home, had the quickest shower ever, and went to meet the crew down at the Lismore.

'Where have you been?' Dougie said as she hurried in. 'We thought you'd gone somewhere else.'

She took a grateful pull of the pint he bought her. 'My bike broke down.'

The Chief gave a sigh.

'My car broke down last month,' she said. 'It was a nightmare. I had to wait on the motorway for forty minutes before the breakdown man showed up.'

But at least you didn't have to push the damn thing all along Dumbarton Road in the pissing rain, Ellie thought. She was still pulsing with angry adrenalin. Mary had perfect hair. It was cut short round her heart-shaped face and amazingly symmetrical. That was annoying too.

'Ach well. Have a drink,' Dougie said. 'By the way, there's a friend of yours here.'

'Is there?' Ellie asked warily. 'Who?'

She looked round the bar, and felt the sad touch in her heart as she recognised him.

As if he felt her stare, the man looked up, smiled, and walked towards her.

'Hi Ellie.'

'Ryan,' she said, smiling. 'How are you? Long time no see.'

'I know. What is it, two years? I'm fine. Still at the Royal.'

She nodded. 'Same old crowd still there?'

'Pretty much. So how are you?'

'Fair to crap,' she said, grinning. She leaned against the bar. 'Is this your local?'

'No. I know Sandra Tallis, from Haematology?' he pointed to a small blonde girl with wide apart eyes. '- and she mentioned they had you working there temporarily. I thought I'd come down and say hello.'

Ellie nodded. She had never seen Sandra Tallis before tonight. She was also pretty sure Sandra didn't know her name. That left only one way Ryan could be sure it was Ellie. Normally, that wouldn't bother her, but it had not been a good day.

'So how are things?'

Ellie looked at him. She no longer felt like smiling. 'Things? Which things would these be?'

Ryan frowned. 'I meant, after your accident. Are you okay now?'

She almost laughed.

'Have you looked at me?'

His face flushed.

'I only meant, like, you're not in pain anymore.'

She just looked at him, trying to hold back the anger. She had no idea where it had come from. It was almost as if it had a life of its own.

'I didn't mean to upset you.'

'I know,' she said. Ryan still had the spiky black hair, the big brown eyes. He had always been drop dead gorgeous. And as solemn as death.

Change the subject.

'So, how's your love life, Ry? You married with kids yet?'

154

He shook his head.

'Courting then?'

He looked up. 'I've been a bit quiet lately.'

She remembered him visiting her in the hospital. He couldn't bear to look at her then, and he was having the same trouble now.

'I sometimes wonder how things might have turned out,' he said.

'What do you mean?'

He glanced up. 'Well, if you'd stayed at the Royal instead of taking the other job.'

'That'd be the road less travelled,' she said in a sarcastic voice. 'The one that makes all the difference.'

Ryan carried on regardless. 'You might never have been in that car.'

'And what? You might still want to go out with me?'

'I didn't mean that.'

'But it's true.'

Ryan looked away.

'Look Ryan, we split up a long time ago. You wanted to get serious, remember? And I wanted to see the world. Well, neither of us got what we wanted, and it's too late now to think about: 'what if?''

She noticed suddenly that the room had gone very quiet. The lab staff were watching them. Ellie sighed, biting back her anger.

'It was nice of you to look me up, Ryan,' she said. 'And I wish you all the best. I think I better go now.'

She walked over to Dougie and Mary, and smiled at them both.

'Thanks for coming out, guys. I'm going to go now.'

Dougie raised an eyebrow, but Mary looked down.

'Good luck, Ellie,' she said. 'And if there's a vacancy in future, I'll let you know, in case you're interested.'

Ellie nodded. 'That's kind of you. Thanks.'

She walked past them, and on the way out, she leaned over the back of Sandra's chair.

'Oh, Sandra,' she said in a light voice, 'The name's Ellie. It's easier to say than Scarface.'

*

By the time Ellie got to Tennents, the rain had turned to sleet.

'What a night,' the taxi driver said as he drew up outside, his wipers working double time.

You can say that again,' Ellie handed him the fare before hurrying out into the miserable night. The pub was heaving as always, and she spotted Lara first, standing in the corner, her arms straight out behind

155

her in the age old gesture of defiance. Ellie stopped dead, heart sinking.

'I should just have gone home,' she said out loud. She felt someone looking at her, and turned to see Hannah leaning against the bar.

'What's going on?'

Hannah nodded towards the corner.

'They're having a fight.'

'You don't say. What about?'

Ellie looked at Hannah's quivering lip. Please don't start crying, she thought.

'It started off about me.'

Han looked back at where Lara was now wagging a finger at Fiona.

'Fee told her.'

'Told her what, that you're gay?'

Hannah winced.

'Oh for God's sake, Hannah, it's not cancer, you know.'

Hannah stared at her, wide eyed with surprise.

'I've had a hell of a day,' Ellie said, 'And tonight doesn't look like getting any better.'

She strode over to where Lara had now grabbed her coat.

'Lara. Laz!'

Lara looked round, her face twisted in anger.

'Don't start!' she said, turning quickly and walking out.

Ellie looked down at Fiona. Her friend looked tired.

'What was all that about?'

Fiona looked up.

'Well, it started off that Hannah doesn't know what she's doing, progressed to the fact that Lara's out of her tree more or less permanently these days, and was rounded nicely off with a tirade about me being worse than her mother.'

Ellie sat down heavily. Hannah hovered, and Ellie handed her a ten pound note.

'Han, get us all a pint, will you?'

Hannah dutifully went to the bar.

'So what made you tell Lara? Ellie said. She noticed that she had clenched her fists, and slowly opened her fingers.

'About Hannah? Lara was telling folk about the club the other week. I just mentioned that she wouldn't be taking the piss if one of her best friends was gay. The trouble is she's paranoid.'

'And what does that make you, winding her up?'

Fiona arched one delicate eyebrow.

'I see you're in a good mood too.'

'The worst. So what's the problem tonight?'

Fiona shrugged. 'It's just one of those nights.'

Hannah returned from the bar. Ellie gave her a quick smile.

'So let me get this straight. Lara's gone off in a huff because you've had a go at her about all the drugs. Hannah's nearly in tears because you decided to out her, and you've got a face like a wet weekend because-?'

Fiona looked up angrily.

'Well what about you? You've been as miserable as sin ever since you came back from bloody paradise island.'

'Ah, right,' Ellie said. She felt herself grow very calm. She had not been this angry in a long, long time, and suddenly everything became very clear.

'You've had your results, haven't you?'

Fiona looked away.

'Fiona? Tell me.'

'I'm all right. Okay? There, you had to know, now you do. It's not me. So that was a great idea of yours, wasn't it? What do I do now?'

Fiona stood up, close to tears, and Ellie looked past her. Lara was standing in the doorway with Fiona's husband. Fred only needed the horned helmet to pass for a Viking, with his dazzling blue eyes and thick straw-coloured hair. As usual, he looked subdued and morose, and Lara, amphetamined up to the eyeballs, was telling him some story at a hundred miles an hour. Fiona saw her husband and hurried over, and Ellie followed.

What the hell am I doing here? Ellie thought. A few weeks ago I was on a beautiful island, with a beautiful man, and nothing could spoil it. Now, everything's turned completely to shit. Her face began to itch angrily, and she gritted her teeth.

'Not a word,' she hissed, 'Not a word!'

Who? Us? As if we'd ruin your wonderful night.

'Hello Ellie,' Fred said, directing his gaze at her right ear, as always. Suddenly the anger fountained up uncontrollably and she felt her teeth clenching. Fiona touched her arm and she pulled it away, hard.

'Ellie, don't-' Fiona began.

'Do you remember that film,' Ellie said, 'The one with the line: You! You can run, but you can't hide!'

Lara stared at her, confused. Fred looked wary.

'That's you,' she said. 'All of you. You've all got problems you could easily sort out. But you don't. You hide from them. It's pathetic, and it's time you sorted it out. I'm sick of it!'

Fiona moved so she was next to Fred, as if she could protect him from Ellie's words.

'That's fine coming from you,' she spat back. 'All you ever do is run

157

away from things.'

'Yeah, and you know what?' Ellie shouted, 'It's doing something. It may not be very positive, but at least it's not sitting around hoping things will improve, when deep down you know they won't. Look at you all! Lara's terrified of dying, and so she tempts death every day. Hannah's scared of everyone finding out her secret, at the same time wishing they would. And you, Fred, you're afraid that if there's something wrong with you it'll mean you're less of a man.'

There was a heavy cold silence, full of the echo of the terrible words.

'I'm leaving now. Sort it out, all of you. Just sort it out.'

She shoved past into the night, where the sleet had now turned to snow. There was a taxi at the kerb, but she ignored it and began to walk down Byres Road to her empty flat, her heart pounding, and hot heavy tears at the back of her eyes.

Well. What a display!

Running away, she thought, clenching her fists against the insidious inner voice. I'm running away, because what else can I do? I can't stand and fight-

Or perhaps I can.

'I could have you removed. Permanently.'

But you won't

'You want a bet?' she said loudly. A couple coming out of the chip shop stared at her, and she winced, looking down. She listened carefully, but the scars had no more to say. Maybe that was the answer, after all.

TWENTY SEVEN

Griff was worried.

He had now left six phone messages and sent Ellie over a dozen e-mails, none of which had been answered. His worry was that Ellie hadn't replied not because of some phone problem or computer glitch, but because she didn't want to.

Yet he could still dismiss the idea. Whatever his brain might tell him, his heart knew that she loved him. He knew it deep down, with the same certainty that he knew he loved her. He had now been in LA for ten days. He had to get out of here.

Everything was sorted. Money had changed hands, the helicopter was sold, and he was ready to leave his home town for ever.

He had told Dave that this was his last night, and his friend had just looked at him sadly. They agreed to meet up for dinner later, and Griff took a last drive up Mulholland Drive to pass the time, easing the Lexus round the winding curves and gazing at the million dollar homes built into the hills. All this could be his, he knew, if he wanted it, if he just shut up and toed the line. He searched his heart again, but found no desire there for his former lifestyle. He had moved on. On an impulse, he parked in a fire road and got out, walking down through the brush and stunted trees to a clearing. From there he could see all the way across the valley. The sun was going down in a dark amber sky, and a gentle breeze brought the smell of someone's barbecue. The sound of the freeway was a constant rush. Baranpay could almost be another planet. Griff felt his heart lift at the thought of it.

He turned to go, and heard a sudden rustling noise to his right.

Hey man, I don't want no trouble. Just gimme the wallet.'

Griff stared at the kid. He was no more than sixteen or seventeen, but he looked raddled. He had pale green eyes that bulged from a thin acne-marked face. He was wearing grey combat trousers designed for mountains and snow, and a plain white T shirt that should have been washed days ago, or, better still, thrown away. Griff wondered if the boy had been sleeping up here in the bushes.

'I mean it!'

Griff noticed the knife then. Curiously, he felt no fear. The kid looked scared, as if he'd never done anything like this before. Griff noticed he held the knife in his left hand.

'Son, I'll give you some money, but you can't have my wallet.'

The kid looked Griff up and down, taking in his clothes, making a decision. Griff knew what he was thinking. A rich dude. He wanted the wallet. He reached slowly into the back pocket of his jeans and took out the wallet.

'Slowly man. Toss it over here.'

'I said you can't have it.'

He opened the wallet, not taking his eyes away from the boy, reaching inside for the paper currency. The boy's eyes were drawn to the money, and Griff felt sorry for him.

He had ninety dollars in the wallet, and as he pulled it out he saw the kid's eyes change. The boy looked up at him again and lurched forward out of the brush. He made a grab for the wallet with his right hand, and Griff snatched it back, dropping the notes, which were caught by the breeze and carried over the edge. The kid gave a frustrated yell and slammed forward, and the knife went into Griff's right side.

At first he thought the boy had punched him. A bloom of anger rose through him and he launched out with his right hand, connecting with the boy's chest. The kid was skinny and off-balance, and he fell hard

159

on his back. He looked up at Griff, terrified, put his arms down and tried to shuffle backwards. The ground was littered with broken glass, cigarette ends and empty beer tins. Griff took what he hoped was a menacing step forward, and the boy's eyes focussed on his shirt. Griff saw the fear on his face. The boy yelped as his hand came in contact with the glass. He managed to get his legs under him, then took one last longing look at the wallet still in Griff's hand before running back up the track.

Griff just watched him go, letting the anger slowly subside. Now that it was over, he could feel his heart pounding, the adrenalin pumping through him, making everything around him seem crystal clear. He looked down at his wallet, and realised that had just been a really stupid thing to do.

'No hypes in Baranpay,' he said aloud. He shook his head, breathing hard, and went to put his wallet back in his pocket. That was when he felt the sudden pain, and only then did he notice the blood soaking his pale blue shirt. He remembered the punch, only it hadn't been a punch at all.

'Shit,' he said, starting up the track for the car. The pain seemed to arrive all at once, and a fresh surge of blood welled from his side as he took a step. It was no more than fifteen feet to the car, but it was all uphill. Griff forced himself to do it, slow step after slow step, his heart thudding and his breath coming in harsh gasps. With every step it felt as if the knife was still in his side. He wondered if his young buddy would be waiting for him up there, ready to rip him off if he lost consciousness. Another agonising step brought the roof of the car into view. He was getting lightheaded, and knew he had to hurry.

He suddenly thought of Ellie. She had never told him the details of her accident, but he imagined her, trying to get out of the burning car, fighting to survive, and in that instant he realised how strong she really was. The pain seemed farther away now, and he knew he was losing too much blood. Another step, and another. He gritted his teeth. Just a couple more and he'd reach the car door. But he was beginning to feel numb. He just wanted to sit down, go to sleep. One more step. He reached out and touched the car door, fumbled for the handle.

He had locked the car.

His legs gave out and he crumpled to the ground. He could hear music coming from above, one of the big houses up there. Maybe it was the people having the barbecue. The breeze brought the words to him:

'you need to know that I'll be watching over you'

He had fallen against the rear door of the car, and now he reached into his jeans pocket for the car key. His fingers felt like sausages. He

160

touched the keys, but couldn't quite close his hand round them. He felt for the button that unlocked the door, pressing it in the hope that the car would respond. Nothing. The sensor must be facing the other way.

'I nearly got out of here,' he thought.

He couldn't keep his eyes open, couldn't think.

'you need to know that I am always here for you.'

He didn't know the song, but the lyrics seeped into his brain, and he felt a sudden surge of warmth.

Ellie,' he said, staring out at the fire road, the trees silhouetted in the sunset. His shaking fingers closed round the keys and he dragged them out of his pocket, still pressing the button. The locking system beeped twice. He reached up for the door handle and pulled. He fell into the gap as the door opened, but managed to get his arms inside the car. The phone was in the glove box. He struggled to open his heavy eyes and pulled the little door open. There it was, the pale green display facing him. For a moment he thought the surrounding hills might block reception, but no, the display showed there was a signal. He sighed, grabbed for the phone, and collapsed onto the floor of the car.

*

It was morning in Edinburgh: mist, shiny grey streets. Buildings almost black in the pale light, people hunched over and hurrying through the drizzle. The city smelt of too much rain. It was now November, another month, another city. That morning Ellie had abandoned the Kelvingrove flat and turned in the keys. The letting agency didn't like it much, but that was tough. Ellie had to work, and there was none for her in Glasgow.

he hospital was brand new, white and clinical. Ellie was absolutely certain, however, that once inside, she'd find all the same problems there were in every hospital she'd ever worked: not enough money , not enough staff. From the outside it seemed quiet, although she doubted that was true.

The first thing to do was find the nurses residence. She was going to try and cheek it out. There were always spare rooms in the nurses' homes, and she was getting seriously low on funds. She waited in the rain until she saw two nurses coming out, then hurried over. As expected, they were too busy looking at her face to notice her skipping past them inside.

'Hey-' one of them began, but Ellie had already headed up the stairs, as if she knew where she was going.

It was the standard womens' accommodation. It smelt of talcum powder, disinfectant (it was after all, a *nurses'* residence) and a bare trace of perfume. Ellie tucked her bike helmet under her arm and walked along the corridor, looking for the supervisor's room.

'Hey, I think you're in the wrong place.'

Ellie turned round. A chubby nurse with very red cheeks was smiling at her in a way that made Ellie think it was her only expression.

'Courier deliveries are up at the hospital, ye ken?'

Ellie put on her best smile and walked towards her.

'Actually, I was looking for whoever is in charge of renting a room.'

The nurse's smile didn't falter, and Ellie felt immediately comfortable in her presence. Her broad Edinburgh accent was somehow reassuring.

'You're a nurse?'

'Not exactly.'

The smile got even wider. 'Okay,' she said. 'I'm Allie. Sister Benedetto is in charge of the house, and she's not here. We have got some spares, though. I think. Are you going to be working here?'

'In the labs.'

Allie nodded. 'Oh aye.'

Ellie waited. Allie looked past her down the corridor and heaved a contented sigh.

'You can have the room across from mine, if you like.'

'Don't I have to ask permission?'

'Oh aye, but I'll put a word in for you, if you like. Benny's all right. This is for nurses only, but we can maybe tell a wee fib.'

Ellie started to laugh. 'You're very trusting, Allie.'

Allie looked at her carefully. 'Not really. I just know an honest face.'

'Well. Thanks,' Ellie said, feeling confused. Her face had never been called *honest* before.

Allie started walking back the way she had come, and Ellie followed.

'Which lab ye in?'

'Biochem.'

'Oh, Norrie's lab. You'll like him. He's a scream.'

And she started to laugh. Ellie said nothing, bemused. Her scars were also silent, annoyed at the lack of attention. The two of them climbed to the second floor, by which time Allie was out of puff.

'I must lose some weight,' she said amiably, between deep breaths.

Allie was fat, but, not 'two seats on the bus' fat. She was fat in bits. Her bottom half was big and lumpy and full, but from the waist up she wasn't fat at all. It was like one of those children's books where top and bottom halves are interchangeable. Allie had just got someone else's bum by mistake.

162

'Why bother, if you're happy,' Ellie said.

That brought a quizzical look from the nurse.

'You got much luggage?'

'No. A couple of bags. I'm a light traveller.'

Allie stopped at a door and turned the handle. The door opened and she walked in.

'It needs a bit of an airing, but it's all right.'

Ellie looked round. Single bed, pine-effect wardrobe, chest of drawers with a mirror on it, bedside table with a lamp. Small, but sufficient.

'Where's the bathroom?'

'Two doors down. You have to share, I'm afraid.'

Ellie shrugged. 'It's fine,' she said.

Allie nodded, still smiling.

'Aye well. I just popped back because I got caught short, that time of the month, ken? I'd better get back to work. Make yourself at home, and we'll sort it out with Benny later.'

Ellie thanked Allie as she walked off down the empty corridor. She grinned. That had been incredibly easy, maybe her luck was changing.

Allie stopped suddenly. 'Oh, me and my pal Cerys will be hitting the pub about five, if you're up for it?'

Ellie laughed. Some things never changed.

'Absolutely. Which pub?'

'Out of the hospital, second road on the left. It's called the Griffin.'

Ellie's smile froze on her face. Griffin. It was like a stab to the heart.

'All right?'

'Yes. Fine,' Ellie managed, before going back inside and sitting on the hard little bed.

Tears roared up out of the depths, and she was powerless to stop them. She stood up and walked to the window, looking out at the car park and the rain.

*

The Biochemistry lab was a large prefab at the back of the oncology unit. She walked in and found a counter. She heard someone hurrying towards her, and heard his voice before he appeared.

'About time! What's the matter, do ye no' want tae get wet or someth-'

He stopped when he saw her.

'Sorry lass. Thought you were the porter. He gets later every day.'

Ellie shook her head. 'They're all the same.'

'Ah. You'll be Ellie, then.'

163

She smiled. 'You have a job for me?'

'Aye, that I do. Maternity leave, it is, and between you and me, the job's yours. I doubt she'll be back, ken?'

He tapped his nose conspiratorily. 'Come along, we'll get you kitted out. Here. You can have this locker. I'll order you a lab coat, but for now you can borrow Tara's. Like I say, she's not likely to miss it.'

He carried on talking without a discernable break for breath. Ellie said nothing, not that she'd have got a word in, but it was nice. He was funny and friendly. She guessed he was in his late forties, with dark brown wavy hair going grey at the temples. His eyes were a very dark blue, and he had joined-up eyebrows that reminded her of Murd. She followed him through the lab, introducing her to the workers and showing her the equipment. The scars preened a bit at some of the looks they got, but Ellie ignored them.

'So. What do you think?'

Ellie nodded, looking enthusiastic.

'It's fine. Everyone seems nice, and I'm familiar with most of your stuff.'

His face fell.

'Aye, I know. Some of it's shamefully out of date. Look at that Centrifichem. Tch tch.'

He shook his head. The analyser was at least twenty years old.

'It still does the job.'

He looked at her carefully.

'So now for the sixty four thousand dollar question,' he said.

Ellie looked at him warily, her heart beginning to race. The scars sat up and begged.

'Are you buying the pints?'

Ellie laughed, more in relief than anything else.

'I think that'll be a definite aye,' she said. 'I met a nurse earlier, Allie?'

'Och, the whole hospital knows Allie,' he said, grinning. 'She's already told you where the pub is?'

Ellie nodded. 'Five o'clock?'

They walked back down the row of benches.

'Aye, we'll all be there. All except poor Ronnie-' he tapped the man on the shoulder.

'-who's on call.'

'Aye, I can still come to the pub, though.'

Norrie shook his head in a gesture of well, I suppose. He winked at her.

'See you later then,' As Ellie walked out of the building, she heard him whistling.

TWENTY EIGHT

Griff was hot, and for some reason, he couldn't seem to get rid of the bedclothes. He tried to push them off, but they wouldn't move. He could feel the sweat trickling down his face. He opened his eyes, but, like a dream in which he thought he was awake, nothing happened, he saw only the darkness of his eyelids. He struggled for a while, thinking he could hear someone speaking a long way away. Then he felt himself drifting off.

Eventually he managed to open his eyes. It was too bright to make anything out, and his head was pounding, so he closed them again, and concentrated on his other senses.

There was no sound, at least, nothing discernable. He was in bed, but knew it wasn't Ellie's house. Where was he? He tried opening his eyes again, squinting through the lids.   Window. Flowers. Cards.

Hospital.

The memory hit him hard. The kid, the stabbing, the painful trip to the car, all these were as nothing. He had woken up thinking he was in Ellie's house. He raised a hand to his face, wiping sleep from his eyes. His tongue felt like a leather strap, but he could see no water by the bed. He tried to sit up, and a jolt of pain shot like electricity through his torso. He lay flat again, looking up at the ceiling. After a while, someone opened the door and looked in before leaving again. Griff had no idea how much time had passed. He was suddenly aware of a stocky black man leaning over him. He focussed on him and saw he was smiling.

'Mr Park. Back with us at last. We were worried about you for a while there.'

Griff had only one pressing thought.

'How long have I been here? What day is it?'

'It's October fourteen. Don't be worrying about the time now. You lost a lot of blood-'

'I've been here three days?' His voice broke on the words, his throat was so dry.

The doctor nodded. 'You were lucky. The knife just missed your lung. I'll get you something to drink.'

He nodded, trying to think. The doctor left, and he tried again to sit up. The pain bolted through him, but he was ready for it this time. He managed to prop himself on the pillow, on his left side. He glanced up and saw two cards there. Angling his head, he could see inside.

Neither Dave nor Mel were very good with words. They both carried the same 'hurry up and get better' message, but he smiled all the

165

same, especially at Mel's. Maybe they could actually be friends, now they were no longer going to be married.

Nothing from Ellie, but why would there be? She had no way of knowing where he was. He looked round, but couldn't see any personal belongings. The doctor returned just then and yelled at him.

'If you tear those stitches I'll put them back without an anaesthetic.'

'Sorry,' he mumbled. A nurse had followed him in and gave him a glass of water. It felt wonderful in his dry mouth. He lay back down reluctantly.

Can I have my phone? I need to check my messages.'

The nurse brought him the phone. He had three messages, all three days old and from Dave, wondering where he was. There was nothing from Ellie. His heart lurched.

'When can I leave?'

'Not for a few days. The police want to talk to you. Are you ready for that?'

'I guess so.'

They left him alone then. The police came and went, but Griff was deliberately vague with his description of the assailant. He knew the boy had not meant to hurt him, he was simply desperate.

Time laid heavy on him. He thought about simply getting up and leaving, but every time he tried to stand, a wave of pain and nausea drove him back to the bed. There was a TV in his room, but he didn't turn it on. A while later they brought him some food: a dried up hamburger, a dollop of mashed potato and some beans. He got the nurse to take it away, the smell was making him feel sick. As she left, Dave appeared.

Griff looked up and smiled. Dave walked towards him and said nothing, just looked down at him with a sad look on his face.

'What's up?'

'What's up? Are you crazy? You nearly get yourself killed, and that's all you can say?'

Griff shrugged, then grimaced at the resulting pain.

'I mean, did I kill your sister in a past life or something? Why are you doing this to me?'

Griff felt a wave of affection for his friend. 'You worry too much, mother.'

Dave shook his head.

'So what happened, exactly.'

Griff told him.

'So let's get this straight. Some lunatic, probably drugged to the eyeballs, demands your wallet at knifepoint, and you tell him 'no'?'

'That's pretty much it.'

166

'Crazy,' he said. 'Fucking crazy.'

Griff was suddenly tired of the story. It was more important that he got out of here.

'Dave, I need you to help me.'

'Oh!' Dave had sat on the edge of the bed, but now he stood up and paced the room.

'He has me worried sick for three days, and now he wants a favour.'

'Please Dave.'

'All right. What is it?'

'I can't get hold of Ellie. Something's wrong. I think- I-'

He gazed off into space. What the hell was he trying to say?

'You've still had no reply?'

Griff nodded.

Dave looked at him, and sighed. Griff felt a jolt in his chest.

'Don't say it, Dave.'

Dave made his usual hand gesture. 'Well. It's a possibility. Maybe she's – I don't know- moved on.'

Griff shook his head.

'You don't know her. She wouldn't-'

Dave said nothing for a long minute, and Griff felt a sudden lump in his throat. What if Dave was right? What if she had already forgotten him? No. Dave didn't believe him, but he knew. They had been special. Ellie wasn't the sort of person to treat their affair as casual.

'What do you want me to do?' Dave asked.

Griff sighed. 'I don't know. Is there anything you can do, to help me find her?'

Dave licked his lips carefully. 'Give me the number. I might be able to find something out about the phone account.'

Griff gratefully told his the number which he had now committed to memory.

'I can't promise anything.'

Griff nodded. 'I know, Dave. Thanks.'

Dave had been gone a half hour when Mel arrived. Griff was surprised to see her, and a little guilty. He was slowly coming to terms with the truth that when he had walked out, he had left behind people who really did care about him.

'How are you feeling?'

'I'm fine, Mel, it's nice of you to come.'

She smiled. She looked, as always, as if she had just come from a makeover. Her blonde hair was feathered round her face, her make up carefully natural. She was wearing D&G jeans, a tan coloured shirt and matching suede boots. She looked great. Aware of his scrutiny, she looked away.

167

'You look good, Mel,' he said, looking back at the ceiling.

'Well, I came the first day,' she said, ignoring his last comment. 'But you were out of it.
They told me what had happened, how bad it was.'

She paused, looking down, as if she could see the knife wound beneath the sheets.

'Anyway, I called every day, but they told me your friend Dave was here, so I knew you weren't alone.'

Griff looked back at her. 'Dave was here? What, every day?'

She nodded. 'I think so.'

He sighed. Guilt again.

'When will they let you out?'

'They won't commit themselves. I'm going to have to just leave.'

'Why? Take the time, and let yourself heal.'

He looked at her.

'I don't have the time.'

Let yourself heal, she'd said. Was there another meaning in that?

'You have plenty of time. You're not on a project, are you?'

He wondered how much she knew about him. He remembered the private investigator her lawyers had hired.

'You know, the reason they told me how you were doing was because I told them I was your wife.'

Griff gave a half-shrug. 'You are, still, I mean. For a while.'

She nodded slowly.

'Well.'

'Well what? Mel. What are you saying?'

She sat back and sighed, running her hand through her hair. It fell back into perfect position.

'I don't know. I guess- maybe I'm trying to say you should stay put for a while. You know? Regroup.'

Regroup? What did that mean? He looked into her eyes, searching for meaning. She looked back, and he saw that perhaps she hadn't moved on as much as she had told him.

Whatever she saw in his eyes made her drop hers.

'There's somewhere else I have to be,' he said softly. He smiled, simply at the memory. Mel was a beautiful woman, but his thoughts and dreams were filled with Ellie, her dark wind-tangled hair, her eyes the colour of spruce fronds, her permanent grin, the way she always woke him in the morning. He realised Mel was staring at him, and looked away, shaking his head.

'When I get out of hospital, I'm leaving LA,' he said. 'I doubt I'll be back.'

She looked anxious.

168

'Where are you going?'

'A long way away.'

'Back to where it was you ran away to?'

He nodded. She had said that with a bitter edge to her voice, but it was still true.

'I waited four years for you to love me, and you never did,' she said.

He reached out to touch her arm, but she pulled it away.

'And now you've changed, you've become – I don't know, different. More aware. Kinder. But you still don't love me.'

'I'm sorry, Mel.'

She folded her arms. 'Well, it doesn't matter now.'

'Yes it does. I took four years of your life. I am sorry.'

She looked up again. 'I did railroad you into it,' she smiled then.

Griff chuckled, 'but I let you.'

'Should we just stop apologising for a minute?'

He nodded.

'You've found someone you do love, haven't you?'

Griff smiled. 'Yes.'

She sighed. 'I expect she's really beautiful.'

Griff reached out again. This time she let him take her hand.

'She is. But so are you.'

Their eyes held for a moment. Griff was the first to look away.

'I better go,' Mel said, standing up. At the door she stopped.

'Will you call me? Say goodbye, before you go?'

'Okay.'

She smiled again, and then she was gone. Griff lay back and stared at the ceiling, and thought about what it was Mel had wanted to say, but had not.

TWENTY NINE

The lab was freezing. A bitterly cold north front had blasted down from Iceland, bringing ice and hailstones, and searing winds. The lab heating wasn't working, and various space heaters and free-standing units had been wheeled in, but they were hopelessly inadequate. The five lab crew were working in coats and scarves, but still shivering.

'This is ridiculous,' René said, fumbling a test tube into its slot with gloved fingers. She was a very tall girl with hair so blonde it was almost white, and skin that looked as if the poke of a finger would tear it.

'I know. But what can we do?' Ellie replied. 'At least we're here in the main room. What about poor Malky out there.'

Malky, the most junior member of staff, always ended up with the worst jobs, as was traditional. Today he'd been given the faecal fat test. Certainly the worst of them all.

'But Norrie-' he'd tried to protest, his adam's apple bobbing. He was only eighteen, with carrot orange hair that seemed to have a life of its own. Today it was sticking straight up, as if it had been frozen there, (which, given the weather, it might well have been.)

'Now look, Malky. What if it comes up in your exams? Once you've done the test, you'll know all about it.'

'But they say it's never come up in the exams!'

'"They"?' Norrie said, looking at the others.

Gerry tipped him a wink.

'Well I for one remember it in mine,' he said, folding his arms. Gerry was a very large man. Rumour had it, and Ellie was sure he started the rumours himself, that he had once been a professional wrestler. He was the most senior tech next to Norrie, and Malky worshipped him.

Malky looked down.

'Can't I just read up on it?'

'Yes, of course you can,' Norrie said. Malky looked up at him hopefully.

'Once you've done the test. Now get on with it.'

Ellie had looked round at the grins of the crew. It was a terrible job, but they'd all had to do it. Norrie walked off, and Malky looked round despondently.

'I don't even understand *why* this need to be done.'

Ellie fell for it.

'All right, Malk, I'll explain. Everyone excretes fat. We all eat too much of it, so it's there in the brown stuff. But sometimes it's there because the body's not absorbing fat at all, and that could be because of pancreatitis or bowel disease.'

Malky looked behind him to the terrible room where the samples were stored.

'So the doctor gets them to crap in the tin every day for three days, then we get it, shake it up well, and test it. Understand?'

His lip was curling. Ellie shivered at a sudden draught.

'It's a good day for it, Malk. Believe me, you don't want to be doing it in the summer.'

There was a chorus of murmured agreement.

Malky looked back at Ellie, his face hopeful.

'I don't know how to work the machine.'

Ellie shook her head. She wasn't falling for that one. Gerry walked over to the fume room and looked through the window. The room was small, and housed the mechanisms and chemicals for doing all the less usual tests. Various sized samples were stored on shelves, along with the reagent bottles. There was a deep sink, and a fume cupboard for doing tests in a ventilated environment. There was nothing else in the room apart from the homogeniser.

It was a squat green object, festooned with levers and screw mechanisms. It looked like hell's version of R2D2. There was a flat plate on the front with a screw down lid above it.

'It's easy, Malk,' Gerry said. 'You just put the tin in, screw it down, and the machine does the rest.'

They had all walked over to the room now, and were looking in. Gerry gave Malky a little push.

'On ye go, Malk.'

He looked round the faces, but although there was sympathy there, there was no escape.

The room had an outside window, and so was even colder than the main lab. When Malky opened the door Ellie felt the blast of icy air.

'Jesus!' René said. 'Shut the door quick.'

Malky looked back at them as if he was about to walk the plank.

They watched him lift the first tin off the shelf. It was a plain aluminium can, exactly like a paint tin, with a small green label giving the patient's details. It was clearly heavy. Malky put it down gingerly on the plate, and stepped back to work out how the machine worked, rubbing his hands against the cold.

Ellie looked at her colleagues. 'Let's leave him to it, he's nervous enough.'

Gerry and René both grinned, and they all walked away. Ellie had the glucose analyser again today, the most boring job in the world. She set up the machine, her fingers growing ever more numb,

171

dreaming of her warm little room.

Allie had been as good as her word. Ellie didn't know what she'd said to the sister, but she had been handed a letter offering her the room, no questions asked. She figured that any money coming in was fine, regardless of the source. This was, after all, the NHS.

And the people were fun. There was plenty to do. It was a very busy hospital, and, as she had surmised, they were short of staff. So there was overtime if she wanted it, and she was on-call twice a week. She had found that the best way to keep her angry scars and broken heart quiet was to work hard and play harder. Unlike the Children's Hospital, the crew here were all serious party people. Gerry and René were both single, young Malky had just discovered drinking, and Norrie was separated from his wife. Allie, the nurse, was seeing one of the anaesthetists, Tom, who drank even more than the rest of them, and they were always in the pub with another nurse, Allie's best mate Cerys.

So there was hardly any time to remember soft sand and warm island winds, and gentle Americans.

'Malky! No! Turn it off! Turn it-'

Ellie abandoned her daydream and rushed over to the little room. Norrie was standing with his hands on the glass, shouting. The others hurried over in time to see Malky leaning hard against the wall, arms outstretched, staring in horror at the green machine. The homogeniser made a noise like a lawn mower on speed, and was vibrating in the corner like something out of a Stephen King story. Ellie could see that Malky had not screwed the tin down hard enough, and it had worked its way half out.

'Why doesn't he turn it off?' René said.

'Because it's going to blow any second,' Gerry murmured in fascinated horror.

The violent motion was too much for the flimsy tin. A thin line of brown liquid had appeared round the edge of the lid, and a second later, the tin exploded out of the machine, arcing across the room followed by a comet's tail of noxious semi-solid gloop. Everyone hit the floor as the stuff hit the glass. There was a long moment in which nothing could be heard but the machine still vibrating uselessly and the slow dripping of liquid, and then, slowly, all of the lab crew rose up to peer through the glass.

Malky looked like a large novelty easter egg. His red hair had somehow escaped the deluge, and still stood on end like a wire brush.

'Jesus,' Gerry whispered.

Ellie looked round at Norrie, whose single eyebrow was creasing. She couldn't read his expression, but Malky saw him, and bit his lip, an action he immediately regretted.

Ellie couldn't help it. The laugh started somewhere deep inside, and roared out of her like a tornado. She laughed so hard she could hardly breathe, until her stomach muscles howled in protest. She looked round, but the others were completely in the grip of it as well, even Norrie. She looked in at Malky again and suddenly he too started to laugh. It went on for some time, until at last Norrie got a grip of himself and shouted through the glass.

'Go and have a shower. No, on second thoughts, get this cleaned up first, then you can have a shower.'

Malky looked round at the mess, and they all started to laugh again.

'And turn the damn machine off!'

'What about the test?' Gerry gasped, wiping his eyes. 'Some poor sod's going to have to shit in a tin for three days again.'

Norrie looked in again. 'No, they won't. Scoop it back in the tin, Malky,' he said. 'You'll have to start all over again.'

That sent them all off again. Ellie felt her scarred cheek itching desperately at the unaccustomed exercise. *And the unaccustomed lack of attention,* she added cheerfully.

*

Griff looked out at the hospital garden. It had been landscaped at one time, but then simply left to its own resources. The patients in rooms such as his own had clearly opened the windows to have a sneaky smoke, and thrown the stubs down. It was a cigarette graveyard.

He stood up and walked carefully to the door. The doctors wanted him to stay longer, but that was impossible. Dave would be here in a minute to drive him back to his flat, where he could pack up a few belongings and take off. He looked out into the corridor, but there was no sign of his friend.

Over the last few days he had wondered if fate was somehow conspiring against him to keep him here, perhaps to save him from the bad news waiting for him. Last night he had opened his laptop and looked back at the e-mails he had sent Ellie, from the first, explaining what had happened, and that he would be back soon, to the last hopeless cry, just a few days ago:

Ellie, where are you?

He saw Dave rounding the corner, and looked back inside the room. There was nothing he needed apart from the computer. He picked it up, determined not to wince at the sharp stab in his side.

'You ready?' Dave said.

He nodded. 'Let's go.'

They walked slowly down to the car park, and out into daylight.

'You all right?'

He nodded. Breathing was painful. Dave had thoughtfully brought Griff's Lexus, easier to get into than his own Boxster. Griff eased himself in, and breathed out heavily.

'Sure you're all right?'

'Will you stop saying that?'

'Sorry.'

'Did you find out anything?'

Dave looked at him, then turned his attention to the road.

'The phone's still listed to her, but it's a no-contract phone. You buy vouchers to pay for talk time. She could easily have given it away.'

Griff shook his head. Why would she do that? It didn't sit right. Again he cursed himself for his foolishness in not knowing about the number stored in the phone. He wondered if she'd ever believe he could have been so stupid.

'You're still determined to go?'

Griff nodded.

'Well, I think you're crazy.'

He looked up. Dave was staring straight ahead. They were at the junction of Sunset, and a couple of street girls approached the car, calling out. Dave drove on without looking at them.

'I don't know what I'd have done without you,' Griff said.

Dave looked at him then. Griff saw the sadness in his eyes, and something else, something he couldn't quite identify. He felt a pain in his chest that had nothing to do with his injury.

'Griff,' Dave said quietly. 'I want to-'

Griff's phone rang, and he grabbed it out of his pocket, forgetting about the injury and wincing hard as he stretched the torn tissue.

'Who is it? Is it her?'

Griff looked at the number. He didn't recognise it. He looked up at Dave.

'I don't know.'

'Well answer it then!' Dave yelled.

Griff put the phone up to his ear. 'Hello?

'Griff. You'd better come. He's asking for you again. They say this is the last day.'

Mother.

Griff looked down, and felt his shoulders sag. He remembered that earlier thought, about something conspiring to keep him here.

'I already said goodbye.'

'Goddammit. You're as bad as he is! He says he's got something to

174

tell you.'

Griff closed the phone, aware of Dave's curiosity.

'That wasn't her?'

'No. My mother. My father's asked me to go see him again. She says he's close to death.'

Dave hesitated. 'Will you go?'

Griff looked at him.

'Would you?'

Dave shrugged. 'I really don't know, Griff. You went already, what did it prove?'

Nothing, Griff thought. Nothing, except that maybe I'd have been better not going at all.

He sighed.

'Turn around Dave. Cedars is back that way.'

THIRTY

It looked as though the entire hospital staff were packed into the Griffin Bar. It was three deep at the bar, and everyone was doubling up on their drinks. Malky had pride of place, even if he still did smell of disinfectant. He had become an overnight hero, once the 'fume room incident', as it had come to be called, had gone round the hospital. He was now very drunk, and trying to listen attentively to Cerys, who was telling him the plot of her latest story.

'So then the policeman says to the prostitute, 'well, why don't you be a brain surgeon, you can be whatever you want to be', and then she says-'

Ellie tuned her out. Allie was raising her eyes to the sky.

'This is the worst one yet.'

'Actually, I thought it was all right.'

'Ye Gods. The trouble is, if she marketed them as humour, she'd sell shedloads.'

Tom came back from the bar with a loaded tray.

'It's hell up there,' he said, sitting down. Everyone dived in to the tray. 'What's going on tonight?'

'Word of Malky's shit-shaking technique has got round,' Gerry said.

Ellie laughed. She was sitting between Allie and Norrie, feeling pleasantly drunk. It had been a long time since she had felt so content.

'That was the funniest thing I think I've ever seen,' Norrie said. 'The way he just stood there with it all over him-'

'Except his hair,' Gerry said, laughing. 'It never touched those ginger locks.'

Malky looked up at them and grinned. Cerys frowned, annoyed at the interruption of her story.

'So I was thinking,' she said to Malky. 'Would you mind if I used what happened to you in a story?'

Malky shook his head.

'Jesus,' Tom said, shaking his head. 'What sort of story features someone getting covered in crap?'

Cerys gave him an indignant look, which she was very good at.

'Well, you'll just have to wait and see.'

Everyone grinned, but no one said anything.

Cerys's literary ambitions knew no bounds. She never felt the tearing doubt that no one would be interested in her work, never read someone else's great story and thought, I may as well give up now. Even the incessant derision of the hospital crew never dampened her certainty in her talent. She was going to be the next J K Rowling. The next small, bespectacled, lesbian J K Rowling. Ellie wondered how that would go down at Hogwarts.

It was Thursday night, unofficial start of the weekend.

'Are you working Saturday?' Ellie asked.

Allie shook her head. 'It's my dad's birthday, and we're all going to see Mama Mia.'

'Oh God,' Gerry said. 'Abba'.

'Hey, can't fault them,' Rene said, swirling her beer. 'Is your dad *the* Doc Savage?'

'I'm afraid so.'

Ellie felt a blast of déjà vu. She knew the name, and not just from the obvious reference. She looked into her glass, watching a bubble run around the rim, and tried to pin down the memory.

'You all right?'

She looked up. Norrie was watching her.

'Yeah, I just- bit of déjà vu.' She grinned. Rene and Allie started to sing *there was something in the air that night, the stars were bright…*

Tom stood up and began to waltz Cerys round the tables. Malky's eyes were slowly closing. Ellie laughed, looking back at Norrie. He looked suddenly sad.

'What's up?' she asked. He looked back, surprised.

'Och, nothing, I'm fine.'

He smiled at her, but she saw how bleak his eyes were.

'No, really,' she said, 'What?'

He finished his pint and swapped it for a fresh one from the tray.

'It's the damn solicitors. You know, Mary and I were all set to go our separate ways, had it all worked out. Then they come along and tell her she could get this, that and the next thing. Now she wants the shirt off my back.'

He took an angry pull of his pint. Ellie sighed.

'I suppose they have to give her the best advice they can.'

'Aye, but she doesnay have tae take it.'

Ellie had noticed that stress brought out his accent. She didn't reply.

'It's that song, as well. Fernando. They played that at our wedding, y' ken.' He shook his head.

'I don't know. One of these days-'

'What? One of these days what?'

He grinned suddenly. 'One of these days I'm going to jack it all in and travel round the world.'

'Really? That sounds scary.'

He sat back, looking up. 'I'll do it the hard way. Over land. There are places I'd love to see. That crater in Africa, you know? And Maccu Piccu, and of course the Pyramids.'

177

He sighed. 'One day.'

Ellie had no conception of 'one day'.

'Well, why don't you do it?'

He shrugged. 'Aye, when I've saved up, once we've got more staff in the labs, once this divorce is sorted. I'll get to it.'

'No,' she said, 'Why don't you do it now?'

'Now? Och I can't just drop everything and go!'

'Why not?'

He looked at her as if she was daft.

'It's not that simple.'

'I've never found it a problem.'

She saw the expression that crossed his face, and looked away. The scars woke up.

Oh gimme some more of that old fashioned sympathy!

'Shut the fuck up.'

Oh. Nice.

'I know what you were trying to work out, earlier,' Norrie said.

She was confused, earlier-?

'When you said you had déjà vu. It's Allie's father. He's the leading light in corrective

laser surgery. No pun intended.'

He smiled, and Ellie tried to smile back, her heart suddenly beating hard. Now she remembered, the e-mail Jim had sent her, it seemed about a hundred years ago. *I know you might not want to think about this right now-* he'd written. He'd given her the name of Doctor Graham Savage. She nodded to herself. Coincidence. She sensed Norrie looking at her.

'You're right,' she said. 'Someone gave me his name.'

'He's the best,' Norrie said.

Ellie said nothing, looking up at Allie and Tom dancing. There was no room, and they were rebounding off other drinkers. Sooner or later, someone would get angry. Ellie felt all the warm contentment being slowly sucked out of her. She lifted her glass. 'Here's to better days,' she said.

'I'll drink to that,' Norrie replied.

There was a dull thump, and they looked round in time to see Malky sink slowly to the ground.

'I think I better let him stay with me tonight. His parents'll go spare otherwise.'

They manhandled Malky back on to the seat, and Norrie went outside to call his parents. Ellie finished her drink.

Well, that put a damper on the evening.

'Aw, shut up, will you? Just leave me alone.'

Just making an observation.

She got up and walked past the bar. She caught Allie's eye and gestured that she was going. Then she grabbed her coat and walked back to the nurses' home. The streets were slick with ice, and once out of the glare of the streetlights, she could see a zillion stars. Just like home, she thought. Home. Hah. Fooling herself again. All the same, she searched for the patterns of stars that Griff had shown her, not finding them. Even the skies had moved on, she thought bitterly. They were no longer there.

*

Carl Park was no longer on the third floor. Third floor residents still had some hope.

Griff's father was now in bed, and it looked as though his frail skeleton was held together by a load of tubes and lines. A machine in the corner monitored his vital signs, while a cheery nurse bustled round, tucking in the bedclothes and making small talk, as if it would make things more comfortable. It didn't. Mother sat reproachfully in the corner, staring at him. She had spotted the way Griff was walking, and was curling her lip. She obviously thought he was using it as some excuse.

'What happened to you?'

He ignored her, walking over to the bed. Carl's eyes were closed, but he sensed the shadow over him and opened them.

'You came.'

The words didn't come out, but Griff saw what them on the old man's lips. A thin arm came up, pointing to the bedside. Griff remembered how dry his own throat had been in hospital. He reached for the water jug, but mother had beaten him to it. She poured out a glass and held it to the old man's lips. Carl sipped the water, and Griff could almost trace its path through his emaciated body. He nodded that he'd finished, and looked at his wife.

'Please leave us a while,' he said.

Mother looked up at Griff, an angry refusal on her face.

'Please,' Carl said again. She looked back at him, and was about to say something, then changed her mind. She grabbed her purse from the back of the chair and stormed out.

'She hates me too, you know,' Carl said, a faint smile on his face.

Griff sat on the edge of the bed.

'I wanted to see you. Last time, I did it all wrong.'

'I know,' Griff said.

'You were always such a smart boy. And your writing! I never knew

179

where you got that talent. It sure wasn't from either of us.'

He coughed, and Griff heard the machine beep grow a little faster. Carl reached out and touched Griff's hand. His own was ice cold.

'I'm sorry, son. I know it does no good now, but I'm sorry. I wish I could say that to Peter too, but-'

Griff said nothing. The old man's gaze wandered off.

'I don't suppose you know where he is? What happened to him?'

Griff swallowed a surge of anger. Here was the old bastard who had made his childhood miserable, and his brother's appalling, saying sorry now at the end, as if it would make everything all right. He wanted to tell him the truth, that Peter had died an ignominious death in a sad hotel room, that his whole life had been tainted by the violence visited on him by this man and his wife. He looked into the cloudy blue eyes, saw the hope there.

He shook his head.

Carl sighed.

'I don't expect you to forgive me for what I did, for what I let happen by doing nothing. But I believe that, wherever I'm going, I'll be paying for it. And that's OK. I deserve it.'

He lifted his hand, and Griff fetched him more water.

'I'm real tired now, Griffin,' he said. 'My little dragon.'

Griff felt something reach in and touch his heart. He remembered that endearment from when he was a small child, before the anger. Before the bitterness.

'You go leave me now. And thank you. Thank you for letting me do this.'

The old man folded his hands over his stomach, and closed his eyes.

'Goodbye, father,' Griff said softly.

'Bye son.'

Griff walked to the door, the pain in his side matched by the irrational pain that went deeper. Before he got there, he stopped.

Griff didn't know what he believed, whether there was a God, or a hell, or if this was all there was. But Carl believed. And if there was one thing Griff knew for certain, there were no second chances. Ever.

'Dad?'

The old man's eyes opened.

'I forgive you, dad,' Griff said.

He turned to go, and heard a soft sound from the bed. The old man was crying. Griff quietly opened the door and stepped out into the dark corridor. His mother was sitting by the wall, reading a magazine. She stood up as he passed, but didn't speak, and neither did he.

THIRTY ONE

Ellie woke up with someone banging on her door. She had that moment of deep existential dread that follows every heavy drinking session the night before, and then the door swung open to reveal Cerys.

'Wake up, Ellie. It's gone half past eight.'

'Oh, shit.'

She had forgotten it was only Friday. She got up too quickly, feeling dizzy, and hurried down the corridor to the bathroom. It was a mess, with empty shampoo bottles and wet towels left lying on the floor. It looked as though everyone had had a good night last night. She had a thirty second shower and rushed back to her room.

She looked in the mirror.

Good morning. Not feeling so good today.

'Me neither,' she said aloud. The scars were red and painful-looking, although she could feel nothing. The redness only emphasised the ridges and valleys, the alien landscape of her left cheek. It was like the surface of Mars.

There was no time for this.

She got to the lab at a few minutes after nine. Norrie and Malky were there already, Malky, pale and staring, sweating in the cold. He was holding a mug of tea in both hands, which were shaking.

'Ah. Morning Ellie. First to arrive. Well done.'

She grinned. 'You're not looking too good, Malky,' she said, winking at Norrie. 'And you've still got the rest of those faecal fats to do.'

Malky groaned and closed his eyes. Ellie went to put the kettle back on and get her lab coat out of her locker.

'Hey, Ellie? Got a new girl starting tomorrow.'

Norrie was holding a sheet of fax paper.

'Not before time,' she said.

'They're sending her over later so we can have a look at her.'

Ellie shook her head. They were so desperate for staff that anyone willing to don a lab coat would do. Of course, they'd also have to be willing to get rat arsed drunk every night.

Allie came sauntering over at ten o'clock, her usual happy grin seriously curtailed.

'My God, that was bad last night,' she said, leaning her head on her arms. 'Let's go grab a cup of tea.'

Ellie had set her machine up to do its thing. She decided she could spare ten minutes.

The canteen tea was famous for its strength. Two sips got your heart racing. It was making Ellie feel sick, and she pushed it away.

'God, I feel bad.'

'How's Tom?'

'Tom? That sod's got the constitution of an ox. He was on the phone waking me up at six.'

Allie shook her head, but her smile was back. Ellie felt a pang of something – not quite jealousy, more like regret.

'You guys are really good together.'

The smiled got wider. 'We really need to get you a decent man, Ellie.'

She laughed. 'You'd be better setting Cerys up. Get someone else to listen to her stories.'

'Gay folk are too difficult,' Allie said. 'I can never tell if they are or they're not.'

Ellie took another sip of tea. Grimaced.

'Anyway, I can't believe you've not been snapped up already.'

Ellie stared at her. 'Allie, have you looked at me recently?'

'What? Your face? So what. A decent man wouldn't care.'

No, Ellie thought, heart sinking. *You're right there.*

'Sorry,' Allie said. 'I've struck a nerve, haven't I'

Ellie smiled and looked away.

'There was a good man, once,' she said.

'But you let him slip away?'

'Something like that.'

'Oh you're a tight lipped one. Come on, tell me more.'

Ellie examined her memory, wondered if it could stand the telling. Perhaps not.

'I can't. At least, not right now. I better get back.'

Ellie could see the look Allie was giving her. She ignored it.

'What are you doing later?'

'Not drinking.'

'It's Friday night!' Allie was outraged.

'Well, we'll see. Anyway, I must go.'

She hurried back to the lab, but the test run was just finishing. She sat down and waited till her heart slowed down. The canteen tea was something else.

Or maybe it had been the talk.

'Why is it I can never talk about personal stuff? She thought.

Because it's personal, the scars replied.

She shook her head. It was because as soon as she thought about things, they seemed to take on a physicality, to rise up out of the depths of her memory and become capable of inflicting actual pain. Because she felt that if she spoke her thoughts aloud, they might all gang up on her and take over, and Ellie would be gone.

A feeling of vague unease fell on her, and stayed all morning. She was just thinking about going for a sandwich when she heard the tortured-air sound of a helicopter, and she entertained one wonderful moment of unqualified hope. Griff had come for her. She hurried to the back of the lab to look out at the patch of grass that doubled as a helipad, and her hopes were dashed. The scars had a good old laugh.

It was a Sea King, a huge yellow beast with twin rotors, but it touched down on the grass as gently as a bird.

'There goes lunch,' said Norrie, beside her. Ellie nodded.

Ellie wondered where the sea king was coming from, what had happened to the passenger, who was even now being stretchered out. The hospital grapevine would provide all the answers later today, but in the meantime Ellie was catapulted back to Iowyn's bike and Donnie's quiet fag in the toilet. Donnie had insisted he would not go to hospital, and Ellie understood. Imagine the story going all round the hospital, all round the *mainland*, instead of just round the island, which was bad enough.

'Penny for them?'

'Uh?'

Norrie smiled. 'You were miles away.'

Hah, she thought sadly, In more ways than one.

Gerry came and stood at her other side.

'LFT's for definite,' he said.

Ellie sighed. She was on the Liver Function Test bench.

'I'll go set up.'

A porter arrived within ten minutes. He already knew the story: an oil rig worker had become trapped in some equipment. At least it wasn't a fisherman, Ellie thought. Too close to home.

She was just about to phone her results through when Norrie arrived again. He had someone with him she didn't know, and Ellie remembered about the new girl.

'This is Ellie, our-' Norrie began.

'Oh my God! What happened to your face!'

Ellie blinked. The girl had a look on her face as though she'd just stepped on dog shit. Ellie looked down and chuckled softly to hide the sudden stab of pain in her heart.

Nice to be appreciated!

'Good to meet you too,' Ellie said. Norrie was looking at the girl as if she were from another planet.

'Gosh, I'm sorry.'

'No problem,' Ellie said, picking up the phone with shaking hands. Norrie took the girl away, and Ellie could feel his eyes on her back, but she didn't look round. She phoned the result and then went to the locker room. There was a mirror on the wall, and she looked into it. A large tree on the lawn outside cast shadows through the window and on to the glass. It made the scars look as if they were moving, changing places on her face. She tried to slow down her breathing, but her heart was thudding. She sighed.

'Not a good day,' she said.

Oh, don't say that. We've enjoyed it!

'Yeah, I'll bet.'

She realised they were not alone. Norrie had his head round the door.

'Who are you talking to?'

'No one.'

'Are you all right?'

'Yeah, fine.'

'Look, I'm sorry about-'

'Norrie, it's not your fault. Anyway, no harm done.'

He walked in.

'I know it's probably not my place to say this, but you should speak to Graham Savage. I've been told his work is amazing.'

Ellie looked at him. 'I look that bad, hmm?'

'I didn't mean that. If you had treatment, you'd be able to avoid scenes like we just had with that idiot girl.'

Ellie looked past him to the tree outside. It was bare and dark, with empty branches swaying in the wind. Her heart felt exactly the same.

'I'll think about it,' she said.

THIRTY TWO

The funeral was depressing, not the least because Griff was made to wait almost another week. As far as he was concerned, he and his father had made their peace. He didn't need to stand at the graveside looking sombre. Mother, of course, sobbed through the entire affair.

'I thought you said they didn't like each other?'

Dave had come along for moral support. The two of them were standing at the back of the small gathering. It was a beautiful California day, winter round the corner, but the chilly wind the only real sign of it. Mel had come too, and she was standing on the other side of the grave, looking stunning in a black two piece suit, a silver grey blouse. She caught Griff looking and smiled.

The service finished, and the grieving widow was escorted away by women Griff vaguely recognised as his aunts. They looked at him with solemn, accusing eyes as they passed, as though Carl's death had been his fault. Mother had never made it as an actress, but she was putting up a reasonable performance right now.

'It's time to go,' Griff said.

Dave looked at him. 'Right now?'

'Right now. Before anything else can go wrong.'

'Don't you think-'

'Nope.'

Dave drew his lips into a thin line.

'Well. Let's get your things together.'

'You can ditch most of my stuff. I won't be needing it.'

He started walking back along the path towards the gates. Dave hurried to keep up, and Griff noticed Mel trying to catch his eye again. He remembered his promise to her to say goodbye, and stopped. She looked at him, uncertain. He took a step towards her.

'I'm going now, Mel. You take care of yourself, you hear?'

'Going? What, can't you, I mean-'

She looked confused for a moment, then it turned to sadness.

'Don't cry, Mel.'

He wanted to add: you'll ruin your make-up, but it was a cold, unnecessary thing to say, something the old Griffin Park, below-average film director, would have said. He kept silent.

'I'll miss you,' she said.

'Me too,' he said, and was surprised to find that he meant it. Mel looked at him, and after a moment she smiled. Griff held out his hand, and she took it. He pulled her into a loose hug, and then he smiled and let her go.

185

'Bye.'

'Bye, Griff.'

He turned and walked quickly down the drive, Dave following.

Back at the car, Griff sat down carefully, still wary of his damaged side. Dave was looking at him.

'You're certain you want to do this? You think this Ellie girl is right for you?'

'No,' Griff looked out at the dispersing crowd. 'I know she is.'

They drove in silence back to Dave's apartment. Griff changed out of his charcoal grey suit and hung it up with his others. He wouldn't be needing them again. He packed a sports bag with a few items, and took his laptop.

'You can get rid of anything I've left,' he said.

'Maybe I should keep it, just in case.'

Griff shook his head.

'Sure you won't stay at least for tonight? It's been a hell of a day.'

Dave's dark eyes were sad. 'I'm hurting everyone again,' Griff thought, feeling a dull ache in his chest. 'Everything I do seems to hurt people.'

'Then we'd have to say goodbye all over again tomorrow. I have to go, Dave, I have to find Ellie and sort my life out.'

Dave looked down. 'What do you want me to do with the Lexus?'

'Keep it.'

Dave smiled. 'It's not my style.'

Griff smiled back. 'Well, trade it in for something else. Better still, buy a motor cycle. You ever ridden a motor cycle, Dave? They're a lot of fun.

'You're full of surprises. All right, let's go.'

They drove to LAX in silence. Griff looked out at his city as he left it, and an old poem came to mind. He smiled.

'What you thinking?'

Griff sighed.

'For always, night and day
I hear lake water lapping with low sounds to the shore
While I stand on the roadway, or on the pavements grey,
I hear it in the deep heart's core.'

'Is that a poem?'

Griff nodded.

When they arrived, Dave reached for the door handle.

'Wait,' Griff put his hand on Dave's arm.

'I'll take it from here,' he said. 'I hate long goodbyes.'

Dave tried a smile that didn't quite work.

'Listen, Dave, I'd like you to come out one day, maybe soon, if it all

186

works out.'

'What, to your lost island?'

Griff nodded. 'I'd like you to be my best man. Again.'

Dave shook his head. 'You sure have got it bad. I guess I could do that. Hell, I might even like it, want to stay myself.'

Griff chuckled. There was no chance of that happening.

'I'll keep in touch. I mean it.'

'You better.'

Dave leaned over and hugged him. The skin pulled tight around Griff's side and he grimaced at the sharp pain, but he didn't pull away.

As he walked towards the terminal, he heard Dave shouting after him:

I'll keep the suits. Just in case.' Griff raised a hand in farewell and walked into the airport.

He was waiting for the New York flight to board when his phone rang. He grabbed it, his eyes searching the display. The number was not one he recognised, and his heart began to pound as he wondered, yet again, if it could be her.

'Hello?'

'Mr Park? Hold please for Mr Hayter.'

Hayter? Griff looked up at the departures board. They were calling his flight. He didn't know anyone called Hayter. He felt a warning knell. This was something else contriving to keep him here. He reached for the end-call button, just as the voice appeared.

'Griffin Park?'

He lifted it reluctantly to his ear.

'Yes.'

'Hello Griff. It's James Hayter.'

James Hayter. The famous director. Now he knew. Hayter was up there in the same ranks as Coppola, Spielberg, Kubrick.

'Are you there?'

'Uh, yes,' he said.

'Well, sorry if I caught you at a bad time, but I'm trying to get a project off the ground, and wonder if you could help me.'

'Mr Hayter, I've pretty much given up on directing.'

A soft chuckle. 'I was kind of hoping to do that job myself. No, I wondered if you could help on the writing front. I've heard a lot of good things about your writing.'

Griff looked again at the departures board. Second call for New York was being announced. He felt his heart begin to race.

James Hayter wanted him to write for the film he was directing. It was like asking a struggling artist to help Leonardo da Vinci with his sketches.

'What's the film about?' he said. His heart was beating faster now.

Hayter began to lay down the plot and characters. It sounded good. Meaningful. A story of betrayal, cruelty, and ultimate redemption.

'So what do you think?'

Griff closed his eyes. He could almost see the road dividing in front of him. The road less travelled, he had told Ellie. He was standing there now, the decision hanging in the air like a thunder cloud.

'Griff?'

The last call for New York came over the PA. The phone felt like lead in his hand.

'Griff, can we set up a meeting?'

Griff looked across the airport concourse. At the departure point, they were closing the gate.

*

It didn't take long for the new girl's outburst to become known to all and sundry. Louise, her name was, and she was only twenty two.

'But that's no excuse,' Allie said, her perennial smile lost from sight.

'She's just a daft lass,' Tom replied. 'Anyway, Ellie doesn't seem to mind, do you?'

Ellie shook her head. They were in the Griffin again, and the discussion had moved on from the oil rig worker in Intensive Care to the new lab rat. Ellie had a full pint in front of her. She didn't dare touch it. Her emotions were too close to the surface, bubbling under like lava and alcohol would bring them blasting into the open. She looked up and saw Norrie watching her.

'You had enough last night? I know the feeling.'

He too was nursing an almost full pint. She smiled.

'I must be getting old. Can't hold my beer.'

'Hah. If you're getting old, what does that make me?'

She thought she heard her name mentioned, and glanced round. At the bar, a group of nurses looked away as she turned.

They're watching us! Oh we love the limelight!

Ellie felt her shoulders slump. She could almost taste the sympathy in the air. She thought back to what Norrie had said to her, why didn't she get the treatment? It couldn't be that bad, not after everything she'd already put up with. And hadn't she already thought about it, before she came here?

And why was it okay for her to make jokes about her scars, but not for anyone else to?

That's your problem, dear, not ours.

She ignored the sudden ache in her head. Norrie was still looking at her.

'It makes you about ripe for your trip round the world,' she said.

He grinned, shaking his head.

'It's about time I was leaving as well.'

'What? You only just got here!'

She hadn't even thought about leaving until the words were out. Now, it was as if the decision had been made long ago. She felt instantly better, and picked up her pint.

'Are you serious?'

She nodded. 'I'm not good at staying in one place for too long.'

Except for the eight months in Baranpay.

Bloody scars.

Anyway, let's get out of here. We don't like this talk about laser treatment.

'Don't go,' Norrie said. 'I'm serious. I think it would be good for you to stay, and anyway, you're the best tech I've had in years.'

She smiled. 'Thanks. I'm not just a pretty face.'

Norrie shook his head, but the line wasn't funny. Not any more.

She went back to her room early, and sat on the little bed looking at her laptop. She had still not checked her e-mails. She had been too busy with travelling, getting set up, working. It was denial, she knew, but the excuses helped.

But now perhaps she might take a look. She was alone now, and it didn't matter if her emotions spilled out. And she could think about Griff, and perhaps there'd be some e-mails from Jim and the gang, and they would remind her of better days. Of course, there might also be one from Griff, beginning: *Dear Ellie...*

She gritted her teeth, and switched the machine on. There was a commotion in the corridor, and a moment later her door flew open. Allie came hurrying in.

'What happened to you? I went to the bar and you'd gone?'

'Oh, I wasn't in the mood.'

Allie closed the door and came and sat on the bed.

'Norrie said you're thinking of leaving?'

She wished she'd had the foresight to lock her door.

'But why? Don't you like it here? It's not because of what that stupid girl said, is it?'

She shook her head. 'It's just, I don't stay places very long.'

'But why?'

'I don't know,' she said, looking away.

'Are you running away from something?'

'Oh, so now we're a psychologist?'

'No, I'm just concerned.'

189

'Well, you're probably right, but I'm still going.'

'Is this about the man?'

'What man?'

'The one you're eaten up about.'

Ellie looked at her, feeling suddenly faint. 'I am?'

'Of course. It's obvious. You love him, and it's breaking your heart.'

She gave an uneasy laugh. 'You make me sound like a sad Mills and Boon.'

'What was his name?'

Ellie looked down at the laptop. The blue Dell logo had come up, and the cursor was on the AOL icon, ready to connect.

'Griffin Park.'

'Sounds like a place.'

'He's American.'

'So what happened?'

Ellie looked at Allie. Her smile was still there, but it was sad now. The last thing she wanted to do was talk about this, but she couldn't hurt Allie's feelings. She winced as her headache grew suddenly worse.

'Not much,' she said, trying to be nonchalant. 'We had a good time together, then he had to go.'

'Oh come on, there's more to it than that!'

Ellie smiled. Wasn't there just.

'We met on Baranpay. It's a tiny island in the Highlands. We spent all summer together, then he got a call that his father was dying, and he had to go back to America.'

'And you never heard from him again?'

Ellie shook her head.

'But then, you left too, didn't you? You told me your last job was in Glasgow. How do you know he didn't go back there looking for you?'

Ellie sighed. 'Because that's not the way it works, Allie, not in real life.'

'You don't know that.'

She shrugged, feeling completely drained. She pressed the button to shut down the laptop. The e-mails would have to wait for another day.

'Did you at least call him?'

She shook her head again.

'But you do love him?'

More than the world, she thought, her heart pounding. 'Allie, I'm really tired, and unlike you, I'm working tomorrow. How about we continue this some other time.'

'All right,' she replied, standing up. Ellie heard the mattress groan in

190

relief.

'But continue it we will, ken?'

She just nodded. 'Whatever.'

As Allie was leaving, Cerys appeared at the door.

'Oh, I'm that glad I caught you both. Listen to this. I've had a great idea for a story.'

Ellie tried not to groan.

'Cerys, why don't you tell us tomorrow?' Allie said.

'No, I'll have forgotten by then. It won't take a moment, see, it's about this woman who wants to work on the oil rigs, so she pretends to be a man to get the job-'

Ye Gods, thought Ellie.

'Cerys, let's go,' Allie said, grabbing her by the elbow.

When Allie had gone, Ellie turned out the light and lay back on the bed. She hadn't closed the curtains, and the yellow streetlight outside was swaying in the wind. She listened to the usual sounds, nurses coming in from the pub, cars in the A&E car park below, the stereo playing in the room next door. Ellie had a sad, wry smile as she listened to the words:

On the trawled seabed of my heart
Nothing remains

THIRTY THREE

Griff was dreaming. Peter was chasing him through an abandoned tenement. He ran past men selling drugs and women exchanging them for sex, through pools of stagnant water, tripping over a young girl's legs. The girl was holding a cigarette lighter under a piece of foil. She looked up, and her eyes were black, without iris or cornea.

'They call it chasing the dragon,' Peter called, laughing. 'Just like I'm doing, chasing my brother, the dragon.'

'It's a griffin, not a dragon,' he shouted back. 'Not the same thing.'

He slammed through a door and was in Grand Central Station. Griff had never been there before, but it was familiar from all the movies that had used it. It was empty apart from a homeless man rifling through a garbage can. Griff looked behind him, but Peter was gone. He turned back, and his father was standing there, in his hospital gown.

'You didn't tell me,' he said.

There was a strange noise, someone speaking. The words seemed to come from a distance.

'Sir? Wake up, sir?'

He opened his eyes. The flight attendant was smiling at him.

'Sir, I need you to put your seat belt on. We're coming in to land.'

He looked out of the window at the patchwork brown and green of rural England.

The airplane circled, and he could make out a village with a church, a lake, the river winding away from it north and south. The sky was completely opaque, and a steady drizzle was falling.

'Ah, cheery England once more,' the passenger in the seat next to him said in a rueful English accent. Griff smiled.

'At least the rain makes everything green.'

'Well, there is that, I suppose.'

Griff had not spoken to the man previously. As soon as the plane had taken off he had fallen asleep. All the way from LA he had worked feverishly on the laptop. When Ellie hadn't answered his e-mails, they had changed from messages into diary notes, into tales of last summer. Now he had a whole raft of stories, all interconnected. And what's more, he knew it was good.

He had told James Hayter that he was leaving the country, and didn't know when he'd be back. Even before the words were out, he knew he was right. Hayter had been disappointed, but asked if he would keep writing. Griff had said he would and Hayter told him to keep him in mind for the future. And Griff had ran for the flight gate, elated that he was going back to Ellie, and that he still had hope for his career. If a man like Hayter would buy his writing, he didn't need to worry about making a living.

It would be a screenplay, he knew. It was a story now, but he could adapt it, and then he would do something he had never been able to do before: he would send it off into the world and wave it goodbye, like a grown up child that no longer needed him.

And he even had a title. He would call it: *The Road Less Travelled.*

'Are you vacationing?'

Griff shook his head. 'No, I'm moving to Scotland. I have to get yet another flight now.'

'Really? I often fly to Glasgow from Chicago, myself.'

Griff stared at him. 'You can fly from Chicago to Glasgow?'

The Englishman grinned in that condescending way Griff knew the English had off to a tee. 'I get the impression you left in a hurry.'

Griff ran his fingers through his hair. He felt grubby and needed a shower and a shave. And a haircut. By contrast the Englishman looked dapper, his lightweight suit barely creased. He was obviously a businessman and used to long-haul flights. Griff sighed. There were more important things right now than whether his hair was too long.

There were no more flights to Inverness from Gatwick that day. He had to take a train into London, and then get on the tube system to get to Heathrow. And he had not been prepared for the cold. It was late October, and the wind was bitter. There was a shop at the airport selling lambswool sweaters, and he bought a dark green one, thinking he could give it to Ellie later. It would match her eyes.

LA was eight hours behind. He was losing time even as he travelled. He thought about the Englishman telling him he could have flown to Scotland from Chicago. Like a fool, he'd simply got on the first flight going east, to New York, then London. If he'd just thought about it, he could have been in Scotland by now, but he dashed that thought away. He would still have had to get from Glasgow to Inverness. He remembered how basic the Highland airport was, and changed some currency before he got there. It was a long wait for the flight, and, tired out, he set the alarm on his mobile phone and tried to sleep. But it wouldn't come, and in the end he opened the laptop again and went back to his story.

He thought about his strange dream, and put it down to too much emotion over the last few days. Griff always tried to write his dreams down, never knowing when they might create a spark of a story. He looked up from the screen and gazed absently at the people walking past. He noticed a teenage boy screwing up his face in disgust, and followed the boy's gaze. A man was sitting in the second row opposite,

193

reading a newspaper. An ugly dark red birthmark was splashed diagonally across his face. Griff noticed that everyone who walked past stared at the man, either in fascination or horror, or disgust, and it filled him with a sudden fury. He stood up, and only then hesitated. What was he going to say: stop staring? The man had noticed him, and was giving him a curious look, quite unconcerned by the stares of others, and in that instant Griff remembered lying on the beach with Ellie, she telling him she couldn't go away with him, not because of what the stares would do to her, but what they would do to him. He sat down heavily, filled with a desperate aching need to see her, to hold her, and, yes, to keep her from those fascinated stares. He realised now how right she had been about him, about the world.

At long last the flight was called, and he walked out on what he hoped would be his last journey for a long time. He couldn't have been more wrong.

*

Saturday morning was quiet. Ellie and René were the only ones working, but there wasn't a vast amount to do. Plenty of time for Ellie to brood about things. She had intended to bring the laptop in and check her e-mails in the lab, but had chickened out at the last minute. She finished work at lunchtime, and decided to take a ride out on her bike. The freezing cold weather had moved off, and it was a clear crisp autumn day, the sun low in the sky, high torn clouds in a bright winter blue sky. She filled up with petrol and rode out over the Forth bridge and up into Fife.

And the scars were hidden behind her helmet, and had nothing to say.

The country up here was soft and fertile, and when the hills rose, they did so gently, as if a more benign geology had been at work. Ellie rode up into Perthshire, taking time to just roam. She followed the winding path of a river as it bustled along, tumbling over rocks, and stopped by a sudden cut in the land where the water fell a hundred feet into the valley below. She took off her helmet and felt the cold wind on her face. God, she loved this country. There was a standing joke that the Scots lamented about being far from their beloved home before they'd even left, and Ellie figured you had to actually be Scottish to understand that.

By the time she got back, it was already dark. She took off her leathers and showered, changing into jeans and a baggy shirt. She had two choices tonight: the Griffin or her lonely room, but the ride out had made her feel better. The mountains had a way of doing that. She

194

thought of the time she and Griff had lain on the dragon's mountain and looked for the stars.

Ah Griff. She had told Allie that miracles didn't happen in the real world. But then a handsome Hollywood film director meeting up with a disfigured lab technician wasn't real world stuff either. She decided to try the pub.

Cerys was there, with Gerry and the new girl. They seemed to be getting on very well, and Ellie stayed at the bar and left them alone. Cerys had her back to her, and Ellie didn't make any move to attract her attention.

'Hey Joseph. You're quiet tonight.'

The bar manager picked up a glass. 'Aye, it's early doors. Be busy later.'

She ordered a half-pint, a vague attempt at cutting down the alcohol intake.

'Hi Ellie.'

She looked round. Allie was there with an older couple, all of them dressed nicely. Ellie remembered: the trip to see Mama Mia. Then her heart skipped as she remembered something else – this was the famous Doc Savage, the saver of faces.

'This is my mum and dad: Liz and Graham.'

'Hello,' Ellie said, 'Happy birthday.'

'Och, Allie's told you. Tell you the truth, I try to forget them these days.' He smiled, and Ellie smiled back, keeping her right profile to him.

'So, I take it you do like Abba?'

Graham Savage laughed. 'Not really, but Allie does.'

'Dad!' Allie said.

'Well, I like them,' the woman said. Liz was in her fifties, with steel grey hair cut in a severe bob. She had a very round face and the haircut was all wrong for her.

'I'm sure you'll enjoy it. I hear it's very good.'

Graham paid for their drinks. 'Do you want to sit down?' he said, looking at Allie.

'I suppose so, but I must warn you about Cerys-'

Ellie grinned as they walked away.

'Will you not join us?' Liz said, looking back.

'Oh, I'll be fine. I'm sure you have lots to catch up on.'

She turned back to the bar before she could be persuaded over.

Joseph leaned over and winked.

'That's the man of bronze, you know.'

'The what?'

'Man of bronze. Doc Savage? Och, I suppose it's before your time.'

195

Ellie did know. It was one of the useless facts she'd accumulated over the years. The world's first superhero. She smiled to herself. Norrie arrived just then, and she signalled Joseph back.

'Just a quick half,' Norrie said. 'I'm on call, ken.'

Ellie paid for the drink, as Cerys finally spotted her.

'Oh hello Ellie. Sorry for butting in on you last night.'

Ellie shrugged. 'Did you remember your story this morning?'

'Yes I did! And I've written it already.'

'Cerys, what do you do with these stories?'

'I send them to magazines, like.'

'Have you had any published?'

'No,' she hesitated for an instant. 'But I'm sure it's only a matter of time.'

Ellie nodded. 'I'm sure you're right.'

Cerys went back to sit with Gerry and Louise, totally unaware that she was being a gooseberry. Norrie looked at the new girl.

'They've started called her 'Lousy', you know.'

Ellie frowned. 'I wish they wouldn't.'

Norrie shrugged, glancing over at Cerys, who was telling Louise another of her plot lines.

'There's nothing can dent Cerys's iron confidence, is there?'

Ellie nodded. 'I envy her that.'

Norrie was about to speak, when Graham Savage appeared. His wife and daughter had gone off to the toilet, leaving him hanging about.

'We're off then, to see this allegedly wonderful show.'

'Oh aye, Mama Mia,' Norrie said.

Ellie sniggered. 'It'll be better than you expect, you'll see.'

The doctor looked over her shoulder and smiled absently as he saw Allie waving.

'I'd better go. Ellie, is it?'

She nodded. 'That's me.'

He chuckled.

'You might want to come and see me sometime? I think I could do something for you.'

Ellie felt the scars roaring in outrage. The rest of her face grew red in sympathy.

'Is that a proposition?' she said hurriedly.

Graham laughed outright this time. 'Sorry, I could have phrased that better -yes, I'm coming dear – I'll be seeing you.'

He left, and Ellie and Norrie looked at each other in an awkward silence for a moment.

'Do you think Allie asked him here for that?'

'I don't know,' Ellie said. 'If so, it's kind of her, but I wish she wouldn't bother.'

Norrie finished his drink.

'I better go.'

'Hmm. Me too.'

But instead, she stayed and had another drink with her scars. And poor company they were too, hiding in the dark from the man of bronze.

Later she returned home, but couldn't face her lonely room. She went to the deserted TV lounge. On Saturday night, everyone who wasn't working was partying. The lounge was a big room with a mish-mash of furniture, none of which matched. There was a TV and an old video machine, no DVD. In the corner was a PC, switched on with the geometric shape screensaver going. Ellie chose the lumpy blood-red sofa nearest the TV and switched on. She flicked around for a few minutes, eventually stopping on a film from a few years ago. It was strangely recognisable, although she couldn't remember having seen it. The actors had been unknown when the film was made, and the two female leads had gone on to brighter and better things.

It was a story about two women fighting over one man, but the twist was that both women were dead. One of them had become a dark angel, and wanted the man dead so he could be with her, while the other did everything she could to keep him safe. The film was sentimental, but still worked, like ET. Ellie found herself caught up in it. In the end, the good angel saved the man from death, knowing they would still be parted. She told him she would wait for him, and he told her he loved her.

'I don't love you,' the angel replied. 'You're part of me. You don't love bits of yourself, they just are.'

Ellie felt as if the walls were closing in on her. In an instant she was back in the cottage, with the mist rising from the sea, the terns crying above. And she was telling Griff that very thing, and he was looking at her with a fervour in his eyes that she didn't understand. The tears came in a sudden, sobbing flood, and she was powerless to stop them. Instead she just let them come as the film ended with the man looking up in the dark, sunlit-shot forest, as above him there was the rustling of wings.

The credits rolled, and she flicked the TV off, not wanting to see his name, folding her arms over her stomach for the little comfort that gave.

You're part of me, she'd said, and she had meant it. She still did. He had stormed into her life like a tornado, and when he had gone everything was twisted round. And she knew now why he'd been filled

197

with emotion; because she'd reminded him of his real life in LA, with all the rich and famous people, the beautiful wife he'd said was divorcing him. And in Griff's film, his love was lost to him.

And she reached up and touched her scars, and felt bitterness course through her veins like sour wine.

THIRTY FOUR

If London had been cold, Inverness was the arctic.

Griff walked across the tarmac to the hangar, bent over against the wind. It had been a close thing. The pilot had been reluctant to set down, and in the end the landing had been hair-raising. One of the other passengers had actually screamed at a particularly rough bounce. The landing hadn't bothered him, but diverting to another airport would have been a different story.

He collected his bag and looked for the car rental outlets. There was a Hertz and an Avis, but neither would let him have a one-way option to Ullapool, and he cursed under his breath. After Ullapool, the next stop was Baranpay island, and he wouldn't need a car there. He looked around the airport, which was effectively a big shed, and had decided to take a taxi into the city and find a car hire place there, when a man dressed in a kilt came up to him. He was carrying a card with the name 'Richardson' on it.

'Hullo,' he said cheerily. 'I heard you trying to hire a car. I'm with Moray Rentals. I'm pretty sure my boss would let you have a car that you can leave at the ferry.'

Griff reached out and shook the man's hand. 'Thank you,' he said.

'Och, not at all,' the man grinned. 'I'll just pick up my customer, and we'll be off.'

Richardson turned out to be the elderly woman who had screamed on the plane, and she didn't seem to have recovered yet.

'Are you all right, hen?' the man asked her.

She nodded uncertainly, stepping into the Moray Rentals mini bus. She gave Griff a nervous smile, and he wondered how she'd fare driving on the hair-raising highland roads. The driver whistled cheerily as he climbed in, paying no heed to the freezing weather despite his kilt and open-necked shirt. The wind was getting worse, and as they left the airport Griff could just see the windsock standing straight out in the fading light. If they had been half an hour later, the pilot wouldn't have landed.

Inverness airport has a feature unique to British airports, that it is reached down an unmade single track road with passing places. They bounced down this pitted track, and the driver put on his radio. An accordion band was playing a lively tune, and Griff felt a warm glow begin in the pit of his stomach. He was almost there.

The rental firm was actually the back office of a used car dealership. Griff was introduced to Sammy Vine, the man in charge. He was one of those men who needed to shave three times a day, and his perpetual stubble had worn through the collar of his shirt. He was about thirty, with an easy smile and, despite his young age, deep wrinkles round his eyes.

'You want tae leave it at Ullapool? You'll be going on the ferry then?'

Griff nodded. 'To Baranpay.'

'Baranpay? Och, my sister's husband's auntie lives there, do you know her? Ginty MacPhail?'

Griff smiled. 'Sorry, I don't.'

'Aye well, if you see her, tell her I was asking for her. Now let's see what we've got.'

In the end Griff was given a ten year old Ford Fiesta, a tiny car by US standards. He had to squeeze himself into it, and had a pang of misgiving.

'Are you sure this'll make it?'

'What, to Ullapool? It's only a few miles.'

At least eighty, Griff reckoned, but he said nothing.

'Just you leave it in the harbour car park, I'll send Wullie to fetch it when he gets round to it.'

Griff nodded and thanked the man, then drove off towards the Moray Bridge. The wind buffeted the light little car, and he felt a pang of regret for his lost Lexus. It took him a while to find the bridge road, but at last he could see the pillars of the beautiful bridge off to his left, and there, finally, was the signpost. That was where his heart sank. The wind was too strong. The bridge was closed.

'Shit!' he said. He had to turn round at the traffic island and head back into the city. He found the car radio and twiddled with it until he found a weather report.

'-gale force six off the western isles. The wind is likely to veer south over the next twelve hours, and the following pressure system –'

Twelve hours! Griff let out a groan. He pulled to the side of the road and got a map from his bag, searching for another way north. There was a way around the Moray Firth, a twenty one mile detour, but it was that or wait in an Inverness hotel until the wind died. Twenty one miles. Sammy would think that was a short hop. He drove out and hunted for the road.

He drove through the darkness, almost alone on the road. The car bounced around in the wind, making him glad of the lack of traffic. Despite his detour, he knew perfectly well that the chances of the ferry running were non existent, but the thought of coming so close just to sit and do nothing was unacceptable. The road rose steadily, passing through tiny villages until it reached a bare plateau between the mountains, and there the wind came at the car head on. The little car struggled on valiantly, and Griff gritted his teeth and kept his foot to the floor. The radio died, the signal blocked by the mountains, and he felt as if he had entered some strange limbo, no sound but the wind, nothing to see but the empty road ahead. The Scottish twilight zone.

At last the bleak terrain gave way to a softer landscape, and by the time he reached the turn for Gairloch, trees surrounded the road, providing a little shelter. Griff reached Ullapool just after ten o'clock, and drove around looking for a hotel.

Ullapool was the departure point for the ferry to the Hebrides. Smaller ferries ran to the other islands, and in the summer the little town was filled with people. There was a harbour-front row of shops selling tartan nonsense: shortbread and postcards and cuddly loch Ness monsters, and there were lively pubs and restaurants with live music playing. Small boats took tourists dolphin watching, and the harbour was filled with yachts and brightly coloured fishing boats. There was a steady stream of people coming and going, and the air was filled with noisy banter and laughter.

In the winter, it was shut.

Griff stayed at a small pub on the sea front. The landlord was surprised to see a tourist this late in the year, and he left Griff in the bar while he went to sort out accommodation. Griff looked round at the only two other customers: an old man and his dog.

'Evenin'' the man said. He had white hair and a fisherman's face, as lined as the nets.

'It's blowin' a bit.'

'It is that.'

'You come far?'

Griff smiled.

'Inverness.'

'Ah.'

He laid his hand gently on the dog's head, and Griff saw the black labrador's tail swishing the carpet at the old man's touch.

'What do you think?' Griff said. 'How long will this weather last?'

The old man drew in his breath.

'They're saying another day, but I think it'll have blown itself out by morning.'

The landlord returned.

'Now then, I have a small room that might do, if you like?'

'Absolutely. Thank you.'

'Och, not at all. I'll take your bag, then you can have a dram and I'll fetch you something to eat.'

Griff couldn't remember the last time he'd eaten. He was suddenly starving. The landlord's wife served him shepherd's pie, and he drank

201

whisky with the couple and the old man, while they quizzed him about his journey.

'This is really good of you. I mean, me turning up at nearly closing time-'

'Think nothing of it,' the landlord said. His name was Tommy.

'We can't have you starving to death, now,' said Elaine, his wife.

'So where did you say you came from?'

'Los Angeles.'

'That's in America?' the old man said. Griff had not yet discovered his name.

'Never mind old Peter,' Tommy said, 'He's not as daft as he makes out.'

'We don't get many tourists this late,' Elaine said. 'It's nice to have the company.'

'Thanks a lot!' Tommy said.

They laughed, and Griff bought everyone another drink. He was starting to feel warm again, which was partly down to the alcohol, but also because of the friendly people. After a moment of silence, old Peter spoke again.

'You're going to Baranpay, aren't you?'

Griff raised an eyebrow. 'How did you know that?'

'My son told me there was an American on the island in the summer. I'm thinkin' that was you.'

Griff nodded.

'Aye, Donnie said you had to go, but he knew you'd be back.'

'Donnie? Donnie MacLeod?'

'That's his name, yes.'

Griff felt something warm curl up in his chest.

'Peter here lives in the residential home,' Tommy said.

'With his lady friend,' Elaine added.

'Ach, away wi' ye, lady friend!'

But he was grinning all the same.

Griff felt his eyelids dropping suddenly.

'The man's exhausted,' Elaine said, standing up. 'Come on and let him get to bed.'

'Aye, I'll take you back, Peter.'

'Och, I'll be fine.'

'You will not. You'll be over the harbour wall in this wind, and then what'd happen to Cahal here?'

The dog's tail wagged again at the sound of his name. It was only when the old man stood up that Griff saw the dog's harness and realised Peter was blind.

He climbed the stairs and fell into bed in the little room, feeling happy and hopeful. Tomorrow he would reach the island, and everything would be all right. After all, what else could go wrong?

THIRTY FIVE

December came, and the staff notice boards and the hospital website were full of posters for upcoming parties. Even the pub had stepped up a gear. Last night there had been a Karaoke, at which Cerys and Allie finally had to be asked to sit down and shut up. There was a horse racing night planned, and live bands, even an Ann Summers party in the snug. Ellie watched it all happening and felt nothing.

There were some things Ellie just knew instinctively. For example, she knew that working around pain and death all day gave the hospital staff the urge to enjoy life to the full.

And she knew that there was no way she would ever love anyone the way she loved Griff. *Tae a' the seas gang dry*, as they say. All her friends had noticed the sudden change in her, and yet she was unable to do anything about it. It was getting harder and harder to smile, never mind crack jokes. Christmas was going to be a nightmare.

And so the job on the website was a Godsend. She had heard one of the lab techs from Haematology talking about it.

'Switzerland,' she was saying. 'Christmas in the Alps. Fantastic!'

'Yeah, and I bet they pay well too.' Touch of bitterness there. 'I'd go like a shot if I'd passed my exams.'

So she had looked it up on the TV lounge computer. It was an exchange trip, from University Hospital Geneva. They would send one of their techs and a Scottish tech would go there, ostensibly to compare methods, technology, techniques. They wanted applications on-line, and Ellie did it there and then. It was perfect. It would get her somewhere no one knew her in time for the worst part of the year, and she needn't feel guilty about leaving Norrie without a tech.

So long as she got the job. But she felt confident. After all, who else would want to be in a strange country over Christmas? Not the people with families.

She had never enjoyed Christmas. At least not since she was a very small child. They were always miserable affairs with people pretending to be having a good time, all the time feeling utterly miserable. It was a time that reminded you of all you didn't have.

Word came through two days later. As expected, Ellie had been the only applicant. Norrie called her into his room that morning.

Ellie sat down. She was not long out of bed, and still half asleep. 'What's up?'

'I've been asked to give you a reference.'

He held up a sheet of paper. Ellie sat up straight.

'For the Geneva job?'

He nodded. 'Ellie, why are you doing this? You'd be better staying here.'

'But you'll get someone to replace me-'

'That isn't the point.'

She sighed. 'Norrie, It'll be great. Haven't you heard everyone else talking about it? Christmas in the Alps, and so on.'

He looked at her. 'And you can ski, can you?'

'Well, no. But I can learn. And there's all that apres ski. They serve beer in tankards with lids so you can't spill it-'

'That's Germany.'

'Oh. Well, I'm sure they have something similar.'

'It's Switzerland. You know what they're famous for? Cuckoo clocks.'

'And chocolate.'

He nodded. 'Chocolate, granted. And you won't know anyone there.'

Ellie's heart was beating faster now. She was determined to get the trip.

'So the person who'll come here in my place, you lot won't take them to the pub, get them involved?'

'Of course, but-'

'The techs in Geneva will be just the same.'

Norrie sighed. 'You're determined to go through with this.'

'Are you going to give me the reference?'

He put the paper down on the desk and looked at it.

'On one condition.'

'What?'

'That you come back here afterwards.'

Ellie looked at him. She had no intention of lying to him.

'Deal.'

He looked hard at her, checking for deception, but after a moment he looked away.

'You can go now.'

'Gee, thanks.'

Ellie wandered through to the reception counter, where a porter had left the morning's samples. Sorting them was Malky's job, but he hadn't arrived yet, and with a sigh she pulled up a stool and began to look through the various bags. She looked up at the sound of footsteps and saw a teenager in a blue porter's coat that was too big for him.

'Hullo,' she said.

'I've come from Microbiology,' he said nervously. No more than sixteen, she thought. Straight from school, first job. She knew what

205

was coming.

'What can I do for you?'

He swallowed, uncertain. Ellie gave him a reassuring smile.

'I've to take back a fallopian tube.'

Ellie didn't change expression. She nodded seriously, then rolled the stool over to the door.

'Hey Gerry, you there?'

'Yeah. What?'

Gerry sauntered over, a contented grin on his face. Things were obviously going well with Louise.

'Micro' have sent this chap here over for a fallopian tube.'

Gerry put his hand to his chin and shook his head. 'Tch, tch. I don't know,' he said.

'They can be dangerous. Have you handled one before?'

The new porter shook his head violently. His eyes had widened at the word 'dangerous'.

'Well. I'll let you have one, but you'll have to be careful. Wait there.'

He walked out of reception and Ellie followed him into the fume room, where they both cracked up.

'That's a new one, a fallopian tube! I wonder who thought that up?'

'What can we give him?'

Gerry looked round the room at the bottles of reagents.

'You fetch a glass burette. We'll fill it with copper sulphate. That ought to look impressive.'

It took a couple of minutes to funnel the dark blue crystals into the long, thin tube. It did look impressive.

'Ready?' Ellie said.

Gerry nodded, and wiped the grin off his face. He lifted the tube in both hands, holding it in front of him carefully, as if it were a tray loaded with drinks. The boy was still at the reception counter.

'Here you are,' Gerry said, and he very gently handed the glass tube over. The boy took it, staring at it as if it might explode.

'Now you walk slowly, and hold it very gently. Any rough movement and it could combust.'

The boy looked up, terrified.

'Keep away from other people, and if you see any doctors coming, tell them they're to keep back, because you've got a fallopian tube.'

The new porter nodded, and turned achingly slowly.

'I'll get the door for you,' Ellie said. Gerry nodded and hurried back into the lab, no doubt to tell the others. She watched the poor lad walk at a funereal pace across the path and towards the main drive of the hospital. She saw faces appearing at windows as the joke went round the hospital, and shook her head. It was funny, it really was.

So why wasn't she laughing?

*

Old Peter had been right.

By the time Griff got out of bed and looked out of the tiny window, he could see the clouds sweeping fast across a pale blue sky. He could still hear the wind, but it was no longer the storm it had been. He was elated. He pulled out his phone and tried Ellie one more time, in case being this close might somehow make her answer, but there was still nothing but a lonely ringtone on the other end.

Elaine laid on a huge breakfast for him, but he felt too wound up to eat, so instead she made him up a pack of sandwiches to take with him. Griff said goodbye and drove the
car down to the harbour.

He had to find the ferry from memory, as there were no signs indicating it. Two men were loading items from the back of a pickup. Among them were a pair of large glass doors.

'Hi,' he said.

'I need to get to Baranpay. Is Cameron around?'

The youngest man shook his head. 'He's gone down to see his sister in England. But Scott here's taking the boat over.'

Scott nodded. 'Aye I can take ye, once we're loaded.'

He had the typical fisherman's wiry build and wind-tanned skin. He smiled at Griff as if they were old friends.

'Can I help?' Griff offered, and then spent the next hour loading boxes and beer barrels.

'I've not been able to get over for two days. The wind's been that strong,' Scott said.

'Do you live on the island?' Griff asked, lugging a case of beer.

'Och no. I'm Ullapool born and bred. It's a wee bit remote for me out there.'

They were ready to leave by ten o'clock, by which time Griff was sweating. However it was a different story out on the loch, with the wind still sweeping south, and Griff in nothing but a shirt and sweater. Scott found him a set of oilskins, but it was still bitterly cold.

Still, it was a far more hopeful journey than the last ferry trip. The boat came out of the estuary and turned north, and minutes later there it was, a dark smudge, exactly like a sleeping dragon, with the tiny westernmost island sticking up like the tip of its nose. He felt his blood quicken at the sight. He was going home.

The boat approached the harbour from the eastern side, where the water was gentler and the rocks less hazardous. He stood on the deck

207

and watched Jim's house come into view, with Mairearadh's donkeys down on the beach, watching him. Then round the wingtip with its warning buoy and into the sheltered harbour. There were no boats; everyone was making the most of the break in the weather, and no people around except two men Griff didn't know. Scott shouted to them, and they caught the boat ropes and tied up. Griff grabbed his bag and leapt on to the harbour, shouting a 'thank you' to the boatman.

He was running by the time he hit the cliff road. The northerly wind was behind him now, pushing him along, and he kept going until he could see the little white house at the mountain's foot. The door was closed, but then, it was not a day for open doors.

He hesitated. He had been desperately anticipating this moment for so long. He smiled to himself, took a deep breath, and knocked.

There was no reply, so he tried again. Still nothing. He walked to the cliff edge, perhaps she was down on the beach. He felt a sharp tug inside himself as he saw the rocks where they had first met, but there was no sign of her. The rowing boat had been pulled tighter up the beach. The cliffs were quiet.

He dropped his bag, feelings of dread now rushing in. He reached into his pocket for his phone. She had never answered any of his other calls, why would she answer this one? But it was worth a try.

The wind was whipping the grass, roaring in his ears. He listened to the ringing tone. There was no reply.

Then he heard it.

There was a phone ringing. He looked back at the house, started to run. He reached the door. Yes, the sound was coming from inside. Relief flooded him. She must be in the shower or something. He knocked again, and this time reached down and lifted the latch. The ringing got louder as he opened the door. He walked in, slowly.

The room was clean and bare. There were no papers, no jackets, no empty coffee cups.
No muddy boots. No washing up. Nothing.

Except the phone, alone on the windowsill, forlornly ringing, and the amber pendant abandoned on the table.

He clicked the stop button and the sound died. He didn't need to check the bedroom to know that no one lived here anymore. The wind banged the front door against the wall, then came rushing in behind it. Griff felt colder now than he had on the boat over. Ellie was gone. He picked up the necklace and stared at it.

'Griff? Is that you?'

He looked round. Jim was silhouetted in the open door. He pulled it shut behind him and came in.

'Hello, Jim.'

Jim was dressed properly in layers, with a heavy fleece on top, and a woolly hat. He looked sad, and Griff could barely meet his eyes.

'I couldn't convince her,' Jim said quietly.

'When did she go?'

'Not long after you did.'

'It's all my fault. I should never have left.'

'Griff, come on. Let's go down to my house. We can talk there.'

Griff looked round the empty cottage, and the memories looked back at him. There was the couch where they'd fallen over one night, both of them too involved in each other's lips and skin to notice. There was the little table where she'd joked that he was the best cook on the little island. There was –

'Griff?'

'Yeah.'

He followed Jim out to his Land Rover, closing the door behind him.

THIRTY SIX

The thing about Switzerland, Ellie thought, as she sat looking round the Irish bar, was that there were hardly any Swiss. There were British and French and German, and loads of Americans with their heart-stopping accents, but very few natives. The bar was packed out like a United Nations convention, but there was none of the raw edge found in Scottish pubs. Everything, even the shouting, was very civilised.

'I want to know what you're thinking. I can tell it's not good.'

She looked up. Guillaume was grinning.

'What makes you say that?'

'I can just tell. I am good at that sort of thing.'

She grinned back. 'I was just thinking how nice everyone is. No one's drunk, or fighting and swearing.'

'Ah. Yes. The Genevois are very – what is the word?'

'Repressed? Anal retentive?'

He laughed.

'Exactemente?' she offered.

'Oh please, Ellie,' he shook his head. 'Don't speak French. My language, you torture it.'

'Thanks a lot.'

Guillaume smiled, and it was a killer smile. He was dark, very French, black hair and eyes, wide mouth, angular features, seriously handsome. He was also very short, barely taller than Ellie's five foot three. In less charitable moments she wondered if that was why they had hit it off: both of them different. They had met on her first day, when he explained that he was nearly the one to exchange for her, but he changed his mind at the last minute. When she asked why, he simply shrugged.

And the job. Well it wasn't much of one. Basically she had visited all the labs in the hospital and discovered that Scotland wasn't quite as backward as everyone thought. Much of the equipment used was exactly the same, and they even had some analysers that Ellie remembered from her very first job, years ago. The techs were nice, very serious people. Ellie knew she could never tell them about poor Malky's nightmare with the homogeniser.

But Guillaume was friendly, seemingly glad of her company. He had given her the sympathetic look when they had met, and Ellie had waited to see the next reaction. It was a smile, and she couldn't see anything behind it. She had been confused at first, unable to read whether he was interested in her romantically, or whether he just needed a friend. Now she was pretty sure it was the latter, and that was fine with Ellie.

No point it all ending in tears again, hmm?

She told the scars to shut up and finished her drink.

'How come your English is so good?' she asked.

'My mother is English. I grew up speaking two languages. Another?'

She nodded, and he got up to fetch the drinks. She looked around the bar, which was decorated in faux American-Irish, lots of false beams, barrels, and sawdust on the floor, about as authentic as a movie set.

'Damn,' she thought, as the reminder hit home. 'Where are you now, Griff?' she wondered. The part of him he had left behind knotted inside her, She found herself looking inwards at the damaged place, much as a crash survivor might look at the wreck of his car. There was nothing to be done.

'Ellie? Are you all right?'

She blinked and smiled. 'Sure, Gui. I was miles away there for a minute.'

'What is this 'gooey' you keep calling me?'

He was smiling.

'Shut up. You like it really,' she said, picking up the drink.

*

At the weekend, Ellie did the tourist thing, which she did in every new town. What was great about this one was that it was cold, and the trend this season was for Sherlock Holmes hats, the ones with the cheek pieces. Everyone seemed to be wearing one, and hers covered the scars nicely.

You can hide us, but we're still here.

'Who cares?' Ellie said, 'out of sight out of mind.'

But she knew that wasn't true.

She bought a map and went to see the jet d'eau, which she thought was disappointing although her fellow tourists oo-ed and ahh-ed at the enormous plume of water. All in all, it was still just a big fountain. Ellie chided herself for being cynical.

Geneva was truly beautiful though, flanked on one side by the Jura mountains and on the other by the Savoy Alps. She looked at those mountains and felt a familiar pang inside. She would have to go up there. She was beginning to accept that Baranpay had been the best time of her life to date. She did not believe in going back, but she knew now that no city would ever have the appeal for her that the wild places had.

She took the map back to her hotel. The St Victor was a step back in

211

time, with its wooden floors and chandeliers. Her room was small, but neat, with a wash-hand basin against one wall, and a view from the window of a building with gold minarets. The concierge had told her it was the Russian Church, and she had taken a walk to look at it. The Church was made of white stone. Delicately carved arches led into the dark interior. It was romantic and beautiful, out of place in the commercial city. Ellie had walked down narrow cobbled streets where shuttered houses towered above her, through medieval market places and past gothic churches, but this little church was different. Ellie could not remember the last time she had been inside a church. Probably Fiona's wedding.

She glanced at the brittle winter sun gleaming on the gold domes before turning back to her map. She had decided to go up into the mountains the next day, and was trying unsuccessfully to decipher the French when the telephone rang in her room.

She answered it and the concierge said she had a visitor. Ellie's heart took a leap.

You really enjoy setting yourself up for a disappointment, don't you?

'Shut up!' she hissed.

'Pardon?'

'Oh, sorry, I don't- I'll come down.'

She tried to walk nonchalantly down the stairs. After all, the scars were right. What was she expecting, Griff to have traced her here and followed her? Griff was in LA, enjoying his jet set lifestyle. He had probably forgotten all about her by now.

'Hello, Ellie.'

'Gui. What, are you bored?'

He laughed. 'Not I, but I thought you might be? Would you like to have a drink, maybe?'

Ellie smiled as her heart decelerated.

'Sure, why not. Wait. I'll bring my map. You can help me with the French.'

They went to a café in the Rue Vautier, which was packed with drinkers sitting on long carved wooden benches. There wasn't enough room inside, and people had spilled onto the street. But it was more homely and pub-like than the Irish bar Guillaume had taken her to before. They grabbed a seat as a group got up to leave, and Ellie spread her map out to show him where she wanted to go.

'Ah. From that ridge you can see all the way to Mont Blanc.'

'Really? Great.'

'But there will be much snow. Can you ski?'

'Of course not.'

He grinned. 'But you are Scottish. There are many mountains in

Scotland.'

'I was born in the city, Gui. Not many mountains there.'

He shrugged, and she got up to fetch more drinks. One of these days soon, she told herself, I'm going to quit drinking.

Yeah. Like that's going to happen.'

When she got back, Guilllaume was trying to fold the map and finding it difficult, as she had folded it awkwardly earlier when she was doing her sight-seeing. She smiled.

'Sorry. I was being a tourist earlier.'

'Where did you go?'

She reeled off the usual attractions, finishing with the little church.

'The Russian Orthodox. It is strange, no?'

She nodded. 'Very. I liked it though.'

'You are religious?'

'No.'

'Of course. You are a scientist.'

She gave him a curious look. 'What does that mean?'

He held his hands out as if it were self explanatory. 'Scientists know the universe does not need a God to make it exist.'

'Just because a God is not required, does not mean there isn't one anyway.'

He leaned his head on one side. Looking down at the pitted wooden table.

'Where I live, in Meyrin, it is near CERN. Do you know what that is?'

'Of course. The underground accelerator. The place the internet was invented.'

'Oui. And you can go inside and look around.'

Ellie was intrigued. 'Have you been?'

He nodded.

'I have stood inside the tunnel. The place where they send the particles down to collide with others and create still more. The place where space and time and matter and energy are broken down and re-created, and yet they are the same as we are. They are what we are.'

Ellie said nothing. Guillaume smiled again.

'I stood there and felt what the devout feel when they believe they are close to their God.'

She waited while he relived the moment. His face was full of joy.

'You see, there is no such thing as a religious experience. There are only human experiences.'

She nodded then. 'And you live there? Near the accelerator?'

'Oui. I have stood in the field while matter and energy are interchanged beneath my feet.'

She chuckled. 'That must be something.'

213

He smiled again, but it was back to normal now.

'So what of your experiences, Ellie?'

She looked up, wary. 'What about them?'

'I sense that you are very sad.'

She sighed, and reached for her drink. Guillaume put his hand on top of hers.

'You want to talk about things? Talk to me. Anytime. I will take you to the place where everything can be changed. I will take you to sit on top of the universe.'

He grinned, and Ellie found herself grinning back.

'Deal,' she said. 'Now change the subject.'

He held his hands up in front of himself, 'ça va,' he said, laughing.

'I hope that means: 'more beer', Ellie replied.

*

Griff looked out at a sky the colour of dry sand. Dove grey and purple clouds streaked across it like horsetails, their edges turned pale gold by the setting sun.

He had never forgotten the sunsets here. Every night he'd watched the LA sky turn to fiery splendour, he'd thought of here. Jim was looking at him, but he waited until the sun had finally left the sky, the light turned off behind the clouds, before turning to him.

'Here.'

Griff took the whisky and sipped it, but it tasted wrong. He knew that was nothing to do with the drink. Everything was wrong. Ellie was gone.

'What happened?'

Jim sat down and looked at the fire burning in the stove.

'When you left, she didn't think you'd ever be back.'

Griff told him about the frozen bank accounts, his mistake over the disrupted phone. In frustration he got to his feet and walked over to the fireplace, looking at his reflection in the mirror above.

'I phoned the pub. I spoke to Murd. It was his birthday.'

Jim frowned. 'Did he not tell you she had gone? That was the day she left.'

Griff recalled the memory. What was it Murd had said: *och, she's away.*

He closed his eyes, then took a deep breath and turned back to Jim.

'I have to find her. Where did she go?'

Jim looked at him sadly.

'Griff, she said Glasgow, but I don't know. She won't get in touch

214

with us either.'

He sat down again, and looked out at the darkening sky.

'This is my fault. I never should have gone. But I don't understand. How can it have all gone so wrong? We were happy, both of us. We didn't -'

He realised he was rambling and shut up.

Jim leaned forward.

'Griff, did Ellie ever tell you about her past?'

'Bits of it. We didn't talk about the past much.'

He looked up. 'Is this about her face? About her scars? Because I don't-'

'Partly,' Jim interrupted. 'But there's a lot more to it than that. Ellie never learned to trust, Griff. No one ever told her the truth.'

Griff picked up the glass and drank the whisky. It burned a trail down his throat, snapped him awake.

'Ellie adored her father, but he walked out on her when she was nine,' Jim said.

Griff simply listened while Jim told him the story of her life, all the broken promises, all the let-downs, all the lies. He felt something deep inside tear itself into pieces. He should have known this. He never should have left.

And he thought again about her strength. He wondered if he would have made it through all those slaps in the face. And he realised that while he had not talked about his life simply because it was a problem he didn't want to address, she had not talked about her past for a deeper reason. Her silence was her self defence.

'What are you thinking?' Jim asked. Griff looked up. The sky was dark now, and there was nothing to see but the slowly turning light of the warning buoy on wingtip point.

'I'm thinking about why she never told me these things,' he said. 'She couldn't tell me, could she?'

Jim nodded. 'Ellie thinks that if she bares her soul, she will lose herself. She believes she would be destroyed. So she chooses to ignore her demons. But not confronting them does not make them go away.'

He watched the tiny light flashing in the dark, alone and brave.

'I have to find her,' he said.

'It won't be easy. I managed to work out that since she lost her job as a rep, she's moved about every few months. Staying on the island was the longest she'd spent in one place for a long time.'

'Nevertheless,' Griff said, swallowing hard. 'I found her once, I'll find her again.'

Jim simply nodded. 'I'll help you all I can.'

215

They both looked up as Mairearadh opened the door.

'Come and eat,' she said. 'Both of you.'

Griff smiled, but it didn't make it to his eyes. 'Thanks, Mairearadh, but I'm really not hung-

'You have to keep your strength up,' she said, looking fixedly at him until at last Griff relented.

*

Next morning was bright and brittle, the sky the clear pale blue of tropical seas. The wind was bitter, and Griff had borrowed one of Jim's coats as he walked up the mountain path. He had taken the long way, round the eastern side of the island, so as to avoid the harbour, and having to speak to people he knew. It occurred to him that this was how Ellie must feel all the time, wanting to avoid embarrassing encounters. The wind strafed his nose and throat as he climbed, tugging at his hair and reminding him that it needed cutting, and his feet sank up to the ankles in the boggy ground. He made it at last to the top, and stood looking at the mica shining in the black rocks, like hidden gems.

There was only one ferry per day in winter, and he had missed it. When he realised this, Griff had thought about asking one of the fishermen to take him to the mainland, but they were all out already, and he felt bad about asking them to make another trip after a long day's work. So he stood on the mountain top and looked out at the rough waves, and thought hard about the last few months, and what it all meant. And he searched his heart for doubt, for any suspicion that everything he had done since spring was just madness, a crazy idea whose time had passed. He decided that it was not. He walked past the waterfall, past the place where he and Ellie had lain and made love, and watched the clouds, and just touched, and he remembered what she had said to him:

I suppose you'll be going soon.

And he had. But he was back now, and he would find her, and bring her here. Bring her home. He took the path down the mountain that led to the cottage, to the secret wood, and he wondered now, why she had shown him that place. Was it because she knew he would leave, or was it that she was beginning to open up to him, to share all her secrets. He gritted his teeth.

There was the usual 'stranger in town' silence as he entered the pub, but as his eyes grew accustomed to the gloom, he heard his name called, and someone tapped his shoulder.

'Oh. So you're back then,' Murd said, in his cheery way.

'Griff! About time, man. Where've ye been?'

Archie grabbed his hand and pumped it, smiling in apparent delight at seeing him.

'Hello Arch-'

'No helicopter this time?' Roy said, grinning.

'Not this time,' Griff said. He felt a sudden pang of annoyance. He could have hired one, and have been here sooner. But then, he had not thought he'd be in need of one to get off the island again. He thought he was here to stay.

'Well, you'd best have a drink, now you're here.'

He looked up and saw Donnie looking sadly at him.

'For I doubt you'll be staying long, hmm?'

Griff nodded. 'I'll be back though.'

Donnie smiled.

'Well, don't come back alone, will you?'

THIRTY SEVEN

Glasgow was filled with Christmas shoppers, and Griff ducked into the side streets to avoid the crowds. He checked in at the Moat House Hotel and asked them for a phone book. He had both his own and Ellie's phone in his pocket, and he was going to work them both hard.

He had hitched a ride with Donnie when the boat next went out, not wanting to wait for the ferry. Jim had told him that in the winter, the ferryman made the trip whenever he felt like it. At least going on the fishing boat would give him something to do. Donnie had not asked him to help with the catch, knowing it was hard, dirty work, but Griff didn't care. The work was exhilarating, enjoyable. The crew were happy to have an extra hand, and when Donnie let him off at Ullapool, he shook his hand.

'You ever want a job, I could use you.'

Griff grinned. 'I'll think about that.'

'Be seeing you soon.'

Griff nodded, and walked down the harbour to the road. There he had gone into the same pub he'd stayed in three nights before, and asked Tommy if there was a taxi service. A little while later, (an hour – a relatively short time in Highland terms), the driver appeared. He was a tall rangy man, with white hair and bright pale green eyes. He could have been anywhere from fifty five to seventy.

'Duncan MacLeod,' He introduced himself.

'There sure are a lot of MacLeods round here.'

Duncan smiled. 'That's a fact. Where are we going?'

'Inverness. And if you drive fast as you can, I'll pay twice the going rate.'

Griff climbed into the car, realising too late that he stank of fish.

'Sorry. I came over on Donnie's boat, and –'

'Aye, I know. He told me you were a canny worker. So you can forget about the going rate.'

Griff digested this.

'Are you related to Donnie?'

'Uncle,' he said.

Griff smiled. It was a safe bet that Duncan already knew everything there was to know about him, so he shut up. That was fine, because Duncan talked the whole journey, in the best taxi driver tradition. He complained about the lack of fish, the bloody EU, the state of the roads and the disproportionate council tax they had to pay considering what few services they got. It was all entertaining stuff, despite the fact that Griff understood about half of it. They reached Inverness in less than an hour and a half, and Duncan took him to the train station. He refused any money for the trip, but Griff insisted on paying for the petrol.

As he closed the door, Duncan shouted at him.

'Hoy, Griff.'

He turned to look back at the older man.

'I hope ye find her.'

Griff smiled and waved. He felt as if he was a man on a mission, as if all those people back there were with him, willing him on. It was a good feeling, and almost smothered the feeling of guilt, that he had driven Ellie away, and the fear that he might never find her.

And now he was in Glasgow, and scrolling through Ellie's numbers. They were all names, nothing to identify whether they were other than just friends. He saw his own number there too. He remembered the names of her friends: Fiona and Lara, and thought that might be a good place to start, but then he saw the name 'Janice Agy'. It was the only name with an apparent surname, and he thought about that. After a minute he decided to try the number. The phone was picked up after two rings.

'S&M Recruitment.'

'S&M?'

There was a sigh. 'Yes, I know. It's an unfortunate name.'

'Can you tell me what it stands for?'

'Scientific and Medical. What branch are you looking for?'

Griff paused and looked back at Ellie's phone.

'Is that Janice?'

'Yes it is. How can I help?'

'Janice, I'm trying to trace a friend who might be a client of yours.'

'I can't give out confidential information-'

'Can you at least tell me if she is a client?'

'What's the name.'

He told her, and there was a short pause.

'And what's your name?'

'Griffin Park.'

'All right, Griffin. Ellie might be a client of ours, but that's all I can tell you.'

Griff felt a surge of excitement. At least things were moving.

'I understand. But if I give you a number, if she calls in, can you give it to her? Get her to call me?'

'Yes, okay.'

He gave her the number, and Janice was about to hang up when Griff thought of something else.

'Tell me, you recruit people for work where, just Glasgow?'

'Och no, we do all over Scotland. Even Europe.'

Griff noticed that England was clearly bunched in the 'Europe' category.

'So she could be working anywhere.'

'I'm afraid so.'

Griff clenched his fist in frustration.

'Look Janice, I understand your position, but I really need to find Ellie, and I know she wants to find me. Can you at least tell me which city to look in?'

'I shouldn't give out that sort of info-'

'Please Janice. It's really important.'

There was a long pause, and Griff wondered if she was checking a computer screen.

'All I can tell you is that she is working in Scotland.'

Griff sighed.

'Now I have to go, Mr Park.'

She hung up, and Griff lay back on the bed and looked at the ceiling. He knew he was a long way behind her, and needed to catch up fast. He grabbed the phone again and scrolled down to her friend Fiona. The phone was answered right away.

'Hello, Fiona?'

'Who's this?'

'My name's Griffin Park. I'm a friend of Ellie's.'

'Oh yes?'

Cagey. Griff wondered what Ellie had told her about him.

'I'm trying to find her. Can you tell me, is she in Glasgow?'

A long pause. 'Why don't you ring her?'

'She left her phone behind. On Baranpay. If she has another phone, I don't know the number.'

Another pause.

'Well, I'm sorry Mr Griffin, but Ellie never mentioned you.'

Griff felt like he'd been hit by a baseball bat. She never mentioned me? A sea of hurt and anguish rose up and almost carried him away, but Fiona threw him a lifeline.

'But that explains why she's not answering my calls. Leave me your number and I'll pass it on. *If* she ever bothers to phone me.'

A little chink of hope opened up. There was stuff between Ellie and this girl, maybe enough that she would not share her thoughts and feelings with her.

'Do you know where she is?'

'Tell you the truth, I don't. But then I wouldn't tell you if I did.'

'Would any of her other friends know where she is?'

'Same thing applies.'

220

He sighed. 'Well, thanks, Fiona. I hope I might meet you, someday.'
That floored her, and she said nothing. Griff hung up.

He glanced out of the window over the river Clyde. He touched his fingers to his neck to the pendant he had taken from Ellie's cottage. Then he pulled his laptop towards him and booted it up, opening the folder named *Ellie*. There were still copies of his e-mails to Ellie, but they had grown. Here were his memories of the sunsets on the island, the feelings he had, sailing in Ellie's dinghy, watching a dolphin leap, its eyes level with his, the way the mist rolled in every morning from the sea, like the curtains opening on a fantastic stage. It had become a story, and now it was more than that.

He still didn't know the ending, he could only hope.

*

It was the 12th of December, and Ellie and Guillaume were walking through the cobbled streets of the old part of town, following the procession. The occasion was the festival of the 'Escalade', and commemorated a seventeenth century invasion attempt by the Duke of Savoy, which was unbelievably foiled by some woman throwing vegetable soup over the invading force. The Genevois made little soup pots out of chocolate to celebrate this occasion. Both Ellie and Guillaume carried the little pots, only theirs were filled with beer.

'This has to be the daftest festival in the whole world,' she said.

Guillaume shrugged. 'Possibly.'

There was a lot of laughter, but there was none of the reckless abandon of street parties anywhere else. Everyone's historical costumes were too perfect. Everything was a little too restrained. Ellie smiled to herself. After all, who was she to talk about other people's restraint, when she was the biggest control freak of all. She finished her drink and caught Guillaume's eye.

'Let's go to the stoning.'

He laughed. 'All right.'

They ended up walking past the Promenade des Bastions, down roads Ellie did not know.

'Where are you taking me?' Ellie asked.

'There is a good pub by the old cemetery.'

'Don't tell me, the beer's dead good.'

'The spirits are better.'

'Ha ha.'

The cemetery was filled with old trees and shrubs, and it reminded her of Highgate in London.

'Anyone famous in there?' She asked.

221

'Oh yes. Borges is buried there.'

Ellie looked at him.

'You have not heard of Borges? Come, I will show you his grave.'

Ellie sighed. 'I'd rather you bought me a beer.'

'Come on, it won't take long.'

He had clearly been there before. Ellie followed him slowly. She never felt comfortable in cemeteries. She'd already been close to death, albeit briefly, and didn't want to rekindle that relationship. She looked back at the gate.

'Come on Ellie. What are you doing back there?'

She sighed. 'Procrastinating.'

'What? Procr-what does that mean?'

She grinned. 'I'll tell you tomorrow.'

The single tombstone was not what she had expected. She had imagined a mausoleum, or at least a tall edifice, maybe a statue or two. Not this simple stone. She read the inscription. '*Ond ne forthedon na*'.

'What does it say?'

'It's a quote from a poem. The commander of a peasant army hopelessly outnumbered tells them to fight bravely. It means: 'don't be afraid.'

Ellie frowned. 'On a gravestone? I don't see the point.'

'Borges wrote about the choices we make in life, and how they affect our future.'

'The road less travelled,' Ellie said softly.

'Exactly. Everyone can look back and see where the road of their life reached a fork. Everyone wonders what would have happened if they had taken that other road.'

Ellie looked at the grave. What if? She thought. There were too many what ifs in her life.

'You know that poem, the Robert Frost one?'

'Yes, I know it.'

'I learnt it at school. Everyone thinks it's about a man looking back and being smug about taking the less trodden path. It's not. The man never took the road less travelled.'

Guillaume nodded, looking at her.

'Very few of us do,' he said.

He looked back at the gravestone, and then he turned and sat on the grass. Ellie joined him.

'When he was an old man, Borges was blind. For a writer, that must have been very hard. I think the quote is talking about that, that despite everything being difficult, maybe even hopeless, you have to hold fast.'

Ellie looked at him.

'Is that why you brought me here?'

Guillaume smiled. 'I don't know. Maybe.'

Ellie looked down the little hill to the street below. She felt suddenly at the cusp of time, as she had before. What she did now would change things inexorably, yet she was almost powerless to decide. It was like being in a dream in which everything happened around her, and despite it being her dream, she was left uninvolved.

'Who broke your heart, Ellie?'

She looked at him. 'A man called Griff,' she said quietly.

Guillaume nodded. 'Tell me about him.'

She looked down at her hands. She could see all the lines there, the fine hairs on her wrist, the greenish glow of her blood flowing under the skin. Griff, she thought. She waited for the tears to come, but they didn't.

'He was an American I met on an island,' she said, and as she started to speak, in a rush the whole sorry tale came flooding out. Guillaume said nothing, letting her tell it. Ellie leaned against the grave of the master of 'what if?' and wondered where Griff was now.

After she had finished, Guillaume was silent for a long minute.

'I think you left too soon,' he said.

'What?'

'How do you know he did not come back for you?'

'He didn't.'

'Have you spoken to your friends there, on the island?'

'No, but-'

'Then how do you know for sure?'

She stood up. 'I know. He's rich and famous. Back there he has everything-'

'But he was trying to get away from it. Don't you see?'

She shook her head. 'He's handsome. In California everyone is beautiful.'

Guillaume said nothing.

'It's gone now, in the past,' she said abruptly.

'And so you keep moving from place to place,' Guillaume said, standing and wiping the grass from his clothes. 'Why is this?'

She shrugged.

Because of us! The scars said smugly.

Yes, she thought. Because of you. All of you.

'Too many scars,' she whispered.

'The scars on your face,' he said, 'they can be fixed. You know this, don't you?'

She looked at him. She had not meant for him to hear. Eventually

223

she nodded.

'Then why do you not fix them?'

She shrugged. The scars whispered their secret truths to her.

'You are a beautiful woman, Ellie,' he said. 'With these scars or without them.'

She gave him a cynical smile. 'Doesn't quite work, does it.'

He raised an eyebrow.

'Then why not do it to avoid the looks, the sympathy? I can see how much you hate that.'

She nodded. 'I expect you're right.'

'Ellie-' he reached out and took hold of her arm as she tried to walk away. Ellie felt a jolt at the contact. No one had touched her since-

Well. She smiled to herself. Maybe Guillaume was right. She felt the edge of time looking in at her again, felt the road beneath her feet beginning to divide. If her face was no longer scarred, what would happen to the rest of her? Would the other scars, the deeper, angrier ones, remain?

Of course they would.

Can't get rid of us that easily!

But at least she could avoid the stares, the fascinated horror on children's faces, the pretence that she was as normal as the next person. Hah, that was a joke. She could pretend she was normal, but you can't lie to yourself, not forever.

She looked up and smiled.

'I think you're right, Gui,' she said. 'I ought to get them fixed.'

He smiled warily. 'Are you serious?'

She nodded. 'I have a friend in Edinburgh. Her father is a laser specialist. I'll go and see him when I get back.'

Guillaume threw his arm around her. 'I am so happy you are going to do this.'

She hugged him back, absently.

'It is a good thing for you, Ellie. It will help you move on.'

'I suppose.'

He laughed.' And if you meet your American friend again, he will not be able to resist you!'

Ellie laughed back dutifully, but as they walked out of the cemetery towards the bar, she felt a deep ache inside at the truth. It was easy to love beautiful people, but Griff had loved her, despite the scars.

Despite everything.

THIRTY EIGHT

It was while he was eating a solitary curry that the solution occurred to Griff. It was pretty easy, really. He'd just call all the hospitals. Ellie had said she had worked at the Royal Infirmary, and then others, as and when. He would ring and find out if they had someone called Ellie working there. He felt so energised by the idea, that his appetite disappeared, and he left his plate half full. The waiter gave him a concerned look, but Griff assured him that the food was excellent, he had just remembered something he had to do.

He had bought a new coat in a mountaineering shop in Argyll Street, and the bitter wind was no longer the enemy it had been. He caught a cab back to his hotel and turned on the TV, grabbing a vodka from the mini bar. The news washed over him, none of it sticking. He opened his yellow pages to 'hospitals', and pulled the phone close. No time like the present, he thought. He checked the time and saw it was just past nine o'clock. He called the first hospital on the list, but was told there was no one in the labs at that time of night. If there was an emergency, the person on-call would be paged. The operator had no access to staff records, and suggested he call back in the morning.

Frustrated, Griff put the phone down and lay on the bed. He couldn't escape the thought that Ellie could be right here, perhaps even only a mile away, but he couldn't find her. The local news was playing on the TV now, and he listened to the anchorwoman reading in her soft accent. Graham Stott, a noted Scottish actor, had died, and they showed footage of his home on the shores of Loch Ness. Griff watched hungrily, hoping for more of the scenery. Ellie had said there was something about the highlands that drew people in, a siren song that called people back and held them. He was willing to believe there was something in that. The feature ended and the weatherman came on, bantering with the news team.

'I was very sorry to hear about Graham Scott,' he said.

'Graham *Stott*,' the anchor woman said testily.

'Oh goodness, I've been doing that all day!' the weatherman said, shaking his head. He was very tanned, and the TV lights made him look like someone had daubed him with orange paint.

'If you're listening, Graham, I'm very sorry.'

Griff cracked up laughing. He lay back down and realised that was the first laugh he'd had in a long time. His chest ached, and he knew it was the empty place inside. Ellie, everything reminded him of her. The phone rang and he grabbed it, looking at the number. He tried not to feel disappointed.

'Hi Dave. What's up?'

'Griff? You all right?'

'Sure.'

'Just thought I'd check you were still alive.'

He grinned. 'Afraid so.'

There was a pause, and Griff knew what his friend wanted to ask.

'I've had a bit of a setback,' he said.

'Why? What's happened?'

Griff told him. He tried to keep the guilt from flooding his voice, but it was there all the same.

Dave said nothing for a long moment.

'Hell, I'm sorry, Griff.'

'It's OK. I'll find her.'

'You sure she wants to be found?'

Griff swallowed. 'I'm sure. I know more things now, Dave. Stuff I didn't know before. It explains what happened. I'll find her.'

There was another pause. Griff heard the little electronic bubble noises on the open line.

'You working?'

'Lunch,' Dave said. 'Got a new assistant. He's good. I actually had a day off last week.'

Griff said nothing, he was too surprised. Dave, the workaholic's workaholic, had an *assistant?*

'You still there?'

'Yeah. I'm just picking myself off the floor. What's all that about, an assistant?'

Dave sighed. 'I thought about some of the things you told me. I thought maybe it would be nice to, well, travel a bit, see places, you know? Have time off now and then. Maybe the law isn't everything.'

'Jesus!'

'It's nearly everything,' Dave added hastily.

'Well that's great, Dave. I hope your first trip's going to be Scotland.'

Dave said nothing, and Griff closed his eyes.

'Good luck, Griff, man,' Dave said. Griff could almost sense him shaking his head.

'Yeah. Speak to you soon.'

He hung up and flicked the TV off, finishing up the vodka. He looked out of the window again, towards the river far below, invisible in the darkness. He closed his eyes again for a moment, and then he pulled the laptop over and booted up.

I remember the first time I ever saw her, he wrote.

She looked like a mermaid trapped in the rocks. The sea surrounded her, and the wind was tugging at her dark hair. And I could tell that she belonged there, as much as the shingle on the beach or the high granite cliffs. She was part of it all. She turned her face to look at me, and smiled, and in that moment I was part of it all too. So it doesn't matter where I go or what I do, I will be called back. I will always be called back.

*

In the morning, Griff was up early and skipped breakfast, instead he manned the phone. He called the Royal Infirmary without success, and then tried all the hospitals in alphabetical order. It took him quite a while to reach the Sick Children's Hospital. He tried the Haematology lab first, and the chief there hesitated when he heard Ellie's name.

'Sounds familiar,' he said. 'But she's not in my lab. Have you tried the others?'

Griff felt the excitement bubbling inside him.

'No. Can you patch me through?'

'Och no, I don't know how to do that. I can put you back to the switchboard, though.'

Griff thanked him, and waited to be connected to Biochem. The chief there was a woman.

'Biochem. Mary Law.'

Griff rolled out his spiel.

'My name is Griff Park. I'm over from the States on vacation, and trying to trace a friend I think might be working there?'

'What's his name?'

'Her name. Ellie Woods.'

'Oh Ellie. I'm sorry, you've missed her. She left last month.'

Griff felt all the energy drain from his body.

'Where did she go, do you know?'

The woman paused. 'I don't think she had anything lined up when she left. She was only here temporarily while one of my people was off sick.'

Griff said nothing. So close…

'Have you tried her agency? She's with S&M.'

'Yes, thanks,' he said. 'They're reluctant to tell me where she is.'

'Well that's silly.' Mary put on her best schoolmarm voice.

'Would she only be working in Biochemistry?' Griff tried.

'I don't know what her experience was,' Mary said. 'Not necessarily. Look, hold the line and I'll have a word with the crew here, see if anyone's still in touch with her.'

Griff waited, gazing out at the opaque wintry sky. The forecast was for snow, and it didn't look far away. He realised his hands were shaking.

'Hello? Mr Park? One of my people seems to think she may have gone to Edinburgh. I'm afraid that's all the information I have.'

'Well, thank you anyway.'

'You're welcome, and I hope you can meet up with her before you go back.'

Go back, Griff thought, closing the phone. He shook his head. He was a long long way from going back.

*

Griff decided he had a better chance of finding Ellie in Edinburgh if he went there, rather than just phoning from his hotel. He called a hire firm and arranged to rent a car. It was a small SUV, or what the British called a 'people carrier'. Quaint, but it was a far cry from the last car he had rented in Inverness. The snow had started to fall by the time he set out, and the M8 was slow and clogged with traffic. It reminded him of the 10 back in LA, except it didn't snow in LA. Period.

By the time he got to the capital city, he was starving, and he checked in at a very grand looking hotel and went across the road to a friendly looking pub where he ate something called a *bridie.* It was a kind of meat-filled pastry, and surprisingly delicious. Then he returned to the hotel to work the phone.

He got lucky on only his second call. The lab chief answered the phone and Griff rolled out the 'on vacation' speech. There was a silence.

'Aye well, Ellie is technically here,' he said.

Griff stood up, his heart beginning to race.

'Technically?'

'Aye. She's on a fact finding mission for the hospital, ken? A sort of exchange thing,'

Griff had no idea what he was talking about. And why was he calling him 'Ken'?

'Where is she?'

'Geneva.'

Griff sat down again. Fuck, he said to himself. Fuck, fuck, fuck.

'Aye but she'll no' be long. She'll be back in a week or so. How long are you here for?'

Griff's mind was reaching for straws. He couldn't think of anything to ask.

'Thanks,' he said, and hung up. He grabbed the car keys and tore downstairs. The receptionist gave him a quizzical smile.

'Have you got a map of the city?'

'Er, no sir, but if-'

'I need to get to the hospital. Can you direct me?'

'Are you all right, sir? I could call you a taxi-'

'I just need directions. I need to visit a friend.'

Without another word the girl pulled out a piece of paper and drew him a map. He thanked her and hurried out.

'I hope your friend's all right,' she called after him.

The famed Scottish helpfulness, he thought, smiling grimly as he got into the car. He had half expected the girl to get in the car and drive him herself.

The hospital was a new, white edifice, set in a green field site next to an ancient ruined castle. Griff parked and went in, searching the boards for directions. He had no luck, and ended up accosting a passing nurse and asking her. She was an overweight girl with a cheery grin, and she gave him a look as if she knew him. She sent him in the right direction and a few minutes later he walked into a reception area. A man was sitting on a stool reading a technical journal. He looked up at Griff with startlingly blue eyes beneath a single eyebrow that ran across his forehead. Griff, like Ellie before him, immediately thought of Murd.

'I telephoned this morning-' Griff began, then stopped, hesitating.

'You'll be Mr Park,' the man said, 'I'm Norman Colquhoun.'

'Mr Colquhoun,' Griff said. Now he was here, he hardly knew where to start.

'Do you want to give me the whole story now?'

Griff felt his face reddening. The story hadn't been much good, but there was a seed of truth in it. Not one that would grow, however. He sighed.

'Do you know Ellie well?'

Norrie shrugged. 'Well enough, ken. I know she's got a few problems, and I'm guessing you're one of them.'

Griff hesitated. 'It's Griff,' he said. 'My name's Griff.'

Norrie gave him a funny look. Griff looked at the man and tried to get a feel for him. Norrie looked back placidly, the way a father would look at a child having a tantrum, just waiting for it to pass.

'It's a long story,' he said.

'You'd better come into the office then.'

Griff gave him the abridged version. They had met, fallen in love, he had to leave, when he got back, she had gone. Unlike Dave, Norrie made no comment about Ellie not wanting to be found. Griff sat in the tiny, freezing cold office that smelt of strange chemicals, and watched the older man tapping a pencil on the desk.

'She's a great one for running, is Ellie,' he said at last. 'I didn't want

229

her to go to Switzerland, but she was adamant. I did get her to promise she'd come back here once she was through, though. That's partly because we are all her friends here, but also partly selfish. We are crying out for staff, and Ellie is very good at her job.'

Griff sighed. 'I'm going to have to go to Geneva.'

Norrie smiled then. 'You can't wait a fortnight?'

He shook his head. It was unthinkable. He had left her alone long enough.

Norrie stood up and opened a filing cabinet, pulling out a folder. He opened it and spread some papers on his desk.

'This is the reference I gave them for Ellie. Here we are.'

He wrote something down and handed the paper to Griff. 'Phone them first. Might save you a journey.'

Griff looked at it, then back at Norrie. His heart started to pound again.

'You think she's coming back here?'

Norrie held his arms out by his side.

'Who knows?'

Griff opened the door and walked out. A man and a teenage boy were working on a nearby piece of equipment, and they looked up at him.

'Good luck,' Norrie said, shaking his hand. 'Although if you find her, I don't think you'll be doing me any favours.'

He smiled, and Griff returned it. He left clutching the paper and headed back to the car. The snow was falling fast now, and as he trudged through it his feet were soaked in seconds. Back in the car he pulled out the mobile and called the number.

'Bonjour, L'Hopital Université.'

Griff realised too late that he couldn't speak French.

'Uh, English? Does anyone speak English?'

'Oui Monsieur. Can I help you?'

'I need the Biochemistry Lab.'

There was a long pause, and he was put through to someone else.

'Hello?'

'Is that Biochemistry?'

'Bio- pardon?'

'Bioche-' Griff wondered if it was called something else there.

'The laboratory, where they test the blood?'

'Ah, oui. Un moment.'

He waited and was patched through to someone else.

'Hello?'

'Could I speak to Ellie Woods?'

A long pause. 'I do not know this Ellie Woods. Is she a doctor here?'

'No. In the labs.'

'Well, she is not in my lab.'

'Well, can you put me through to one of the others?'

This went on for some time. In the end, he reached what he worked out was the Haematology lab.

'I do not know this person,' the woman said. Her accent was so thick he could barely make out her words.

'Please, I know she is there, somewhere. Could you please ask in the other labs for me? I think she's in Biochemistry, only you don't call it that there.'

'Bioch- ah, je comprende. Un moment.'

'No, wait, I-'

But it was too late. He was put on hold again, and he gritted his teeth, watching the huge flakes of snow building on the windshield. The sky was the same dull grey as his laptop, and he pulled it towards him. Perhaps he could go online and find details of who he needed to speak to. As he opened the computer, the voice came back on the line.

'Hallo? Sorry, but no one is there. I leave message, say them to phone you, okay?'

Griff left his number and then stared out of the car, trying to keep calm. He turned on the wipers in time to see a car fishtailing out of the car park. Maybe he'd better leave, or he could end up stuck here. He drove slowly back to the hotel, the car fighting him all the way. He had never driven in snow, the worst he'd had to put up with had been the flash floods of a few years back, when the water was literally pouring down the roads like a river. The last thing he needed now was a crash. Unconsciously he touched his side where the stab wound was almost healed. He'd get back to the hotel and boot up the computer, try and find who was in charge in Geneva, and maybe book a flight. That's if anything could fly through this.

The Christmas shoppers had more or less disappeared now, and the decorations in the streets looked forlorn without people around. There was a crash in the street ahead, and a police car blocked the road, the officer out in the snow diverting the traffic. The man's face was grim under his hat, and Griff thought he knew how he felt.

THIRTY NINE

The flight was tense, what with the weather. Ellie had paid no attention to the upcoming forecast, and the blizzard came as a surprise. She wasn't concerned about the way the plane was pitching and rolling, although most of her fellow passengers were white faced, clutching their arm rests and speaking in frightened whispers. In fact she quite enjoyed the hair-raising flight, facing the fact that there was nothing she could do about it.

The whole East coast was blanketed in snow, and the plane couldn't land at Edinburgh, and was diverted west to Glasgow. Ellie collected her small bag and went out to the main terminal. She supposed she'd better get a train through to Edinburgh, get back to work.

Instead she found a Starbucks and sat watching the planes for a while, nursing a latte.

She had left Geneva early, as the lab had plenty of staff, and her departure would not cause them any problems. The chief had been polite and kind, thanking her for coming and for all her help, although she felt as though she had contributed very little and told him so.

'You have made recommendations,' he told her with a quiet smile. 'We will certainly get new equipment now.'

So she had thought hard about what to do, and decided to go home. She had talked herself into having the treatment, only now she wasn't so sure. Gui had been delighted by her decision, and that was hard to understand. She put it down to his strange fascination with decisions, and their consequences. Maybe he liked the idea that he had somehow changed her life. In any case, she wasn't sure.

Thank God for that!

She pursed her lips. 'You're back, are you?'

Never been away.

She drank the sweet coffee and watched a small jet coming in to land. Maybe she should just cut her losses and move on. The guys in Edinburgh were great, but they knew too much about her now.

That was it, wasn't it? She hated people knowing about her, the truth about her.

And what truth is that?

'Why don't you shut up,' she said. A woman walking past gave her a sharp look, and Ellie felt her insides lurch. She hadn't realised she'd spoken aloud.

'Maybe I will get you removed.'

Fat chance.

232

'We'll see.'

She pulled out her mobile and called up the hospital, checking her watch. Allie was on early shift, so she ought to be home, if the weather was anything to go by.

She was put through to the nurses' residence, and a girl she didn't know answered. She heard her calling Allie's name and Ellie heard her footsteps approaching.

'Allie? It's Ellie.'

'How ya doin? How's Switzerland?'

'Um. It was good, but I'm back now.'

'Back? Where are you?'

'Glasgow. The flight was diverted.'

'I should think so. It's like bloody Lapland over here.'

'Well, listen, Allie. I was thinking of maybe seeing your father, you know, see if-'

'Great idea, Ellie. He's the best. I'm pleased you've decided.'

Ellie said nothing. Decided, have I? She thought.

'And you're in the right place, too.'

'What?'

'Glasgow. He's based over there now. I'll give you his number.'

Ellie heard her ferreting about. She watched a plane taxi along the runway, and thought about fate.

'Here we are. Call him now, Ellie, because he's quiet at the moment. He'll fit you in.'

She took the number and thanked Allie.

'I'll see you later,' she said.

'Ellie? You are coming back, aren't you?'

She hesitated. No lies, she thought.

'I don't know, Allie, I really don't. I'll let you know.'

'Make sure you do, ken? I'll tell Norrie what you're doing.'

Ellie hung up, smiling to herself at Allie's accent. She wondered what Griff would make of it. That stung, and the scars had a bit of a laugh, until she picked up the phone again and called the hospital.

'Doctor Savage's office.'

'Hello. My name's Ellie. I wonder if I could either have a word with the doctor, or make an appointment?'

'Have you seen the doctor before?'

'We've met, yes.'

'No,' the woman said impatiently. 'Have you had a previous appointment?'

'Oh. No.'

'Well, he's rather busy at the moment.'

'That's not what I heard. Look, could you just tell him Allie's friend

Ellie is on the line, and see if he wants to speak to me?'

'Hold.'

Polite, she thought. I don't think. The plane roared by and took off, destination unknown. Ellie watched it go, and felt a surge of pleasure in the thought of just taking off like that, not knowing where you were going.

'Ellie. I was wondering if you'd call.'

'Oh, hello, doctor. Sorry if this is a bad time.'

'Not at all. It's a good time, in fact. When can you come in?'

Ellie shrugged. 'It's up to you.'

'Day after tomorrow?'

'That fast?'

'Sure. Why not? Sooner we get going, the better. Don't you think? Those scars have been there quite long enough.'

I hope you're listening, Ellie thought savagely. The scars said nothing.

'Well. Okay.'

'Fine. Come in for two o'clock.'

'Um, do I need to do anything, like not eat, or-'

'No. It's an outpatient procedure. You'll be surprised, I think, how easy it is.'

'Well, okay,' she said again.

She hung up and wondered what to do now. Her bike was back in Edinburgh, and there was no point going there to fetch it, if the weather was so bad. She'd never dare ride it back. She decided to book into a hotel for a couple of nights. Stuff the expense. She had no idea how much the laser surgery would cost, but it was likely to clear her out. She remembered the bond she'd given the flat rental people. She'd left before she'd had a chance to reclaim it, and she decided to give them a call, see if they'd pay up.

She watched another plane taxiing up. This one had Qantas on the tail fin. Australia. There was a thought. Maybe with her new face she could go somewhere completely different. Somewhere no one knew her at all.

We'll still be here.

She sighed.

You can scrape us off your face, but you can't scrape us off your heart.

'We'll see,' she said again. 'We'll see.'

*

Ellie stayed in a room two floors down from where Griff had spent

234

the last few nights. Then she opened her laptop and once again declined to check her e-mails. She considered looking up laser surgery to see what was involved, but decided it would only induce her to change her mind.

She lay back on the bed and glanced out of the window. The sky was grey and overcast, and it looked like the snow was finally moving west. Maybe she should just have got on one of those flights yesterday. Maybe she could have gone to America.

Maybe not. The thought of Griff was still too open a wound. She could hear music coming from the next room. It was the perennial *I wish it could be Christmas every day.* What a thought. Christmas. She had almost forgotten about it. And what about Fiona and the girls? She hadn't spoken to them in weeks. And then there were the Baranpay crowd. Guilt came soaring up in a wave. She was ignoring all those she loved.

She sat up and reached for her phone.

'Fiona?'

'Oh it's you. I wondered when you were going to show up.'

'Yeah, I deserve that,' Ellie said with a sigh. 'Sorry. How are you anyway?'

'Fair to crap.'

Ellie hesitated. 'I'm in town. You want to meet up?'

'Not particularly.'

'Fine. I'll meet you in McGinty's at seven.'

'If I must. Where have you been, anyway?'

'I'll tell you later.'

'You, uh, want me to bring the crew?'

'Sure,' Ellie said. 'Why not?'

When she hung up, she left the hotel and went into town, braving the Christmas shoppers to buy her friends presents. Hannah got a voucher for her favourite hairdresser, Lara got a silver four leaf clover on a chain, and Fiona got a bottle of her usual perfume. Not very adventurous, Ellie knew, but they were presents her friends were guaranteed to like. In the Buchanan Centre, a man was demonstrating a model helicopter, making it take off and land. Ellie watched it solemnly. Maybe if Griff had stayed she'd have been buying one of these for him. The man caught her eye and gave her a sympathetic smile. Ellie smiled back, without thinking.

*

McGinty's was busy with Christmas parties, and Ellie winced. She hated Christmas, all the forced jollity. She spotted Fiona at the bar and made her way through a group of women wearing reindeer antlers and singing along incongruously to *in the summertime.*

'Hi,' Ellie said, squeezing into the bar.

'Hi yourself.'

Ellie did a double take. There was something different about Fiona. It took her a moment to spot it. The smile. Her smile was back. Ellie felt her own lips curving in response.

'You look good, Fee.'

She shrugged. 'What's been happening?'

'Lots. I'll tell you. But you first.'

Fiona shrugged again, but she was still smiling.

'What?'

Fiona's smile became a laugh. 'Fred and I have been to the hospital.'

Ellie began to laugh too.

'Oh Fee!'

Ellie spotted the tears in her friend's eyes, and pulled her into a hug. Fiona hugged her back for a moment, then released her, wiping her eyes.

'Fred had a benign cyst. None of the tadpoles were getting through.'

Ellie laughed. 'They've fixed it?'

Fiona nodded. 'They did this microsurgery on him. They say it's gone, and he should be fine.

'I'm delighted, Fee. So can I be godmother?'

'You're a bit premature.'

'Ha ha.' Fiona just looked at Ellie for a long moment.

'It's because of you,' she said.

'What is?'

Fiona looked down. 'What you said the last time we met up. Why didn't we all sort it out. Well, it did the trick, and not just for us.'

Ellie frowned. She vaguely remembered being angry, having a bad day, getting drunk and shouting. Fiona looked over Ellie's shoulder and waved, and Ellie turned in time for Lara to pull her into a bear hug.

'Is this a Ellie I see before me?'

Ellie laughed. 'Lara, you tart.'

'Famous for it.'

Lara looked great. She had lost the dark circles under her eyes, and her skin was no longer stretched so tight it looked as if it was a size too small.

'What's happened to you?' Ellie said, amazed.

'Me? Nothing. I'm fine. You look like you could use a good man, though.'

Ellie found herself laughing. 'Laz, you look great.'

236

Lara shrugged. 'No change there, then.' But her eyes were shining.
'So where have you been? Tell us all.'

'Let me get a drink first,' Ellie said, turning back to the bar.

She told them about Edinburgh, about the lab crew there, and Switzerland, and Gui, and finally she admitted what she was doing back here in Glasgow.

'I'm seeing a face guy. A laser surgeon.'

Fiona and Lara looked at each other, then back at Ellie. Fiona sighed.

'Well, it's about time.'

'What?'

'It's about time. You should have done it ages ago.'

Ellie looked into the depths of her pint, but could see no help there.

'Fee's right,' Lara said. 'But none of us could tell you.'

Ellie looked up. Of course they couldn't. She wouldn't let them.

Lara grinned at her.

'Listen, Ellie, it's great to see you, and let's meet up in a couple of days, but I gotta dash.'

Ellie nodded, looking back to where a man was waiting for Lara. Probably her latest dealer.

'You take care, Laz,' she said.

When she had gone, Ellie looked at Fiona.

'Laz cleaned up her act a bit?'

Fiona nodded. 'That's her boyfriend, Carl. He's a policeman.'

'No!'

Fiona laughed. 'She met him when she lost her driving license, remember?'

Ellie giggled. 'Well, there's nowt as queer as folk.'

'Speaking of queer-' Fiona said softly.

'Ellie! Hiya.'

Ellie looked round. Hannah had her hair dyed in different streaked shades of blonde. It looked very trendy. Ellie pondered her own use of the word 'trendy'.

'I wondered if you were going to turn up,' Ellie said, grinning.

'I wouldn't have missed you, Ellie,' she said solemnly.

'Oh Han. Lighten up, Ellie laughed, pulling her friend into a hug. 'Come and sit down.'

Hannah laughed. 'I hope you don't mind, but I brought a friend.'

Ellie looked round. A red haired girl sat down beside Hannah, smiling hesitantly. Ellie crinkled her brow, knowing she had seen her somewhere before.

'This is Ruth,' Hannah said. Ellie saw her turn to look at the girl. Saw the look in her eyes, and remembered. The club. The jazz night.

237

Lara's outburst.

'Hello, Ruth,' she said, smiling. Then she leaned over and nudged Hannah, and when she turned, blushing furiously, Ellie grinned.

'So everyone's happy,' Ellie said to the world in general. 'I go away for a few weeks and look what happens.'

Fiona grinned. Ellie looked at her friends. She was amazed that they had all seemed to have sorted out their problems. All except her. She wondered if saving her face would also save the rest of her. Doubtful. The thought of Griff came back to haunt her. Even if her face was restored, she knew deep down that no other man would love her unconditionally, not the way Griff had.

They piled out of the pub around midnight, into the cold clear night. The wind had blown all the clouds away, and the stars were crisp and bright even through the street lights. Ellie looked up and thought absently of Andromeda, chained to the rock, and Perseus coming to rescue her. Hannah waved goodbye, and walked off down Byres Road, arm in arm with her friend.

'Where are you staying?' Fiona asked.

'The Moat House.'

'Nice.'

Ellie smiled. 'It's only for a couple of nights.'

'And then where are you going?'

Ellie looked at her. 'I don't know, Fiona.'

Fiona studied her face and slowly nodded.

'We just need to get you sorted out now, Ellie,' she said, and then she smiled.

'You want a lift?'

Ellie shook her head. 'You're going the opposite direction. I'll catch a cab. Go on home to Fred and jump on his old bones.'

Fiona laughed.

Ellie looked into the street and saw a cab coming. She flagged it down and got in.

'Phone me, once you've had the op.'

'I'll try,' she grinned.

'And don't take off again without telling me. Please Ellie.'

Ellie looked away guiltily. 'I'm sorry, Fee.'

'It's not just me you do this to. Someone phoned me looking for you, you know.'

Ellie's heart felt as if it had stopped.

'Who phoned? Who, Fee?'

'Some bloke called – oh I forget. It was Welsh, I think.'

The name sat on the end of Ellie's tongue, but she dared not say it.

'Are we going, love?' the cabbie said.

Ellie looked at him as if he was mad. She got out quickly.

'I'm sorry,' she said. 'I've changed my mind.'

'Please yersel''

He drove off, and Ellie stood staring at Fiona, whose face looked as though she'd just sat through a weepy film.

'What was his name, Fee?'

'I think it was something like Glynn, or Griffith-'

'Griffin.'

'That's it. Griffin.'

Ellie felt her knees buckling. Griff had phoned Fiona looking for her. That meant he had her number, and that meant he had her phone. And if he had her phone, it meant he had been back to Baranpay.

FORTY

Griff walked down Princes Street, looking in shop windows, but not seeing their contents. He was grounded by the weather, which showed little sign of clearing, and once more stuck in a hotel room waiting for things to happen. At least he knew where Ellie was, he thought. At least I can go there, as soon as the snow stops. He absently wished he still had the helicopter, but knew that was stupid. He could no more fly that through the snow than he could concentrate on the Christmas window displays.

It was late afternoon, and in the darkening sky Edinburgh castle was a squat black lump high on the hill above. This country was full of the past, and it was a dark and bloody history, but he thought he had an idea of why its people fought so hard for what they had.

He turned into a side street, thinking about finding a movie theatre to take his mind off things, when his phone rang. He stopped and grabbed it out of his pocket. He didn't know the number. His heart began to pound. He put the phone to his ear.

'Hello?'

'Mr Park?'

'Yes?'

'Hold please, for Mr Hayter.'

Hayter? Calling me again?

Of all the people he might have expected, he wasn't even on the list.

'Griffin, it's James. How are you?'

Griff was taken aback. 'I'm fine. Thanks.'

'Good. You're still in Scotland?'

Griff wondered how he knew. Maybe Leo had told him, or Dave.

'Yes.'

'Well, it so happens I'm in London, and I thought we might be able to meet up and talk about a few things?'

Griff was flattered, but beneath that, he felt annoyance.

'Look, I'm sorry, but I'm waiting for someone, and I might have to fly out to Geneva very soon.'

'I hear the weather's bad.'

'It is.'

'Well, since you can't fly out, couldn't you catch a train down here?'

Griff caught his breath before he said something he would certainly regret.

'It's probably a four hour journey, and I'd just have to come back here afterwards. Anyway, I'm really pushed for time. I'm sorry.'

'Uh huh.'

There was a long pause, and Griff wondered how Hayter knew where he was. He also had the irrational fear that perhaps Ellie was trying to call him at that very moment, only to find the line busy.

'What are you working on?' The man said.

Griff sighed. 'A novel, probably destined for a screenplay.'

'Run it down for me.'

'I'd like to, but there just isn't time.'

'I see.'

'Look, if you're really interested, I could e-mail you a synopsis.'

'Do that.' Hayter gave him the address.

'Where are you staying?'

'A hotel in Edinburgh, uh, the Glasshouse.'

'All right, Griff. We'll speak soon.'

He hung up and Griff sighed. That had been absolute career suicide, but he really didn't care. The only thing that mattered was finding Ellie.

Still, at least it gave him something to do. He caught a cab back to his hotel and booted up the laptop. He re-read parts of his story, and knew it was good. It took him twenty minutes to summarise it, and he included a patch of dialogue he was particularly pleased with. He sent it down the ether to John Hayter's computer, and then went back to the story.

Of course the synopsis had no ending. How could it? He looked at the phone as if he could will it to ring. He thought of all the messages he had left, in Glasgow, in Edinburgh, in Geneva, in Baranpay. Surely she must have picked up at least one of them? He had managed to convince himself that her laptop was either broken or she no longer had an account with an ISP, but the lack of response to the messages was worrying. It was getting to the stage where he woke in the small hours of the night, with the little voice telling him that she knew he was looking for her, but she didn't want to be found.

Griff closed the computer and went to find a bar.

When he woke up next morning, he had forgotten to close the curtains, and the sky above was blue. Griff got up and looked out at the clear day, the snow still lying in drifts, and felt a burst of hope. At least now he could do something. He showered and dressed, skipped breakfast as usual, and was about to call the airport when the phone in the room rang.

He answered it.

'Mr Park. You have a visitor, a Mr Hayter.'

Griff sat on the bed. Talk about the mountain coming to Mohammed.

241

'You better send him up,' he said.

James Hayter smiled when he opened the door. 'I liked your work,' he said.

Griff said nothing, but motioned him inside. Hayter was a small man, no more than five eight or nine, and with his receding sandy hair and pale complexion, he looked more like an accountant than a film mogul. But he had an intense presence about him, which most people found intimidating. Griff watched the man looking round his room with distaste, and realised he had probably never been inside a hotel room that wasn't the presidential suite. Griff pulled the chair out from the small table for him to sit on.

'You like to live ascetically,' Hayter said.

Griff grinned. In his opinion, the hotel was both beautiful and luxurious.

'Not really, I don't think about it. And I'm not planning on being here long.'

Hayter nodded.

'Um. Can I get you a drink or something?'

'I'm fine.' He sat down in an armchair, pale grey eyes scanning the blue sky above. Griff sat on the edge of the bed, feeling uncomfortable.

'So what are you going to do with this new script?'

Straight to the point. 'I don't know yet, it's – well, it's not finished yet.'

Hayter smiled. 'I guessed as much. I am intrigued by your story, and by the events in your life recently.'

Griff looked up warily. Hayter was still smiling.

'Come on, Griff, you know Hollywood. Gossip is rife. First your wife leaves you, then you lose your brother to drugs. You storm off set when another director is brought in, then you disappear off the face of the planet for months. You come back, bury your father, tidy up your affairs, and then you're gone again. People are saying unkind things about you.'

'I'll bet.' *And you'll be one of them,* he added to himself. He shrugged. At this moment, he couldn't care less.

'So, I like interesting stories, and yours is interesting, believe me.'

Griff felt a wave of irritation rising inside him. He had had just about enough, and the world's greatest film maker turning up to tell him he had problems wasn't helping.

'Your point being?'

Hayter laughed. He had a good laugh, rich and booming, and, Griff thought, under other circumstances, probably quite scary.

'Ok, Griff. I'm sorry. I didn't come here to upset you, to try to drag

242

you back to LA. I came here because I believe you are a great writer, and I want your story.'

Griff looked at him. He knew his story was good, but not that good.

'I expect this has to do with the fact that a lot of it is true.'

Hayter smiled. 'It helps.' He stood up and walked to the window, looking out.

'Griff, many years ago now I had a decision to make; to either go with the flow, and very likely make a very large sum of money, or to try something different, and make none.

I tried something different. As it happened, it led to other things, and I ended up making a great deal of money anyway, but at the time, it was a hell of a decision.'

He sat back down, looking at Griff again. Griff saw his face had softened, he no longer appeared the ruthless entrepreneur.

'I think you've just done the same thing, and I admire that. It takes a lot of guts.'

No, Griff thought, it didn't. It was simple. But he said nothing.

'*The hand on my shoulder* was a magical film. I loved it. But it became a cult film almost upon its release. You were never going to persuade a producer to support you on the back of it. *Twisting and turning* was okay, but you didn't write it, there was no spark there.'

Griff said nothing, looked out of the window as his career was dissected.

'And *Passages*, well. I read your original script, which was superb, but again, it wasn't going to bring in big bucks-'

'I didn't care.'

'Exactly. The trouble is, your films were never going to make enough money to make you autonomous, and you were never willing to compromise your work so they would make money. Catch 22.'

Griff was suddenly back in the board room, the producers introducing a young man, Griff's heart sinking as they told him he was here to 'help with the script'. Griff looked up. James Hayter was watching him.

'I understand your dilemma. Why should you compromise your work? Why not make the best thing you can? Something with value, with meaning. Integrity is a hard thing to live with, Griff.'

Griff stood up.

'You want this story, I'll give it to you, but I won't let you change it.'

James smiled. 'I wouldn't dream of it.' He stood up, and looked up hard into Griff's eyes.

'You go and find your Holy Grail, Griff, whatever and whoever it is. Then you finish the story and let me make it into something that people will remember for a long, long time.'

243

Griff swallowed. 'You're going to direct it?'

He nodded. 'No offence, but I'm better at it that you. You just stick to the writing.'

Griff felt a sudden surge of joy, and he had no idea why. Maybe it was because his work was going to be made into a film by this, the best and most influential director on the planet. Maybe it was because he didn't have to direct it himself, a task fraught with stress. And maybe it was because Hayter had put his finger on the truth. The Holy Grail. Salvation. Griff smiled.

'It's a deal,' he said.

'Good. Now I'd better get back to London. The weather seems better. I'll fly.'

'Uh, thanks for coming.'

Hayter raised an eyebrow, a rueful smile on his face. 'There didn't seem to be any choice.'

He opened the door. 'Good luck, Griff.'

'Thanks.'

When he was gone, Griff went back to the window and looked out. A wintry sun reflected on the drifts of snow, blinding him. He felt as if he was at the beginning of a new road, one that would take him through gentler weather, one that he would be happy to walk.

'*But one man loved the pilgrim soul in you,*' he said aloud;
'*And loved the sorrows of your changing face.*'

As long as there was Ellie to walk it with him.

FORTY ONE

Ellie sat down on the kerb.

'Ellie? Ellie, you're worrying me. Who is this man?'

Ellie looked up into Fiona's anxious face. 'I need a drink. Is the Tennents open?'

She got up and walked across the road, Fiona following. They found a pub still open and went in, and Ellie ordered a large MacCallan.

'Tell me what's going on,' Fiona demanded, looking down at her pineapple juice and grimacing.

Ellie recalled telling Gui the story, remembered how it had hurt but helped, all at once. But she didn't want to be helped.

'What have I done?' she thought.

'Ellie?'

She looked at her friend, and hesitated.

'What did he say, exactly?'

Fiona looked into her drink, thinking.

'I don't really remember exactly. He said he needed to get in touch with you. Wanted to know if you were here, in Glasgow. I told him I'd never heard of him and wasn't telling him anything.'

Ellie groaned.

'Well, what was I to do? You weren't answering my calls either.'

'I know. I'm sorry Fee. What else?'

'That was it, really. He sounded foreign, Ellie. American, I think. He could have been anyone. I wasn't going to give out your details. Not that I knew where you were anyway.'

Ellie threw back the whisky. It burned angrily down her throat.

'Who is this man, Ellie?'

Ellie looked up slowly. Fiona looked more worried than anything else. All the times she had denied that Griff wanted her, all the times she'd run away without telling her friends, telling anyone. It had all backfired at last in spectacular fashion, and it was all her own fault.

'He's-' Ellie looked at her friend. Fiona looked sad now, as if she sensed Ellie's despair.

'He's the man I love.'

'Oh Ellie!'

She called up another shot, and drank that back as well. Her scars had got their friends round and were having a party. They were all listening to her now, and laughing.

Yeah, well, wait till tomorrow, guys.

'Where did you meet, on your island?'

245

Ellie nodded. 'He had to leave, and I thought- I thought he'd never come back.'

'But he did.'

Ellie took a deep breath and pulled herself together.

'Maybe not,' she said. 'Maybe he was just checking I was OK.'

Fiona looked skeptical. Ellie suddenly couldn't talk about this.

'I need to go now, Fee. I've got this operation tomorrow, and –'

Fiona looked at her. 'We'll meet up after it, and talk,' she said firmly.

Ellie simply nodded. The way things were, she had no idea where she'd be after tomorrow. For a moment she considered that running away had caused all her problems, and now she was thinking of doing it again. Then reality asserted itself. She had no choice.

Where to this time, then?

I don't know, she told the scars.

But I know one thing. I'm going alone.

*

Back in her hotel room, Ellie opened her laptop. The hotel had helpfully provided a modem socket, and she plugged in and listed to the electronic dial-up.

You have e-mail! The PC announced. She looked at her inbox. She had a spam filter to weed out the junk mail, but there were still hundreds of messages.

You really don't want to do this…

'Shut up,' she said aloud. 'I'm doing it. I'm fed up listening to you.'

She called up the list of mails, looking for anything she might recognise. She saw mail from Jim, Gethyn, Fiona, Hannah, and Janice, the recruitment agent in Glasgow. There were still a load of crap mails offering to sell her Viagra or show her get-rich-quick schemes. And there were a lot from one address: GPF@filmnownet.com.

Her hands were shaking as she reached for the keyboard. She checked the date on the last mail, sent three weeks ago. Before she could think about it she pressed 'read', and looked at the message. It was one simple line:

Ellie, where are you?

Her heart was beating against her chest like a trapped insect. She scrolled up to a previous entry and read that:

I'm real sorry it's taking so long. I don't want to bore you with the details, but I have to wait another few days. My father died, and the funeral is next week. Will you not call or mail me? I'll be home soon! Love you!

246

Ellie closed her eyes.

'What have I done?'

All the way back here she had convinced herself that Griff had merely called Jim, who had given her Fiona's name, and he had traced her from there. She hadn't asked if Griff had called Fiona's home phone. If he had called her mobile, that theory was shot.

Well, it was stone dead now. She looked back at the message and felt the tears rolling down her cheeks.

She got up and fetched a bottle of water from the mini-bar, sat on the bed, and thought hard thoughts. It was time to sober up. Tomorrow she would have a new face, or at least the beginnings of one. After that, things should be different. But as she stared at the blank wall, she realised that there was no reason for things to be different. The scars on her face weren't the real problem.

It was time to confront some hard truths. The past may be a different country, but it was one with borders that she herself had closed long ago. Once again, she felt herself standing at a crossroads, with decisions waiting before her. She could have her face fixed and go back to Edinburgh, try and be normal. She could have her face fixed and run away again. Or, she could leave those scars where they were, and stay, or run. The decisions floated before her in the air.

We prefer the last one.

'I'm not listening to you.'

And then there was another idea floating there: a terrifying one. She could sit here tonight, and open those borders, visit those closed off cities of memory, and walk among the horrors of the past. She was too drunk, she knew, and in the morning everything would be different again. There would never be another time like this, and maybe, just maybe, if she could get through it, she could leave them behind, forever.

If she could get through it.

This is a crap idea.

Maybe.

She ignored her pounding heart, the dryness of her mouth. She had never felt brave, but if ever there was time for courage, this was it.

She sat down and took a deep breath, then closed her eyes and let her mind drift, back through the years, along a mental track with many turnoffs. Some of them led to sunlit groves. Some led to dark places. She felt the tug of the first, and instinctively pulled away, fear making her breathless. She opened her eyes and breathed in again deeply.

I have to take the chance, she thought, *I have to.*

She closed her eyes again, and let herself follow the road down, into the past.

'Where's daddy?'

'He's not here.'

'Why are you crying? When is he coming back?'

'I don't know. Stop asking me questions and go to bed.'

'But mummy-'

'Look, he's not coming back, all right?'

'Why not?'

'Hah! If I knew that-'

'Doesn't he love me any more?'

'He doesn't love either of us anymore. Now go to bed, Ellie, will you?'

She opened her eyes again, and the tears poured out. She tried to close down the vicious, desperate thoughts, but the gates were opened now, and the memories came flooding through:

'I'm leaving.'

'What? You can't leave! What are you-'

'I'm going, mother. You stay with him if you want, but I'm off.'

'Please don't do this, Ellie! Don't leave me!'

'I have to. I can't stay here like this.'

'Please, Ellie-'

She fell back on the bed, the memories bearing down on her like lead weights. She desperately wanted them to stop, but they swirled round her in cruel glee, free at last.

The screaming of metal against metal, the splintering of wood, then a sudden stop, jerking forward. The sound of the ticking engine, the smell of petrol. 'Jesus Christ!' and looking round, and the sound of the seatbelt clicking open, and the door opening, the suspension rocking as the driver got out. Slowly reaching for the seatbelt. Can't find the button, then, the noise, the ticking noise, and out of the left corner of her eye, the bloom, the orange flower of flame, and the sound, the roar, the flames coming towards her, a bright chrysanthemum unfolding its petals. The smell of her hair sizzling, the sudden agony. Fumbling with the button until at last it gave way. Climbing across the gearstick, grabbing the door, pulling herself out as the flames caught her clothes. The smell of burning fabric and wet grass, grabbing the aluminium barrier. Headlights in her face. 'Oh my God! Oh my God! Get an ambulance. The cold wet road, so kind against her face. 'Is there anyone else?' No, just me. 'What happened?' He promised, yes he did, he promised…

The bottle of water fell out of her hand and emptied, unnoticed, on the carpet.

The bright white. Fluorescent lights. The mirror. The lie.

'What do I do now?'

'Well, we'll let them settle down a bit. There are other treatments-'

'But they said- they said there wouldn't be scars! Not like this...'

'Sometimes – well, sometimes the treatment works better than others.'

'And that's it? I just have to live with it?'

'Like I said, there are other treatments-'

'I'm supposed to believe that now?'

Ellie groaned, and rolled on to her side. Her arm hit against the laptop and woke the computer up. She opened her eyes and stared at the screen:

I'll be home soon. Love you!

The sobs started deep inside, and came rushing out, taking her breath, her strength. The tears were blinding, and though she tried to sit up, she couldn't. She was back on the clifftop. He was kissing her, telling her to wait. She was telling him to go. She fought for breath, in the grip of the grief of all the years. She curled up like a child, eyes tightly closed against the pain. She was lost. Pandora's box had been opened, and all the sad truths had escaped, and there was nothing left, nothing at all. Not even hope.

Not even hope?

She opened her eyes, and raised her head. The computer still held its message, waiting for her to look.

I'll be home soon. Love you!

Then, all at once the tears stopped, and Ellie struggled for breath as the sobs began to subside. She sat up, staring at the screen.

There was a moment of perfect clarity. It felt as if she had finally woken up from a long and nightmare-filled sleep. She looked at the words and saw at last what she had done.

And it was all right. She understood it now: every wrong assumption, every wrong decision, every desperate escape. It all made perfect sense. She stood up and picked up the water bottle, absently fetching a towel from the bathroom to soak up the spill. She opened the curtains and then the glass doors, walking on to the balcony and breathing deep of the freezing air. She could smell the river below, see the hotel lights reflected in its surface. The sky was clear, the stars winter-brittle. There was Orion, the hunter. Sirius, his beloved dog, following him across the sky forever. An airplane roared off overhead, and she closed her eyes.

Not even hope? She thought, and then she smiled.

FORTY TWO

Griff woke with his phone ringing. He grabbed it and read the number. It was coming from another country.

'Hello?'

'Hello. Mr Park?'

'Hi there. My name is Guillaume Levret, from the University Hospital in Geneva. I am a friend of Ellie's?'

Griff's heart leapt. 'Is she there?'

'Oh no, she has left. Where are you?'

Griff sighed. Why was he surprised?

'In Scotland.'

'Then you will see her soon!'

'Guillaume, where is she going? Back to Edinburgh?'

There was a pause. 'Yes, I think so. The place she was before.'

Griff realised he was grasping the phone as if it were a wild animal. 'When did she leave?'

'Oh, it was- let me see, two days ago?'

'Then she's back already. Thank you. Thank you so much!'

'You are welcome. You know, she told me about you. I wish you good luck.'

Griff hesitated. 'She did?'

'Oh yes.' He laughed. 'But you will meet her soon and she can tell you everything.'

Griff closed the phone and got up. Ellie had told this man about him, and he seemed very cheerful. Was that a hopeful sign? He checked the time; it was almost eleven, he'd worked long on the story last night, and had slept very late. He had a quick shower and checked out of the hotel, then he drove back along to the hospital, trying to control his pounding heart.

It was the sort of day where the sky was the blue of Caribbean seas, yet the air froze breath into misty clouds. Griff sat in the car for a long moment. In a few minutes he was going to see Ellie again. He would find out the truth. He knew he would see it on her face as soon as she saw him, and that moment would have the power to change his life. He was impatient to go, but at the same time reluctant. What if he was wrong? What if she had been running from him, as well as from everything else?

He took a deep breath. There was only one way to find out. He looked at himself in the rear view mirror, checking the red veins in his eyes. The harsh sunlight turned the lines round his eyes into harsh grooves, reminding him that he was six years older than Ellie.

With a final sigh he got out and walked into the cold air.

His mouth was bone dry by the time he reached the Biochem reception. There was no one there, and he pressed a bell, hearing laughter coming from inside. Footsteps approached. Griff licked his dry lips.

'Hello.'

It was the young man he had seen on his last visit. He was painfully thin, with hair as orange as the fruit. He looked no more than fourteen, but his eyes were clever and keen. He smiled.

'Are you in the right place?'

'I hope so,' Griff said. 'I'm looking for Ellie.'

'Oh, Ellie. Well, you and everyone else.'

Griff could have cried. The weight of all the anticipation was too much. He leaned against the wall.

'I thought she was back,' he said, hearing the bitterness in his own voice.

'Oh, she is. But we don't know *where* she is.' The boy turned and shouted: 'Norrie!'

Norrie appeared. From the look on the man's face, Griff knew he must look terrible.

'Away back to your glucose, Malky,' Norrie said softly. 'You're back then.'

Griff almost laughed. The Scots loved stating the obvious.

'I spoke to someone in Geneva-' Griff stopped. What was the point? It was pretty obvious that she must now know he had been searching for her. She clearly didn't want to be found.

'Are you all right? Come and have a seat.'

Norrie lifted a section of the reception desk to let him in. Griff sat in the office looking round at the boxes. Norrie had been packing.

'You're leaving?'

Norrie smiled a strange smile.

'Aye,' he said. 'Ellie convinced me it was a good idea.'

'You've seen her?'

'No. Not since she went to Switzerland. Look, she wasn't due back here until after Christmas. Maybe she's having a holiday.'

Yeah, right. Griff thought. He could see from Norrie's face that he didn't believe it either.

'How do you know she's in the country?'

'She spoke to one of her friends who's a nurse here.'

Griff could see there was more that wasn't being said.

'Did she say she was coming back?'

Norrie sighed and ran a hand through his thick hair.

'The truth, Mr Park? The truth is she said she didn't know.'

Griff just nodded. The chances were that she was already gone, somewhere else, maybe even farther away than Switzerland. It was over. Griff felt his shoulders slump.

'Well, thanks, anyway,' he said, standing up.

'Look, if she comes back, or I hear anything, I'll let you know. I've got your number, and I'll be here another fortnight.'

Griff tried a smile. 'Where are you going?'

Norrie smiled brightly. 'Around the world. Ellie said I should follow my dreams before it's too late.'

Griff looked away. What dreams was Ellie following? What dreams did he have left?

He glanced down at his mobile. Unsurprisingly, there were no battery indicators left.

Outside, his frozen breath misted as he stood and looked over at the castle. It was a great ugly grey building, but all the same he began to walk up the path leading to it. Let's face it, he had nothing else to do. Two nurses smiled at him as they walked past him, but he couldn't manage to smile back. The cold air felt as if it were creeping into his bones. He stopped and looked up at the forbidding walls and felt them closing round his heart.

*

Ellie looked out over the river, watching the sun gleaming on the waves. The morning had a strange feel to it, as if Winter had less of a grip today. She had the doors open and the air was still cold, but there was a scent underneath it, not quite spring, but the feel of things not dead, but waiting. She smiled to herself. The chill air stroked her scars, and she turned her damaged cheek to the north. The smile did not want to leave her face.

Last night the world had ended and begun again.

In confronting the past, she had somehow burst through the walls of doubt and insecurity she had built around herself all these years, and now she could see the truth. A lot of it was unpleasant, but she could accept it now. She could do something about it.

Ellie had read all the e-mails from Griff until they were emblazoned in her mind. There was no point in regretting what she had done. No point in beating herself up over the fool she'd been. She understood, now. She had avoided all the bottled up pain, but at what cost? It was time now to try and put things right.

She went back into the room and booted up the laptop. Her first job was to reply to Jim, who had e-mailed her over and over, desperate for her to get in touch. She thought for a long moment and then began to

252

write:

Jim. It's me. I'm sorry.

Look, I've been a fool, but things have changed. You were right. I think I'm going to be all right, now, and I know now what I need to do.

I'm back in Glasgow, right back at the place where I started! There's something I need to do, but I promise I will be back on Baranpay soon.

I don't know if Griff will still want me, if he's still interested, if he's even in the country, but I have to try. I've never stopped loving him. I don't know if I ever can.

She pressed 'send' and then she closed the laptop. In another hour she was due at the hospital. She had a lot of calls to make first. Apologies to make, and promises to keep.

And miles to go before we sleep

She smiled. 'Exactly.

FORTY THREE

The hospital car park was busy, and Griff sat for a while watching people coming and going. He watched a couple helping their teenage daughter out of their car. Her left leg was completely encased in a plaster cast, and they were all laughing as she struggled to get out. Behind them he saw three men, one of them with a towel wrapped round his arm. The towel was soaked with blood, and the man's face was as white as the surrounding snowdrifts. His mates hovered round, not touching him, but ready, knowing he was close to collapse. They walked into the hospital and a couple walked out. They were holding hands so tightly their knuckles were white. Griff looked into their faces and saw only pain.

How could Ellie work amongst all this sadness, he wondered. And did it rub off? This was a place of misery. He looked down at his own empty hands.

It was time to go. He heard laughter again and looked up. A family were loading a people carrier the same as the one he was in. The two women, younger and older, were fitting a baby carrier in, their faces filled with light. The older man held the hand of a young boy of about six, who was craning to see the baby. The younger man looked down at another child, a daughter of three or four, and suddenly he crouched and hugged her tight. His eyes were closed, and he was smiling.

A place of misery, Griff thought, but also joy, also hope. Maybe he was wrong. Maybe it was that hope that kept Ellie going. And perhaps it could keep him going too. His phone bleeped and he looked down at it. Low battery warning. The charger was in his bag, but there was nowhere to plug it in. He threw it on the dashboard and pulled the laptop towards him. At least now he knew the end of the story. He moved the cursor towards the desktop icon behind which his work was stored, but then he passed the AOL icon.

Hope, he thought. It was a wonderful thing. He looked at the phone again. There might be enough juice left for a connection. He attached the modem link and logged on.

You have e-mail!

He scanned the list. The phone bleeped again. There was nothing but spam. No wait, there was a mail from Jim. Quickly he opened it. It was just one line.

Griff. Read this!

There was an attachment. The phone bleeped anxiously. Griff moved his finger over the computer plate, positioning the cursor over the link. He pressed go.

The phone died in mid-bleep.

*

She walked up to the hospital. It was a beautiful day, and the Christmas shoppers were out in force. Ellie walked through them with her head held high. Every pitying look, every grimace, every horrified stare she met with a bright smile. A bunch of lads spilled out of a pub, laughing. They saw her and their laughter faded. But Ellie grinned. Nothing could hurt her any more.

She stood for a moment outside the hospital. Her very first job had been here, back in the days when she was only flawed, not broken. It felt good to be back here again, as if the circle was complete, and perhaps some of the damage could be repaired. She could cope with being only flawed again. After all, who wasn't?

Graham Savage smiled as she walked into his consulting room. 'Are we all right?' he asked.

Ellie gave a soft little laugh. '*We* are fine.'

She sat and listened while he described the technology, the procedure. He showed her the CO_2 laser, explained the science.

'Are you going to anaesthetise me?'

'No. It will be uncomfortable, but not painful. It will feel as though I'm flicking your skin with an elastic band.'

Ellie nodded. 'Okay.'

Graham stood up and looked at her. Ellie knew he sensed something different about her, even though he didn't know her at all. And she was different. She had opened the door into hell, and as she stood in the flames, all her own demons had defected.

'I'm ready,' she said. 'Let's go.'

FORTY FOUR

Griff had his foot to the floor. The car was doing a hundred and eight miles an hour along the M8, passing everything in sight. He was getting close to Glasgow, and the traffic was building up. He looked at his hands, shaking on the wheel. He had to hurry. He didn't know why, he just knew. The words of the e-mail were ringing in his head, and his heart was trying to rip itself out of his chest.

'I'm back in Glasgow', she'd said. 'Right back at the place where I started!'

And he thought back to the day they'd met. All the rubbish they'd talked while they were busy looking at each other, while their hearts were occupied with more important things.

'My first job was as a hospital porter,' he'd told her. 'I was in college, and needed some money. It was a terrible job.'

And Ellie had laughed. 'My first job was in the Royal Infirmary, in Glasgow. They were good times.'

He knew she was there. She *had* to be there. He took the turnoff and followed a motorcycle down the ramp. The bike turned in front of him towards the hospital, and he took that as a good omen. He parked the car and hurried out.

The hospital was big and black and foreboding, and smelled like hospitals everywhere. Without even attempting to look at the direction signs he immediately ran towards a nurse.

'Excuse me. Where is Biochem?'

She gave him directions, and he ran up the stairs. The place was busy, nurses hurrying along corridors, patients sitting outside closed doors, harried looking young doctors. He was vaguely aware of piped Christmas music as he sprinted along a corridor that smelled of something horrible being cooked, and there, at last, it was: Biochemistry.

He stopped at the door. Through the frosted glass he could see people moving around. He swallowed, aware that this was the very end of the line.

I know she's here, he told himself. And she does want me.

He remembered that morning after the gathering, the words that he had written about feelings that, until she had spoken them, he had never known:

you're part of me

He opened the door. A man about his own age, with an easy smile and hazel eyes looked up.

'Hi,' he said. 'Can I help?'

'Is Ellie here?'

His brow creased. 'Ellie? You mean Dr. Shawcross?'

Griff shook his head, resisting the urge to strangle this man.

'Please. She must be here.'

'What's up, Luke?'

The hazel-eyed man looked round. Another man had appeared, this one about Ellie's age. He had a disapproving look.

'Ryan, Do you know anyone called Ellie?'

The young man's eyes changed. He knew her all right.

'Where is she? Please! I know she's here.'

Ryan was seriously checking him out, but Griff didn't care. If this was an old boyfriend of hers, he didn't care. His heart was racing, and he felt his fists clench in frustration.

'Ellie Woods?' he said, as another two lab techs appeared, both women. One of them had her hair tied up with pink tinsel.

'Ellie? Is she coming back here?' she said.

'I haven't seen her,' the other, Luke, replied.

Ryan kept his gaze fixed on Griff. For a long minute they stared each other out, then Ryan looked away.

'She's not working in the labs,' he said.

Griff turned and leaned his forehead against the wall. He wanted to cry.

'You're sure she's here? In the hospital?' Luke said.

Griff closed his eyes and nodded. This was pretty much the last straw. How could he have been so sure, and so wrong.

'Are you all right?' the tinselled woman said. Griff said nothing.

'Why would she be here, if she's not working?' Luke shook his head.

There was a long embarrassing silence, then:

'What about Graham Savage?' Ryan said.

'What? Oh,' one of the women said. 'Yes. That's a possibility.'

Griff looked round. 'Who is this Graham Savage? What are you saying?'

The younger woman looked at him with pity. 'She might not be working here,' she said. 'Ellie might be a patient.'

Griff stared uncomprehendingly.

'Doctor Savage is a consultant dermatologist,' Ryan said, watching him.

Griff said the words over in his head until at last they made some sort of sense. Dermatology. Skin.

Skin. Scars.

'Where can I find him?'

'I'll take you,' Ryan said.

257

They ran up the stairs, the Christmas music making Griff angry. He knew he was close, and the younger man's attitude confirmed it. He knew she was there.

'I'm Ryan, by the way,'

'Griff. How much further?'

'It's just through here-'

Griff was right behind him. This was a more exclusive corridor, with no one walking aimlessly about, and everything very silent.

'Um. They don't expect you, do they?

Griff looked at him.

'Didn't think so.'

Ryn knocked quickly on the door and pushed it open. A tight faced woman in a severe navy blue suit looked up in annoyance. She glanced at her computer screen as if she had been caught out in something.

'Can I help you?'

Griff ignored her, pushing past Ryan and heading for the door at the rear of the office. It had frosted glass, but Griff could see there were figures moving behind it. The woman began to yell angrily, but he barely heard her. He pushed the door open and held it, looking, feeling his heart about to explode, and time holding his breath.

A fair haired man was standing there, leaning over a patient on the bed. He had a complicated instrument on the table next to him, and was wearing a protective visor over his face. Behind the visor, he looked not only surprised, but somehow expectant, as if he might have anticipated the interruption.

'Doctor, I'm sorry-'

It's all right, Margaret,' the doctor said. He was still looking at Griff, and all at once he smiled.

The patient on the bed had long dark hair. He could see a snake of it falling over the edge. Lots of people had dark hair. It meant nothing.

Then the patient moved, removing something from her own eyes, and turned, and looked at him.

He had no idea how it happened, but all at once they were there, together. In each other's arms. Ellie was crying, kissing him and crying, and Griff could barely breathe. She was grabbing at his skin, his clothes, his hair, as if she could somehow get inside him.

'It's all right,' he said, choking. She cried and cried, holding him so tightly he felt utterly trapped, utterly content. There was nothing to say. Everything that had happened since they had parted was gone, and all his fears with them. They were together again. His heart was so full he thought that it might physically burst. He felt as if he had wrung all the emotion out of the entire world. He leaned in and laid his face down on

258

her hair, smelt the cold winter wind there. It was like coming home.

He heard a cough, and reluctantly looked up. Both Ryan and the doctor were looking at him. Savage was smiling. Griff took a deep breath and leaned back, putting his hands on her shoulders. God help him, he didn't want to let her go.

'Ellie. Ellie, love.'

She took a deep breath, and then another. And then she looked up into his face. Griff looked into her eyes and felt tears leaping into his.

'I'm so sorry,' she whispered.

'Hush.'

She rested her head on his shoulder. Her fingers found the amber necklace round his neck and she smiled.

'I'll never leave you again,' he said. The tears were rolling down his cheeks now, but he couldn't care less. Ellie was shaking. He knew she couldn't speak. He looked up at the doctor, who held both hands up in a 'what can you do' gesture.

'Ellie, we can do this another day,' Savage said softly.

Ellie looked up. Griff looked into her sad dark eyes, and put his hand on her ruined cheek.

'What were you doing, Ellie? Having this removed?'

She nodded, still unable to speak. He smiled.

'Carry on, if that's what you want.' He smiled. His fingers traced the long ridge of scar tissue that ran from her ear to her jaw. He had never cared about these scars. They were part of her, and she was far more than them.

'Either way, I don't care,' he said.

She reached up and touched his cheek, and her fingers closed round the tear they took from it, as if it were a rare diamond.

'Let's go home,' she said.

FORTY FIVE

'I can hear the boat coming round the wingtip,' said Archie.

'Ach away with ye,' Murd spat. 'You cannae hear last orders in the pub.'

'That's because you never ring the damn bell.'

Murd gave his friend a sour look, and they both looked back at the empty harbour. The whole island had turned out to see the boat coming in, but for now they were standing round nonchalantly, as if they had nothing better to do, and might as well wait to see if anything was happening.

Both men looked round as Flora came to stand beside them. Archie smiled at her, and Flora smiled back.

'No sign of them yet?'

'I can hear them, coming-'

-round the wingtip. Yes, Archie. You've said.'

'Och, you've a miserable head on you today. More than usual, I should say.'

'Ach, I'm fed up of waiting,' Murd said. 'I think I'll go in and open up.'

'Please yourself.'

But Murd made no move to leave.

'You know, I think I can hear something,' Flora said. Almost as she spoke, the spokes of the mast of the *Heron* became visible above the rocky harbour wall. There was a sizzle of excitement in the air.

'Here they come,' Conor said, looking down at his girlfriend and taking her hand.

The boat chuffed into the harbour, and they could see Donnie at the bow, waving.

'Hello!' he called. Everyone on land waved back. The boat nudged the jetty, and Donnie leapt off to tie up.

'Where is he then?' Archie said.

'I thought he was bringing- och, there they are,' Murd said.

And as Angus and his grandfather walked across the deck, Ellie began to applaud.

Conor took it up, and in a few seconds everyone was clapping. Angus beamed in delight, careful to walk slowly for the sake of the old blind man. He had brought his dog with him, and the black Labrador's tail was sweeping the deck, as if the applause was just for him.

'Welcome back Angus,' Murd said. 'And you, Peter. It's good to see you.'

The old man looked up and sniffed at the good air. He smiled.

'Let me go now, Angus, and go and see your fans.'

'Och, granda!' Angus said, looking up hesitantly.

'Well done, young Angus,' Flora said. 'Our very own Kenneth MacKellar.'

Ellie laughed. 'More like our own John Lennon.'

Angus blushed furiously. He climbed on to the harbour and looked around, the grin fixed permanently on his face.

'Are you opening up, Murd? I would like to buy everyone a drink.'

'For that,' Murd said sincerely, 'I'm opening up.'

And as they trooped inside, two small children ran shrieking through the adult legs, to disappear round the corner.

'Bloody kids,' Archie said, catching Flora's eye. She didn't look at him, but her face lit up in a smile.

Angus touched Ellie's arm.

'I have you to thank for all this,' he said.

Ellie shook her head. 'No, Angus, not me. You did it all by yourself.' She laughed.

'A platinum album! You know everyone on the island has your CD, in fact, probably everyone in the highlands does. You're a national hero.'

'Och, away with you.'

Ellie laughed again, looking up at the wispy afternoon clouds. Spring was here again, and with it, life.

'You made me believe I could do it, that I could really write songs people would want to hear.'

Ellie smiled. 'How long are you staying?'

'How long? I'm not leaving! This is my home.'

She nodded. Things had changed a lot in a short time. She saw Conor and his girlfriend, arms entwined, laughing together as they stood at the bar.

'Conor's staying too,' she said.

'Aye, I know. They're going to have the old postie's cottage. And I hear incomers have taken the bottom house, by the church.'

Ellie nodded. 'They're nice. Got kids, too.'

Angus sighed. 'It feels as if I've been away for years, not months. It's good to be back. And what about you, Ellie? How are you?'

She smiled at him. 'Oh Angus, I'm absolutely great.'

'Really?'

'Really. Now let's go. Your fans are thirsty.'

It was late, and the night air was cold by the time Ellie left the pub and started the climb up the track to the clifftop. Angus was playing his songs for the locals, making them join in. He was going to be a superstar, she knew, despite his island naïvety. She stopped at the top of the track, and looked back. The once empty cottages that looked out to sea had lights in the windows once again, lights to pull the fishermen home from the waves.

It was Griff who had done that.

His book, and the film that was made of it had touched something deep inside many people, a long forgotten sense of purpose, of hope, of searching for something long forgotten; something good and true. It wasn't just Baranpay. People were coming back to all the highlands, like the descendants of those long dispossessed, returning home.

She reached her cottage, and looked out at the sea, where the birds were also returning, to find a mate and rear a family, and send them out once more into the world alone. And up above, the stars were bright, and Ellie remembered another spring, when Griff had named them all for her: Arcturus and Polaris. Rigel, Bellatrix and Aldebaran. She loved to hear their exotic names.

And there, out towards the west was another star, brighter than any other. She stared at it for a long moment until at last the sound arrived, the low hrumming roar of the rotors, and she felt her blood begin to surge through her heart. The star grew impossibly bright, and Ellie began to run across the clifftop, towards the entry to the secret wood. She clambered over the rocks as the noise grew louder and then died away, the rotors still beating at the air though the engine was turned off. The door opened, and in the starlight she saw him climbing out, running as he hit the ground, and she ran too. She leapt into his arms, hearing his delighted laughter, joining in. He held her tightly, and she wound her legs round his body. They kissed and he touched her hair, her face, and she looked into his gentle eyes.

'You're very late,' she said.

He laughed softly. 'I'm sorry.'

She dropped to the ground, and he reached gently and touched her swollen belly.

'Are you all right?'

'*We* are,' she grinned.

All of us.

Yes, she agreed.

And arm in arm, they walked across the clifftop to the little cottage on the dragon's back. Above them, as if in celebration, the aurora appeared, dancing its fluorescent colours across the sky, shifting and alternating like an eightsome reel, the different paths leading different ways on their journey across the sky to their many destinations, in the dark and hopeful world below.

Visit Jeanette's website at:
www.jeanettemccarthy.co.uk